BLOODHEART ROY...

She was almost boyish i... ...pposite of
Stella. She was pale; her complexion was the envy
of the Burgher ladies who considered that the paler
a woman, the better her birth.

The silken locks of her hair were dishevelled,
spread in a swirl of gold over his arm that served
as her pillow. Gold curls of damp downy hair
sprouted where his eyes feasted. His throat
tightened and he gazed at her, enraptured. She
opened her eyes and giggled.

Bloodheart Royal
RICHARD TRESILLIAN

SPHERE BOOKS LIMITED

SPHERE BOOKS LTD

Penguin Books Ltd, 27 Wrights Lane, London W8 5TZ (Publishing and Editorial)
and Harmondsworth, Middlesex, England (Distribution and Warehouse)
Viking Penguin Inc., 40 West 23rd Street, New York, New York 10010, USA
Penguin Books Australia Ltd, Ringwood, Victoria, Australia
Penguin Books Canada Ltd, 2801 John Street, Markham, Ontario, Canada L3R 1B4
Penguin Books (NZ) Ltd, 182–190 Wairau Road, Auckland 10, New Zealand

First published in Great Britain by Century Hutchinson Ltd 1986
Published by Sphere Books Ltd 1988

Made and printed in Great Britain by
Richard Clay Ltd, Bungay, Suffolk
Set in 10/11 pt Compugraphic Plantin

'The British, being desirous of adding the Kingdom of Kandy to their conquest of Ceylon, enlisted the help of princes who were rivals of the King, enticing them with the false promise of placing one of them on the throne in the King's place. When the Kingdom fell and the King was exiled, there arose the problem of what to do with the princes who expected to succeed him.'

From: *My Ceylon* by Lancelot Ryall, London, 1907.

For
K.P. Neel Jayantha

CONTENTS

PROLOGUE

THE FAR HILLS OF KANDY
1814–1815

CHAPTER ONE

'Another prince of the royal blood!' exclaimed General Brownrigg, the Governor of Ceylon. 'Dammit, D'Oyly, how many princes are there in that tyrant's kingdom?'

John D'Oyly, who had been in Ceylon for twelve years, ten more than General Brownrigg, permitted himself a slight smile at the Governor's exasperation.

'Very few remain, Your Excellency. Prince Gamunu's defection is a blow the King will feel keenly.'

'Is it?' General Brownrigg considered the information, drumming his fingers impatiently on the top of the large teak desk that trapped him in the confines of his small office. 'By Jove! Does that mean he's losing his influence?'

'Yes.' D'Oyly resumed his habitual expression of dedicated concern.

He was a civil servant devoted to his work. He thrived on reading and writing reports, on interpreting events rather than creating them. General Brownrigg, a soldier who had seen action in America and Europe and seemed to yearn for more, offended his gentle nature with his bellicose manner.

'However,' added D'Oyly hastily when he saw the gleam that entered the Governor's eye, 'it does not mean the people of Kandy have turned against their King. Prince Gamunu's defection has to be investigated.'

General Brownrigg rose to his feet in agitation. 'D'Oyly,' he said. 'You are renowned for the efficiency of the intelligence network you have built up in Kandy. I appreciate your efforts. The Prince Regent does. Now we want action!

'There must be some way we can exploit the situation in Kandy to Britain's advantage. We have waited long enough for Kandy to fall.'

3

The Governor moved away from his desk and turned towards the window. The view from it was of the distant hills surrounding Colombo, the colony's capital. He looked towards them as he spoke.

'We were foiled in our attempt to take Kandy twelve years ago because the campaign was ill planned and because the people supported the King.' He paused to give emphasis to his words.

'I am preparing a new campaign. Kandy poses no immediate threat to British possessions, to our Maritime Provinces, but I am determined to take that kingdom in the hills. Without it, we do not have Ceylon.'

He swung around and glowered at D'Oyly. 'Interrogate this Prince Gum – '

'Gamunu, sir. Prince Gamunu.'

'Gamunu, parvenu, whatever the brown devil's name is. Promise him anything so he will help us. I must have that kingdom soon, before the Prince Regent changes his mind.'

'Yes, sir.' D'Oyly bowed his head, giving no clue to his feelings as he edged out of the room. He found the Governor's air of belligerence disconcerting, as though General Brownrigg lusted only to prove his manhood after the two years he had spent as a deskbound administrator.

Despite his distaste at the Governor's attitude, D'Oyly was confident he could restrain him. The General required assurance that victory was certain before he would attack the King's stronghold. John D'Oyly was the only man who could give him that guarantee.

He was deep in thought as he entered his palanquin. The conveyance was raised off the ground and its supports hoisted onto the shoulders of the four men who carried it. They trotted forward at a word from his boy, a fussy middle-aged man, who commanded them to take him to his quarters at the other side of the Colombo Fort.

He sat back on the cushions, calmed by the swaying of the palanquin after the disruptive atmosphere of his interview. He had been obliged, as soon as the royal defector had been brought to him, to inform the Governor. The number of

4

Kandyan nobles seeking British intervention was increasing.

Earlier that year, the first *Adigar*, or Prime Minister, had been deprived of his post by the King. He had crossed over to the British who controlled the littoral surrounding the Kingdom of Kandy.

The *Adigar's* defection marked the turning point in the long wait of the British to possess the whole island. Other nobles followed the Prime Minister into exile, offering their aid to the British for the overthrow of the King.

D'Oyly was the British expert on Kandyan affairs. He spoke Singhala and was versed in the etiquette of Kandyan life and of the Buddhist religion that governed it. With each new defection he evaluated the situation to see what measure of support existed among ordinary Kandyan people for a revolt against their King.

It was natural that the nobles who were stripped of their privileges by the King should turn against him. The *Adigar* wanted to be king himself, but he had been unable to raise the popular support to start a rebellion.

Prince Gamunu's defection was different. D'Oyly learned that the prince had not been in conflict with the King and was a member of his own family. His arrival in Colombo could be the opportunity the Governor wanted, if the prince had the support of the people.

D'Oyly's thoughts were interrupted as the palanquin was lowered to the ground with a jolt outside his quarters. He hurried from it to his office, followed anxiously by his boy.

'Bring the monk to me,' he said when he had settled down behind his desk.

D'Oyly knew very little about Prince Gamunu. They were the same age, forty, but he had nothing else in common with him. Somehow he had to establish a speedy rapport with the prince so he could discover if he was the man they sought.

Prince Gamunu Raja Singha – Royal Lion – was a grandson of a brother of a former king. He was a cousin of the present monarch, King Sri Vikrama Raja Singha who was himself the son of the late king's wife's sister. Tenuous threads linked Gamunu to the throne in several directions.

D'Oyly rose from his chair as the prince entered. He bowed his head, putting his palms together in the traditional Buddhist greeting of respect.

The prince, who was dressed in the bright saffron robes of a monk with his right shoulder bare and with his hair cropped close to his skull, arrogantly waved aside the greeting. He sat down opposite D'Oyly without waiting to be asked.

'Do not be fooled by my disguise,' the prince snapped. 'It is for convenience only. A *bhikku* is invisible, but I do not have the temperament to be a monk.'

His forthright attitude unnerved D'Oyly. He returned to his seat so that the desk was between him and the prince. Despite the modesty of the prince's disguise, there was no mistaking the force of his personality. He was a man accustomed to having his own way.

'You speak English very well,' said D'Oyly to cover his confusion.

'In Kandy,' said the prince, 'we are not savages.'

D'Oyly was stunned by the rebuff. 'Some people consider your King is,' he said defensively.

'How can a king rule if he is not strong? His people are his people. They do what he wills. If they do not, they die.'

'You have chosen to leave your king. Is that because his will is not yours?' D'Oyly asked pointedly.

'I am not afraid of death!' The prince's eyes flashed with anger then, without warning, he laughed. It was a surprising sound, a deep throated, mocking laugh that contained the self-confidence of his royal upbringing. It alarmed D'Oyly.

'How eager you British are!' Gamunu laughed again. 'You seek division so you can exploit it. I suppose you hope to use me as the instrument to overthrow my kinsman?'

'Prince Gamunu,' said D'Oyly sternly, in an effort to take control of the interview. 'If you have popular support we can help you. You have taken a risk. If the King finds out . . .'

'He *will* find out, Mr D'Oyly. He will do what is necessary.'

'You are safe here.'

'That matters not. The King has summoned me. I chose not to obey his summons. It is my risk, my choice.'

6

'Your wife . . .?'

'She is in Kandy. And my son.'

D'Oyly frowned, trying to understand the prince's motive. 'Won't they suffer? The King has a reputation for barbarity.'

'Yes, they will suffer.'

'Why, Prince Gamunu? What is your reason for coming here?'

'I have studied the British. You interest me. In Kandy, we are too isolated, too traditional to progress. The priests rule us.' He shook his robe irritably.

'You surprise me,' D'Oyly said, voicing his doubts aloud. He was overwhelmed by a feeling of disquiet inspired by this large, dark-skinned man.

The monk's robe had misled him into seeing Prince Gamunu as a gentle, humble person. If he had seen him in his royal regalia, his ruthlessness might have been more apparent. There was no warmth in the prince's eyes, only an evil that made him uneasy. He stood up.

'You will be given accommodation,' he said curtly, anxious to bring the interview to an end to impress upon the prince that he was his superior. 'You are welcome to stay as the Governor's guest.' He held up his hand when Gamunu tried to speak.

'I shall interview you again. I shall expect information on what support you have for a rebellion. We can, of course, be of great assistance to each other. A king on the throne of Kandy who is a friend of the British would be more valuable to us than one who isn't. We could help put you there.'

He smiled to indicate his meaning as he walked to the door and opened it. He held out his hand in the British manner.

Prince Gamunu took it without hesitation and shook it energetically. 'I was told you are an honest man.'

His cynical laugh echoed along the corridor as he swept down it, his monk's robe rustling around his ankles. D'Oyly flushed, feeling insulted. He was pleased that he had lied to the prince with his false hint of British support to regain the throne.

There was only one prince the British wanted on the throne

7

of Kandy. That was George, Prince of Wales, the Prince Regent himself.

John D'Oyly was a man of simple tastes. His long stay in Ceylon, and his fondness for oriental languages and his appreciation of the Singhalese character, were singular enough to make him the subject of uncharitable gossip among his fellow Europeans. He ignored them and pursued his duties with dedication. He knew his sympathy for the Kandyans would win their kingdom for the British.

Most of the nobles were in contact with him clandestinely and the King had no inkling of their treachery. D'Oyly understood their motives and played them off against each other.

Despite his familiarity with Kandyan ways, he remained ill at ease with Prince Gamunu. The other nobles at least feigned respect for the British, Gamunu did not. He was mild mannered when he was interviewed but D'Oyly was not deceived. He knew that for the prince to have survived in Sri Vikrama's Kingdom, he was as cruel and as heartless as the monarch himself.

Two months after the prince's arrival in Colombo, D'Oyly received the report he had been dreading. He read it with revulsion. He disliked Prince Gamunu but he had to wait several minutes before he summoned up the courage to send for him.

'I have some bad news for you,' he said, endeavouring to hide his disgust behind a mask of officialdom.

'I know,' Gamunu said coldly. 'I wondered how long it would take you to find out.'

D'Oyly stared at him, unable to speak. His eyes dropped to the report on his desk. The King, on learning of Gamunu's defection to the British, had arrested his wife and son.

According to the report, Prince Gamunu's wife pleaded that she, her son and her absent husband were innocent. At the same time, she submitted herself to the King's pleasure, offering up her own and her son's life in the fervent hope that Gamunu would benefit by the sacrifice.

'It's awful!' D'Oyly was annoyed by the prince's impassive

8

stare. He wanted to shock him into expressing dismay at what had happened. He held the report in trembling hands and read aloud from it.

'It says here that your wife was taken to stand between two areca palm saplings. Their trunks had been bent so that the tops of the trees were secured by ropes to pegs in the ground. She was tied by her left ankle to one tree and by her right ankle to the other.

'The executioners, acting in unison, severed the ropes that held the trees to the ground. They sprang apart, splitting her in two.'

Prince Gamunu remained unmoved.

D'Oyly sighed before continuing. 'A lad of fifteen, your son, was taken to another tree. While two men held his arms, the executioner cut out his navel with the point of a sharp knife. It was secured to the trunk of a tree with a nail. The boy was driven round and round the tree until his guts were wound around the trunk.'

'The King's will,' said Gamunu calmly.

D'Oyly shuddered. 'The Governor will not be pleased.'

'Good.' Gamunu beamed. 'He will take action.'

'Is that what the death of your wife and son mean to you?'

'Why else should I deliver myself here? Now General Brownrigg must capture Kandy.'

'You sacrificed your wife and son because you want to be king!'

Gamunu shook his head vigorously in the ambiguous way that to the Singhalese means agreement but to a European indicates denial. 'Tell me, Mr D'Oyly,' he said curtly. 'When will the Governor march?'

By the end of 1814, all preparations for an invasion of the Kandyan Kingdom were complete. Every chief of importance was in league with the British. Most notable, after Gamunu, was the King's new *Adigar*, Molligoda.

'The King's a heathen and a tyrant!' said General Brownrigg when Mr D'Oyly informed him what had happened to Gamunu's family. 'This is a good reason for us to move against him. Prince Gamunu is our ally.'

'He is not. He is using us for his own ends.' Mr D'Oyly withstood the glares of the army officers gathered in the Governor's office.

'My information is that there will be no resistance to an invasion. Gamunu and Molligoda and the other nobles will arrange that. However, there will be no support from the people. We need a proper pretext, not butchery by the King of his own relatives.'

'By Jove, what for? Once the Kingdom's ours, the Secretary of State won't quibble.'

'Your Excellency!' D'Oyly exclaimed reprovingly. 'It is the Prince Regent's express instruction. There is to be no punitive action unless *British* people or territory are involved.'

'What about that recent disturbance in the south, near Galle?' one of the officers asked. 'A young settler chap called Bloodheart had his house burned down.'

D'Oyly pursed his lips in annoyance at the interruption. 'My information is that it was a domestic disturbance over a land title, not a matter of State.'

Major William Willerman, an able staff officer who had drawn up the technical aspects of the invasion plans, leaned across the table. 'With respect, sir,' he began, forcing D'Oyly to withdraw. 'I have a suggestion.'

'Go ahead, Major,' said the Governor gratefully.

'It is in His Excellency's power to determine what constitutes an invasion of British territory, is it not, Mr D'Oyly?'

'Yes.' D'Oyly felt a trickle of sweat run down his chest under his silk shirt. He shifted uncomfortably in his seat.

'The Galle incident is perhaps too slight. However, the King's troops recently chased a band of insurgents across the Sabaragamuva border into British territory.'

'By Jove, Willerman, that's it!' General Brownrigg pounded his desk with satisfaction. 'Violation of British territory! Mr D'Oyly, prepare the proclamation. I shall lead the regiments myself. We *will* have Kandy!'

*   *   *

The proclamation dated 10 January, 1815 was issued in Colombo when General Brownrigg was already leading his troops into the hills around Kandy. It announced that the war was being undertaken on behalf of the oppressed Kandyan people who were to be protected from the depredations of their ruler.

Governor Brownrigg had hopes of victory in a spectacular battle that would establish his name. The Kandyans had other ideas. As the invading forces of two British and five locally recruited regiments advanced, the Kandyans melted away. Mr D'Oyly's intelligence proved correct. There was only token opposition to the British and no support.

Kandy fell in forty days, and with it Ceylon's independence came to an end. Victory was achieved because of the technical skills and ingenuity of the military engineers in transporting artillery through the jungles and mountains to the Kingdom. As the army approached the city, Molligoda's force offered resistance only until the *Adigar* and his family safely crossed over to the British.

King Sri Vikrama was captured on 18 February and on 2 March, the Kingdom of Kandy was formally ceded to the British. The Convention document was drafted by John D'Oyly and signed by the priests, the chiefs and by Molligoda. Prince Gamunu refused to sign it.

'It would be to your advantage,' said D'Oyly when he confronted him in his office in Colombo.

The prince was no longer alone as he was during all their earlier interviews. A soldier stood on either side of him as guards. He had discarded his monk's disguise and wore a cloth of white tied below his chest so it covered his body to his ankles.

'I will not sign away my kingdom!' Gamunu's brows were heavy with rage. 'I should be king! That's what you promised.'

'My dear chap,' D'Oyly said patronisingly. 'It's the British who took Kandy, not you.'

'I gave you my support! Your forces have deposed the King. Nothing more is required. Tell the Governor he should leave Kandy now.'

'We acted to protect British interests, not yours.' D'Oyly

smiled at the prince's anger. 'Just sign the Convention and you will be favourably treated. You will be honoured as . . . as . . .' he paused, thinking of an appropriate title. 'As a friend of the British!'

'Can I return to Kandy?'

'Certainly not.'

'I won't sign.'

Mr D'Oyly sighed. 'Then I'm afraid there is no alternative.'

'You won't execute me. That's not the British way.'

'You are right. We won't.'

'Who will rule my kingdom?'

'I will, actually. I am to be the British Representative in Kandy. The *Adigar* Molligoda and his ministers will answer to me.'

Prince Gamunu spun around on the balls of his bare feet and tried to walk out of the room. He was restrained by the soldiers. 'Release me,' he shouted. 'I will go to Kandy!'

'Oh, dear, no.' D'Oyly fussily shuffled the papers on his desk. 'You really cannot do that. I believe you might try to turn the people against us.'

'Hah!' Gamunu's eyes blazed with scorn. 'They are against you anyway. Kandy can never be British as long as a prince of the blood royal lives in Ceylon.'

'Indeed?' D'Oyly nodded his head. 'I guessed correctly. Molligoda *was* acting under your instructions.'

Prince Gamunu lapsed into silence.

D'Oyly signalled to the two soldiers. 'Take him away.'

'Where are you sending me?'

'The King is retiring to India. We will spare you exile with him. You will be sent South, to our fort at Galle. You will be comfortable there and too far away from Kandy to be a nuisance.'

'Galle?' A slow smiled spread over Prince Gamunu's face. 'Why, thank you,' he said mockingly. 'That is not exile.'

His eyes glittered with menace. 'That is another chance.'

CHAPTER TWO

When Thomas Radley was appointed by Governor Brownrigg as the first Collector in Galle, he regarded the promotion as a sinecure, a reward for his long service in Ceylon. He looked forward to a life of ease as the district ruler, with a pleasant bungalow and a retinue of servants.

The position was newly created. Up to 1815 there were only six Collectors in the Maritime Provinces and Galle fell under the jurisdiction of the Collector of Customs in Matara. The seat of the Colonial Government was in Colombo. Since senior officials did not tour the provinces, Thomas Radley was delighted with the arrangement for he would be free of supervision by any superior.

He realised that his duties, outlined in his letter of appointment, were formidable. As Collector, he was responsible for the administration of the district; everyone, except the military, came under his control.

He would be the only British official in the area and would enjoy immense power and prestige. It made him confident that he would be able to lead the life of luxury he had craved since coming to Ceylon ten years earlier.

Before he took up the new post, Radley wrote to his wife and daughter in England asking them to join him. His daughter, a child of fourteen, was virtually a stranger to him. His wife was ailing and he thought the climate would suit her. His plan was to set up house with his family and enjoy the perquisites the posting would bring him.

He was dismayed when he discovered his duties were more than collecting customs revenue and supervising local officials. He was expected to perform every major function himself, including that of judge. He was required to act on his own initiative, instead of leading an easy life protected from people and problems by the files and ledgers of a desk job.

His enchantment with the posting changed to resentment. He was forty-five years old and felt he deserved the comforts of his age. He found Galle, despite its being the island's main port, a depressing and enervating place. The heat caused him to be drenched in sweat day and night, and the damp turned his clothes and papers green with mildew. His first act when he took up residence was to petition the Governor for an assistant.

The district that his ill-fortune had brought him, extended thirty miles northwards along the West coast to Bentota and along the South coast to Matara. Inland, the boundaries were the settlements of the lowland territory of the Kandyan kingdom.

Originally, Galle was the trading port for that Kingdom. It had been wrested from the Singhalese by the Portuguese in 1587, fortified by the Dutch after they captured it in severe fighting from the Portuguese in 1640 and then, in 1796, ceded to the British.

Radley regarded the walled town without enthusiasm. The ramparts of grey blocks that encircled it, on both the land and sea sides, made it like a prison. The blocks came to Galle as ballast on ships. The ramparts were built by Negro slaves who worked in chain gangs under the Dutch. A spell of hard labour in Galle was a favourite punishment of the Dutch courts. Radley wondered what crime he had committed to be banished there too.

He saw no beauty in his bungalow set in the ramparts by the Akersloot bastion. Although it overlooked the sea and had a breadfruit tree growing in its garden which was said to be one of the first introduced into the island by the Dutch, the aspect did not inspire him. There was a telescope and eight mounted guns in the pretty garden. He would gladly have fired the guns if it would brighten his despair.

His exasperation increased when he had to deal with the officials who ran his departments. None of them were British. Those who masqueraded as white were really Burghers,

14

descendants of the Dutch and their Singhalese concubines.

To compound his dislike of his posting, three months after his arrival in Galle, Radley received a dispatch signed by Governor Brownrigg. It filled him with foreboding and anger.

'Why me?' he demanded in outrage of his empty office.

His shout brought his houseboy hurrying into the room, bobbing his head and trembling.

'Get out!' he shouted at him without raising his eyes from the dispatch.

It was an order instructing him to prepare quarters for Prince Gamunu who was to be detained within the fortified town at the Governor's pleasure. The Collector was to treat Prince Gamunu with the respect due to his rank, to treat him as a guest, not as a prisoner, but to see that he did not leave the fort.

'That's for the military!' Radley exclaimed aloud. 'I can't be responsible for guarding a prince day and night.'

He pushed back his chair and paced his office, racking his brains to see how he could avoid this preposterous demand. The only way was resignation.

He sighed, returning to his desk and burying his head in his hands. Even the thought that his wife, Mildred, was on her way to Galle did not console him. He knew she would hate the town with its heat and flies and its population of conniving Moorish traders and cunning Singhalese clerks.

To Radley's relief, the fort's Military Commander received a similar dispatch about the exile of Prince Gamunu to Galle. They met and discussed where their guest – not a prisoner, Radley was rudely informed by the meticulous Commander – was to be housed. Since officers of the 83rd Regiment were quartered in a Dutch-built mansion in Church Street, it was decided that there would be both secure and convenient as a home for the Prince.

The morning of Prince Gamunu's arrival was a difficult one for Radley. He was uncertain what to wear, what protocol to adopt and how he should conduct himself. His anxiety, coupled with the heat of his heavy formal clothes, made him bad tempered.

He was reluctant about taking part in a special ceremony for the prince's arrival, yet he did not want the Military Commander to outshine him. So he stood dressed in his Sunday best morning suit, the sweat pouring down his face and his eyes blinking at the brightness of the sun as he waited at the fort's gate to receive the Prince.

An escort of soldiers accompanied the prince's palanquin across the drawbridge over the moat that surrounded the landside of the fort. When the troop passed through the archway under the ramparts, they came to a halt. The soldiers presented arms, Thomas Radley adjusted his hat, mopped his brow with his handkerchief and stepped forward.

His first sight of Prince Gamunu was of a bare, brownskinned and hairless leg that protruded from the curtain of the palanquin. He gaped as the leg became a man who stood in front of him draped in a white cloth that left his chest and shoulders exposed.

The prince's outfit was completed with a flat, broad hat covered in white muslin ornamented in gold. He wore a large gold band in each ear. He was a tall man with a narrow nose and a supercilious stare.

The two of them eyed each other. While the Military Commander saluted, Radley deliberately kept his hands stiff at his side. He had no intention of shaking hands with this half naked savage, nor was he going to greet him in the native style of praying hands.

'Who are you?'

Radley blinked. The prince's deep voice and his careful enunciation of the question in English took him by surprise.

'I am the Collector,' he said haughtily. 'The Government Administrator for Galle and the surrounding district.'

'Hah! My gaoler!'

'You are in Galle as a guest of the British.' Radley flushed at being put on the defensive by the Prince's scornful manner. 'I trust you will . . .'

'Enjoy my stay here?' interrupted Gamunu gazing around him with interest.

A crowd was gathering, drawn by the prince's bearing. He returned the silent greetings of his countrymen who bowed their heads low, keeping their hands clasped together close to their brows in worship.

'I'm sure I shall,' he said mockingly. 'You must be Thomas Radley. Please show me my residence.' He gestured at the crowd. 'My presence is causing some consternation. Do you think your soldiers can control them?'

'Commander!' Radley gestured irritably at the crowd pressing around them. 'This is your responsibility!'

The prince began to move up the street, forcing Radley to chase after him. 'Follow me,' he said as he reached Gamunu's side. He wanted to make it clear that he was in command.

The prince looked at him with amusement. 'Mr D'Oyly told me about you.'

Radley was disturbed by the prince's leer. He was being treated like servant, like a little boy.

'He said you will see that I am accommodated comfortably and supplied with whatever I need as a guest of the Government. Is that your understanding of my presence here?'

He was so amazed at the prince's arrogance, he could only nod his head in agreement. Suddenly his elbow was seized and held in the firm grip of Gamunu's fingers. He halted, the sun beating on him as he was forced to stand in the centre of the street where there was no shade, and look up into the prince's eyes.

'Radley,' Gamunu said softly so that he had to move closer to hear him. 'I know you don't want me here any more than I want to be here. We are obliged to tolerate each other. I am a prince without a kingdom yet I have feelings, here.' He released him and clutched his bare chest.

'I am human, like you, even though I dress differently.' He glanced up at the sun and smiled. 'Perhaps more sensibly.'

He resumed his walk, leading him into the shade of a suriya tree. 'We are both men, Radley, with the needs of men.'

'You want women!' Radley uttered the words without thinking, shocked at what the prince had said.

A frown crossed Gamunu's face. 'How typical of your attitude towards us Singhalese for you to think so. It is not women a man needs, Radley, but friends. I was born to

17

power, you have it thrust on you by promotion. It is friendless being powerful.

'If you want my help, Radley, I shall be your friend.' He smiled condescendingly and gazed beyond him to the ramparts.

It was only afterwards, when the prince was safely installed in the mansion and he was sitting on his own verandah, that Radley realized what he had done. With a few words, the prince had laid down the terms of their relationship as well as humiliated him in front of the entire population of Galle.

'Damn!' he said, glaring at the sea as it gently lapped the rocks surrounding Gibbet Island in the centre of the harbour. Prince Gamunu's arrival had spoiled forever his hope of a peaceful sinecure.

The harbour of Galle is a sight that impresses all travellers from Europe when they gaze on the lush tropical scene of the bay and the wooded hills that encircle it.

Havis St Valle was affected by the view as he scanned the bay eagerly from his position on the foredeck of the ship beating into the harbour. To the vessel's right were the granite walls of the fortified town, rising magnificently from the sea.

The look-out towers on each bastion resembled pepper pots. Havis saw the heads of soldiers watching the ship from the battlements. The sea broke in waves of spray on the rocks below the ramparts, softening their harsh lines. This was where he was to be stationed.

He looked in wonder beyond the peninsula – the Point de Galle – where the fort was built, to the hovels of the native quarters beyond its walls. There, thatched huts nestled at the edge of the jungle. The ferny silhouettes of coconut palms leaning over the water drew his eyes, then he saw the mauve, red and white of the flowers growing at the shore's edge.

He raised his eyes to the mountains, thick with jungle of perennial green. In the distance, the far hills of Kandy were lost in a purple haze. The sacred mountain of Adam's peak was enveloped in the clouds.

'Isn't it marvellous!' he exclaimed to the sad eyed girl standing at his side. 'I'd throw my cap in the air for the sheer joy of being here, but it will probably fall in the sea and I'd have to dive in to rescue it.' He laughed with pleasure, and because he wanted the girl to laugh too.

She turned her dark eyes on him and gazed up at his face. He fell silent immediately to listen to her.

'I want to thank you, Havis. You have been kind.'

'No more than any gentleman would be for such as you.' He felt proud and squared his shoulders. 'You will soon be reunited with your father. The worst is over.'

'Is it?' She looked at him doubtfully.

'Why, of course. You are to begin a new life!'

'Yes.' She bit her lip.

'Come now, no tears. You don't want your father to be ashamed of his little girl.'

'I am almost fifteen,' she said archly. 'Three years younger than you. Does that make me little?'

'That's the spirit!' He laughed, pleased he had managed to distract her attention away from her sadness. 'You are not little in my eyes, Raven. You've borne yourself like a young lady of poise and maturity.'

'You are funny,' she giggled. 'I shall miss you.'

'We'll see each other often, maybe every day.'

'I doubt it. I am sure young ladies in Ceylon are expected to lead very discreet lives.'

'So are young government officials.'

'Look!' Raven touched his arm in her excitement and pointed to a group of people standing on the wharf below the entrance to the fort. 'There's daddy, in the white breeches and the blue top coat.' She waved but the man on the wharf kept himself stiffly correct as the ship dropped anchor.

'He hasn't seen you,' Havis said. 'He looks super in his kit. I bet he's hot standing in the sun.'

'Yes.' Raven giggled again. 'It makes him so bad tempered when he has to dress up for official occasions.'

Havis sensed her sadness evaporating in the excitement of seeing her father. The time had come for him to go. 'Goodbye,

Miss Raven,' he said softly, stepping away from her side.

He looked back but she did not notice he had gone. He was dismayed at the lump in his throat. Then the shouts of the natives distracted him as they swarmed around the ship in their dugout canoes.

He waited patiently on deck until it was time to be ferried ashore. Raven went ahead, escorted by the captain. When it was his turn, he was delighted to see that she was still on the wharf. She had been delayed by the official greetings.

She glanced at him shyly while the captain was talking to her father.

'Mildred?' Havis heard the Collector say incredulously. 'Dead?'

This was the moment Havis had been dreading. He smiled his encouragement at Raven, willing her to be brave and not give way to weeping. Her mother had died at sea from some lingering illness a month before. He had comforted her while she grew accustomed to her loss. He was sorry for her having her grief revived as her father learned the news.

He watched Mr Radley turn to Raven. He seemed more angry than sad and looked at her as though it was her fault. 'You've come alone.' he said accusingly.

'I'm all right, daddy,' Raven's bright voice sounded forced to Havis. 'Mr St Valle was great comfort to me.'

The Collector looked baffled.

Havis wished Raven would keep him out of the conversation. Her father had enough to worry about. There would be time to make his acquaintance later.

Raven beckoned him to her side. 'Daddy, I want you to meet him. This is Mr St Valle.'

The Collector ignored her and cleared a path with his swagger stick through the mass of near naked natives. Havis heard the splashes of men toppling off the edge of the pier as they were brushed aside. He hurried after Raven before the crowd closed in and he was pushed off the wharf too.

The natives were as fascinated by him as he was by them. Several people touched him. He could not understand their jabbering and assumed they were commenting on his clothes and the smooth whiteness of his skin. They were smiling so he smiled back enthusiastically.

The mob, carrying him in its centre, passed through the archway under the ramparts and entered the fort. Raven and her father were standing in the middle of the street.

'Where's my palanquin?' Mr Radley demanded of the crowd swarming around him. 'None of these natives ever do what they are told!'

'If it is not far, daddy, I would prefer to walk.'

'The sun, Raven. A lady does not walk in the sun.'

'I don't mind. See,' she said smiling. 'I have my parasol.'

Havis stepped forward without thinking. 'Allow me, Miss Raven.' He extended his hand to hold the parasol.

'What do you mean, sir!' Mr Radley looked furious. 'That's a slave's duty.' He frowned at Havis. 'Who are you, anyway?'

'I told you, daddy . . .'

'Were you not informed, sir?' Havis spoke as politely as he could. 'A dispatch was sent a month before I left England.'

'What dispatch?' Mr Radley sighed loudly. 'What are you talking about, young man?'

'I am your writer, sir. I have been appointed to train under you, as your apprentice.'

Mr Radley stared at him, his face showing his lack of comprehension. Then he groaned. 'I asked for an assistant, not an apprentice!' He clapped his hand over his brow. The crowd, startled by his gesture, fell back.

'Mr St Valle is very well connected, daddy. The Prince Regent himself is his patron.'

'Prince?' The word set off a spasm of shaking in Mr Radley's body. His hands quivered and his head shook from side to side. 'By God!' he said, raising his eyes hopelessly to the heavens. 'Is my life to be plagued by princes?'

He strode up the street muttering to himself. Havis exchanged an anxious glance with Raven and then, clearing a way for her through the crowd with her parasol, escorted her along the street after him.

BOOK ONE

THE MEASURE OF THE MAN
1815–1817

CHAPTER THREE

The lantern burned low, adding to the heat in the room. By its glow, the flickering shadow of the tall Dutch almirah with its heavy scroll-work, loomed over the bed. The room was small and airless; the wooden shutters of its only window closed for privacy. The stifling atmosphere created by the ponderous furniture, the heat and the glowing lantern distracted Bart. He was unhappy at being confined within four walls.

The woman's hands caressed his naked body as he lay facing her. She leaned over and murmured soothingly in his ear, 'Bloodheart . . .'

'Damn!' he said, giving vent to his discomfort. He pulled away, ignoring the grasping of her hands and swung his legs over the side of the bed. He stood up.

The square red tiles of the floor were cool to his bare feet. He felt like stretching out on them. 'I must have some air!'

He crossed the room and pushed up the wooden bolt that secured the shutters. They swung open and hit the outside wall with a bang. The sound of laughter – the ribaldry of hearty men drinking – surged into the room. He glanced through the wooden struts that barred the window. At the other side of the courtyard, Madam Gudde was in her parlour entertaining clients. He breathed deeply, relaxing as the inhibiting feeling of claustrophobia lifted.

'Someone will see.'

He turned back to the woman. She was watching him from the bed. By the lantern's dancing light he saw her pout of concern. His eyes took in the sight of her breasts. They were beautiful, taut alabaster white, blooming to dark pink tips that resembled hibiscus buds.

She placed her hand shyly to cover her bare thighs.

He laughed at the gesture. 'How can you be shy in this place, Stella?' He walked slowly over to the bed. 'I like to see you naked.'

'Well turn down the light, Bart. Madam Gudde will charge her clients to watch us if you leave it burning.'

He laughed again, raised the lantern from the table beside the bed and blew out the flame. 'Is that better?'

'Come here,' she said coyly. 'I'll show you it is.'

He lay on the bed beside her, listening to the shouts of the revellers while her fingers fluttered over him. The sight of the night and the flow of air through the open window calmed him. he felt his body responding to her skilful touch.

He seized her waist with firm hands, pulling her to him. He edged between her thighs and she moved to accommodate him. In the darkness he smiled, entering her easily. His restlessness eased and he began to make love to her with long and deliberate strokes.

It was not always like this. Stella was a whore, one of Madam Gudde's newest. He had been persuaded to try her several weeks before by Gretchen Gudde herself. He was reluctant because of the love he had for his wife. He was also suspicious of affection that had to be paid for.

'If I want a wench,' he had told Gretchen bluntly, 'I have black and brown girls on my plantation who'd open their legs for a bolt of cloth.'

Gretchen Gudde had looked at him with a knowing gleam. He had met her six years previously when he arrived in Galle from England with his mother and sister. He was a lad of nineteen then, eager to prove himself. In the years that followed he had achieved his ambition of owning a large plantation. He had also married Jessica and incurred the bitter enmity of her stepfather, the odious Marcus Van Dort.

'Believe me,' Gretchen had said. 'Stella is different from my other girls. She is from a respectable Dutch Burgher family. She really cares for you.'

Bart's response had been to look scornfully at Gretchen and laugh at her.

'It's true, Bart,' Gretchen insisted. 'You need the company

of a young woman like Stella. She can show you she cares for you by the warmth of her pleasuring.'

'What about Jessica – ?' he began to protest.

'You will be doing your wife a favour.' Gretchen smiled persuasively. 'You must give her more time to recover before you sleep with her again. After what happened . . .'

That night, Bart shared Stella's bed. He was drunk, nervous and suspicious. Stella seemed to understand. The next morning, instead of feeling ashamed, he awoke with a feeling of contentment.

He had returned to her the next night and then every night during his stay in Galle. He learned the story of how she had been raped by Marcus Van Dort a few months before. As a result, she was thrown out of home by her strict father. She had been destitute and friendless when she turned to Gretchen Gudde for help.

Bart's affection for Stella increased when he realized her feeling for him was genuine. Her delight when he came to see her made him enjoy being with her. As a result, he visited Galle often.

His love for his wife, Jessica, remained strong. She was nervy and hated him to touch her and he understood why. If he had tried to make love to her the way he did with Stella, she would have had a breakdown. He was grateful to his mother for the patient way she was nursing Jessica back to health after the dreadful night of the uprising. (*)

Bart rolled over on his back and sighed at his problems. Stella's hand gently stroked the whip scars on his chest.

'Why are you worrying?' she asked sympathetically. 'I thought you were asleep.'

'I was thinking of you, and of Jessica, and of all that's happened.' He brushed her hand away from the weals that crisscrossed his skin, etched there by the same Negro who had ravished Jessica.

'Don't worry, she'll get better soon.'

He was pleased she sounded genuinely concerned about his

(*) See: *Bloodheart*

wife. Then he remembered that Stella too knew the agony of being forcibly debauched.

'Give her time,' she said. 'At least she has you and your mother to care for her. You don't make her feel she's an outcast.'

'Why should we?' He opened his eyes and stared at Stella in the dark. 'I love her.' He spoke without considering the effect his words might have on her.

'She's very fortunate.' The trace of irony in Stella's voice was lost on Bart. She drew away from him to the other side of the bed. He was surprised and wondered idly if she was upset about something.

Despite the open window, it was sweltering in the room and the sweat lay on him like a film of dew. He remained motionless, reluctant in the heat to move or to touch Stella. The noise of Madam Gudde's clients receded as they were led off to their rooms around the courtyard by the whores they had chosen for the night.

He sighed again, this time because of Stella's affection. He knew she must have other clients. Gretchen Gudde was a hard-headed business woman. She would require Stella to earn her keep and to contribute to the profits of the bordello.

He was unconcerned. As long as her affection for him was genuine, he was satisfied. He was known as a courageous man with a warm heart – that was why the natives called him Bloodheart. He was forgiving by nature and this was recognized by the Singhalese as a strength, not a weakness.

The harsh shriek of a woman's forced laughter as she passed the window with a drunken customer grated on his nerves. How long would it be before Stella would lose her naturalness and become false and calculating like the other whores?

As he tried to dismiss the question from his mind, the spectre of Marcus Van Dort haunted him. It was because of Van Dort that Stella was a whore; it was because of Van Dort's orders that his house was burned down, his sister killed and his wife raped.

The mattress shook. He frowned. Stella's side was quivering. He listened and realized, as the slight movement sent a tremor through the bed, that she was sobbing into her pillow. He rolled over to comfort her. He was immune to a whore's

28

tears but his hatred for Marcus Van Dort obliged him to show concern for someone who was his victim.

'Stop that weeping, woman,' he said gruffly, putting his arm around her shoulders and hugging her. 'You're keeping me awake.'

'What's going to happen to me?'

He scowled, pleased she was unable to see his grimace in the dark. It was the sort of question he preferred to avoid. 'What would you like to happen?' he asked to divert her self-pity.

She wriggled around so she was facing him. Her body was slippery against his. Its proximity stirred him.

'I don't want to stay here.'

'Where can you go at this hour?' His joke was wasted.

'I mean forever! Bart, you know I'm not like Madam Gudde's girls. They enjoy what they do. Some of them are saving to open places of their own, some plan to return home with a fortune. I'm only here because . . .'

'I know,' he said gently, fondling her breasts. He lowered his head and kissed her nipple, drawing it into his mouth.

'Please listen!'

He raised his head. 'I am.' His hand stroked the moist inside of her thighs.

'I want to leave here.' She shuddered as he probed her with his fingers. 'I wish you'd buy me,'

It was too late for him to stop. His body throbbed with desire as he thrust himself against her. She grasped him, stroking him vigorously.

'I can't buy you,' he gasped. 'I don't have the money. The rebuilding, the . . .' He gave up trying to speak and groaned with pleasure instead.

'Will you when you have the money?' she said. 'Give me some hope.'

'Yes . . . yes!'

'I love you, Bloodheart,' she whispered, wrapping her legs around his waist with a practised twist of her body.

'Damn Van Dort!' he muttered as he plunged into her.

'You and Stella make a fine couple.'

29

Bart stared unhappily at Gretchen Gudde over the brim of his bowl of coffee. The steam made his eyes water and the bowl burnt his fingers. He sipped at the scalding black liquid, torturing himself awake. The shutters of the parlour were closed, only the door to the courtyard was open and the brightness of the sunlight disturbed the gloom of the room. He blinked and sipped again.

Gretchen Gudde, in the robes an ample lady wears to disguise her uncorseted figure at such an early hour, sat opposite him. A glass of gin was in her hand and she was waiting for his reply.

He said nothing, continuing to sip at the coffee while he gathered his thoughts. She raised the glass to her mouth, drained the measure of gin in a single gulp, and smacked her lips with relish.

'That's what a widow needs to rouse her.'

'Widow? Did you once have a husband?' Bart asked the question reluctantly. He had the feeling that whatever he said would make no difference to what was in her mind.

'I had one last night. He died on me so I threw him out.' She laughed raucously. 'He paid in advance, like all my clients.'

Bart returned his attention to his coffee. Stella had brought it for him after he dressed and was preparing to leave the bordello. Gretchen's joining him in the parlour was unusual. She was accustomed to sleep until the afternoon.

'Sometimes,' said Gretchen as though musing aloud, 'I do take credit . . .'

Bart fidgeted under her gaze. He finished the coffee and placed the bowl on the table. He had drunk it too quickly and his throat was raw. 'What are you hinting at, Gretchen?'

'I know your situation, Bart. Van Dort's nearly broken you financially.'

'I have no money to buy Stella from you, if that's what you mean?'

Gretchen frowned at his outburst. 'You can look after yourself. It's Stella I'm worried about. I'm not asking you to *buy* her.'

He sighed with relief. The conversation the night before had

30

worried him. He would like to rescue Stella from her unhappy lot as a whore. It would be a victory over Van Dort. Yet without funds it was impossible.

'She can stay here, Bart.' Gretchen seemed to be reading his thoughts. 'As my companion, not as one of the girls. It is not necessary to pay for her now. She can be yours alone, whenever you want her.'

'Why, Gretchen? Why do you want to help me?'

'You?' The gust of her scornful laughter jolted him. 'I'm thinking of Stella, I told you, and Jessica. You think only of yourself. Like all men, Bart, you can't see beyond the end of your prick.'

He glanced at the closed door to the outside patio wondering how he could escape Gretchen's lecture.

'Stella's a trusting girl. If she believes you'll take her away from here some day, when you've re-established yourself, she'll survive. If you pleasure yourself with her, instead of pestering Jessica, then your wife will have a chance to recover too.'

'Have you finished?' He stood up and stretched.

Gretchen muttered crossly, shaking her finger at Bart. 'You don't believe me. You're as pig-headed as Van Dort himself.'

'I'll think about it.'

'Payment can wait. Your credit is good with me.'

'Hah!' He grinned cynically. 'Your clients must be paying well if you're prepared to accept a promise that I'll buy Stella. You'll have to wait a long time before my sugar crop makes me rich.'

'I can wait.' Gretchen smiled up at him as she reached for the gin bottle. 'Won't you join me?'

He shook his head. 'I have five miles to walk to the plantation. I sold my horse yesterday.'

'I know.' Gretchen drank quickly and belched.

'You're very smug this morning. Is the Kandyan prince one of your clients? Only gold or a royal title would make you so pleased with yourself.'

She pooh-poohed the idea with a wave of her hand. 'Have you never heard of romance, Bart?'

'You are in love?' he said mockingly.

31

'It's you and Stella. You're so suited.'

'I'd rather it was the Kandyan prince's custom that put you in a good mood instead of that foolish notion.'

'The Prince doesn't like women.'

The silence was ominous. Bart wanted to leave but his curiosity detained him. 'How do you know?'

'I can tell.'

'I've never seen him.' He walked towards the door, pausing with his fingers on the handle. 'If he doesn't like women, what about his wife and child? The King of Kandy killed them.'

'Yes, because Prince Gamunu wanted it to happen.' Gretchen's face showed her horror. 'The child wasn't really his. His wife loved another.'

He snorted. 'You're making it up.'

'If you want to know about affairs of state, own a brothel. I hear everything from my girls.'

'Maybe you do.' He wrenched open the door. The sun ousted the darkness in the room, causing Gretchen to shield her eyes with her hands.

'Stella will wait for you, Bart. She's yours.' She turned her face away from the glare. 'Now get out and shut that door, for God's sake. The sun's not fit to be seen in here.'

He laughed and closed the door behind him. He was in a thoughtful mood as he crossed the patio to the outer door set in the high wall that blocked off Madam Gudde's establishment from the prying eyes of people in the Street of Moorish Traders.

During the day that street was a busy thoroughfare. Muhammadan ladies, deeply veiled and shawled, walked in pairs, hurrying past the white painted walls of the brothel with their eyes lowered. The servants and clerks were less circumspect. Few of them could afford one of Madam Gudde's whores and they eyed the men coming out of there with envy.

Bart unbolted the door, pulled it open and swaggered into the street. He was Bloodheart again, the public man. The sight of him stepping out of a house of ill-repute was in keeping with the image the natives had of him as a loose-living, fearless English man.

He paused, surveying the street both ways. It was thronged

with a motley of the fort's inhabitants. The sunset coloured robes of shaved headed monks contrasted with the black *buibui* cowls of the Muhammadan ladies. There were houseboys in white sarongs covered with red dust from the streets, and patrolling soldiers in scarlet tunics. Colourful saris, revealing plump brown midriffs, clashed with the drab dresses of Burgher ladies perspiring under their high bodices and long sleeves.

Bart was about to loose himself in the crowd when he glimpsed an unusual sight. Coming towards him, shaded by a parasol held over her head by an anxious young man, was a white woman he had never seen before.

She was exquisite. She wore a bonnet swathed in pink muslin that, whilst concealing her face, revealed the mirthful curve of her lips and the daintiness of her petite nose and proud chin.

She promenaded down the dusty street as though gliding on a carpet of flowers, heedless of the clamour and filth around her. Her serenity and poise made her unusual. Bart stepped back into the doorway as the crowd milling around her reached him. He tried to hide behind a tall Muhammadan in a white embroidered skull cap so the young woman would not see him outside the brothel.

'Who is she?' he murmered in awe to himself.

The Muhammadan turned and flashed him a toothless grin. 'The Collector's daughter,' he said. 'A mango ripe for picking.'

Bart bridled, clenching his fists and restraining himself with difficulty from knocking down the loathsome man. He looked at the woman again, at the very moment she glanced in his direction across the heads of the crowd.

Her lips quivered and her eyes, hidden by muslin and the shadow of the parasol, seemed to widen with reproach. She turned her head haughtily and glided on her way.

Bart stared after her, unable to move from the brothel's door until the heat in his loins subsided.

CHAPTER FOUR

The ninety acres that comprised the fortified town of Galle contained many houses as well as the garrison's barracks. Since the days of the Portuguese, the fort had been more than solely a military post. The harbour gave it the commerce that necessitated a civilian presence. There were merchants' warehouses, chandleries, and several churches including a Dutch one and one for the Caffres.

The houses ranged from the substantial granite block Dutch mansions of the establishment figures such as Marcus Van Dort, to the red brick and tiled roof cottages of lesser personalities. There were also the makeshift *cadjun* hovels of palm leaf thatch that housed the native tinkers, hucksters and drifters attracted to the town by the presence of the British garrison.

Bart liked Galle in preference to the sprawl of Colombo, sixty miles overland along the coast to the north. It was the main port for the island and most visitors bound for Colombo spent a few days in the town before attempting their journey elsewhere.

Bart avoided them. Some settlers in Ceylon regarded themselves as exiles from Britain and craved the company of fellow Britons. For Bart, Ceylon was home and he was indifferent to newcomers.

As he threaded his way through the crowd in the Street of Moorish Traders, past the single-storey houses of the Muhammadans where brightly coloured cloth, gems and tortoise-shell trinkets were on display, he was lost in thought. He acknowledged the greetings of the natives with an absent-minded wave of his hand, without pausing.

He turned from the frenetic activity in the street to the

somnolence of Church Street with its grand mansions and government residences. Here people promenaded sedately, some attended by slaves bearing parasols. There was a stir of interest among the strolling whites and Burgher gentry at his appearance in their midst. He ignored them. Since his arrival in Ceylon six years previously, Bart had been the subject of gossip. The nickname of Bloodheart that he earned for his recklessness in moments of crisis, and for his forgiving, warm nature, added spice to the scandal of his conduct.

On the wide verandah of the mansion next to the Dutch Reformed Church, two men were watching him as he turned right down the street leading to the fort gate. He caught a glimpse of them although their identity did not register in his mind at the time. He was preoccupied with the memory of that young white lady who had eyed him so reproachfully as he left the brothel.

He passed through the archway under the ramparts, nodding to the sentries. The road along the beach, skirting the harbour where ships bobbed at anchor in the choppy water, was crowded with natives, bullock carts and Caffres, the Negro slaves owned by the government for the upkeep of the town.

The rhythm of his marching was disrupted by this throng of people. He was impatient to get beyond the shadow of the ramparts and into open country so he could walk at his own pace and devote his thoughts to considering that self-assured young lady.

He analysed in his mind what made her different from other English women sightseeing in the bazaar on their arrival in the town. Her proprietorial air could have been one reason; another was the mystery in her half-hidden face with its air of aloof sadness, and of a yearning as yet unfulfilled. That such a girl should look at him with disapproval in her eyes caused him to suffer a fit of pique. What right had she to judge him?

His brisk pace took him beyond the fort and the mud huts of the natives outside its walls to the path that meandered through the coconut groves lining the shore. He entered the shade of the palm trees eagerly and stepped up his pace for the five mile walk to the plantation.

It was then he remembered the two men who had been watching him from the verandah of the villa where the British officers were quartered. 'Why!' he exclaimed aloud to himself. 'That was the girl's father.'

Bart had met Thomas Radley on two occasions and the encounters had not gone well for either of them. He found the Collector fussy and a typical example of English bureaucrats – arrogant and incompetent. Now that he knew the Collector had such an intriguing daughter, he was prepared to regard him more charitably. The other man on the verandah, he realized, recalling his impressive demeanour in his costume of white and gold, was undoubtedly the Kandyan prince.

It was a band of Kandyan marauders who, with some of Bart's own Caffre slaves, had attacked him and set fire to the mansion he had laboured lovingly to build. His sister had died in the blaze rescuing his baby son, Garth, and her own daughter, Ranita. Her husband also died in the attack.

Although he had no proof, Bart knew the attack was inspired and financed by Marcus Van Dort. The Burgher, a descendant of a liaison between Dutch and low-caste native ancestors, was formerly the Registrar of Galle. Bart had caused him to lose his position and the man had vowed to drive him from Ceylon for revenge.

As he marched along the trail, he pondered the outcome of the Kandyan prince's presence in Galle. Van Dort, always keen on mischief-making, would probably befriend him. Bart guessed that Collector Radley was going to be busy with his new charge.

He abandoned his thoughts on the intrigues of the town as the beauty of the trail distracted him. Every few hundred yards along the path, there were villas set among the coconut trees. They had fine views out to sea, with rambling gardens overgrown with bougainvillaea and wild plantain trees. The foliage embracing the villas disguised their decay. The Burgher and Singhalese owners were no longer prosperous. After the British conquest twenty years before, the cinnamon trade that was their source of wealth declined.

The Burghers became clerks while the Singhalese land-owners depended for their livelihood on coconuts instead. The tree was a versatile provider. As well as products from its timber and leaves, there was copra and coir fibre rope from its nuts. Even the sap extracted from its flowers was utilized and drunk as toddy or distilled into arrack, the island's famous coconut brandy.

It is said in Ceylon that the coconut palm only thrives within the sound of human voices. Where the area of the decaying shoreside villas ended, the groves of palm trees gave way to the thick vegetation of land being reclaimed by the jungle.

The road to Bart's plantation lay alongside a lagoon shielded from the sea by a broad sandbank. The original river path had been widened and the boulders removed so that bullock carts, horses and elephants could use it without difficulty. Bart had sold his horse to raise cash to buy provisions which was why he was walking. It enabled him to take a narrow, over-grown short cut through the jungle instead of using the road.

He knew the path from the day he first climbed it and discovered a vast plain where deer grazed undisturbed. He vowed that day the plain would be his. Now sugar-cane grew where wild animals roamed and two thousand acres of jungle had become Bloodheart Plantation. The land was given to him by the former Governor, Sir Thomas Maitland, who believed the prosperity of Ceylon lay in the hands of settlers from Britain.

Bart's choice of sugar-cane as the crop that would make his fortune – he was unconcerned about Ceylon's prosperity – was natural. He had been raised on the sugar plantation of his American-born father in Barbados. When his father died and his mother was dissatisfied with life on her return to England, Ceylon offered a chance for a new start.

The soil of the land he had claimed was lusher than that of Barbados so Bart reasoned it would produce better sugar. With his mother's inheritance he had built a fine mansion and a mill by the river that formed the plantation's eastern boundary. He imported slaves from Madagascar and Mozambique and ran the plantation as if he was back in Barbados.

The slave uprising the previous year had halted his plans. He regarded it as a temporary setback. The idea of abandoning the plantation and returning to England never occurred to him.

He emerged from the jungle trail and blinked in the sunlight. Ahead of him were acres of green and gold sugar-canes waving in the breeze that wafted over them from the distant mountains. He smiled at the sight. He was hopeful that his second crop, almost ready for cutting and boiling, would be more successful than the first. He needed the money to build another house, to pay his debts to the provision merchants and, perhaps, to buy Stella's freedom from the brothel.

In the fresh air of the plain with the sun warming his face and the sweet scent of his land tingling his nostrils – instead of the smell of gin and fleshy whores – Gretchen Gudde and her whorehouse and Stella seemed far away. He chuckled to himself.

He loved his land with the passion a man feels for a woman. He touched a cane tenderly, grasping the shaft in his hand and fondling the ribbons of green. He possessed that land: he had changed it from a wilderness to a plantation that would support himself and his family and be an inheritance his son could be proud of.

He gazed across the fields expecting to see the mansion with Jessica at the upstairs window watching for him. Nothing remained. The burned out shell with its walls of river stone had been dismantled. Now Jessica and his mother lived in the guest pavilion. Its red tiled roof was just visible above the bougainvillaea bushes whose leafy blooms of pink, yellow, mauve and white, contrasted with the carpet of green waving canes.

'Tissa!' Bart cried with delight at the sight of his overseer who appeared at the other side of the cane field.

The young man smiled and walked towards him, holding the hem of his sarong in one hand to prevent it snagging in the grass. He was shirtless and barefoot with his long black hair hanging loosely to his shoulders. His skin was a light bronze colour and his eyes, in the sunlight, were amber. He moved gracefully along the rough track. At first sight, with his dazzling smile and girl-like features, he looked fragile and feminine.

Tissa's softness was deceptive. His slender body concealed a muscular strength that with his experience and commanding manner made him a leader among the Singhalese. He was a slave, a year younger than Bart. He was also the father of Ranita, the child of Bart's dead sister.

'I feel like I've been gone five months instead of five days!' Bart grasped Tissa's hand, feeling in his handshake the stump where Tissa's fingers had been chopped off when he saved Bart's life in the uprising.

'Did you sell the horse?' Tissa asked hastily. 'Have you bought provisions?'

Bart laughed at him. 'You sound like my mother.'

'It was Mistress Charlotte who asked.' Tissa lowered his eyes. 'She said you should have kept the horse because it was your own.'

'That is why I sold it. The proceeds are my own. It frees me from borrowing more from her.'

'Frees you for a time.'

The doubt in Tissa's voice made Bart look at him sharply. 'Whatever happens, Tissa, we'll survive. Van Dort won't chase me away from here.'

'You are not knowing him like I do. I was his slave before. He's like an elephant, he never forgets. He's vowed vengeance for the disgrace you caused him. He won't give up until he succeeds.'

'The cane!' said Bart, dismissing the matter breezily. He fingered the stems as he strolled around the field with Tissa. 'It is ripe. We must begin cutting.'

'How?' Tissa shook his head sadly. 'You have only four Caffres.'

'Even with only four, we'll do it. The houseboys, Nimal and Jagath, can help, and Daisy and Little from the kitchen.'

Tissa sniggered. 'Why not ask Mammy as well?'

Bart sighed. Mammy Sobers had been a wedding gift to his mother. They had brought her with them from Barbados. She had grown fat in Ceylon and ruled the household. She loved Bart's mother, Charlotte Taylor, but there were limits to what she would do.

'You need more Caffres, Bloodheart,' said Tissa patiently. 'Only Negro slaves can do that sort of work.'

Bart refused to feel discouraged. 'We can do it ourselves!'

'You and I?' A frown settled on Tissa's smooth brow. Ahead of them was the guest pavilion where Jessica and Bart's mother were sitting on the newly built verandah. He indicated them with a nod of his head. 'Will you ask your wife and mother to help too?'

'If necessary!'

Bart hid his frustration. What Tissa said was true. With only four trained slaves remaining out of his original twenty, it would be impossible to harvest the cane crop, Yet he needed the sugar to pay off his debts. It was a planter's maxim: no slaves, no sugar, no income.

He shrugged aside his despair and hurried towards the villa.

His mother and Jessica rose when they saw him coming. He embraced his mother, pleased at how well she seemed. In London, she had many suitors following the death of his father. Even after the ordeal of the uprising, she retained the youthful beauty that belied her age and made her so attractive.

'We missed you, Bart,' Charlotte Taylor said, her eyes radiant. She whispered in his ear before pushing him away from her. 'Kiss Jessica!'

He was startled by her command but he knew better than to query it. He turned towards his wife, hesitated, then opened his arms.

'Jessica?' he said softly in case he alarmed her.

She came to his outstretched arms nervously. He stroked her hair. It calmed her. She slipped her hands around his waist and hugged him.

He held her close, surprised at her affection. Slowly he lowered his head and brushed his lips against her cheek

'Jessica,' he murmured into her ear. 'I love you.'

She was weeping and her frail body shook in his hands. He wiped the tears from her cheeks with his fingers, crooning sympathetically. 'Why the tears, Jess? I'm home now. Don't cry.'

'I'm so happy,' she said. 'I thought . . . I thought . . .'

He held her away from him, catching sight of his mother's nod of approval. He was guided by it.

'Thought what, Jess? That I'd leave you? You are my wife. *I love you.*'

Bart had long ago discovered the magic of those three words. After the trauma Jessica had suffered at being raped, she needed encouragement to believe in herself again. He had spoken glibly but in his heart he knew it was true. He did love her.

He brushed aside the gossamer strands of blonde hair that were caught in the moistness of her cheeks. Gently he led her back to her chair.

'Forgive me, Bart,' she said, seizing his hands. 'You have been so understanding.'

'It was worth it!' He beamed at her proudly. 'You've recovered a lot in the five days I've been away.'

'It was because of your absence, Bart.' Charlotte Taylor sat down and signalled Jessica to do the same.

Bart pulled up a chair between them. He had difficulty keeping his eyes off his wife. The change in her recalled how she looked before the dreadful rape. He pushed the memory of it out of his mind.

'Jessica and I had a talk,' explained his mother. 'She agrees with me that you need our help.'

'You won't stay in Galle overnight again, will you?' she asked anxiously.

He was surprised to feel Jessica touching his arm. He grasped her hand and squeezed it.

'I may have to stay . . .' He broke off when he saw the glimmer of unhappiness in her eyes. 'No,' he said warmly, forgetting Stella. 'I won't. I belong here with you.'

CHAPTER FIVE

'You must take her carefully, Bart. She wants you but she's scared.'

'I will!' He nodded at his mother, embarrassed by her frankness. 'I know how she's suffered.'

'No you don't. How can you?'

He grinned at the rebuff. He was sitting with her on the verandah. Jessica had gone to bed. He did not know which room she had chosen: his or that of his mother. Since the uprising, she had slept with his mother every night.

Fire during the uprising had destroyed everything they possessed, except for his mother's chest – the treasury – which Mammy Sobers with her customary presence of mind had dragged from the blazing building. They were fortunate in having the pavilion to live in. Using materials salvaged from the ruin of the mansion, Bart and the remaining slaves built a parlour and a verandah around the two bedrooms.

The verandah, which faced south, was broad. The deep pitch of the roof and the trees that surrounded it gave shade when the sun slanted at sunrise and sunset. Large double doors opened into the parlour. It had thick walls and a very high roof. It was a huge room that served as lounge, dining room, office and sewing room.

As soon as he had sold his sugar crop, Bart intended to add to their cramped accommodation. There was so much for him to do. It could not be as grand as their former mansion but it would be sufficient for him, Jessica, his mother and the two children.

'You're remarkable, mother,' he said, pulling the lobe of his ear in a characteristic gesture of bewilderment. 'You have put up with so much since we came here yet you never show any sign of regret. If anything, you look lovelier than you did when we were in England.'

'I adore your flattery, Bart, but it's unwarranted. We chose Ceylon together. I would regret it if you were to give up when we are beginning again. You have another chance.'

He wondered whether she was referring to Jessica or the ripening sugar cane. Her face gave no clue. It was stern. Her hair, cut short, revealed the masculine bone structure of her proud face. She had kept her trim figure, despite her love of rum punch. She was a sympathetic listener and the slaves and the Singhalese adored her.

She was a redoubtable woman whose determination never wavered in her battle to do the best for her children. It was she who forced through the marriage of Bart to Jessica because of its advantages for him. At first she distrusted Jessica but the crises they had shared made her a fighter on her behalf too.

'What should I do?' Bart asked anxiously. 'I don't want to frighten her.'

'Let her trust you.'

'I wouldn't hurt her!'

'You are a man. You cause her hurt because of your sex.'

'Mother!' He sat back, shocked by her remark.

'Your father taught me about men and their needs. You are in his mould. You think Jessica neither knows nor cares about your visits to that place in Galle? You are wrong. She was born in Galle, she speaks the language. She has friends who delight in telling her everything you do when you are in the town.'

'How can she know about Madam –'

Charlotte Taylor held up her hand imperiously and he gulped into silence. 'Say nothing,' she said, her voice husky with anger. 'Neither to her nor to me.'

She rose from her seat and with a swirl of her skirt stalked off towards the door. Bart scrambled to his feet. She was inside the living room before he could explain.

He walked to the edge of the verandah and gazed out. In the soft light from the half moon he could see the field of sugar-cane that shimmered beyond the lawn and the bushes of bougainvillaea. The field extended into the darkness, representing casks of sugar, money for his debts, if he could only harvest it. He sighed, preferring to think of Jessica.

Was she really ready to lie with him again? Gretchen Gudde was right about men being guided by their pricks. He was relieved Jessica had recovered her vitality but worried in case she knew about Stella.

He struck his open palm with his clenched fist. There was nothing he could do. Jessica would continue to sleep with his mother until he charmed her into forgiving him. It was a situation he hated. He glared into the night at the sugar-cane and sighed once more. *By the devil*, he thought, *I'll harvest the cane even if I have to cut every stalk myself.*

Bart pushed open the door to his chamber. Nimal was at his side with a lantern. He shook his head at the houseboy.

'Go to sleep,' he said. 'Take the light. I don't need it.'

He watched Nimal pad barefooted across the cool red tiles of the parlour floor and out onto the verandah. He and the other houseboy, Jagath, slept on reed mats laid out on the verandah floor. When he observed Nimal's slim hips under his loose fitting shirt and sarong, he knew instinctively that the boy would be useless as a temporary cane-cutter. It was a task that needed the mindless brawn of a gang of Negro slaves.

He closed the door so the bedroom was in darkness. It was sparsely furnished and he could find his way around it without a light. He closed his eyes and walked over to the window without bumping into anything. He flung open the pair of shutters and let the breeze from the hills soothe his troubled mind. There was a vague scent of perfume in the room that pleased him.

He opened his eyes and gazed up at the sky visible through the gaps in the overhanging suriya trees. He could not see the delicate yellow flowers of the trees but assumed the scent came from them. He watched the stars, marvelling at their sparkle in the deep midnight blue of the sky.

He recalled the days when he and Jessica slept in the open

on the plain as they were building the mansion. Their love was sharp then with the zest of discovering new delights in each other. He feared that now, through his dallying at Madam Gudde's, he had destroyed his chance to recapture those moments.

He bit his lip with regret and turned away from the window. His four-post bed, with tester of muslin draped over its carved wooden frame, was within reach of his hand. He leaned against it while he eased off his boots, breeches and shirt. Unlike most British settlers, he preferred to sleep naked instead of wearing the same clothes day and night for a week or more. He took a final deep breath of the mountain breeze, drew back the muslin drapes and slipped into bed.

'What the devil!'

His shout disrupted the silence. He reared up and tried to leap out. He was trapped by the muslin canopy.

A hand touched his shoulder. 'You'll wake Charlotte with your noise.'

'Jessica!' He sank back onto the mattress and reached for her in the dark. 'How? What?'

His protest was smothered by her lips closing over his mouth. He submitted willingly to her kiss, puzzled by the fierceness with which she clutched his body. When he touched her to restrain her, he discovered she was naked. Her perfume overwhelmed him as she rubbed her breasts against his chest.

'I want you, Bart,' she whispered into his ear.

His nerves tingled with the sigh of her breath against his cheek. She toyed with the soft hairs at the nape of his neck, sending shivers down his spine.

He squirmed out of her grasp and held her firmly, hoping to calm her. The feel of her body in his arms stirred him and he was becoming roused. 'Why, Jess . . .?' he murmured, withdrawing from her.

'Love me, Bart!' She sounded close to despair. Her fingers plied him, seeking out the sensitive parts of his body with unerring accuracy.

He was baffled by her ardour and although he tried to

control the heat soaring through him, there was little he could do. He remembered his mother's words to take her with care yet she was demanding him with fury. He faced her, held her close and kissed her.

He made love that night like a stallion. He was fired by Jessica's need and responded eagerly. Her loving was greater than any he had known and, after the first moments of caution, he abandoned himself to her without restraint.

Hours passed in this blissful manner, neither of them aware of the time until they lay satiated, arms around each other, their bodies moistly together, and stared out through the muslin drapes at the lightening sky. Bart knew then the joy of fulfilment; his wife content, with a smile on her face, snuggling trustingly in his embrace.

Jessica amazed him. Gone was the reserve he had grown to expect of her. Instead, through her natural desire, she showed a greater intuition of how to satisfy him than Stella did. He revelled in it and was glad that after so long she had brought him happiness.

He longed to probe, to find out the reason for this change in her attitude after months of living in shame. As he framed his question, she sighed with sleep. He closed his eyes and slept too.

When he woke, the sun was high. Nimal or Jagath had considerately closed the shutters from the outside to keep the brightness from disturbing them. There was enough light in the room for him to see Jessica clearly. He gazed on her nakedness with interest, intrigued that so much frenzied passion was contained within her frail body.

She was almost boyish in figure, the opposite of Stella. She was pale; her complexion was the envy of the Burgher ladies who considered that the paler a woman, the better her birth.

The silken locks of her hair were dishevelled, spread in a swirl of gold over his arm that served as her pillow. Gold curls of damp downy hair sprouted where his eyes feasted. His throat tightened and he gazed at her enraptured. She opened her eyes and giggled.

'Good morning,' he whispered, leaning over and kissing her. 'Or perhaps it's good afternoon.'

She murmured contentedly and embraced him.

'I must leave you,' he said. 'The cane harvest . . . We've stayed abed so late, mother will be shocked.'

'Yes?' Her dreamy tone made him look at her quzzically. He longed to ask what had brought about the change in her. She giggled again.

'You look so pompous,' she said. 'You're the one who's shocked.'

He feigned astonishment. 'Me?'

'Hush!' She placed her finger on his lips. He kissed it which seemed to please her for she smiled and said, 'I suppose you've done so much, Bloodheart, that nothing shocks you.'

'No,' he said quickly, wondering what she meant.

'Have you lain with a lot of women?'

The question was not what he expected. He stared at her.

'I know I'm not as good as those whores,' she said, sounding sad. 'If you teach me . . .'

'By the devil!' He was dismayed by her mood. He pulled her close. 'What's got into you, Jess? Don't you know I have never loved a woman as much as you, never could. You've taught *me*!'

'You're just saying that.'

'Why should I?'

'Whores are skilled in making love. Surely they satisfy you more than I.'

Bart considered his reply carefully. Jessica was incapable of guile, her face was open and genuine. He supposed her questions were asked because she was worried about his visits to Madam Gudde's. Was that why she had made love to him so recklessly, to compete with his whores?

'What's worrying you, Jess? Don't you trust me?'

'Oh yes, Bart, I do. It's me I don't trust.'

'That's foolish.' He laughed and kissed her lips, but she pulled away before his tongue could enter her mouth.

'I hope it is,' she said. 'After what Daniel did, I was so ashamed . . .'

It was the first time she had referred to the rape by the Negro slave. Bart stroked her cheek tenderly, waiting for her to continue. 'Of course, you were,' he murmured. 'I understand that, we all do.'

'You don't.' She hesitated, her lips trembling. 'You think I was ashamed because of what happened.'

'Yes.'

'I wasn't, Bart. I was ashamed of . . .' She paused and looked at him imploringly. 'You won't be cross with me?'

'How could I!' He grinned and she seemed reassured.

'I was ashamed of the way I felt. I wondered if there was something wrong with me. You showed me last night that there isn't, that it's natural for me to enjoy being with a man.'

She reached down to his thighs and cupped him in her hand. 'Bart,' she said, 'I *loved* it! I loved the feel of that Caffre inside me.'

He shuddered as the warmth of her hand stirred him. He barely heard her words. He reached for her and pressed his mouth to hers, forcing open her lips with his tongue. He vowed then that he would never leave her for another woman again.

The revelation that Jessica was more amorous than he thought her to be, and its consequences, penetrated Bart's mind slowly. He was halfway through his bowl of scalding strong black coffee, without sugar, when it occurred to him that it was quite improper for a genteel wife to be so passionate.

It was Mammy's frown of disapproval at the lateness of his appearance in the parlour that caused him to question Jessica's behaviour.

'I was tired, Mammy,' he said lamely, to excuse himself.

She stood with her arms folded over her plump bosom, eyeing him witheringly while he sipped his coffee.

'Sometimes even I need a rest.'

Mammy's snort of scorn echoed in the cavernous living room. He gazed around him bleakly, pondering how he was going to cope with Jessica's change from being untouchable to insatiable.

'You does have too much to do to rest, Mas Bart.' Mammy

unfolded her arms and admonished him with a wag of her finger that set her podgy arm quivering. 'Same as me.'

He frowned as the oddness of Mammy's presence finally dawned on him. She was a creature of convention; there were certain things she would do and certain things she would not do. She did not wait at table; Nimal and Jagath did that.

So why, it gradually occurred to him, had Mammy brought him his coffee? He glanced at her suspiciously. Her heavy jowls were sombre, showing no sign of her customary cheerfulness.

He realized something else was wrong. Usually there were people moving around the small house. Jagath silently dusting, or Daisy polishing the floor, or his mother sitting in a corner by the window with her needlework. Today there was only Mammy.

He placed the coffee bowl on the table and stood up. He saw the glint in Mammy's eyes. 'What's going on?' he demanded anxiously. 'Where is everybody?'

Mammy enjoyed his alarm. 'Miss Jessica is in your chamber.' Her fat lips tightened in a mocking smile. 'You and I does be here. And here,' she added emphatically, her grin fading, 'is where I stayin'.'

He fought back his cry of exasperation, aware that Mammy was deliberately goading him. He strode over to the window and gazed out at the back of the house, confirming that none of the house staff were in the garden or in the kitchen cabin.

He rushed across the room and thrust open the double doors onto the verandah. He blinked and glanced along its length: it was as deserted as the rear of the house. He strode across it and stood by one of the columns, running his hand down that to reassure himself that at least the house was there.

Mammy waddled after him. 'I ain't goin' to dem fields even if Mistis Charlotte herself beg me!' she said defiantly.

He gazed at her as though she had gone mad. Mammy raised her finger and pointed accusingly in the direction of the river. Bart stared.

A whole cane field had been cleared. The sugar-cane lay in bundles waiting for the bullock carts to carry them to the mill.

Directing the work was his mother, with her head crowned by a wide bonnet to protect her from the sun. There were a score of Singhalese men, with their sarongs tucked up around their waists like loin cloths, hacking at the canes with cutlasses.

He saw Tissa in the middle of them, with Nimal and Jagath at his side. The four Caffre slaves were swinging their cutlasses expertly, showing the Singhalese how the work should be done. Daisy, Little and some native women were carrying the cut canes in bundles on their heads to a bullock cart.

'Tissa done ask me go'n carry cane too,' Mammy said indignantly. 'Mas Bart, I stayin' here.'

'I ain't!' His heart was heavy with shame that Tissa and his mother had started the work for him while he was still in bed with Jessica. He stripped off his shirt, flung it in Mammy's face and ran down the trail to join them.

The sugar harvest had begun.

CHAPTER SIX

Galle fascinated Havis St Valle. Every evening, however tired he felt after running hither and thither for Collector Radley, he sat on his bed with his journal open on his knees, quill and inkpot to hand, and recorded his impressions of the town.

It was a strange experience for a seventeen year old youth to be transported from the fringes of court life in London to this humid outpost in Ceylon. It was through his grandfather's connections as a physician to the Prince Regent that he had secured the post.

He realized that had he been less enchanted by his surroundings – and by the company of the Collector's daughter – he would have found it irksome being apprenticed to a choleric and inefficient government official. By nature he was a thoughtful young man, modest in his aspirations and anxious to acquit himself well and be a credit to his sponsors.

He knew that if he survived the period of his apprenticeship he could look forward to a post with the establishment. He would be one of the British elite with a substantial salary and pension that would enable him to enjoy a comfortable independence after a lifetime serving the colony.

Recruitment to the Ceylon civil service came under the personal control of the Secretary of State in London. No educational or other criteria were laid down for the selection of recruits, termed *writers* after the Indian fashion. Patronage was the sole determinant.

Writers were recruited young with the intention that they should mature in the environment where they were to serve in virtual exile. Havis was satisfied that his future, provided he did nothing to disgrace himself, was secure. The ignorant manner in which Collector Radley conducted his affairs, although exasperating, was insufficient to deter him from enjoying his good fortune.

He confided his thoughts and his impressions with gusto to his journal. 'The groups,' he wrote, 'collected about the landing place and lounging in the streets and bazaars of Galle, exhibit the most picturesque combinations of costume and races.'

He smiled to himself as he recalled his confusion at the first sight of those exotic looking people. After a few weeks he had learned to identify them.

'As well as the Europeans in their white morning undress, shaded by japanned umbrellas, there are Moors, Malabars and Malays, Chinese, Caffres, Parsees, and Chetties from the Coromondel coast, the latter with their singular head-dresses and prodigious ear-rings. There are Buddhist priests in yellow robes, and Moodliars, Mohandirams and other native chiefs in their rich official uniforms with jewelled buttons, embroidered belts and swords of ceremony.'

He omitted the more unpleasant aspects of life in Galle: the unbearable humidity that caused him to wake at three in the morning, his pillow soaked with perspiration and his body itching with prickly heat. There was the stench from sewers that hung heavy in the hot air until the tide came in, washed the sewers and banished the smell. There was the babble and bustle of the bazaar, and the constant appraisal of him by inquisitive natives.

He asked himself, as he laid his journal, the inkpot and pen on the table beside his bed, snuffed out his candle and stretched out to sleep, how Raven tolerated it. He had his career and his duty to his patrons to sustain him should he feel homesick for England; Raven had nothing.

His thoughts were often of Raven when he lay on top of his bed, struggling to sleep in the closeness of his chamber. Although the ceilings were high and the walls thick in the Collector's bungalow, the atmosphere even at night was unbearably hot. With the shutters open the ceaseless pounding of the sea on the rocks below the battlements added to his discomfort. How did Raven fare, he wondered.

After being her companion on the long voyage from England, he knew she was a strong-willed girl. She had borne the death at sea of her mother, to whom she was devoted, with fortitude. She showed courage and despite her sorrow declined to give in to her despair. He had expected her to find consolation with her father but after so many years apart, Mr Radley was as much a stranger to Raven as she was to him. In fact instead of sharing her feelings now she was reunited with her father, she became aloof.

He sighed in the darkness of his chamber. His room adjoined the courtyard, isolated from the main house where Mr Radley and Raven lived. Days would pass without him catching a glimpse of her. They dined separately and his duties prevented him idling in her company on the verandah. He suspected it was her father's wish to keep them apart.

The Collector's resentment of him was obvious. Mr Radley wanted someone to do his work, not a boy he was supposed to train. Havis tried hard but he lacked experience. Mr Radley offered little guidance which made him doubt whether the Collector was competent to handle the duties of his position.

Despite Mr Radley's shortcomings, and Raven's apparent preference for solitude, Havis was undaunted. He turned his pillow over, dismayed that already it was wet with sweat from his brow. He resolved in his heart to be a dutiful apprentice to the Collector, and a reliable friend to his daughter if ever she needed him. It was all he could aspire to at present.

He woke early, roused from a fitful night's sleep by the heat. The door eased open and a barefoot boy in a sarong glided in, softly calling his name. The boy placed a jug of water on his dresser, opened the shutter and, seeing he was awake, bowed before sidling soundlessly out of the room.

The town was stirring as Havis sluiced himself with the water. He walked to the open window and gazed out. His view was across the harbour to the hills at the opposite side of the bay, shrouded in shadow as the sun rose behind them.

He glanced at the vessels at anchor in the harbour. There were the dhows of the Arabs, the petamars of Malabar, the dhonies of Coromondel and the grotesque seaboats of the Maldive islanders. Darting between them with surprising velocity were the canoes of the Singhalese, fashioned from a single hollowed-out tree trunk with a log attached parallel to one side as a stabilizer.

The jangling of bullock carts trundling along the mud streets, accompanied by shouts and the crack of switch against hide, disturbed his contemplation of the idyllic scene. Cocks were crowing, foraging crows squawking loudly while birds in the shade trees whooped and warbled with daybreak.

From the battlements came the sound of guards changing duty. The streets were noisy with the early morning bustle of people emptying slops, hawking phlegm loudly, and greeting their neighbours.

Havis dressed with care, discarding his damp nightshirt and donning the drab outfit his position required. The undergarments, he found to his relief, reduced the effect of wearing so many clothes in the heat. Although he perspired constantly and had to keep a handkerchief to wipe his brow, he could not think of appearing among the natives in anything less than formal wear.

He regarded himself in the looking glass, brushing his curly hair flat across his forehead. Within minutes, the curls sprung back, making a mockery of his attempt to look neat and official. His tousled hair and sympathetic grin lent him a natural affability at variance with the stern manner he felt he should adopt.

His eyes, a greenish-grey in colour, were frank and friendly and attracted attention among people whose predominant colour, both of skin and eyes, was brown. Despite the care with which he dressed and groomed himself, and his efforts to remain unnoticed, he found it difficult to merge into the background as Collector Radley's writer.

He was not good looking, and he attributed Raven's lack of interest in him to his plain features. His teeth were crooked and he kept his mouth shut when he smiled so the defect would be hidden. His nose was too long, his chin too prominent.

He rubbed his hand over his jaw and peered closely at it in the mirror. He would need a shave soon where the down on his chin and cheeks was casting a shadow on his smooth, pale skin. With a final sweep of the brush over his hair, he turned away from the looking glass and went to the room Mr Radley used as his office. The houseboy had put a bowl of coffee for him on his desk. He sipped it slowly and reviewed the diary for the Collector's appointments that day. The morning was free. He was relieved, because he could use the time to copy letters.

He had been working diligently for an hour when a movement in the courtyard caught his eye. He was rewarded with a glimpse of Raven as she sauntered from her bedroom to the dining room for breakfast. He stared after her, captivated by the brief sight of her onyx-black ringlets and her moodily expressive face. Her complexion was a delicate pink from her deliberate exposure to the sun when she should have protected herself under a bonnet and parasol.

He observed that she walked across the grass without shoes or stockings. He was shocked and delighted, but fearful at what her outraged father would say if he knew. At times Raven positively delighted in defying her father. It made life difficult for him because Mr Radley vented his anger on him instead of reprimanding his own daughter.

Raised voices from the dining room warned him that the day was beginning badly. He winced, wondering how someone as outwardly sweet and charming as Raven could inspire the Collector to such wrath. When he heard Mr Radley shout his name, he jumped up hesitantly. He was being summoned to the dining room where he would at least see Raven, but the shame of being rebuked by her father in her presence made him reluctant to go.

He paused as Raven emerged from the dining room. She glanced in his direction, tossing her head as if to say her father's temper was nothing to do with her.

'Miss Raven . . .' he called softly. She ignored him and strolled coolly across the lawn to her room. He pursed his lips with disappointment and hurried in the direction of Mr Radley's loud voice.

The Collector was striding the length of the verandah. It was unusual for him to be agitated early in the morning and Havis feared the consequences. There was a messenger, a government Caffre, standing in the hot sun with his head bowed.

'What the devil does the boy want?' asked Mr Radley. 'How many times have I given instructions that I am not to be disturbed outside my official hours of duty?'

'Many times, sir,' Havis said politely, relieved that the Collector's temper was directed at the Negro slave and not at him. He crossed the verandah and stepped down into the yard, drawing the Caffre out of the sun with his hand on his bare shoulder.

'Do you speak English?' he asked, trying to put the Caffre at ease. Mr Radley was muttering threateningly in the background.

'Yessa,' said the Negro with a glance of scorn. 'Dat why I does be here.'

'Where's your message?'

The man looked baffled. He tapped his head. 'Here, sah.'

Havis grinned and the Negro smiled back with a flash of brilliantly white teeth.

'You should beat the boy with a horsewhip instead of indulging him.'

He ignored Mr Radley's outburst and tried to look serious. 'Tell me what it is quickly. The Collector will send you to the stocks if you upset him.'

'He goan be upset.' The Caffre scratched his ear. 'De prince want him. He say come twunce.'

'Twunce?' Havis repeated the word doubtfully. 'At once? What is wrong with the prince?'

The Caffre shook his head, relishing his ignorance. 'You have change, sah? I ain't eat.'

Without thinking, Havis opened his purse and gave the man a coin. There was an outburst of disgust from Mr Radley on the verandah. The Caffre ran off quickly.

'You're not claiming that tip on government expenses!'

'No, sir,' Havis kept his exasperation hidden. 'Prince

Gamunu presents his compliments and requests a visit from you, sir, with utmost urgency.'

'I heard what the slave said.' Mr Radley snorted at his attempt to mollify him with his smooth tongue. 'The prince is the bane of my life. I'm not going!'

'But sir –'

'You remind me of my duty? I am the Collector of Galle, not handmaid to a deposed princeling with ideas above his situation. He's a savage, Havis, and a tiresome one. You go to him and tell him I said so. I shall call on him every two weeks and no more. If he has any complaints, let him put them in writing, if he can write English, which I doubt.'

'Now, sir? Go now?' Havis was delighted at the chance to escape Mr Radley's wrath.

'Yes, yes!' The Collector waved his hand and dismissed him.

'You!' exclaimed Prince Gamunu, glaring with hard eyes at Havis. 'A boy is the Collector's emissary!'

Havis was so fascinated at being in the prince's presence, he was undaunted by the man's fierce expression. He stood in the centre of the large room that formed the prince's quarters and studied him.

The prince wore a white cloth covering his body from his chest to his ankles. On his head was a hat resembling a mortar board, flat with a veil of golden threaded muslin. He was sitting on a Dutch upright chair as though it was a throne.

'The Collector presents his compliments . . .'

'I know that, young man! The British obsequiousness is as shallow as the Kandyan. What did the old chap really say? That I harass him too much with my constant demands for attention? Is he not a civil servant? Should he not serve me civilly?'

Havis was unable to suppress his grin. The prince, who was obviously sharper than he looked, roared with laughter.

'What a guileless messenger you are, sir,' he said gleefully. 'Your face reveals you agree with me. Come,' he beckoned with his hand, indicating a chair at his side. 'Sit with me and tell me about yourself.'

Havis sat down, keeping his back straight. The prince

towered above him and it was then he realized that the prince's chair was elevated by a makeshift dais.

The room was furnished in Dutch fashion, with wooden chests, long elaborately carved wooden couches with wicker-work upholstery, and ponderous mahogany almirahs. Behind a curtain that billowed in the breeze wafting in from the open windows, was a four-poster double bed. It occurred to Havis how solitary the prince must find his enforced confinement.

The prince questioned him with the intensity of someone eager for company. He was particularly interested that the Prince Regent was his patron. 'Have you met him?' he demanded. 'What manner of man is he?'

'Alas, Your Highness,' said Havis fulfilling the role of a courtier, 'I have not. My grandfather is one of his physicians. He says he can be a very impatient patient.'

Prince Gamunu chuckled. 'You are a better companion than your miserable Collector,' he said. 'Can you believe that I who am worshipped by the nobles of the Kandyan kingdom, have been placed in the care of a man whose caste is that of a clerk!'

'The Collector is the most important civilian in the district,' Havis said correctly, hiding his smirk of agreement. 'Mr Radley is the district representative of the Governor himself, even if he is not of the upper class.'

'It is as I say,' Gamunu grinned ruefully. 'He is a clerk with a fancy title. Why, you have more breeding than he has. Your patron is the British prince. Are there no British nobles in Ceylon, people I can converse with as an equal?'

Havis kept to himself Mr Radley's view that Gamunu was a barbarian and a savage. He had respect for the prince's shame. 'I will convey your request to the Collector,' he said solemnly. 'I can understand how isolated you are.'

'I believe you do.' Gamunu beamed again. 'You are a sensible young man. I, who was born to ride the royal elephant the length and breadth of my family's kingdom, am denied the right to stroll through the streets of this foreign devil's fortress. Why? What alarm can I create?'

'I will explain your desire to promenade and for occasional

conversation with people of aristocratic status.'

'What a young diplomat! You could have done well in Kandy.' Extending his arm as though offering his hand to be kissed, the prince flicked his fingers towards himself in the Singhalese gesture of beckoning.

Havis rose to his feet and approached cautiously. There was a curious scent emanating from the prince, an odour of spice that was pleasant to his nostrils.

'Yes, Your Highness?'

Gamunu stood up and embraced him, holding him tightly. Havis was nonplussed and tried to wriggle free.

The prince gripped him firmly with his hands on his shoulders, staring into his eyes as he spoke.

'One day I will be king and you shall join my court! Do my bidding, and you will be noble. You are already, in my heart.'

Havis broke away, blushing furiously. He backed out of the room in haste, too embarrassed to speak.

CHAPTER SEVEN

A musky aroma lingered in Havis's nostrils long after he left
Prince Gamunu's chamber and reported his conversation to
Collector Radley. It was a startling smell, sweet and spicy,
hinting at the mysteries of an exotic eastern world of which he
knew very little.

It was a fragrance stronger than the frangipani trees that
grew in the courtyard, although it resembled it. He attributed
the stirring that occurred in his body when the prince held
him in his arms to that piquant odour.

He kept from Collector Radley the information that
Gamunu had hugged him. It would have made Mr Radley
even more scornful of the Kandyan. For Havis, though, it was
an incident charged with meaning. His physical arousal, the
tingling of his loins, he associated with desire and forbidden
pleasure. That he should feel that way at the touch of the
prince convinced him that Gamunu possessed a sorcerer's
power.

The smell of the frangipani flowers as he walked beneath
the trees in the courtyard was evocative of the Kandyan. He
plucked one of the blossoms and held it to his nose. It was a
white flower with five petals overlapping where they had
opened out from the bud. He inhaled deeply, closing his eyes
as he pictured the prince's strong, copper coloured body and
his proud features. His senses quivered and he felt Gamunu
was with him.

'Are you composing a sonnet?'

He opened his eyes and saw Raven watching him as though
she understood what was on his mind. He blushed. There was
a shrinking sensation in the pit of his stomach.

'I declare, you must have more than daddy's dull office

ledgers in your mind to be strolling in the garden smelling the flowers.'

He let the blossom fall to his feet and stared at it, uncertain what to say. It was the hour after dinner when the Collector was sleeping. Usually Raven stayed in the cool shadows of her chamber in the afternoons. He was surprised to see her in the courtyard garden. She was hatless, her black ringlets hanging loosely over her shoulders and shimmering in the sunlight.

'You should be careful of the sun. It could burn your skin.'

'I hope it does,' she said peevishly. 'Isn't the frangipani flower prettier pink than white?' She snapped off a bud from one of the trees. Its white petals were tinged with pink.

'You are pretty enough, Miss Raven, without changing your colour from white to pink.'

'Havis, save your compliments for your sonnet.' She began a circuit of the garden, keeping to the far end of the courtyard, away from her father's chamber.

He followed her, delighting in the rare chance to talk. 'I was not composing a sonnet,' he said to break the silence. 'I was merely enjoying the flower's perfume.'

'You're a romantic!' Her eyes sparkled. 'Tell me about the prince!'

He was startled by her abrupt demand.

She laughed at him. 'Such surprise on your face! I can read your mind. Do you disapprove of me? Is your visit to the prince a state secret?'

'No.' He shrugged his shoulders. 'The prince said my thoughts are revealed in my face. Am I to develop a deceitful mien to preserve my secrets?'

'Yes! If you want to be successful in the civil service you're not allowed to show, or even have, feelings.' She pouted. 'Daddy doesn't.'

'I'm sure he does. He has many problems in his position.'

'The prince is the main one. Tell me about him, please.' Her winsome smile made him weak.

He clasped his hands behind his back and walked with her, describing his meeting with the prince. To Collector Radley he had outlined only the gist of their conversation, to Raven

61

he related every word, except for the farewell. He could not understand his own reaction to Gamunu's exuberant embrace. He was not prepared to tell Raven about it until he could.

When he finished, there was silence. He glanced across at her. She was frowning.

'What does he look like?' she asked suddenly. 'Is he handsome?'

'In a swarthy fashion. He is well built, muscular, not given to fat.'

'Like a warrior? Like an ancient gladiator?'

'Perhaps . . .' He tried to follow her thoughts but her face gave no clue. She was inscrutable, and it troubled him that she seemed so much wiser than he was.

'What is daddy going to do?'

'Nothing. He said the prince is a prisoner and if he does not wish to speak with commoners he is not obliged to.'

'He must be very lonely.'

'He is. He craves company, not officials like your father or the army officers but people of his ilk.'

'There are no other princes here.'

'That's what your father said. I don't believe he wants princes to talk with. Someone who is independent and of noble manner would suffice. It seems sensible to try to grant his wish. He will only get more troublesome if we don't.'

'Is he allowed visitors?'

'Oh, yes. He is not a real prisoner. I've seen the Governor's instructions. He is a *guest* of the Government. He can entertain, even promenade around the town, as long as he has a trustworthy companion like your father as his escort. Unfortunately, your father refuses to be bothered.'

'Daddy's scared of him.'

Havis frowned, wondering what should be his reaction. He chuckled. 'I think I am too. He has a sort of evil magic about him. I can imagine him influencing simple natives to do what he wants.'

'Ah . . .' Raven's sigh was echoed by the wind that stirred the branches of the frangipani trees. The perfume from the flowers wafted over them both. Havis caught his breath. It was as if the prince was at his side.

'Do you want to help him?' Raven asked softly.

'If I can.'

'Do you remember the man we saw when we were walking in the bazaar? I asked you his name and one of the natives told you.'

'Bloodheart?'

'Daddy says he is related to an English earl.'

'Have you met him?'

'No.' She tossed her head, setting her tresses glimmering in the sunlight. 'Not yet . . .' She smiled with determination.

'I'll suggest it to your father.'

'That will spoil the plan! He disapproves of anything he has not thought of himself. Go to Bloodheart's plantation and tell him what you've told me. He'll understand.'

'You said you've never met him.'

'I haven't.' She paused under a tree and reached for a flower, holding it to her nose. She twirled it and glanced at him coyly. 'I know the measure of him from what I saw in the bazaar. He is the prince's man.'

She sighed again and the breeze seemed to sigh with her, giving Havis the impression that Gamunu was agreeing with everything she said.

The making of sugar is a painstaking process. As well as skill, it requires a large number of labourers to cut the cane; to carry it to the mill while it is succulent and not withered through remaining too long in the hot sun; to crush it, and to tend it from vat to vat during the boiling and cooling process. Bart and Tissa had the skill, it was the labour force that was lacking.

Bart's reaction when he saw his mother supervising the men in the canefield was one of astonishment. Unknown to him, Tissa had persuaded the Singhalese who were encamped on the plantation boundaries to join with the Caffres to get the cane cut.

The settlement of Singhalese had sprung up by itself. The

men were accustomed to performing duties for Bart, mostly clearing the jungle with their elephants and burning the undergrowth. That they were willing to cut cane in the heat of the sun surprised Bart, for it was not their usual work. He had overlooked the respect they had for him, after a few days they were working as hard as the Caffres. Because they were not compelled with a whip, they worked happily. Their pace was not as fast as slave labour, but the job was being done.

Bart formed them into gangs, making one responsible for feeding the canes into the massive grinding stones turned by the waterwheel. The juice extracted from them was channelled in wooden troughs to the interior of the millhouse where it flowed into vats. Another gang, under Tissa's supervision, boiled the juice in those vats over fires made from the squeezed and dried stalks of the cane.

Bart or Tissa judged when the liquid was boiled enough to be drained from vat to vat and gradually transferred to the cooling chamber. There it was placed in pots on griddle shelves to cool so the molasses crystallized into sugar. It was a hot, sticky, sweaty and smelly process that left Bart drained of energy when he returned to the villa at night. Because of the help from Tissa's Singhalese friends, the household staff were not needed in the fields, much to Mammy's relief. She was as exhilarated by the cane harvest as Bart was exhausted.

'You doin' somethin',' she announced boldly to Bart when he was preparing to leave for the fields one morning.

'You does be a man 'gain.' She beamed at Jessica who was on the verandah to see him leave.

Bart reflected on the double meaning of Mammy's words before he kissed his wife and walked off to the fields. Whatever Mammy was referring to, he was sure she was right.

His renewed relationship with Jessica and the start of the cane harvest had added zest to his step and given him confidence in the future. He had no idea how he could pay the natives and deliberately said nothing to Tissa. Let the cropping be finished first, he thought. The harvest was nearing completion and Bart was pleased. The dust from the cane and the cloying aroma of the boiling molasses sickened him. It pervaded his clothes and, although he bathed in the river every evening, followed him to bed at night.

Jessica drenched herself with perfume to smother the smell as he lay with her. He did not know whether the stench of the *frangouline*, the sugar liquor, or the smell of verbena and vetiver was worse.

He estimated that the remaining cane would take three more days to cut. He was walking slowly through the fields of stubble back to the house. The sun had set and dusk was descending fast. Fireflies with emerald sparkling on their tails were visible as they darted among the branches of the *suriya* trees surrounding the villa.

He approached the house wearily, thoroughly exhausted by his day in the mill. He was ready to sleep. The glow of the lanterns being hung in the verandah by Nimal cheered him.

He was jolted out of his relaxed mood by the sight of a stranger sitting on the verandah with Jessica on one side and his mother on the other. An odd sense of jealousy stirred in his breast.

For weeks, the three of them had lived without visits from anyone except the Singhalese families who were their neighbours and workers. The unexpected presence of a white man on his verandah threatened the intimacy that had developed between him, Jessica and his mother. He resented the man's intrusion.

He paused at the edge of the bougainvillaea bushes and studied the man without being observed. He was gesticulating as he spoke and Bart saw from Jessica's delighted smile that she was enchanted with his repartee. Incensed at seeing her happy because of a stranger, he burst from his hiding place and leapt onto the verandah with a shout. The man stopped speaking and rose to his feet immediately.

'Bart!' exclaimed his mother, startled by his sudden arrival. 'This gentleman is a newcomer from England.' Her voice was deep with caution, a warning to him to show politeness.

He halted in his headlong rush and stared at the visitor with embarrassment for his hasty reaction. He saw from the fine down on his face and the flicker of fear in his eyes that he was no more than a youth, despite his formal garb. He swallowed his anger and thrust out his hand.

'How d'ye do, sir,' said the youth, his thin voice squeaking as he shook his hand nervously. 'I beg your forgiveness for my unexpected visit.'

"This is Havis St Valle,' said his mother. 'He is newly apprenticed as writer to Collector Radley.'

'Is this an official visit?' Bart released the youth's hand and collapsed into a chair with a loud sigh to disguise his displeasure. 'You see a working man before you, sir, not a civil servant with salary and pension as a reward for pen pushing and incompetence. I have been in the fields since dawn. I regret I am too weary to be much of a host.'

'You are welcome nevertheless, Mr St Valle,' said his mother firmly. 'It is many months since we had company. You will stay the night, of course.'

'Where?' Bart held up his hands in mock despair. 'We have no guest chamber.'

'No doubt Mr St Valle is aware of our circumstances,' said Jessica sweetly. 'He can share our room while I sleep with mother.'

'You see the straits we are in, eh?' Bart was oddly pleased that the youth was embarrassed too.

St Valle's cheeks reddened and he was fidgeting, trying to say something but lacking the courage to speak out of turn. Bart wondered what bad news the Collector had entrusted to such an inexperienced messenger.

'Please . . .' said the youth with a squeak in his voice. He coughed, blushed, and began again. 'I have come without the Collector's knowledge, a private mission. I do not wish to cause any inconvenience. I am happy to spend the night here.'

He gestured at the verandah floor with such helplessness, Bart hesitated in forming a bad impression of the young man.

'I have to return to Galle before daybreak,' he continued. 'I'm a hard working man, too, in my fashion.' He grinned ruefully. 'Unfortunately, the Collector is not an understanding master.'

Jessica and Bart's mother murmured sympathetically, won

over by the young man's naive charm. To his surprise, Bart found himself warming too. His shy grin and frank expression were genuine.

Bart remembered how insecure he had been at the youth's age when he arrived in Ceylon. He felt sympathy for Havis St Valle if the Collector was anything like Marcus Van Dort had been.

'What brings you here, young fellow?' he asked, modifying the gruff tone of his voice. He noticed his mother gave him a glance of approval.

'Before you two men discuss business,' she said, 'how about a glass of punch for our visitor? A bite of supper too?'

'Please . . .' began Havis St Valle, rising to his feet as Bart's mother and Jessica stood up.

'Sit down, young fellow,' Bart interrupted him. 'Havis, is it?' He smiled, stretching out his legs and sitting back with his hands clasped behind his head.

'Well, Havis, you ought to know that when a man's mother and his wife decide to do something, protest is useless. You have been invited to drink, to eat, and to have my own bed for the night. You have created a favourable impression indeed.' He watched his mother lead Jessica inside the house. 'I had no idea,' he added with a smile, 'how starved for company we have all become.'

'I was talking with your mother about London,' Havis said. 'My grandfather is acquainted with friends of hers.' His lopsided grin and hopeless attempt to smooth down his tousled hair seemed familiar to Bart.

'I can see why my mother has taken to you,' he said. 'It's the maternal instinct.'

Nimal emerged from the house carrying a tray on which were two glasses of rum punch, the colour of purple bougainvillaea. He smiled as he offered a glass to Havis.

'You are honoured,' said Bart. 'This is made from an old recipe by our cook who cames from Barbados. You won't have a drink like this anywhere else in Ceylon.'

'I really don't drink, sir.'

'You must! My mother will be offended.' He was amused

67

by Havis's politeness. It reminded him that he too was starved of company.

'Do you have any, er, female friends in Galle?' he asked, hoping to lead the conversation around to Madam Gudde so he could ask about Stella.

'I am newly arrived, my work . . .' Havis spread his hands from which Bart understood the pressures he was under as Mr Radley's writer.

'I am acquainted only with the Collector's daughter,' he added shyly. 'Miss Raven Radley.'

'By the devil!' Bart sat up, thoughts of Stella chased from his mind. 'Now I remember where I've seen you before. You were holding her parasol.'

He noticed Havis's blush and raised his glass. 'Let's drink to that young lady's health!' He sipped his punch with relish and watched Havis cautiously do the same.

'Is she as beautiful as I remember?' he asked to encourage Havis to speak. 'She was hidden by her bonnet and your damned parasol when I saw her. It was impossible to see her clearly.'

'She is, she is!'

He wondered if the deepening flush in Havis's cheeks was due to the punch or to a yearning for the Collector's daughter. Again he experienced a pang of jealousy. It was odd that he should envy the young man for his relationship with a girl he had seen but once.

'Are you very friendly with her?' he asked gently, implying it was a question of no importance.

'I wish I was!' Havis's sigh showed how he felt. 'She keeps to herself. We lead a lonely life in Galle, not like you here with your family. Your mother and good lady have made me more welcome than I have been since leaving England.'

The talk continued in this fashion until Bart had to urge Havis to explain the purpose of his visit. Jessica returned to the verandah as he did so, and sat without a word in her seat. The rum punch served to loosen Havis's tongue.

'It was Miss Raven who suggested I visit you,' he said eagerly. 'She understands these matters better than her father does . . .'

'What matters?' Bart prompted.

'How the prince feels. Prince Gamunu is in virtual solitary confinement not by law but because Mr Radley refuses to spend time with him. He longs for people of intelligence and breeding to converse with. He is forbidden Singhalese visitors in case he stirs up trouble. There are no British settlers in Galle who could call on him. Only you.'

'Why me?' Bart pursed his lips, intrigued by the suggestion.

'The prince will respect you, according to Miss Raven. She referred to your background, and daring.'

'Raven seems to be a very astute young lady.' Jessica spoke with a tone of scorn that made Bart flinch.

'Could you call on the prince when you are next in Galle? It is very bold of me to make the request. I feel sorry for him, and Miss Raven did suggest you . . .' Havis's voice trailed off and he sat back in his seat and stared from Bart to Jessica and back again.

'To please Miss Raven,' said Bart gaily, 'I would be delighted to visit Prince Gamunu.'

'So would I!' said Jessica in a voice that brooked no denial and caused Bart a tremor of disquiet.

'That is not necessary, my dear,' he said. He was hoping to call on Stella during his visit to Galle. If Jessica accompanied him he would be unable to go to the brothel.

He felt Jessica's eyes on him. She was smiling coldly. 'If you are going to Galle, Bart, I am coming too.'

CHAPTER EIGHT

The expedition set out at daybreak. What Bart originally intended to be a simple march, the five miles to Galle and back the next day, was a grander affair. Jessica made sure of that. Although she was born in Galle, her childhood there with her step-father, Marcus Van Dort, had not been happy. She had been content since her marriage to avoid the town.

Havis's talk of the new Collector and his daughter, of the Kandyan prince, and of the colourful dress materials, gems and imported goods on sale in the Street of Moorish Traders, made her yearn to visit there again, and her suspicions about what Bart might do if he was allowed to go alone, added to her resolve. She had an ally in Bart's mother who decreed that if Jessica was going to Galle, she was going too.

It was a party of eight that set out for Galle when the sugar harvest was over. Because both she and Charlotte were making the trip, the children could not be left on the plantation. Malika, Tissa's sister, who was their nurse, accompanied them. Daisy, the pretty Caffre slave from Mozambique, was enlisted as a maid for herself and Charlotte.

Bart insisted on taking Tissa, claiming he needed his help in arranging to ship the sugar, which was his reason for going to Galle. In addition, there were the drivers of two bullock carts and a dozen Singhalese of various ages who joined them for the joy of making a journey.

Jessica was excited. She sat in the cart opposite Charlotte and smiled with triumph because, despite Bart's protests, they were at last on their way. The cart lurched forward and she clung to the side of the seat to stop being thrown out.

The cart was designed as a passenger vehicle with two leather seats stuffed with coconut fibre facing each other. An awning of leather kept off the rain and the sun. There were brass brackets at both sides to hold candle lamps for night riding, and a step giving access from the rear. But for the bullock that pulled it, and the bare-chested driver in loin cloth who crouched on its shafts, it could have been a carriage in London.

Jessica's mind was full of fantasy that morning. She had never left Ceylon. Since she and Bart were reconciled she was content with life on the plantation. Bart treated her well and seemed to love her. He was a husband again in every sense.

Her fantasies included him. She imagined they were driving in state to visit the Prince Regent who would commend Bart for his pioneering and guarantee him a good price for his sugar.

She understood how important it was that the sugar should sell for a high amount in England. She married Bart without a dowry and blamed herself for the disaster which had befallen him because of her step-father. If there was anything she could do to restore Bart's fortune, she would do it willingly.

She noticed that Charlotte appeared to be thinking too. It was impossible to converse with the swaying of the vehicle and the noise of the natives chattering excitedly as they ran alongside the carts. The determined expression on Charlotte's face meant she would refuse to acknowledge the discomfort of the ride, however much she was suffering. Jessica admired her.

When she married Bart, his mother had resented her. Their shared misfortunes had brought them close though until they understood each other perfectly, especially where Bart was concerned. She saw in Charlotte a formidable woman, too proud to admit when she was wrong and fiercely loyal to her family. It was Charlotte who gave Bart his backbone.

'We will have a splendid time,' said Charlotte loudly, breaking into Jessica's contemplation of her. 'We deserve to leave the plantation for a few days. We have let Bart's obsession with sugar become ours.'

'He is anxious to sell it for a high price to repay you.' Jessica shouted in reply.

'We are not destitute yet.' There was a twinkle in her eye. 'Better to let Bart think we are. Men like to be chivalrous. It is not Bart's nature to depend on a woman.' A sudden lurch by the cart cut off the conversation.

For their stay in Galle, Tissa had arranged the temporary renting of a single storey house belonging to an impoverished Burgher couple. The house with its gloomy interior – despite the bright sunshine outside – reminded Jessica of her childhood home at the corner of Church and Rampart Streets. The Burgher couple knew her and treated her with awe. They gave up their own room and moved into their deserted slave quarters to act as servants during their stay.

Jessica was sorry to see these once proud descendants of Dutch and Singhalese families reduced to penury. Since the conquest of Ceylon by the British, they existed by letting their home to visitors. She was therefore relieved when Charlotte pronounced herself charmed with the house and swiftly set about organizing their occupation. While she worked, Bart slumped with his feet up on a couch in the parlour. He had walked the five miles instead of riding in the second cart with Malika and the children. Jessica let him rest while she helped Charlotte.

There was a room for Malika and the babies where Daisy could sleep too. She and Bart would have the couple's own bedroom while Charlotte took over the guest room at the rear of the house. Tissa would sleep on his mat on the tiled floor.

As Jessica explored the house, aware of the activity of people passing in the street, she hoped Bart would stay in Galle for several weeks. It would be fun to meet her old friends. She was not certain how she would react to seeing her step-father. Since he was sacked from his official position, he spent most of his time in his house engaged in various nefarious schemes.

When she had finished her unpacking, she returned to the parlour. The Burgher lady, Mrs Henricus, brought her a glass of tamarind juice which she sipped quietly as she gazed at Bart asleep on the couch. She suspected he planned to evade her at some stage during their stay in Galle. She was determined that he would not.

'Come, come!' Charlotte burst into the room, clapping her hands, startling her and waking Bart.

72

'Mother!' Bart groaned, opening his eyes lazily. 'After the weeks I've spent in the cane fields, can't I rest for this afternoon?'

'As much as you want, Bart. After you've called on the Collector.'

'Why do I have to waste time seeing that incompetent dullard?'

'Courtesy is never a waste of time. Besides, I have yet to meet him, so has Jessica.'

Bart's sigh acknowledged that he was bound to obey her. Jessica was pleased and hurried to her room to prepare herself. She changed from her travelling gown to one more suitable for calling on the Governor's representative. When she returned to the parlour, Charlotte and Bart were ready and three palanquins were drawn up outside the house.

'This is grand,' she said, worried about the expense.

Bart grimaced. 'Mother says we must do things properly.'

'Of course.' Charlotte led the way out of the house. 'We have to keep up appearances whatever our situation. If word spreads that we neglect to do so, people will have no respect for us.'

Bart held back the curtain of the palanquin for his mother to enter. Tissa helped Jessica into hers and she peeped out to see Bart enter the third one. The palanquin was small with space for only one passenger on its cushions. The curtains that enclosed her provided protection from the sun and from the prying eyes of the people gathered around them. Any unusual activity attracted attention in Ceylon and a procession of three palanquins was a sensation.

Jessica loved the prestige generated by their ostentatious progress through the town. She listened to the voices beyond the curtains and heard the words of awe that were bandied among the crowd when it became known that Bloodheart and his ladies were visiting the Collector.

Charlotte was right. The Singhalese liked pomp and ceremony and trusted strangers who showed style and wealth. It mattered little what their real circumstances were, as long as they appeared prosperous.

Jessica longed to peer through the curtains at the crowd but she restrained herself until the swaying of the contraption and the chanting of the bearers ceased and the palanquin swung to a halt. She heard Havis's voice and glanced up expectantly as he drew aside her curtain.

'Welcome, Mrs Taylor,' he said with a flourish and a bow. She held out her hand for him to help her.

'Please tell your husband,' Havis whispered in her ear, 'to say nothing about my visit to the plantation. Let Mr Radley think he himself is making the suggestion about calling on the prince.'

Bart hurried over. 'What are you whispering to my wife, Havis?' he asked as a joke but his voice had a sharp edge to it. He peered eagerly at the verandah as though looking for someone.

Jessica found Mr Radley livelier than Bart described him. He was a typical English gentleman, practised in small talk and utterly charming. He made a good impression on Charlotte and they were soon talking about mutual acquaintances. She listened with fascination. Bart annoyed her by fidgeting and yawning, despite her glances of disapproval. She was sitting beside him on a couch and rested her hand on his arm to restrain him. She noticed his display of bad manners ceased when the door to the courtyard opened and Mr Radley's daughter entered without warning.

Her first impression of Raven Radley was not favourable. She wondered why Bart was gawping at her. The girl was immature and looked like a peasant with face and arms showing the coarsening effect of the sun. It gave her a dusky appearance, not suitable for the daughter of an important man. Most of all, she was astonished by her dress. It was low cut with a bodice that revealed more flesh than was appropriate to her age and for the time of day.

'Mr Radley,' she said smiling archly, hoping to distract Bart from ogling the girl. 'What do you do about your daughter's education? Does she have a governess?'

Mr Radley sighed. 'Raven is teaching herself. She reads a lot.'

She observed when Raven sat down how she arranged her skirt so that some of her ankle was showing. Bart, judging by his bulging eyes, noticed the flash of white flesh below her hem.

'Your daughter must find life in Ceylon rather dull.' she said pointedly. 'I suppose she'll be returning home to England soon?'

'No, Mistress Taylor.' Raven turned cold eyes on her and spoke in a firm voice. 'Home is with my father.'

'How charming,' Charlotte interrupted before she could think of an apt retort. 'I'm sure you are a source of joy for him.'

'Miss Raven would be that for any man,' gushed Bart.

Jessica looked at him sharply. Raven merely smiled, implying the compliment meant nothing to her.

'She must be helpful in your entertaining?' said Charlotte to revive the conversation.

Bart spoke on cue. 'I hear you are responsible for a reluctant guest, the Kandyan prince?'

There was a noticable stirring of interest in the room with both Havis and Raven leaning forward in their seats. Mr Radley frowned.

'A thankless task,' he said. 'The chap needs constant attention.'

'Would it be possible for me to call on him?' Bart asked casually. 'Is he allowed visitors?'

Mr Radley's face brightened. 'What a splendid idea. You'll find him a pompous charlatan, but if you visit him he can't say we British are neglecting him, what?'

There was an easing of tension and the conversation continued until Charlotte suggested that they should leave. Jessica saw Raven glance slyly at Bart when they were saying their farewells on the verandah.

She was worried by that glance. Raven was young, yet the way she was eyeing Bart had none of the innocence of youth. To Jessica it was the hungry glance of a lustful and scheming houri.

The entrance to the Street of Moorish Traders was visible from the porch of the Henricuses' house. Bart stood on the narrow porch and stared longingly at it. Behind him, all the doors and shutters of the house were wide open. Whatever Bart said could be heard by Jessica and his mother sitting in the parlour. He had his back to the windows and tried to ignore them.

It was dusk, the half-hour when day in the tropics rapidly transforms itself into night. Lamps were being lit in the houses and the people strolling the street were becoming shadows in the gloom.

At the corner of the Street of Moorish Traders, three soldiers gossiped idly. They reached a decision and with much slapping of backs to encourage each other, moved down the street. Bart guessed they were going to Madam Gudde's. He envied them.

He sensed someone standing beside him on the porch. He scowled, thinking it was Jessica. He refused to turn round.

'Jessica is asking if you would like a juice?'

'Thank God it's you, Tissa!' He grinned, putting his arm around Tissa's shoulder and drawing him close. He kept his voice low. 'I thought you were Jessica come to see if she can read my thoughts.'

Tissa stared down the street to the corner and nodded sympathetically.

'She won't leave me alone, Tissa. What am I to do?'

'What do you want to do?'

Bart shrugged. He moved in front of the double pillars so he was one side of them and Tissa the other. Both of them were shielded by the columns from Jessica if she was watching inside the parlour.

'Nothing special,' he replied. 'I'd like to take a walk along the ramparts. Meet some acquaintances . . .'

'Madam Gudde, for instance?'

'Dammit, Tissa! I can't come to Galle without calling on Gretchen.'

'She alone?'

'Tissa!' Bart pretended to be shocked, although he was touched by Tissa's understanding. 'I am a happily married man.'

'Jessica wants you to remain so!'

76

'By the devil, why is she watching everything I do? She wasn't like this before.'

'She is more of a woman now, Bloodheart.' He nodded his head wisely. 'You have made her that way. She is worried lest she loses you.'

'Lose me!' Bart scoffed at the suggestion. 'A man needs a little freedom now and then.'

'Tell her that.'

He shook his head. 'I'll not ask any woman for permission to do what I want. Let's step out into the street, shall we?' He glanced towards the corner. 'Walk with me.'

He moved one pace from the porch, clutching Tissa's arm as though engrossed in conversation and unaware of what he was doing. There was a shrill cry from the doorway behind. He stopped and turned, his eyebrow raised, anticipating Jessica's protest.

'Where are you going, Bart?'

'A stroll, my dear, now it's cooler.' He waved vaguely down the street. 'You know I don't like to be confined inside an airless house.'

'What a good idea!' Jessica smiled brightly. 'I'll come too.'

'Perhaps it's not a good idea.' He stepped back onto the porch, thwarted by her ploy. If she had criticised him for going he could have asserted himself and stormed off in a rage. Her intention of accompanying him made it impossible to deal with her in that manner.

'The roads are muddy, darling. You will spoil your fine gown.'

'Tissa can walk ahead with a flambeau to show us the way.'

'No,' he said. 'We won't go. I'll stay on the porch for a while with Tissa. We have to discuss tomorrow's business.'

'May I bring you a tamarind juice?'

He shook his head without speaking. She smiled simply and glided into the parlour while he rolled his eyes at Tissa behind her back.

'I'm caught,' he said glumly. 'Do I have to wait until she's asleep before I can escape?'

'Be patient.' Tissa looked wise. 'This is her first night.

77

She's nervous. Wait until tomorrow. She and Mistress Charlotte are sure to go shopping. There'll be dozens of things to distract her. You can slip away then.'

'Imagine!' Bart pulled the lobe of his ear unhappily. 'A prisoner of my own wife. You'll have to help me.' He lowered his head close to Tissa's and began to outline a plan.

Bart brooded the rest of the evening as he sat in the parlour with his mother and Jessica after supper. He refused to join in his mother's chatter about what she and Jessica hoped to do while in Galle. However, when she announced that they proposed to accompany him to see Prince Gamunu, he snapped out of his mood to protest.

'You can't come!' he said sulkily.

'Whyever not?' His mother drew back her shoulders and stared at him as though he was a little boy.

'It's not done . . .' He paused, trying to think of a convincing reason.

'I disagree,' said his mother. 'There are no precedents. Mr Radley wants an amenable prince. Who better than two ladies of quality to placate a Kandyan noble? You'll only bully him.'

Bart sighed. 'If you insist. We'll go in the morning.' He sank back in his seat, lapsing into silence.

That night, when they were in bed, he turned his back on Jessica.

'Bart . . .' she whispered in surprise, stroking his spine.

He wriggled his shoulders, moving away from her. 'I'm tired.' he said. 'Go to sleep.' He sensed her shock at his curtness. It hurt him to cause her distress but she deserved it.

Her hand touched his spine again.

'Leave me alone,' he said angrily. 'I want to sleep.'

'What's wrong, Bart. Is it something I've done?' She drew away from him.

'Yes!' The word was out of his mouth with a loud exclamation before he could stop himself.

'Tell me,' she said in a soft, frightened voice.

He did not hear her sorrow, nor heed Tissa's advice to be patient. Something goaded him to utter words he knew would upset her. 'Why are you so possessive?' he demanded.

'Am I?' She was close to tears but he continued without pause.

'Dammit, of course you are! I saw how you were watching me this afternoon at Mr Radley's. You were perfectly spiteful to that young girl because of it.'

She bit her lip and said nothing.

'You behaved very oddly. Raven is just a child on the verge of adulthood. She has the freshness and innocence of youth, she –'

'She was deliberately provoking you. You couldn't take your eyes off her.'

'Why should I?' He sat up, giving vent to his rancour. 'You kept on touching my arm to stop me. She's stunningly beautiful, is that being provocative? Because I enjoyed looking at her doesn't mean I want to seduce her.'

The tears trickled down Jessica's cheek. He felt rotten for causing them, especially when she muttered sorrowfully, 'Forgive me, Bart.'

He felt her hand slip into his. He let her squeeze him, pretending not to notice.

'I was nervous, Bart. She's younger than I am. She's English . . .'

'Dammit, Jess!' He pulled away and stared at her. 'Don't you know you can trust me? You're the one I love.'

'I shouldn't have come,' she said tearfully. 'I should have stayed at home on the plantation.'

'Why do you say that?'

'I've made you cross.'

'Perhaps you have.' He patted her hand, feeling wretched but relieved she knew her mistake. 'I'm not cross that you came with me. We can do lots of things together. But I must be allowed some time to myself. I have to arrange to ship the sugar –'

'You won't stay out at night, will you?'

He tensed, grinding his teeth together. Her hand wound around his own. He shook his head and sighed. 'What a silly woman you are. Why should I do that?'

'I don't know.' She smiled at the change in his attitude. She leaned over and kissed him lightly on his lips, withdrawing before he could push her away.

He considered what she had said. It was a modicum of freedom. He could arrange to see Stella during the day instead and keep his nights free for her. He was drowsy and barely aware of what she was doing. Her head was lying on his chest. He lay back on the pillow, idly stroking the hair at the nape of her neck. The thought of Stella and her reckless loving caused his loins to stir.

He snuggled comfortably into the soft down of the mattress. His hand, with a life of its own, exerted a gentle pressure on Jessica's head. She moved lower without resistance, touching his chest and then his stomach with kisses.

In the darkness, as he drifted in that oblivion of dreams and desire, he could not believe this was his wife whose lips were seeking him. He stroked her hair in a frenzy, pushing her lower, imagining she was Stella.

He was astonished when her mouth closed over him and she began to make love to him with all the fire of a whore.

CHAPTER NINE

The colonnaded mansion with its sweeping verandah and lofty ceilings was an impressive sight. Awnings kept out the sun from the seven round-arched windows of its two upper storeys. Each room commanded views over the battlements to Galle harbour. It was an imposing building, the tallest in the town, and well suited for the incarceration of a prince.

Bart's acquaintance with the unhappy prisoner began when his palanquin deposited him at the porticoed entrance to the mansion and he gazed up to see the prince staring down at him from the top of the steps. He experienced an uncanny sensation of having seen the man before. When their eyes met, he saw a start of recognition on the prince's face. It faded quickly as he turned to watch Jessica and his mother alight from their palanquins.

The prince had Havis at his side and whispered into his ear before pushing him lightly down the steps to meet them. He raised his eyes and stared at the hills at the other side of the bay while Havis escorted them onto the verandah.

Instead of being cowered by this display of princely arrogance, Bart used the moments of waiting to study Gamunu. He sensed in his hard features a conviction that he believed in himself as a man of destiny.

He was standing in profile, the gold ornamenting the muslin veil of his flat hat, sparkling impressively in the sun light. His jaw was tilted upwards, the nostrils of his finely shaped nose quivering as his eyes gazed at a scene of triumph that was yet to be his.

Bart coughed. He had been warned by Mr Radley that the prince would seek to impose his regal status on him, in defiance of his situation as an exile.

'The Prince Regent of Great Britain,' he said loudly to Havis, 'has a reputation for appreciating ladies of noble birth. Are we to assume from the attitude of this prince of the Kandyan kingdom that he is inferior in this regard?'

'Inferior?' The prince's deep voice filled the sweep of the verandah with its shocked tone.

Bart felt the pressure of Jessica's touch on his arm, warning him not to provoke him. He shrugged her off and stepped forward, his hand stretched out. 'A man,' he said, 'even a princely one, who spurns the hand of friendship, may regret it.'

'Ah, yes,' said the prince, turning his gaze on Bart and smiling graciously. 'Yet it is not unknown for those who come in friendship to have a dagger concealed up their sleeve.'

He touched his palms together in the Singhalese greeting, bowing his head to each of them in turn before taking Bart's hand in a handshake that was oddly limp for such a tall and intimidating man.

'Come,' said the prince, tiring of his theatrical posing and becoming a genial host instead. 'Shall we sit here?' He gestured to the chairs set out on the verandah around a table.

'My host, the Collector,' he smiled ruefully, 'has given me permission to entertain on this pleasant verandah. He is prompted by consideration of my visitors rather than of me.'

'If that is so then our visit has brought you an immediate benefit.' Bart's mother beamed at the prince, her voice showing no trace of the irony in her remark.

The prince blinked. 'I have heard from young Havis,' he said as he arranged himself in his chair, 'that I would find you and your brother stimulating company.'

'My brother?' Bart's mother simpered.

'My mother appreciates your flattery,' said Bart crossly. 'You surely do not believe that she is also my sister?'

'Are we not all brothers and sisters?'

'That is an unusual statement for a prince to make.'

Prince Gamunu nodded his head sagely. 'I see you do not intend to flatter me by agreeing with whatever I say.'

'Why should I? Havis has told me of your loneliness in Galle. If you need someone to agree with you, I will send you a looking glass.' He ignored Jessica's glance of alarm at his rudeness.

'Ah.' The prince sounded sad. 'I do not have the confidence to converse with myself without doubting what I say. Do you?'

Bart acknowledged the question with a nod, relieved by the arrival of a servant bearing a tray of fruit juice that prevented him having to make a witty reply. While the juice was handed round and Prince Gamunu turned his attention to Jessica and his mother, Bart watched.

Jessica was soon giggling at Gamunu's small talk, yet underlying his repartee there was a sense that he was holding himself back. He was enjoying the chance to show off but everything he said sounded false.

Bart got the impression he was testing them to see how far he could exploit them for his own ends. Jessica, and to a lesser extent his mother, were enthralled. There was a hypnotic quality about his eyes and his deep voice was reassuring.

A disturbance in the street distracted them. Tissa pushed through the throng of people gathered outside the mansion. He paid no attention to Prince Gamunu, thereby demonstrating his unequivocal allegiance to the British. He addressed Bart directly.

'Sir,' he said importantly, 'you must come at once.'

'I can't.' Bart waved him aside. 'I'm busy.'

'He can wait.' Tissa cast a glance of scorn at Gamunu. 'I found the ship's captain you want to see. He's sailing today so you must come now before it's too late.'

Normally Bart would have reprimanded Tissa for his boldness. However, as a ploy to make the prince feel inferior to the demands of a servant, it was effective.

'Forgive me,' said Bart standing up. 'My servant requires me urgently.'

The prince's supercilious stare masked his reaction to the insult.

'Mother,' said Bart, 'you and Jessica can stay if you wish. Havis will escort you to the Henricuses' house when you are ready.'

'That's all right,' said Jessica, her eagerness surprising him.

He assumed her compliance was the result of their agreement

the night before. He missed the glance she exchanged with Prince Gamunu because he was concentrating on his own deceit.

'I shall visit you again, prince,' he said casually. 'When I have the time.'

The prince's jaw tilted upwards; he said nothing. Bart was pleased he had shown him he was not going to fall victim to his charm like Jessica and his mother.

He squeezed Jessica's hand and whispered, 'I'll see you at the house later.' He nodded curtly at Gamunu and hurried down the steps with Tissa.

'Well done!' he said as soon as they were away from the mansion and walking up Church Street. 'Where's this captain?'

'I'm not sure,' said Tissa with a wink. 'Perhaps he's at Madam Gudde's, unless he's sailed already. You'll have to go there and see.'

'You little devil!'

'You asked me to arrange it so you could see Stella.'

Bart chuckled. 'Jessica is so fascinated by Prince Gamunu she won't give me a thought for a while.'

'He is not an honourable man.' Tissa sounded concerned. 'A Singhalese delights in stealing another man's wife, especially a foreigner's.'

'Not Gamunu.' Bart dismissed Tissa's warning confidently. 'He's not a lady's man.' He quickened his pace, turning off Church Street into the Street of the Moorish Traders. Already he felt the excitement welling up inside him. Sweat was running down his face but he ignored it.

'I should have an hour before Jessica frets about my absence. That's all I need to explain to Stella that I'm not going to buy her.'

Tissa looked at him doubtfully.

'It's true,' he protested. 'I'm determined to be frank with her.'

What he planned to do was not only for Jessica's sake. He was intrigued by his brief meeting with Mr Radley's daughter. He wanted to use his free time from Jessica to see her, instead of Stella.

They reached the door set into the high wall outside the bordello. Bart tried to control the pumping of his heart as he rapped loudly on it. He wondered what Stella would say.

It was morning, the time when callers at Madam Gudde's were rare. He ignored the people on the street who stopped what they were doing and watched him blankly. He was used to the unabashed curiosity of the Singhalese and no longer found it inhibiting.

The door opened. Instead of seeing a slave as he expected, Bart found himself face to face with a plump man whose tiny, bloodshot eyes gazed at him balefully. The flesh where his eyebrows should have been was hairless. It puckered with surprise. His jowls shook and an obscene gobbling sound rumbled in his throat.

Tissa yelped as though struck with the man's stick. He edged behind Bart to hide.

The man's bulk blocked the entrance to the bordello's yard. His pudgy hands clutched the doorjamb and he seemed about to launch himself through the opening like a ball from a cannon.

Bart stood his ground although he was sickened at being so close to the man with his blotchy skin, bloated face, his foul body odour and stinking, rumpled clothes.

'Van Dort!' he said scornfully. 'Just the place I'd expect to see you being thrown out of. Madam Gudde's whores are too good for the likes of you.'

'Bah!' Van Dort raised his cane to Bart's shoulder but he moved aside smartly and the blow missed. His momentum propelled Van Dort through the doorway and into the street. A hat covered his bald head but there was no hiding the malicious glint in his pig-like eyes.

'Does my daughter know you haf business here?' he demanded with a grim chuckle.

'Yes.' Bart lied, challenging Van Dort with his eyes. 'So does my mother.'

The obscene rumbling sound erupted in Van Dort's throat again and the fleshy folds of his face quaked. His mouth plopped open. The tiny globs of phlegm on his lips became a stream of spittle that spat out and smacked against Bart's cheek.

85

Van Dort wheezed with pleasure at the shock in Bart's eyes. He heaved his bulk away and waddled off down the street without another word.

'Now he knows you're in Galle,' said Tissa peeping after him from behind Bart's back. 'He'll do something terrible.'

Bart wiped the phlegm off his face and scowled with disgust. 'Let him try. I'm not worried.' He stepped through the entrance and Tissa followed, glancing behind nervously at Van Dort in the distance. A Caffre slave closed the door.

'Where is Madam Gudde?' Bart asked the Caffre.

'Sleepin', sah.' The Caffre wore a skimpy loin cloth and Bart guessed from his size why Gretchen Gudde employed him in her brothel. He would be a star in the tableaux vivants she arranged for her special customers.

'Call Stella for me,' he said, following the Caffre into the gloomy interior of the parlour. Tissa hitched up his sarong and hunkered down on his haunches to wait outside.

The Caffre rolled his eyes unhappily. 'Miz Stella, sah? She ain't 'vailable to clients.'

'I know that.' He was surprised that Stella was keeping her promise. He expected her to be with a customer. It would have given him an excuse to finish with her. 'Tell her Bloodheart is here.'

The slave backed away towards the door to Madam Gudde's chamber that adjoined the parlour. The door and windows overlooking the entrance yard were closed. Light for the room came from the window that was open onto the courtyard.

Bart walked over to it and leaned out, breathing in fresh air. Two women in undergarments were sitting on a bench in a shaded corner of the courtyard. They were Burghers with dark hair and tallow-white skins, their unsightly bodies rolling with fat. In the bright light, without corsets and face paint, they looked slovenly and repelling.

Bart turned away, thinking guiltily that this was what Stella would become after a few years as a whore.

The Caffre came back into the room. 'Yo' sit down,' he said indicating a chair, reproving him with a glance for being by the window. 'She comin' soon.'

'Is she in there?' He ignored the slave's instruction to sit and strode over to the door. It was ajar behind the curtain. The Caffre put out a long arm and gripped him by his shoulder, halting him.

'Let go of me!' He shoved the Caffre's arm away angrily. He pulled aside the curtain and dashed into the room. 'Stella?' he called, peering into the gloom.

There was a candle burning beside the four poster bed. The muslin drapes were raised and he saw Stella lying naked on the bed with Gretchen Gudde. Their arms were around each other and they were kissing passionately.

Bart stepped towards them only to feel his legs pulled away suddenly. He reached in vain for the bedpost. Stella screamed as he shouted and toppled over with a crash.

He tried to rise from the floor but a blow to the back of his neck felled him again. The Caffre flung himself on top of him, pinning him to the floor with his great weight.

'Let me do him, mistis,' the Caffre begged. 'He done s'prise me.'

Gretchen Gudde sat up in the bed, her pendulous breasts thrown into relief by the candle glow. She kept a grip on Stella, preventing her from leaving the bed and running to him.

'I've waited a long time for you, Bart. Stella has given up hope.'

'Get this damn Caffre off of me!'

'Ah yes, you must excuse Junie for his excessive zeal. 'Release the gentleman, Junie.' At that moment Gretchen relaxed her hold on Stella.

Bart sprang to his feet and dusted down his coat. He pretended to move towards Stella but feinted, swung around and drove his fist sharply into the Caffre's crotch. The slave grunted and collapsed on the floor, clutching himself.

'Oh dear.' Gretchen Gudde sighed. 'I do hope you haven't hurt Junie. He has a performance to give this afternoon.'

'Are you all right, Bart?' Stella tried to touch him but he pushed her away.

He was aware of the flame leaping in his loins at the sight of her naked body. She was an animal; her thighs had a litheness,

87

her breasts a softness and her lips an allure he found impossible to ignore.

He rested his hand on her bosom as he held her away from him. 'So this is what you do?'

'Flesh has its needs, Bart.' Gretchen hauled herself out of bed. Stella left Bart and passed a robe over to her.

'She was distraught waiting for you. Now you're here, you can comfort her yourself.' Gretchen fastened her robe and indicated her bed with a nod of her head. She looked at the Caffre.

'Get up, Junie. I want coffee.' She stalked from the chamber giving no sign that Bart's unexpected arrival had disturbed her. The Caffre followed her out sullenly.

'Don't think badly of me, Bart.' Stella sat down on the bed and spread her hands in front of her to show her despair. 'It isn't what you think. Gretchen is very kind.'

'I'm sure she is.' Despite his shock at what he had seen he was not angry. The familiar tightness in his breeches worried him more than what Gretchen did to Stella. He could not take his eyes off her nakedness. She sat on the bed without embarrassment, unaware of the effect she was having on him.

'I'm glad you came,' she said. The simple trust in her voice added to his discomfort at what he had come to tell her.

'Van Dort wants to buy me.' She shuddered. 'Gretchen tried to shield me from him but he is persistent. That's why Junie threw you on the floor. He thought you were after me too.'

'If I didn't buy you,' he asked with a sinking feeling, 'will you have to go to Van Dort?' He sat down on the bed and she snuggled against his chest. He put his arm around her, dismayed by the situation.

'Yes. But you've come for me so the nightmare is over. I'll go wherever you take me, do whatever you say.'

He swallowed, wondering how to tell her about Jessica. 'Stella –' he began then broke off as her hand slipped inside his shirt and her fingers toyed with the hair on his chest.

He let her remove his coat, knowing that he should stop her but he was loath to cause her hurt. Her faith that he was going to help her made him weak. He lay back on the mattress with his head on the pillow, perplexed about what to do.

She gently opened his shirt to his waist, laying bare his chest. 'I know you've been harvesting the sugar cane,' she said softly. 'I knew you'd come as soon as you finished, so I wasn't worried.'

The touch of her hand made him leap until he thought his breeches would burst. He reached up to stop her and found he was fondling her breasts instead.

Her hands were at his waist deftly unfastening his belt. A draught of cool air from the billowing curtain at the doorway wafted over his thighs as she drew his breeches down to his knees.

'Stella –' he said, trying in vain to protest.

She was astride him, her knees nudging his waist as she rode him, drawing him inside her and bucking up and down with the vigour of a spirited horsewoman.

His protest changed to a groan. He clawed at her breasts, longing to tell her that this must be the end – that he could not buy her – that Van Dort would have her. His sighs became a shout of ecstacy as she smothered his face with wet, passionate kisses.

'I couldn't hurt her!' he exlained to Tissa, feeling angry with himself as they walked down the Street of Moorish Traders on their way to the Henricuses' house.

'You didn't tell her?'

'She trusts me to take her away from there. Van Dort will get her if I don't.'

'Does Van Dort know she's pledged to you?'

'One of the girls told him. He wants her merely to spite me. It would kill her to have to lie with him, after what he's done to her already.'

'Do you want her?'

Bart was halted by Tissa's question. He considered it. His crotch tingled and he felt he was still lodged deep inside her. 'Yes, dammit, I do want her! But then I don't. It would hurt Jessica. She trusts me too.'

'Either way you are going to hurt someone.' Tissa smiled knowingly. 'Better to spoil a whore's dream than destroy your wife.'

'I wish it was as simple as that.'

CHAPTER TEN

As the main port of Ceylon, Galle was constantly busy. Its prosperity and activity depended on the merchant vessels that anchored in its harbour. Travellers from all parts of the East, and from Europe too, were to be seen in the town, exploring the bazaar or promenading along the ramparts.

While Bart pursued his business with the shipping agents, Jessica and Charlotte Taylor were left to their own devices. In the afternoon, when the sun was setting, they joined the throngs strolling the streets. Here they were shaded by the suriya trees whose broad umbrageous leaves and delicate yellow flowers imparted a delicious coolness, giving parts of the town the freshness of walking in a garden.

Galle's development was due to the Dutch while its importance as a port dated back to Biblical times. It was the Tarshish of Solomon's day, where ships from the Red Sea found gold and silver, ivory, apes and peacocks. Galle was the Kalah at which the Arabians in the reign of Haroun Alraschid met the junks of the Chinese. Moorish traders used the port as an entrepôt where they bartered for the products of the East and shipped them to the West.

A legacy of those days resulted in a large proportion of the inhabitants of the town being Muhammadans. They were the dealers in gems mined in the island's interior, and in tortoise-shell products of bracelets, hairpins and ornaments that had been made in Galle since the time of the Romans.

It was natural that Jessica and Bart's mother should find themselves drawn to the bazaar in the Street of Moorish Traders. They viewed the items on sale with excitement, unconcerned by the crowds around them. They flitted from gems dealers to curio stalls where carvings in ebony and ivory inspired Charlotte to ecstatic cries.

'This could command a pretty price in London.' Charlotte picked up a figurine. 'Ask him how much for this,' she told Jessica.

The grey-bearded Muhammadan who sat on the steps of his house stirred himself. 'How much you give?' he asked aggressively in English.

'It is the custom here,' Jessica whispered, 'for you as the buyer to place the value on what you want.'

'Indeed?' Charlotte looked doubtful and put down the figurine. She moved away from the stall and the bearded man shouted after her to make an offer.

'It might be worthwhile,' she said when they had safely edged away from him, 'for Bart to send some of these local productions to England with his sugar shipment. Who knows, there might be more profit in buying and selling gems and ivory carvings than there is in growing sugar.'

Jessica felt a pang of remorse at Charlotte's preoccupation with making money. She suspected it was indirect criticism of her for not having brought a dowry.

'Bart's born a planter,' Charlotte continued, thinking aloud. 'He's not a merchant of knick-knacks. That's something *we* should do.'

'We?' Jessica drew close, wondering if she had heard correctly in the hubbub of the bazaar.

'Why not? Women are more astute than men. Tissa could ascertain the correct prices to offer. We could acquire gems and curios at the lowest price and sell them for the highest price in England. Since the curio merchants in England are men, it should be easy to make a considerable profit out of them.'

Jessica was dismayed. 'You'd be deceiving them.'

Charlotte gave her a quizzical look. 'Men deceive women all the time.'

Jessica followed her patiently as she roamed through the bazaar, stopping at all the vendors and inspecting their wares. Her energy was unflagging. It was typical that she would contemplate taking on the Moorish traders at their own business. She was a woman who would do anything for the sake of her son.

While Charlotte studied a tray of sapphires, ignoring the entreaties of the merchant to make an offer, Jessica gazed idly along the street. She did not share Charlotte's excitement and wished only for the money to buy the fine dress materials that were on display.

Some Europeans from a visiting vessel were in the bazaar and she was amused by the sight of them bargaining for a carved elephant. Her attention was attracted to a door opening in the high wall behind them.

'Why, look!' She seized Charlotte's elbow. 'There's Bart.'

'Good,' said Charlotte, without raising her eye off the tray of gems. 'Call him.'

Jessica hurried through the crowd to catch up with him. She grasped his coat tail from behind to slow him down as he was walking so fast. He turned sharply and his mouth dropped open when he saw her.

'What the devil . . .!'

'I'm sorry, Bart.' She was puzzled by his alarm. 'Your mother is with a gem merchant. She's calling you.'

'You surprised me,' he said. 'I thought you were a whore . . . I mean a hoodlum.' He seemed confused as he took her arm and cleared a way through the throng. 'What are you doing here without a chaperon?'

'Your mother and I are chaperoning each other. You were busy so we thought we'd have a stroll through the town.'

The flash of guilt in his eyes disturbed her.

'Surely you did not expect us to stay at home?' she added, curious about what caused his disquiet. 'I'm sorry if I upset you. We've been perfectly all right.'

'That's not the point. This is not a street ladies of good character are seen in unaccompanied.'

'Whyever not?'

'It doesn't matter.'

She sensed his anger and said nothing, withdrawing her arm and walking ahead of him to where his mother was engrossed in the gem trays.

'You should be careful someone doesn't snatch your reticule, mother,' he said as he joined her. 'This is a bad area.'

'The reticule is empty.' His mother smiled at him. 'Why are you here if it's a bad area? Buying gems too?'

'I, er . . .' He hesitated. 'Tissa told me I could see a captain in one of the houses here. He was mistaken.'

'You were in Madam Gudde's!' said Jessica with sudden insight about whose house it was behind the high wall.

'No, I wasn't!'

'That's her door I saw you coming out of, over there.'

'Is it? I just popped in. A Caffre told me the man I wanted wasn't there so I left.'

Jessica smiled to disguise her dismay at catching him out in a deliberate lie.

The disquiet he felt at being discovered coming from the brothel added to Bart's despair. Every afternoon, while Jessica and his mother were taking tea with Prince Gamunu on the verandah of the grand mansion, he visited Stella. In his heart he knew Jessica would find out sooner or later.

He went to the brothel in defiance of good sense for Stella's sake. Van Dort was unlikely to abduct her when she was under his protection. He racked his brains every time he was with her for some way out of the problem.

If he had the money, he could have come to an arrangement with Gretchen Gudde and had Stella sent away from Galle. He would promise to follow her and hope that, before he did, she would meet someone else and forget him. Jessica's discovery of him in the Street of Moorish Traders added to the urgency of finding a solution.

The next day, at Jessica's request and because he was anxious to allay her suspicions, he accompanied her to see Prince Gamunu. His mother declined to go, saying she would take a walk with Tissa. He was too preoccupied to enquire what his mother was scheming.

Prince Gamunu received them at the verandah steps, surprising Bart by kissing Jessica's hand in the European fashion. He was courteous and affable, showing none of the princely bad manners of Bart's previous visit. He escorted them to his own quarters leading off the verandah and Bart noticed that Jessica appeared familiar with the room.

'This is where Charlotte and I sit,' she explained, taking her place on a settee. 'People can't stare at us from the street when we are here. It's very private.'

He raised his eyebrow but said nothing as he took his seat opposite her. Gamunu lifted the chair that constituted his makeshift throne from its dais and placed it so he was sitting between them.

'It's a delight to welcome you both together,' he said gushingly. 'Usually we have the pleasure of your mother and young Havis as chaperon. Although I am of your mother's generation, I prefer the company of the young.'

'Why?' Bart asked curtly, and received a glance of disapproval from Jessica for his implied criticism.

'The young have hope. I can feel it.' He smote his bare chest. 'It inspires me here.'

'Do the old not have the wisdom of years and experience?'

Gamunu's eyebrows twitched. 'Bart, the folly of youth is often more rewarding than the caution of one's elders.'

'Explain yourself.'

'With pleasure.' Gamunu showed no sign that he was put out by his deliberate hectoring. 'Take you and Jessica as examples. You are both young and in love. Forgive me if I am being personal.'

'You are much admired by the Singhalese for your courage. Bloodheart is a name to be proud of. You won it by recklessness, not caution, by competing with Marcus Van Dort. Your folly has rewarded you with the respect that eludes him.'

Bart accepted the compliment with a nod of his head. 'How do you know about Van Dort?' he asked. 'Have you met him?'

The prince looked owlish. 'You and your family are my only visitors, apart from young Havis and an occasional military gentleman willing to share a bottle of coconut brandy with me.'

'Do you drink?' The unexpected confession distracted Bart.

'Arrack is the only solace left for a man whose liberty is denied because he was promised a throne.'

'I'll bring you a bottle of Bloodheart rum.' Bart grinned at Jessica's shocked expression. 'I'm distilling rum on my sugar plantation.'

'I would be delighted to give it a royal seal of approval by consuming some with you.'

His deep-throated chuckle convinced Bart that he had misjudged the prince. He was an engaging companion and he enjoyed the afternoon's conversation.

It was easy, basking in the prince's charm, to forget that he came from a family of ruthless potentates who considered brutal punishment of innocents an acceptable way of reigning. With his sing-song English, learned from an educated Buddhist monk, and his gracious manners, Gamunu seemed a noble man who had been maligned and wronged by the British.

'I shall regain my freedom and the throne,' he told them with a glint in his hypnotic eyes.

'Through justice,' added Jessica, revealing that she was convinced of the merits of his cause.

'Yes.' The prince's face was stern. 'It will be justice.'

There was a knock at the door. The prince listened as the knock was repeated again, two sharp taps, a pause, and another tap.

'That's young Havis,' he said, his face brightening. 'Come in,' he called across the room.

Havis opened the door and stepped in confidently. His manner became deferential when he saw Bart and Jessica. 'Forgive me,' he said. 'I thought you were alone.'

'You do not disturb us, Havis.' The prince's deep voice assumed a tone of affection. 'Jessica and Bart are our allies.'

'Are we?' A hint of intrigue entered Bart's mind. 'Allies are friends of a special purpose.'

'I knew I could rely on you, Bloodheart!' The prince stood up signifying the interview was over. 'I do hope you'll visit me again soon.'

Bart sniffed, feeling that somehow he was being drawn into a commitment that he knew nothing about. 'I am very busy,' he said. 'Plantation business.'

'Good, good. I wish you success in your ventures. If you cannot come, I hope you will not disapprove of the occasional visit by your wife.'

'If it pleases her.' He glanced at Havis. The young man's

presence reminded him of Raven. He longed to see her again. 'Perhaps Havis will accompany Jessica if I cannot.'

'Of course.' Havis seemed delighted at the opportunity. He escorted them out to the verandah after they had taken their leave of Gamunu. While Jessica was tying her bonnet, he surprised Bart by whispering into his ear. 'Can I see you in a few minutes? By the bell tower.'

Bart's first reaction was to scold him for importuning him in front of Jessica. He was about to speak when he caught sight of the anguish in Havis's eyes. He nodded his head at once and took Jessica by her arm.

He led her down the steps to where the waiting palanquin bearers were stirring themselves under the shade of a *suriya* tree.

'Prince Gamunu is a great man,' said Jessica with a sigh. 'He bears his misfortunes nobly. I hope he becomes king one day.'

'The British will never allow it!' He squeezed her hand, amused by her female gullibility. 'He's a great rogue, Jess, but a charming one. He's harmless.'

'You don't mind me seeing him?' Her winsome smile made him grin.

'I welcome it. At least you're safe in his company. He diverts you from boredom when I'm busy, and places the Collector in our debt because your socializing with him is what he should be doing himself.' He held open the curtain for her while she settled herself on the cushions of the palanquin.

'I will come soon,' he said. 'The bearers will take you home safely.'

Her anxious expression made him feel guilty. 'Don't worry.' He smiled to reassure her. 'I'm going to walk back along the ramparts and watch the sunset.'

She made an attempt to get out. 'I'd enjoy the walk too.'

'Jess,' he said frowning, not wanting to upset her. 'Please don't cause a scene with so many people watching.' He leaned forward and kissed her cheek, ignoring the plea in her eyes. Hastily he signalled the bearers to carry her off.

After dismissing his own palanquin, he strolled casually along the street. The bell tower, another monument from the days of the Dutch, was a few yards away opposite the Dutch church. A bell tolled the hours and six struck as Bart approached it.

Rather than wait where his presence would be conspicuous, he climbed a flight of stone steps to the ramparts. This was a popular walk for people in the early evening as the sun set and the air became cooler. He sat on a bench and pretended to be admiring the view where night was rapidly spreading over the sky above the bay.

Laughing Singhalese girls walked past him in close groups. He admired the way they dressed for its simplicity. The principal garment was a white muslin jacket which loosely covered the figure, leaving a bare midriff above a *comboy* or waist cloth. The girls displayed quantities of jewellery, necklaces, bangles and rings with a casual flair. Some of the gems appeared to be of great value although the cutting and setting was of a rustic quality.

When he smiled at the girls, they giggled and drew closer to one another, the bolder of them flashing him sly glances from under long, fluttering eyelashes. He was buoyed by the innocence of their happiness and nodded gaily at them. His overture provoked peals of laughter, hastily smothered as they hurried past him.

'Dash it!' a voice said at his side. 'So beautiful and yet quite untouchable.'

He looked up to see Havis striking his brow with the palm of his hand in exasperation. 'Why is an English gentleman of good breeding concerned about Singhalese girls? It's as well they are untouchable if you harbour lustful thoughts for them.' He rose to his feet and clapped Havis heartily on his shoulder.

Havis looked crestfallen. 'Am I not a man too?'

'To be sure you are.' He glanced across the road and saw Prince Gamunu standing on the verandah watching them intently.

'Let's walk,' he said, drawing Havis away.

'Yes.' Havis shrugged his shoulders, slipping out of his embrace. 'Please forgive me for troubling you like this. I don't know anyone else I can turn to.'

'You apologise too much. If I can do you a favour, please ask.'

97

'You won't be disgusted with me?'

Bart shook his head, intrigued by the suggestion. 'If you have something to confess, perhaps you should go to the church.' He nodded at the Dutch church opposite the ramparts.

'I've heard a lot of things about you, Bart.' Havis's voice squeaked with nerves. 'I know you go to that place.'

'Place?' Bart frowned.

'In the Street of Moorish Traders. I even saw you coming out of there once, but I didn't know what it was then.'

'Madam Gudde's?'

Havis nodded before continuing. 'In London in the company of other young blades, I sometimes frequented a house in Covent Garden. After the etiquette of Almack's where we flirted with the season's beauties, it was a relief to pleasure myself.'

'Hah!' Bart clapped him on his shoulder again as they walked. 'You are indeed a man! I'll take you to Madam Gudde's if that's what you want.'

'Would you? I'm faint hearted about going there alone. What of the girls, are they clean?'

Bart paused. 'Is this all you wanted to see me about?'

'Yes. It was a good chance to speak in private.'

'This has nothing to do with Prince Gamunu?'

Havis stiffened. 'No.'

'You serve the prince with more dedication than you show Collector Radley.'

'I feel he merits my respect and friendship. He is a wronged and lonely man.'

'He likes you . . .'

'I know . . .' Havis sighed and a faint scowl crossed his lips.

'I understand,' said Bart. 'You are worried about the prince's fondness for you. There are such men.'

Havis blushed.

'I believe I can help.' Bart's eyes were on the Singhalese girls who walked ahead of them, their buttocks rolling provocatively under the thin fabric of their *comboys*.

'I think I know a girl who will suit you admirably.'

CHAPTER ELEVEN

Havis was aware of Raven watching him quizzically as he stood in front of her father. It made him feel ashamed although she could have no idea of what he was going to do. Mr Radley raised his head.

'Have you prepared the briefs for tomorrow?'

'Everything is done, sir. With your permission, I will be back shortly.' He felt Raven's eyes burning into the back of his neck. It made lying impossible.

Mr Radley grunted crossly. He was reluctant to let Havis have the evening off, yet he had no reason to detain him. 'Why does Bart Taylor want to see you?' he demanded.

'Sir . . .' Havis felt the colour deepening in his cheeks. If only Raven was not there he could have lied easily. 'I believe he wants to, er, discuss family matters. His mother knows my grandfather,' he added in an attempt to give his excuse authenticity.

Mr Radley tut-tutted vigorously and scowled. Then he waved his hand in dismissal which Havis took to be consent.

'Thank you, sir.' He bowed and turned to walk out of the sitting room. He could not resist a sly glance at Raven. She smiled at him with gentle amusement and her dark eyes glinted knowingly in the lantern's light.

'Give my regards to Bloodheart,' she murmured, bestowing an importance to Bart's nickname by her sultry emphasis of it. 'And to his wife and mother.'

'Yes, Miss Raven,' he said formally, before hurrying out of the room.

Raven's conduct was a mystery to him. For weeks he dreamed of her as he sweated and twisted on his bed in the humidity of the night. Her dark, impassive eyes and her fleeting smile haunted him. He treasured the moments they were together, even when – with a wild toss of her head and the pursing of her shapely lips – she showed only contempt for him. The more desperate he became for a sign that his feelings for her were reciprocated, the more remote she seemed.

Finally, the pressure was too much. He was worried he would be driven to doing something foolish. Whether it was because of the torrid nights, the tropic heat, the glass of coconut brandy he drank occasionally in the officers' mess, or the profound influence exerted on him by Prince Gamunu, he did not know. He felt himself saturated with lust; he could not look at Raven without an ache in his loins and a desire to crush her in his arms.

He feared the consequences of the passion building up in him. At night, a stickiness glued him to his mattress. His brain was plagued with fantasies that lingered all day. His concentration and will power were weakening. Raven was to blame and his desire for her became a threat to them both.

When Bart Taylor strolled through the streets of Galle, Havis saw him as a familiar figure. He was like the bucks of St James's, gallants who squired the season's debutantes to the *thé dansants* of Almack's Assembly Rooms and to the salons of the *ton*. At night they roistered and rogered with an abandon that made them the talk of society. In Bart, Havis recognized someone who would appreciate his dilemma.

It had taken him time to pluck up the courage to confide in Bloodheart. It was ironical, he thought as he walked the darkened streets of the town to their rendezvous, that having taken the plunge to purge himself of his desire for Raven, she should unexpectedly show more interest in him than at any time since they arrived in Ceylon.

It was too late. Raven's response to his proffered friendship was clear: she was not interested. It was only because he was going out for an evening in which she had no part, that she pretended to be intrigued. She and her father were alike; prone to jealousy if he did not give them his full attention.

The thought of how he was going to break the spell made

him nervous. Often he had eyed the native girls speculatively, wondering if he would ever be able to lie with one. Were they as exciting in bed as they seemed when they shimmied in brightly hued lengths of cloth on the rampart's promenade? Were they different from white women? Would he be forever pox ridden if he rogered one?

His doubts increased as he waited for Bart at the end of the street where he was staying in the Henricuses' house. He could see the house but kept in the shadows out of sight. Bart emerged as the bell in the tower on Church Street rang ten times.

A woman's voice cried plaintively, 'Bart?'

Havis stepped around the corner into the Street of Moorish Traders where Jessica could not see him.

Bart hurried round the corner a few minutes later. 'Dammit, Havis! We'll have to hurry.'

'I hope I haven't caused you any trouble. I heard someone calling you.'

'Jessica.' Bart sighed. 'We had a pact that I would stay with her in the evenings. I told her it's an unreasonable restriction on a man known as Bloodheart.'

'Perhaps we should forget this idea . . .'

'Certainly not. Your need is urgent. I'll introduce you to Madam Gudde then be back in bed with Jessica in a jiffy. She's a good girl but a demanding one. Come on.'

He followed him along the street, guilt-stricken by what he was doing. The urge that had been driving him to distraction for weeks evaporated and he felt a physical shrinking of his body.

'I've been thinking, Bart. I shouldn't be doing this.'

Bart halted in front of a door and knocked smartly on it. 'I saw Madam Gudde this evening after I left you on the ramparts. She's expecting you. Everything's arranged.'

The shutter of the grille set into the door slid open. Havis blinked under the scrutiny of a Caffre watchman and flinched when the door was wrenched open. A push in his shoulder blades from Bart carried him into the garden at the front of the house. He staggered, recovered his balance and glanced unhappily around him.

The trees of the garden were bedecked with coloured lanterns throwing a soft glow on the flowers and on the women seated under their boughs. The sight of the women with their low-cut dresses and predatory smiles of welcome intimidated him. He lowered his head in shame.

'Take no notice of those whores,' said Bart breezily, steering him by his arm into the house. 'They're waiting for their clients. Too old for you.'

He found himself in the parlour of the house, a room hung with velvet drapes to give it a romantic atmosphere. He felt hot and sticky under his collar. A woman sat beyond the light from a chandelier with a glass in her hand. In alcoves of the room men were on couches with their female companions, pawing them and laughing suggestively.

'This is the chap, Gretchen.' Bart introduced him to a large woman with a ravaged face and red-rimmed eyes. 'Where's Stella?'

'Room four. Is it all night, or a quickie?'

'All night.'

'Two of you together? That's double.'

Havis's voice squeaked as he tried to protest. The woman eyed him over the top of her glass of gin. He thought she was laughing at him until he looked directly in her face and saw her smile was sympathetic. She leaned forward.

'You are a lucky man, Havis,' she said in a soft, motherly tone. 'Bart is a friend you can trust. He is giving you his own girl, reserved especially for him.'

'I –' He wished he could speak without his voice rising to a high pitch like a boy's. 'I am grateful to you, madam. Perhaps another night. I've remembered something I must do.'

'Havis!' Gretchen Gudde's voice remained gentle with none of the scorn he expected. 'Relax. You can enjoy yourself here without shame. Let Bart introduce you to Stella. Have a drink with her at my expense before you leave. Then any night, when you have time, you'll be welcome. Just knock on my door and ask for me.'

'You are kind,' he said, warming to her.

He followed Bart out of the parlour into a courtyard. He

102

sensed the presence of couples sitting together in the moonlight and heard the sounds of energetic lovemaking coming from the rooms around the yard. He doubted that he would have the courage to return to this place and take his pleasure with an unknown native woman.

A fair-skinned young lady opened the door of a room in response to Bart's knock. Havis assumed she was Madam Gudde's daughter or perhaps a relative of Bart's who had somehow strayed into the brothel by mistake. She was his own age with a superb figure shown off by her close-fitting gown. She kissed Bart affectionately then turned her gaze on him.

'Hello,' she said, holding out her hand and drawing him into the room when he took it nervously. 'I'm Stella.'

'I see she pleases you,' chuckled Bart.

He was speechless. It was a crime that this beautiful, innocent young lady was available for what he longed to do. 'I don't understand,' he stuttered. 'Is this a joke?'

'By the devil, no!'

Bart told him Stella's story while the three of them sat at a table in the tiny bedroom, sipping arrack. The door and the window were open and Havis felt he could have been on a social visit to a friend. The pressure of having to roger some raddled, dusky whore just to still his craving flesh had vanished.

He relaxed and began to enjoy himself. At the back of his mind was the incredible knowledge that if he wanted her, this girl could be his. His eyes crept to the bed in the centre of the room.

'Take care of him, Stella,' said Bart, draining his glass. 'You'll be saving this handsome young man from the prince's perverted tastes.'

Havis was puzzled by what he meant but he was too excited to query it.

Bart leaned over and slapped him on his knee. 'Stella likes you. Don't worry about me. I'm not a jealous man. You're both the same age. You're better for her than I could be.' He grinned at Stella who was watching him sadly. 'You could have been made for each other.'

'You're going?' He was startled when Bart stood up. Stella rose to her feet too.

'This is your moment, Havis. She's not a whore, you know. Take her under your protection and she's yours.'

His throat was dry and his glass empty. He felt a twinge of panic at being left alone until Stella's hand slipped into his. 'Good bye, Bart,' he stammered. 'And thank you.'

'I'm nervous, too,' Stella said when Bart shut the door and left them alone together. 'I thought you'd be a fat, gouty English man when Gretchen told me Bart was bringing a friend. I'm so glad it's you.'

'You've seen me before?'

'Of course I have. All the Singhalese girls have been talking about you since you arrived in Galle. I never dreamed you'd be interested in me.'

'Oh yes, I am,' he said quickly, guessing that Bart must have told her he had seen her and wanted her.

She was a revelation to him. She had none of the affectation of Raven. She was an exciting, vivacious girl of his own age.

His loins throbbed when he realized he need only give the word and they would be in bed together. It would be for the night, not like the hasty thrusts he paid for in the Covent Garden whorehouses and never really enjoyed.

'Let me take your coat,' she said, moving behind him and helping him remove it. 'More arrack?' She poured a glass of the coconut brandy and held it to his lips. 'Tell me about yourself.'

Soon, he was lying on his back on her bed, an enormous weight pulsing between his thighs, aching for release. She lay at his side, her hand stroking his bare chest. She was naked and the sight of her body in the candle light added to his eagerness to possess her. Her hand slipped lower and brushed against his bulging breeches.

'Stella!' he gasped, seizing her shoulders and pulling her towards him. 'I love you!'

'Yes,' she whispered in reply. 'I love you too, Havis.'

He did not care if it was a lie. He wanted her. He fumbled with his belt to loosen his breeches. Her hands stopped him and held him firmly by his wrists.

'I want to leave here,' she said. 'Will you buy me?'

'Buy you?' Her question startled him. He could feel only the leaping of his crotch and a desperate need to take her.

'Gretchen will sell me to you. You can rent a room for me with a Burgher family. You can came to me whenever you want.' Her fingers pressed against his crotch. He groaned helplessly.

'It won't cost much. Your income is over three hundred pounds a year. I'll be yours alone, as long as you want. Only say yes.'

'Yes . . .' he croaked from the depths of his suffering.

Her fingers loosened his belt and drew his breeches down to his knees.

'Yes, Stella!' he shouted as she sighed and took him in her hands. 'Yes!'

Bart congratulated himself. His scheme had worked out better than he dared hope. He was in such a good humour that he grinned at the Caffre who opened the door to let him out into the street. It was Junie, the black giant who had assaulted him and been kneed in his crotch by Bart in return.

'Thank you, boy,' he said as he sauntered from the brothel. The Caffre scowled and churlishly slammed the door behind him. It did not dampen Bart's gay mood.

There had been the danger that Havis would back out through nerves or even find Stella unattractive. Stella, too, could have spoiled the success of the scheme by insisting that she was saving herself for him and would have nothing to do with Havis. Thanks to Gretchen's stern words of practical advice, Stella saw the advantage of swapping Bart for Havis. She had played her part well.

Bart had released himself from his obligation to buy her, and Stella was safe from Van Dort. Even though Havis was only a young apprentice, he was a person of influence in Galle whom not even Van Dort would risk upsetting.

What was especially pleasing to Bart – and caused him to whistle an air to himself as he hurried along the darkened street – was that with Havis involved with Stella, he would lose his infatuation with Raven. Bart chuckled.

The street was deserted at that hour, close to midnight and the activity of the day was replaced with an eerie silence. All the houses were tightly shuttered and there was no sound, either from stray dogs or rats rooting in the gutters. The moon's vague light served only to define the street by outlining the houses in ghostly silhouette.

Bart was anxious to return home to Jessica. He had been loath to leave her as he knew how distressed she would be. Yet it was worth it to help Havis, and to secure his own release from his foolish commitment to Stella.

He noticed a shape move in the darkness ahead of him. At night, the Government Caffres cleaned the streets, foraging among the rubbish for items useful to themselves, and throwing the rest over the battlements into the sea. Some of the Caffres were descendants of slaves from Africa landed in the days of the Dutch. Others had been imported by the British to serve the army.

In Galle, the Caffres were creatures of the night. By day they slept on the ground in the shade of the suriya trees. At night they prowled the streets ostensibly to clean them but often to engage in dark mischief of their own.

Bart saw another shape move across the street to join the first. There were two of them, almost certainly Caffres, lurking at the corner. Instinctively, he touched his pockets, realizing with relief that he had left his purse at home.

A sense of apprehension shivered through him causing the hairs at the back of his neck to tingle. He glanced behind and saw he was quite alone. He whistled loudly, knowing it was only a few yards to walk to the Henricuses' house.

'Goodnight!' he said boldly as he drew level with the two Caffres. There was a grunt from one of them as though he was surprised to be noticed. 'Waiting for someone?'

One of the shapes drew away from the corner and passed behind Bart's back. He turned to see where he had gone and was instantly aware of the other moving towards him.

He ducked and feinted to his right, rising up quickly and starting to run to his left. A Caffre rose from the darkness in front of him and blocked his path, shoving him in his chest with his fist. He was caught off balance and stumbled back. Someone seized him from behind and lifted him off the ground.

He kicked out with his feet as the night became a swarm of people closing in on him. He heard the yelp when his boots contacted with flesh. The man holding him shook him from side to side like a child worrying a doll.

Suddenly he was released, tossed forward so he sprawled headlong into the mud of the street. He tried to stand but a kick to his waist winded him. He rolled into a crouch to protect himself.

Although his attackers were barefoot, the blows from their feet were sharp and hard. He was outnumbered; there were at least four of them taking it in turns to kick him. They were all Caffres, hissing between their teeth and grunting as they beat him methodically. This was no ordinary attack by footpads or they would have stopped when he was down and fleeced him. In an agonizing flash of horror, he realized they were not going to stop until they killed him.

His horror turned to rage. He grasped at a foot as it flew to his face. Holding it firmly above the ankle, he leapt to his feet and twisted so the man in his grasp toppled over. With the Caffre's leg clasped in both hands, he scythed the ground with his body, bashing him against his attackers and bundling down two of them in the scramble.

He released the Caffre and flung himself at another still on his feet, his hands outstretched for the man's neck. Clutching him around his throat, he brought up his knee to his crotch.

The man whimpered and put his hands on Bart's arms to tear him away. Bart kneed him until he crumpled in a heap at his feet.

'Bloodheart!' a deep voice called from behind.

Instead of running away, Bart turned, ready for another assailant. He was not fast enough to dodge the fist that slammed into his jaw with a force that spun him backwards. The black giant followed him.

Bart recognized him in that instant as the Caffre who guarded the door at Madam Gudde's. He bunched his fists

107

and crouched, preparing to hammer some good manners into him. 'Junie –' he began to shout.

A wooden club smashed against his head, blinding him with a red flash of pain. He struggled to keep on his feet but he knew he was going down. Another blow cracked into his skull, splitting the skin and showering a rush of blood into his eyes.

He hit the ground with a thud. Desperately, he tried to drag himself along it to escape from the blows of the club. His body was afire with pain as his strength seeped from him.

He was angered at the futility of dying in such a fashion. He made an effort to stand, wiping the blood from his eyes with the back of his hand. As he raised himself to his knees, a foot slammed into his backside and pitched him face down into the mud. The Caffres were all on their feet again, honking gleefully as they moved in to finish him off.

'Enough!' A voice cried above the noise of the mêlée. The kicking ceased immediately.

Bart played dead. He did not groan or cry out; he had no energy left for that. He knew he was lying in the street almost unconscious; he longed to resist but his body was too weak. The voice came to his ears from the end of a deep cavern of pain.

'Heh, heh, heh!'

There was the sound of phlegm being hawked up into a fleshy throat then a glob of spittle smacked into Bart's cheek like a pat of bird's dropping.

'Heh, heh!' the voice brayed again, growing distant.

Bart blacked out as, on his short, fat legs, Marcus Van Dort waddled away with his gang of Caffres.

CHAPTER TWELVE

The insistent whoop and caw of a large black crow perched on a branch of the frangipani tree in the courtyard, mocked Bart back to life. He listened to the crow obtruding itself on his attention; its shrieking blending with the ache that split his head. His body was stiff and swollen; he felt he had been pulled apart limb by limb, boiled in hot oil and stuck together again.

He opened his eyes and stared up into the soft glow of the room. The door to the courtyard was open letting the sunlight filter in. His face was puffy and his lips sore but he was determined to speak.

Jessica, sitting at the side of the bed, leaned forward. 'Oh, Bart . . .' she cried with relief.

'Get rid . . . of that . . . bloody bird!'

There was a scurry of feet across the floor and he heard Tissa shoo the crow into flight. He relaxed and concentrated on his pain.

'Praise God, you're all right.' The sound of his mother's satisfied voice roused him. He moved his head gingerly and peered around the room. Jessica put her hand on his shoulder. He winced.

'I'm so sorry,' she said.

He swallowed without speaking and tried to assess his injuries. His head throbbed from a cut on his brow and his body ached from the blows of the Caffres' feet. He tried to move although Jessica wanted to restrain him. After the first bite of pain from the disturbed bruises, the agony calmed and he could bear it sufficiently to consider what had happened.

'I told you not to go out,' Jessica scolded, reaching over to place a poultice on his head.

Her remark annoyed him. He brushed her hand away and tried to sit up. 'I wish you'd leave me alone.'

'He'll get better soon enough, Jessica.' His mother's sensible tones were reassuring. 'He's got his temper back. What happened, Bart?'

'I don't know.' He tried to smile but his lips hurt too much. 'Footpads. They must have thought I had money.'

'I shall report it to Mr Radley right away.'

'What good can he do?' He blinked. 'How did I get home?'

'Tissa found you.'

'Why was he looking for me?'

'I asked him,' Jessica said cautiously. 'When you did not come back as you promised . . .'

'I found you in the gutter.' Tissa sounded proud. 'I carried you home.'

'Did you see anyone?'

'No, Bloodheart. The street was deserted.'

He sat back with a sigh and closed his eyes. He was not surprised at Van Dort's methods. It was to punish him because of his interference with Stella. The Caffres at Madam Gudde's were obviously in his pay. It dismayed him how vulnerable he was. He decided to say nothing to Jessica or his mother in case he alarmed them.

He slept during the morning, unaware of the number of visitors who called at the Henricuses' house as news of the attack spread through the town. Jessica thrived on the attention and he heard her dashing in and out of his room in great excitement. He was relieved she kept the visitors from peering at him so he was able to sleep, letting his mind and body get over the shock.

In the afternoon, he sipped a herb soup prepared by Daisy and began to feel better. He sent Jessica out and called for Tissa.

'Shut the door and open the window so I can breathe,' he said as soon as Tissa entered the room. 'Keep the women away from me. They fuss too much.'

'Jessica was upset last night. That's why I looked for you. She guessed you'd gone to Madam Gudde's.'

'Undress me, Tissa. I want to see what damage is done.'

When he was naked, he inspected his body carefully. From his chest to his thighs, he was blue with bruises. His testicles were swollen and painful.

'No lasting harm,' said Tissa calmly. 'You can't have a whore for a few days.'

'Do you know how it happened?'

Tissa frowned as he helped him put on clean breeches. 'There are Caffres,' he said solemnly, 'who can be hired for any task.'

'It was Van Dort. I heard him.'

'Caffres work for anyone. I could hire some to return the favour. He'll hurt more than you.'

'No.' Bart winced as he raised his arm and Tissa slipped his shirt over his head, fastening it in front. 'He's not worth the trouble.'

'You forgive him?' Tissa was outraged. 'That man deserves some of his own medicine.'

'He'll get it, Tissa.' He stood up and flexed his arms and legs. 'I think I can move now.'

'What are you going to do?'

'Sit in the parlour and drink arrack. Let people see me. Van Dort will soon hear it takes more than a gang of Caffres to put me out of action.'

Each step was painful but he was determined not to remain confined in the chamber. He limped into the parlour with his hand on Tissa's shoulder and was greeted by a group of well-wishers who gasped their concern. He was surprised to see so many people. He waved aside their expressions of sympathy and told Tissa to bring the arrack.

'Do you think you should, dear?' said Jessica coming to his side as he stood by the open door and gazed out into the street.

'Yes,' he said irritably. 'It will dull the pain.'

He chatted briefly with the visitors who speculated on why it had happened. His insistence that he was set upon by foot-pads was accepted. He did not want Van Dort to hear that he knew he was responsible. In time, when his chance came, he would exact his revenge.

He was glad he had left his bed when he saw the Collector's palanquin stop outside the house. He had expected Mr Radley to visit but was astonished when Raven entered the parlour instead, escorted by Havis. He tried to bow in welcome, ignoring the pain. Jessica fussed him back to his seat.

'Daddy wanted to come,' said Raven when she had arranged herself on the settee opposite him. 'He is rather busy so I persuaded Havis to show me where you live.'

'I am honoured.' Bart watched in fascination at the way Raven regarded Jessica. She seemed to disapprove of her.

'Is there anything I can do for you? Daddy said you must tell me. Perhaps some medicines? That cut on your head, does it hurt much?'

'My husband is perfectly all right and well cared for!'

Jessica's frosty retort amused him. 'Please thank Mr Radley,' he said. 'I do have some bruises, that's all.' He rolled up his sleeve and held out his arm so she could see.

She gasped and walked over to him. She peered closely at the bruises, touching one with her finger.

'How dreadful,' she muttered, but Bart found it delightful.

'He won't cure if you prod him.'

Raven released his arm as Jessica rushed over like a frantic hen protecting her brood. Bart wanted to tell her to stop fussing but he was enchanted by Raven's childlike curiosity in his injuries so he ignored her.

'How many of them attacked you?' Raven asked. 'Do tell me!'

He recounted the details of the attack for her, omitting only Van Dort's presence. Her expression of concern captivated him.

'How brave you are!' She gazed at him with admiration.

'It was foolishness that caused it,' Jessica snapped. 'He promised me he wouldn't go out at night.'

Raven turned her eyes on Jessica with scorn. 'Why shouldn't he go out? He's a man.'

Bart chuckled. 'Sometimes it is prudent for a man to obey his wife,' he said ruefully.

'Why? Did she know it was going to happen?'

'Of course I didn't!'

Raven sensed Jessica's dislike of her and made her excuses to leave. Havis had been quiet for most of the visit and Bart noticed there was a trnaquillity in his eyes that was not there before. Neither of them referred to their meeting the previous night although as he left, Havis winked at Bart.

'What a disagreeable child that girl is,' commented Jessica when Raven had gone. 'You can see she takes after her father.'

'Then she must have her mother's looks,' said Bart's mother from her corner seat where she had been observing everything and saying little. 'She's very pretty.'

'Pretty?' Jessica pulled a face. 'I don't think so. Do you, Bart?'

'What?' He was thinking about Raven and comparing her vivacity with Jessica's dourness. 'I don't know, dear,' he said. 'I'm tired.'

'I should think you are. You got out of bed too soon.'

'Then I shall go back to it,' he said sharply. 'I'll thank you to leave me alone whem I'm there.'

Her mouth dropped open with dismay and immediately he regretted his harshness. He wanted to apologize but instead he walked silently across the floor, ignoring the pain that racked his body with every step, and left the room without saying goodnight. He heard his mother making an excuse for him, blaming his bad mood on his suffering.

The row that was hanging over them like a storm cloud at the beginning of the monsoon season, burst with fury two days later. His mother was out with Tissa at the time and he was alone with Jessica in the parlour. The pain had eased and he was feeling restless.

He stood up and walked around the room, casting anxious glances outside. He was keen to see Havis to find out if he had moved Stella into a room of her own. He wanted to warn him to be alert in case Van Dort tried to steal her away.

'I think I'll go out,' he said finally. 'A walk will do me a power of good.'

'Wait a minute, dear. I'll get my bonnet.'

'You've no need to come. I'll go to the ramparts and back.'

'I don't want to stay here by myself.'

'Why not?'

'Would you like it if I left you here alone?'

He shrugged his shoulders. There was nothing he would like more than to be left alone without Jessica watching him possessively all the time.

'Don't be moody, Bart. It was because you went out by yourself that you got attacked. I don't know why you went when you promised you wouldn't.'

'You wouldn't understand!' Her nagging annoyed him especially as he had given up Stella so that he could spend more time with her. 'It was to help a friend.'

'Are your friends more important than our marriage?'

He stared at her, shocked by the bitterness in her voice. 'I said you wouldn't understand. I am going out. Alone.'

'I'm not staying here if you do. I want to go out too. I haven't seen Prince Gamunu for three days because I've been looking after you.'

'He's your friend, is he?'

'Yes.'

'Then visit him. I don't mind.'

'I can't go without a chaperon.'

He laughed scornfully. 'Good gracious, you could spend the whole night with Prince Gamunu and your virtue would be intact. He doesn't like women.'

She stared at him, her eyes moist with tears. 'You don't care about me at all!'

'I do, Jess. We have to learn to respect each other's needs. I need time to myself just as you do.'

'You would let me see the prince without a chaperon?'

'Go to him, Jess. Do what you like. Let him make love to you, if you want.'

'Bart Taylor,' she said, stamping her foot. 'I will! See how you like it then!'

He chuckled to himself as he left the house and walked slowly up the street towards the ramparts. He was confident she would be in the parlour waiting for him when he returned.

* * *

Prince Gamunu showed no trace of surprise when he opened the door of his chamber and saw Jessica. She had hurried through the streets as dusk was falling, avoiding the bazaar where she would be accosted by traders. She had walked briskly with her head held high, defying anyone to challenge her.

She was drawn to the prince by a strange compulsion. Her exasperation with Bart drove her to it. She had waited an hour for him to return then she left to look for him. Instead, she found herself heading for the mansion.

'Come in,' Gamunu said, bowing deeply. 'I was hoping you'd come.' The soft, low tone of his voice caressed her ears.

He took her hand in his and kissed it, his lips lingering on her fingers longer than politeness required. He drew her inside the room. She heard the door close with a finality that made her shiver.

'My dear, are you cold?' he asked solicitously.

She gazed up at his warm brown eyes and was reassured. The room was dark, lit only by two candles burning in a candelabrum on a table in its centre. The shutters were closed. She relaxed as he stroked her hand gently, feeling at ease in the pleasant atmosphere.

'Not cold,' she said, letting him lead her into the depths of the room. She sat where he indicated on the couch, flattered when he sat beside her instead of on his usual chair.

'May I take your bonnet?'

She removed it without protest, noting that he was not wearing the flat hat that she was accustomed to seeing him in. His only garment was the white cloth worn like a sarong. His chest was bare and hairless, his coppery skin glimmering as the candles flickered on the sheen of oil smeared over his body.

'Your hair!' she said, forgetting politeness. She put up her hand. He let her touch it. 'Why, it's soft like a girl's.'

He smiled, his teeth a dazzling white; his eyes flashing hypnotically. His black hair had grown long; he wore it rolled into a coil, drawn back from his brow and bound into a bun at the crown of his head in the manner of a woman.

115

'It is the Kandyan way for hair to be unshorn,' he said. 'Unfortunately, I had to shave it off when I disguised myself as a monk to come over to the British.'

'How you have suffered,' she murmured.

'It is nothing compared with the anguish of a beautiful woman.' He moved closer to her on the couch.

She breathed in the rich, spicy aroma of the oil. Her senses tingled at the proximity to her of this strange, powerful man. She was being drawn to him by a force against which she had no resistance. When his arm snaked along the half-back of the couch, she inclined her head so she was resting on it. The brush of his fingers against her hair thrilled her.

'I heard about Bloodheart's accident,' he said softly. 'And your devotion to him.'

His words were a warning. This was her chance to assume a prim air, sit up, make polite conversation and take her leave. Yet if Bart did not care that she was with him, why should she be worried?

She snuggled against Gamunu's arm, her heart thumping at the firm touch of his fingers on her neck.

'Bart knows I'm here,' she said to excuse her behaviour to herself.

'He is very understanding.'

'He's selfish!'

'Indeed?'

He drew closer and his breath tingled in her ear. It was sweet with the odour of herbs. She closed her eyes, feeling sleepy. For three days and nights she had nursed Bart, caring for him as only a wife can. She was tired, and depressed by his attitude towards her.

The attack had frightened her; she thought she would lose him. Even when he was sleeping, and his body was bruised and battered, she longed to hold him, to smother him with kisses and have him make love to her.

'Would you like a drink?'

She opened her eyes to see Gamunu standing over her, proffering a glass. She took it from him cautiously.

'Coconut brandy,' he said. 'Arrack. The soldiers gave me a bottle.'

'I don't usually drink anything strong.' She took the glass, quivering when his fingers touched hers.

'It will help you relax.'

'I do feel relaxed when I'm with you. I don't have to pretend. I feel you understand me even though you're a prince.'

'Does that make me less of a man?'

His raised eyebrow set her heart fluttering and the tone of his voice excited her. She sipped the arrack and watched him from under lowered lashes. The gold bands in his ears gleamed and his beardless cheeks glowed with oil. There was something odd about him that she assumed came from his princely breeding.

'Bart thinks it does,' she answered suddenly, the words flowing out of control. 'He says you do not have the desires of a man.'

'And you?' he said, holding out his hands and standing in front of her. 'What do you think?'

'I'm not sure.'

The look in his eyes drew her to her feet. She put down her glass without knowing she was doing it and found she was in his arms. She raised her mouth to meet his as his face leaned towards her. His kiss was brutal and demanding. She fought it until pleasure stole through her limbs and she fell weak in his grasp.

As his strong hands gripped her, his touch set off tremors of passion, even through the thick fabric of her sensible gown that covered every inch of her flesh. She moved in a daze with him across the room to the bed.

His lips were at her neck, tingling her flesh; his fingers were on the ribbons of her bodice. She breathed in the exotic scent of his hard, muscular body. Her dress slid down to her ankles, removed from her shoulders with the swiftness and skill of a master.

Their lips touched again and she tasted his tongue as it dove deep in her mouth. She sucked on it passionately, plying his body with her hands, overwhelmed with a need that pitched her beyond control.

117

He was naked. His hand caressed her breasts, thrilling her in a way Bart had never done.

She lay on the bed with her legs dangling over the edge. She gazed at his nakedness, at his huge body pulsing with desire. She reached for him and his eyes glinted with triumph.

He leaned over her and placed his mouth on her nipple, sucking until it was hard. She moaned, her body aflame. His lips traced a line from her breasts to her thighs.

She shivered when his tongue delved between her legs. She squirmed and felt it enter her. She was seized with a frenzy to yield to him. She clutched his head, pulling him closer.

Later, when she lay beneath him and he was lodged deep within her, she began to weep.

CHAPTER THIRTEEN

'So you went to see the prince?' Bart looked up casually from the book he was reading. Jessica stood at the door of the parlour. She seemed uncertain how he was going to react. He grinned affably.

'He made love to me,' she said, unlacing her bonnet and tossing it on a chair. She shook her hair free with a defiant gleam in her eye.

'You do look flushed.'

'You said you wouldn't mind.'

'I don't mind, Jess, because I don't believe you.'

'If you believed me, would you mind?'

'Prince Gamunu?' Bart sniggered and the pain in his head began to throb. 'I'd be honoured. To be husband of a prince's mistress! If he becomes king I could be his prime minister.' He rose from his chair and crossed the room, holding his arms open for her.

'I'm sorry I was so stupid, Jess. I've been miserable alone, waiting for you to come back. I won't treat you so badly again, I promise.' He tried to kiss her on her lips but she turned her head so his mouth brushed wetly against her cheek.

'I'm relieved Tissa brought you home safely,' he said, withdrawing and glancing behind her to where Tissa had entered the room and was bolting the door. 'I sent him to wait for you outside the prince's quarters. He followed you back here. I couldn't risk you being attacked by footpads too.'

'You sent him to spy on me!'

'You're distraught, Jess. I knew where you were. You told me what you were going to do, so why should he spy? Tissa was there to protect you if necessary . . .' He paused, overwhelmed with repentance. 'Dammit, Jessica, I've been foolish.

Something terrible could have happened!'

He took her in his arms and forced her to lean against him, cheek to cheek. He patted her shoulder, expecting her to weep. When she did not dissolve into tears and admit she was wrong, he held her away and looked at her curiously. 'I forgive you,' he said.

'It's true, Bart. Gamunu made love to me. I let him.' Her smile was euphoric.

'Fine.' He released her and chuckled, thinking the tension had passed. 'You look well on it.'

He watched her leave the room, grinning to himself at her dreamlike state. Tissa escorted her to the chamber she was sharing with Charlotte while Bart's injuries healed. He heard her murmur goodnight to him before she drifted inside and closed the door.

Tissa resumed his report when he returned to the parlour. 'She walked back along the ramparts. I was close behind her but she didn't know.'

'Gamunu must be quite a fellow. He's done me a favour. I could spend the night with Stella now and she wouldn't mind at all.'

'Havis might.'

Tissa was right. Bart poured two glasses of arrack and handed one to Tissa. He sipped his own thoughtfully. He had seen Havis that evening. The young man was enraptured with Stella and had arranged for her to live in a house close to the Collector's bungalow. He hoped in time to be able to move in with her. He had negotiated the deal with Madam Gudde and paid cash for Stella's freedom.

'Damned odd,' said Bart, feeling the arrack soothe his aching limbs. 'Just when Jessica seems amenable to my tom-catting and makes jokes about an affair of her own, I don't have a wench any more.'

Tissa downed his arrack in one swallow. 'Shall I help you undress?'

'Time for bed?' Bart yawned. 'Yes, you're right, of course.' He finished his arrack and let Tissa help him to his chamber. He was pleased with himself. His work in Galle was almost finished.

He spent the next few days in the flurry of last minute arrangements over the shipment of the sugar to England. He was eager to return to the plantation. He was mildly puzzled by the change in Jessica's disposition that enabled him to do what he wanted without her nagging him. He supposed Gamunu was responsible. When he was back at the plantation, he expected her to shake off the spell the prince had cast on her and return to her normal primness. A meek wife was no challenge.

He took Jessica and his mother to pay a farewell call on Mr Radley. The Collector received them on the verandah of his bungalow. To Bart's delight, Raven was there but Havis was not. She was more sociable without him. She offered them tea and cake and supervised the serving by a houseboy. Instead of glancing at Bart shyly from a chair in the corner, she sat beside her father and gazed at him openly.

'I am grateful,' said Mr Radley, 'for your visits to Prince Gamunu. He has become an amenable fellow, no trouble at all.'

'My mother and Jessica charmed him,' said Bart, intrigued by Jessica's blush. 'He likes female company.'

'With his ear rings, long hair and skirt he has a lot in common with them!' Mr Radley laughed heartily at his own joke.

'The prince is a man of remarkable intelligence,' said Bart's mother sternly. 'He would make a good king.'

'But a bad husband, what?' Mr Radley was enjoying himself and winked at Bart. 'It was good of you to spend so much time with him.'

Bart saw his mother's eyes take on a look of determination. 'I have,' she said without preamble, 'a chest full of trinkets I want to send to England. Knick-knacks I bought in the bazaar with the help of Bart's headman. I really can't be bothered with the bore of getting permits and licences for them. Do you think, Thomas, that you could give me a special chit?'

Bart was amazed at his mother's lack of finesse and by Mr Radley's response to it. He needed no coaxing and wrote out the shipping permit immediately. Since it would have taken Bart two weeks of shuttling from clerk to clerk to get official permission he admired his mother's blatant approach.

'I do hope,' said his mother as she took the permit, 'that you

121

and your daughter will visit us on the plantation.'

Bart glanced at Raven to see her reaction. She was staring at him boldly. It made him think she was one step ahead of him. Since Jessica was gazing dreamily out at the garden, he flashed her a dazzling smile and winked at her. She turned her head and pretended not to notice.

'We'll be delighted, won't we, Raven?' said Mr Radley.

Bart held his breath and waited for her reply.

Raven's lips twitched. She appeared to be considering the implications of the invitation. 'Are there snakes?'

He laughed with relief. 'No, none where we live.'

'Unless you mean human ones,' murmured Jessica.

'Raven can deal with that kind.' Mr Radley leaned forward and chuckled. 'She saw off my writer with style.'

'What happened?' Jessica was no longer absorbed in her contemplation of the garden but was taking heed of Bart's keen interest in Raven.

'We thought Havis was a respectable young man,' said Mr Radley. 'Raven dscovered he's taken up with a local woman of ill-repute. She insisted he leave the premises immediately. Can't have a man like that living in the same house as my daughter, what?'

Bart smirked and challenged Raven. 'How did you find out Havis was such an immoral fellow?'

'I prefer not to tell you.' Her eyes were cold. 'I believe you know it's true.'

He shrugged his shoulders nonchalantly. 'I do not listen to gossip.'

'Perhaps you should.' Raven sounded innocent but her words had a chilling effect on him. 'Maybe you would learn something about those who are close to you.'

'Maybe, and maybe not.' He stood up to mask his irritation. He had the feeling that Raven, despite her demure expression, was teasing him.

'I'd like to see Prince Gamunu before I leave Galle. With your permission, Mr Radley.'

'Granted with pleasure, Bart. I hope he won't be here for much longer.'

'Why not?' Jessica clutched her bosom as though shocked.

'I've reported to my superiors that he is fermenting unrest here.'

'That's not true.' Jessica looked anxious. 'You said yourself he's no trouble. He is isolated from the Singhalese and has no contact with the Kandyans. How can he stir up unrest?'

'Maybe he's not doing it yet, but I'm sure he's thinking of it!' Mr Radley dismissed her from his mind and turned to Bart. 'Cut off a snake's head before it poisons you, what?'

Bart escorted Jessica and his mother from the bungalow; he was annoyed over her outburst. It deprived him of an opportunity to bid a proper farewell to Raven.

'It's disgraceful, the way the prince is being treated,' she insisted. 'Gamunu is such an understanding man.'

'Then come with me to see him!' he told her crossly.

'No, Bart, I won't.' A sorrowful look entered her eyes as he handed her into the waiting palanquin.

'I thought he was your lover.' He taunted her. 'Don't you want to kiss him goodbye?'

She gazed up at him without blinking. 'Why do you joke about such matters?'

He dropped the curtain on her and snapped his fingers at the bearers to carry her off. His mother followed Jessica to the Henricuses' house in her own palanquin.

He took a short cut through Hospital Street past the gate of the fort and made his way to the officer's mansion where the prince was quartered. He forgot about Jessica's obsession with Gamunu and thought instead of Raven.

He was fascinated by the strong-willed personality concealed beneath her gracious and comely appearance. He pictured her becoming a woman who would be fiercely loyal to the first man who took her. To others she would be either an ardent friend or a ruthless enemy.

Darkness had descended when Bart reached the mansion. It was his plan to leave Galle at daybreak so this was his last opportunity to see the prince.

The door to Gamunu's chamber was closed. Bart remembered the knock that Havis had used and rapped on the door with the same code – two sharp knocks, a pause, another knock – to see what would happen.

When he heard Gamunu call loudly 'Come in,' he pushed open the door and entered the room.

As always, it was dimly lit with the shutters closed. A candle flickered by the bed. The prince was in conversation with a man who sat in the shadows with his back to the door. Gamunu jumped to his feet when he saw Bart and hurried across the room, blocking his view of the guest.

'Bloodheart!' he said loudly, opening his arms to embrace him. 'This is unexpected.' He caught him by his elbow and turned him around, holding open the door with his other hand and hustling him out through it.

'Shall we go on the verandah?' he said. 'I know how you hate confined spaces.' He slammed the door shut behind him before Bart could see more than the bald head of his visitor.

'I thought you were someone else,' the prince apologized profusely. 'Or else I would have greeted you myself instead of leaving you to enter like a slave. I really do need a steward of my own, actually, an aide de camp as you British say. Someone like your Tissa, for instance, such a capable chap.'

Bart was bemused by Gamunu's nervous gabbling. 'It was wrong of me to disturb you,' he said to stop the flow of words. 'I'm leaving Galle tomorrow.'

'Your wife, too?' There was a sudden glint in the prince's eye.

'Of course. She sends her compliments, as does my mother. I bid you farewell on their behalf.'

'Wait here!' The prince pushed him and he fell into a seat wincing with pain from his bruises. The prince rushed over to his door, opened it wide enough to enter so Bart still could not see who was in the room, and slipped inside. He closed the door behind him.

Bart puzzled over the identity of Gamunu's mysterious visitor. It meant nothing to him except that the prince was prepared to let Havis, whose special knock Bart had used, see the man, but not him.

'This,' said Prince Gamunu returning from the room and shutting the door hastily behind him, 'is for you.' He proffered Bart a casket the size of a large Bible. 'Open it.'

Bart hesitated. 'Prince . . .'

'Open it!' Gamunu thrust the casket into Bart's lap and stood back, his hands on his hips. He looked agitated.

Bart slowly raised the lid of the casket, feeling embarrassed by the gift. When he saw what was inside, he closed the lid, stood up and tried to hand the casket back. 'No,' he said, shaking his head. 'This is yours.'

'Take it! That's a royal command. Do you wish to insult me by refusing?'

Bart opened the lid again. The light from the lantern fell on the casket's contents, causing them to sparkle. There were a score of gem stones of all colours, blue, green, and amber on a cloth of gold silk.

'See,' said the prince plucking a stone from the collection. 'This is a blue sapphire, the finest of my country's gems. Only a diamond is harder. This one,' he seized another and tossed it casually in his hand, 'is a cat's eye, black and very rare.'

'Why . . .?' Bart stared at him. 'These are worth a fortune.'

'They are!' Gamunu's eyes glinted. 'I was able to rescue some treasures from my Kingdom.'

Bart closed the lid and tucked the casket under his arm. 'I am not worthy of such munificence.'

'You are. Your wife is! A small gift to remember me by.'

'Small! Is there anything more valuable?'

The prince paused, bringing his agitation under control. There was silence while he scrutinized Bart. 'Yes, there is.' His deep voice was no longer tremulous with excitement.

'We call it the *gaja mutu*. It's the most valuable gem of all. The man who owns it is a king.'

'Then you have one?'

'Yes!' Gamunu laughed, a booming sound that echoed down the verandah and out into the moonlight night. 'I have.'

'Well,' Bart sighed, preparing to leave. 'I mustn't detain you. I know you have a visitor.' He offered his hand. 'Are you sure you want me to have the gems? Might you not need them?' Already he was hoping they were his to keep.

Prince Gamunu put his hands together at chest height and bowed. 'Your need is greater, Bart. I have the *gaja mutu*.'

'Your need is great too. Mr Radley has reported that you're stirring up trouble. He wants to have you sent away. The British won't let you be king, even with your precious gem.'

Gamunu seemed unconcerned. He smiled enigmatically. 'If I live or die here, there will always be a king for Kandy. My blood line will live on.'

'Your faith is impressive,' said Bart wanting to believe him. 'But you have no heir. Your line finishes with you.'

'Bart, you are a planter. Without you, your cane would not yield sugar. I trust you.'

He pulled the lobe of his ear, perplexed by the prince's riddle. 'I'll visit you again,' he said, stepping off the verandah into the street. 'When I'm in Galle.'

With the casket under his arm, he climbed up the steps to the ramparts. He still ached from his beating. Now he had the casket – it was worth more than a season's crop – he did not want to be attacked again. Soldiers patrolled the ramparts at night and he decided to wait for the next patrol to escort him home.

He sat on the bench. The moon was high, its light shining on the boughs of the suriya trees, throwing shadows from its branches onto the ramparts. He hugged the casket close to his chest, baffled why the prince had given him his treasure, and deeply grateful for it.

'Heh, heh!'

The honking snort of evil laughter made his heart leap. He stared across the street in horror as he recognized the man standing on the verandah, the man who had been in the prince's chamber: Marcus Van Dort. Gamunu was shaking his hand enthusiastically, bidding him farewell.

Bart watched with disquiet, disturbed at what was the reason for such a bosom friendship between the two men.

Van Dort hawked gleefully and shuffled down the steps. Four burly Caffres emerged from the darkness where they had been waiting and lowered their palanquin for Van Dort to get in for the ride down the street to his house.

Suddenly Bart realized why Prince Gamunu had given him the casket of gems: to buy his silence.

Silence, he wondered, about what?

126

CHAPTER FOURTEEN

Jessica found it difficult to adjust to life on the plantation after the weeks in Galle. She missed her afternoon walks in the fort's streets and the callers who came every day to admire Garth and Ranita.

Galle was exciting; plantation life was dull compared with it. Knowing that Bart would not be beaten up or attracted to some Burgher whore was a small advantage of being back in the country. However, there was the big disadvantage of no longer being able to see Prince Gamunu.

She was smitten by him. She convinced herself that there was no harm in thinking about him since she was sure she did not love him. She loved Bart.

She was possessive about Bart and affected by his moods. She was happy when he was pleased and saddened when he was downcast.

For Prince Gamunu, by contrast, she experienced a new range of emotions. She longed with an almost religious fervour to serve him. She drew comfort in her loneliness by believing he was with her in spirit.

When she thought back to her evening with him, she was confused. It was a dream and, like a dream, hard to recall. She began to think it must have been another woman doing those things with the prince. Not her.

The night after she gave herself to him, Bart had made love to her. There was a difference, but he sensed nothing. Since then, the routine of their life together blurred the memory of Prince Gamunu, adding to her doubts that he had actually done what he did.

Upon their return to the plantation, Bart was out every day either in the fields or at the mill. First, he floated the sugar down the river to the lagoon where it was safely loaded on ships for the voyage to England. Then he supervised his four Caffres and the natives under Tissa in preparing fields for the new crops.

She saw him only in the evenings when he returned to the house for supper. He was usually dusty, drained of energy and bad tempered. He was an uninspiring companion then. He did not neglect her at night but was selfish in his love making, taking his pleasure without bothering to satisfy her.

She craved him more than ever and it frustrated her when he left her too soon. Her mind and body were undergoing changes; it puzzled her.

With Bart in the fields all day, she had little to do in the house. Mammy ran the kitchen and the two boys, Nimal and Jagath, did everything else. She sought refuge with the children. Garth was the bigger of the two, a placid child unlike Ranita who constantly demanded attention.

Jessica treated them as brother and sister although she was proud when Garth showed himself more advanced than Ranita. In the evenings, the children joined her when Bart came to the parlour. Their presence was usually enough to calm his temper.

'He's growing faster than Ranita,' Bart boasted one evening when she gave him Garth to hold.

Charlotte looked up from the corner of the parlour where she was reading. 'They need a nursery of their own,' she said.

Bart dandled Garth on his knees. 'I have a plan for that.'

Jessica caught sight of the gleam in his eyes and was worried by it.

'Tissa's men are hoeing the ratoons. I'm going to bring the Caffres into the house.'

'What for?' she asked sharply, unable to hide her apprehension.

'To build! Mother's right. We need a nursery for the children. We need a dining room, too, and a guest room. Mammy needs a new kitchen and a store.'

'So soon?' she said unhappily. 'Garth and Ranita are less than two years old.'

Bart ignored her. 'I'm going to make this old guest pavilion like the bungalows in Galle. We'll have a courtyard at the back. Garth and Ranita will have a room where Malika can sleep with them. We'll have a spare room for guests.'

Despite her misgivings about the Caffres being in the house, Jessica was intrigued by the idea. It sounded exciting. 'Who will you invite?' she asked eagerly.

'Mr Radley and Raven will be the first.'

Charlotte was pleased. 'I'm glad you've remembered them. It's important to cultivate Mr Radley.'

Jessica was dismayed. 'Why ask his daughter?' she demanded sulkily. 'She'll hate it here.'

'Nonsense. It will be an experience for her.'

Bart's eyes were unusually bright which made her wonder what other reasons he had for asking Raven.

'Must we inconvenience ourselves for the sake of that spoilt hussy?' she asked.

'She's not a hussy!'

Jessica swallowed her rancour. 'I'm sorry, Bart.' She thought of another objection. 'Where will the money come from to pay for this grand building plan? Your mother?'

The remark was cruel and she knew it. The thought of Raven Radley staying in their house robbed her of sense.

'He can have it, Jessica.' Charlotte smiled at her. 'It's a necessary expense, an investment for the future.'

'Thank you, mother.' Bart tickled Garth. 'But I couldn't ask you for more.'

'It doesn't matter. There are ways to get money.'

Jessica was upset by Charlotte's encouragement of Bart. 'Don't give it to him,' she said. 'Let him wait for the sugar income. We don't need more rooms yet.'

'Mother's right.' Bart grinned at her. 'There are ways. In fact, I've raised the money already.'

'How?' She felt uneasy.

'It's not your concern.'

She was piqued by his attitude but apart from sulking, there was little she could do about it. More rooms could make the tiny pavilion more comfortable. The idea of Garth and

129

Ranita having a nursery of their own too was pleasing.

'Oh, do what you want!' she said peevishly.

He handed Garth to Malika and walked over to stand behind her chair. His hands rested on her shoulders. 'Jess, I know how you miss being in Galle. I see it in your manner. You loved going to the bazaar every day and seeing Prince Gamunu.'

His remark troubled her but she said nothing.

'It will be more fun for you and mother when you can have guests staying here.'

'Can we ask Prince Gamunu?'

He sighed. 'I wish we could.'

'Why not? Does he have to go into exile? Just because Mr Radley doesn't like him.'

'He does . . . unless he escapes.'

'He could escape and hide here with us!' The idea thrilled her, and she forgot her anger at Bart. 'There's that pass to the Kandyan mountains in the hills.'

Bart laughed. 'What would he do if he went into the mountains?'

'Raise up his people so he can get his kingdom back.'

'And attack the British?' Bart's mother looked worried. 'It was the Kandyans who burned down our house.'

'It was the Caffres' fault,' Jessica reminded her. 'Prince Gamunu wouldn't do anything like that. We can trust him. He's convinced he's going to be king.'

'Or that his heir will!' Bart scoffed. 'Even though he hasn't got an heir.'

'You would help him, wouldn't you?' Jessica waited anxiously for his reply. Somehow it was important for her that Bart should share her desire to serve the prince.

'If he's treated unjustly, I would.'

'Bart!' She rose from her seat and hugged him gratefully.

'When Mr Radley comes here to stay,' said Charlotte as though offended by her gesture, 'I will persuade him to be more considerate of the prince's feelings. We can help him that way without plotting his escape.'

'Gamunu's a strange man.' Bart held Jessica away from

him. 'At first I thought he was a fraud. Now I know he's not. I'll do what I can for him, Jess.'

That night, despite her love for Bart, she was unable to respond to his love making. She gasped and squirmed so he would think she was enjoying it because she wanted to please him. She hoped he was satisfied when he rolled off and lay at her side.

In the morning when she woke, Bart had gone. Outside the chamber she could hear him directing the slaves where to dig the foundations for the new rooms. He was determined to complete the building quickly. Then Mr Radley and the obnoxious Raven would visit them.

The idea filled her with nausea. She heaved and to her horror lost control of herself. She leaned out of bed and vomited over the floor.

She was ashamed. 'It must be something I ate,' she explained to Mammy when the housekeeper bustled into the bedroom to see what was wrong.

'You sayin' my cookin' no good?' Mammy sniffed with outrage.

She stood with her arms akimbo staring down at her, making her feel like a naughty child. Her chubby face was wreathed with worry lines. Her tongue, a striking pink against the dark brown velvet of her lips, protruded thoughtfully. She frowned.

'You be like dis before?' she demanded. 'How you feel yes'day mornin'?'

'A little queasy.' Jessica fidgeted, embarrassed by Mammy's inquisitiveness. 'Perhaps I'm sickening for something.'

'Hmm.' Mammy licked her lips. 'You have your menses?'

Jessica wanted to vomit again but Mammy swooped down and seized her in her fat arms. She hugged her joyfully, disgusting her with the smell of her yeasty bosom and the stink of stale cooking that clung to her pinafore.

'Bless you!' Mammy exclaimed happily as Jessica puked helplessly. 'I declare! You does be pregnated.'

*   *   *

131

Bart viewed the birth of another child with pleasure. He was enchanted by Garth and Ranita and spent moments of delight with Malika when she was caring for them. A planter needed children and he was pleased with Mammy's announcement about Jessica's condition.

It explained the difference he had noticed in her behaviour since they had returned from Galle. He had been worried by her coolness in bed – he was too experienced to be fooled by her pretence of enjoyment – and wondered what was wrong. He resolved to treat her considerately, even though it meant giving up making love to her.

Instead, his energies were consumed by the construction of the new wings for the house. He longed to finish the building so he could invite the Radleys. He wanted to persuade the Collector to alleviate Prince Gamunu's conditions of confinement. It was the prince who was responsible for the new wings since the sale of five of his gems provided the money.

Bart's real reason for hurrying the building was so Raven could come to stay. He felt no shame at being attracted to her. After six years in Ceylon he missed the company of personable young English ladies, the kind who were the debutantes at Almack's.

Raven had a zest which Jessica lacked. There was an undercurrent of understanding between him and Raven because of their background. Jessica had never been to England, did not know what Almack's was, and was too serious to appreciate the enjoyment of harmless flirting.

He stopped short of contemplating an affair with Raven. Her company, and the chance to impress on her what a splendid fellow he could be, was all he craved. However, as the nights of his self-imposed abstinence through Jessica being pregnant lengthened into weeks, Bart's thoughts grew ever more lustful. He no longer slept with her, preferring a mat on the verandah floor to risking the temptation of her body in bed beside him. He sensed her growing indifference towards him and the preoccupation with the child she was carrying. He could only hope that after the child was born she would regain her affection for him.

132

He was trapped. He regretted having given up Stella. If he had bought her himself and put her in a villa on the coast, he would have been able to visit her instead of being frustrated every night.

His lust spilled out in other ways. He drove his four Caffres ruthlessly, expecting them to work as hard as he did. When they slackened the pace he set because they did not understand, or through laziness, he was quick to anger.

Delta was their leader, a tall black from Mozambique. Although he was the brightest of the four, he moved slowly in the heat, like a leopard conserving his energy for the kill.

If he were not so pent up, Bart would have respected Delta's idiosyncrasies. Together with Mark, John and the young Romulus, Delta had remained loyal when the other slaves joined in the uprising the previous year.

Bart's urge to finish the building rapidly and his growing tension destroyed his patience. He found the whip he used to use on the slaves when they first came to the plantation.

He shortened its thongs and its handle so it was more convenient for use within the confines of the new courtyard. When Delta faltered in his work, Bart reached for the whip and slashed him across his shoulders.

Although he used it hesitantly, Delta's reaction was immediate. He speeded up his work and encouraged the others to do the same. The foundations for the house were completed even before Bart expected.

He had forgotten the effectiveness of lashing a slave. He had come to reply on Tissa and his followers for the plantation field work. The Singhalese could not be whipped into compliance; it was their nature to take blows without resistance, as fate. Caffres were different from the Singhalese. A stroke across the backside produced dramatic results.

Bart's whip was soon in constant use. He reduced Delta, a grown man of his own age, from a carefree, smiling black to a gibbering, nervous wretch. The slaves became sullen, eyeing him resentfully. But they worked at the pace he set, which was all he cared about.

He worked alongside them, not just showing them what to

do but tackling every task he asked of them. He thrived in burning up his energy in toil. Even when the slaves dropped to the ground at the end of the day, too exhausted to drink the soup Little brought them from the kitchen, Bart worked on.

By the light of lamps at night, while the slaves lay on the ground, he hewed beams for the roof or carved doors. When he wanted help to lift a fresh log to saw, he would kick a slave awake and then let him fall back to sleep again.

This was the way he had built the original plantation house. His slaves had said then that he never slept. He was fired with the same determination, although this time it was Raven who inspired him, not Jessica.

After eight weeks, the new building was finished. It was laid out according to his plan with two wings around a central courtyard. Tissa likened it to Madam Gudde's which made Bart's body ache when he thought of her whores.

In moments of despair, Bart considered his chances with the females in the compound. Malika, the children's nurse, was Tissa's sister, a light-skinned Singhalese girl with straight black hair that reached her waist. She was young and attractive. She doted on the children and was Jessica's closest companion. Bart was ashamed of himself for thinking of her in carnal terms.

The two Caffre girls who worked under Mammy's supervision were Daisy and Little. Daisy was a busty, voluptuous black wench who shared her cabin with Delta. Little, who was so chubby she could have been Mammy's daughter, was loving Mark, the thin Malagash slave who was a skilled fisherman. Neither of the Caffre wenches appealed to him except in his most desperate moments when, even though he was exhausted, sleep would not come and he was forced to imagine pleasures that could not be his.

At last the day arrived that he had been waiting for. It was the day that Jessica, judging by her caustic remarks, was dreading. Mr Radley and Raven visited the plantation.

Raven was everything Bart remembered. She had blossomed into a girl aware of her rare beauty and in awe of it. The first impression she created was of being prideful which could

134

have been why Jessica disliked her. Bart, however, saw beyond her aloofness to a shy, eager girl needing only the right man to guide her to womanhood.

Perhaps guessing what he had in his mind, Jessica took an obsessive interest in Raven for the duration of her visit. She shrugged off the lethargy of pregnancy and busied herself entertaining her.

Although Bart longed for the chance to see Raven without Jessica being present, he never succeeded. After the weeks of thinking of her, she was as far away from him as ever. All he could do was look.

The first night of her visit, Jessica escorted her to the guest room and pointedly instructed both Nimal and Jagath to sleep on the ground outside her door. Bart was left drinking on the verandah with her father.

'Bart!' Mr Radley challenged, startling him from his sullen mood. 'I've been wanting an opportunity to talk.'

Since his mother had gone to bed too, Bart was obliged to listen to him. Mr Radley had begun his stay the way he meant it to continue, in lavish self-indulgence. He over-ate at dinner, complimenting Mammy on her cooking by devouring everything set in front of him. Now he was working his way through a flagon of Bart's best rum.

He was rocking backwards and forwards in his chair, gesticulating wildly. Bart sat opposite him, prepared to be polite for Raven's sake, barely listening to his drunken rambling.

Suddenly, Mr Radley blurted out what was on his mind. 'I want a wench.'

'What?' Bart's jaw dropped. He gazed at the Collector and saw the sweat on his brow and his puffy cheeks flushed with drunken arrogance.

'A wench. I know 'bout planters from when I was stationed in the West Indies. You give your guests a wench for the night.'

'I do?' Bart's heart sank. He wanted a wench himself far more than Mr Radley could imagine.

'No need to pretend innocence with me, young man. Forget I am an official, or remember it if you want to please me. Get me a wench.'

'Er, well . . . why?' Bart asked helplessly.

'Dammit, what a stupid question. In the West Indies every planter wants more slaves, what? He sends a wench to spend the night with his guest. If she has a child he's got a new slave for nothing.'

'It's not that way here,' Bart said gloomily. 'I've only got two Caffre females and I'm not a slave breeder.'

'Neither am I. But I want a wench. You must have one who'll open her legs. Lusty young man like you, your wife pregnant, what do you do?' He leaned forward, spilling his drink.

'I'm not like you,' he whispered loudly. 'I can't go to Madam Gudde's. My position, what?'

'Ah yes.' Bart grimaced as the Collector's foul breath wafted over him. 'You must preserve your respect,' he said, keeping the sarcasm out of his voice.

'Young Havis did the right thing. Gone native and living with a half-breed wench. Ruined his career prospects, of course. I'll see to that myself. But he's rogering when he wants.' He paused, gulped at his empty glass and stared at Bart with his eyes wide.

'I want a wench.'

'Mr Radley . . .' Bart wondered how to turn this situation to his advantage so he could get concessions for Prince Gamunu. 'Words fail me. Have another drink.'

'Nosense, man. You think it's the rum speaking, do you? See there's a wench in my bed tonight, and every night while I'm here.'

The glint in the Collector's eye appalled Bart because he was obviously determined to have his way. 'Excuse me,' he begged, filling his glass from the flagon of rum. 'I'll see what I can arrange.'

He hurried across the courtyard to the kitchen, acutely aware of Nimal and Jagath lying on the ground outside Raven's room. Since he was a small boy he had run to Mammy when he had a problem. If she could solve this one for him there was no end to the favours he could extract from Mr Radley.

Mammy was sitting on a stool in the kitchen doorway, sipping soup from a bowl. She regarded him owlishly.

'Mammy!' he cried in anguish, then lowered his voice so he could not be overheard. 'Mr Radley wants a wench.'

'Aye.' She continued slurping her soup.

'What can I do? He expects it. I never knew –'

'Aye,' she said again.

'I don't even have a bed wench for myself. You must help me.'

'Lor, Mas Bart!' Mammy lowered her empty soup bowl and placed it on the ground beside her. She wiped her protruding lips noisily with her sleeve. 'You ain't ask me before. You go'n take me here on de grass or in my cabin?'

'Not you, Mammy!' He raised his voice. 'This is serious.'

'It sure is, Bart. You gettin' Bondmaster ways. You beatin' your boys like dey sacks of sugar not flesh 'n' blood wid feelin's. Now you wants a bedwench.'

'I'll handle the slaves my way. You beat them too.'

'A cuff on de ear ain't de same as a cut on de rump. Delta scared by what you do him.'

'It makes him work faster.'

'He wastin' work time keepin' his temper less he ups and cuts off your head. I have to tell him let your bad humour pass.'

'I'm in no mood for you to lecture me, Mammy. I must have a wench for Mr Radley to lie with. He'll do me the favours I want for Prince Gamunu.'

'Daisy de one.'

'Daisy?' He stared at her, his loins leaping at the thought of the lissom slave girl. 'She's Delta's woman.'

'Aye. I spoke to her a'ready.' Mammy sighed, her body shaking with the effort. 'When you have guests, Mas Bart, it only polite to offer dem comp'ny.'

He felt sick. 'All the weeks I've been suffering for want of a wench. I could have had her myself!'

'You didn't ask me.' Mammy stuck out her lower lip,

unmoved by his frustration. 'By de by, you go'n lash Delta 'gain? Daisy want to know 'cause if you are, she ain't goin' to de white buckra's chamber.'

'By the devil!' he said, amazed at how easily he had been trapped. 'I should lash you.'

She guffawed. 'You could try, Bart, but you need one long whip to lash me!' She pulled herself to her feet, her vast bulk blocking the entrance to the kitchen.

'Well?'

'The building's finished,' he said defiantly. 'I've no need for the whip now.'

'I call Daisy.' Mammy rolled her eyes, turned her back on him and shuffled off into the depths of the kitchen. Her body shook as she cackled with a laughter that seemed to mock him.

Jessica's son was born three weeks before he was due. He was a big child who cried as soon as Mammy slapped his bottom. She cut the cord, handed the child to Malika and made Jessica comfortable.

She heaved a sigh of relief, congratulating herself that Jessica had survived the ordeal without problems. Mammy had acted as midwife for many babies, including Jessica's first son, Garth, yet she would have preferred a doctor to be present for this one.

When Jessica started in labour, Tissa was dispatched to Galle to find Dr Barry. The baby would not wait. He burst on the world like someone impatient to begin living.

Mammy's worry was Jessica, not the baby. During her pregnancy she had shown a serenity that verged on the fatalistic. She took no interest in guessing whether her child would be a boy or a girl. She seemed to know. She drifted through the last weeks of pregnancy like a zombie.

Bart was no help either. He refused to lie with her as her belly grew bigger, although Mammy told him that was when a woman needs her husband most.

'Lor',' said Mammy, sighing again and straightening the bedclothes around Jessica. She was sleeping, a blissful smile on her face.

'You ain't got no cause to be pleased wid yourself,' she muttered. 'If you don't 'concile wid your husband, you sure go'n lose him. Baby or no baby.'

She beamed at Jessica, remembering the night Bart summoned Daisy from the kitchen. It was the day after Mr Radley's departure from the plantation.

Bart took Daisy out into the garden in front of the villa. The moon was high that night and he led her to an arbour in the middle of the bougainvillaea bushes. Mammy had hurried after them to watch.

At first Bart was tongue-tied, unable to say what he wanted. Daisy knew. She touched him gently on his waist. He shied at her touch, stared at her, and then grabbed her. He pulled her down to the ground and raised her skirt.

Mammy had exclaimed aloud at the speed with which he mounted Daisy. Fortunately, Bart was too engrossed in what he was doing to hear.

He took her that night with a vigour that made Mammy shudder to recall it. Weeks of pent-up passion pounded into the poor girl until she was barely able to move. It was a splendid performance by Bart that made Mammy wet to watch.

After that, there was no stopping him. He came for Daisy every night. Peace reigned on the plantation again as Bart put away his whip and slipped into the slaves' own routine.

It was important for slaves that their master was kept even tempered. That was the wife's role which was why Mammy wanted Jessica and Bart to reconcile their differences.

'Thank de lor' it's a boy,' she said, turning to Malika. 'Dat go'n put Bart in a good humour.'

'Yes, ma'm.' Malika had swaddled the baby in a cotton sheet and was rocking him gently in her arms.

'He sure does be a beauty,' Mammy said happily. 'So white. He does have Jessica's fair skin.'

'Yes, ma'm.'

Mammy was enchanted by the baby and ignored Malika's sulky answers. 'Give him here, girl. Let me hold my child! He go'n be bigger'n Garth for sure.' She took the baby in her arms and chuckled when he cried lustily.

She peered at him with pride. 'He got black hair,' she said. 'Not like Jessica or Bart. His eyes are brown. Such a bonny babe.'

'Ma'm?' Malika said cautiously. 'In Galle they are saying Miss Jessica was loving Prince Gamunu.'

'Tse, girl!' Mammy sucked her teeth. 'Hold your tongue. I hear dat talk. You don't see Bart de boy's father. He's a white baby, see his colour.'

Malika reached up and pulled away the cloth that covered the child's body. He cried louder.

Mammy stared, speechless with horror. Her well ordered world, her hopes for tranquillity on the plantation, tumbled about her.

'What is it?' The baby's crying woke Jessica and she rose up in bed, sensing something was wrong.

Mammy did not hear the question. She saw the baby in her arms, perfectly formed, his complexion the pinkish white of a pure breed, except for –

'Oh, my lor'!' she cried in despair. 'He got black balls!'

Jessica smiled and held out her arms. 'Give me my son,' she said happily. 'This is Bart's royal baby.'

Mammy hastily handed the child to her. 'Don't tell Mas Bart nothin',' she begged. 'Men stupid. P'raps he won't notice . . .'

'Of course I shall tell him.'

'Oh my lor'!'

Malika helped Mammy to a chair. 'Don't worry, Mammy,' she said with sudden understanding. 'Miss Jessica is right. Her son is important. He is Bloodheart royal.'

BOOK TWO

THE ELEPHANT PEARL
1817–1820

CHAPTER FIFTEEN

The new sugar season was in full swing. The chop of the cutlass against cane, the jangle of the bullock carts trundling to the mill, the creak of the water wheel in the river's race, marked the rhythm of each day's toil.

Bart rode through the fields on his new horse, acquired at the cost of one small gem, and watched with pleasure as his four Caffres led the onslaught on the ranks of cane stalks. The wiry Singhalese followed them scurrying to gather the cut canes and transport them to the mill.

The success of running a plantation, Bart had learned from Mammy, depended on establishing a routine and adhering to it. Slaves, whether they were Negroes or Singhalese, disliked disruption. The sugar season imposed its own routine and Bart had little to do except ensure the quality of the sugar was maintained.

Officially, Bart had six Caffre slaves; the four cutting cane in the field in front of him, and Daisy and Little in the kitchen. Mammy was his mother's although it was impossible to consider that wise old owl as anything other than the matriarch of the family.

The Singhalese were not slaves; they were attached to him by their own volition. Many were *salagamas*, the caste who in the days of the Dutch were cinnamon peelers. Under the British, the exportation of cinnamon lost its importance and the *salagamas*, used to the routine of working on the land, became destitute.

Since they accepted their fate as one of toil from birth and were natural workers, Tissa recruited them. Bart was obliged only to maintain them in health, succour them in sickness and apportion their burdens according to their strength.

The *salagamas* lived in *cadjun* shelters, the huts of woven palm leaf thatch on the fringes of the plantation where they grew crops on *chenas*, the land they cleared in the jungle for themselves.

Bart would have liked to understand the manner in which they lived but found it better to channel all contact with them through Tissa. He regarded their customs as curious especially as their women were forbidden by their caste to cover their breasts. He left them alone, content that they worked well and without supervision from him.

Bart understood the Caffres better. They had no culture beyond the vaguely remembered mumbo-jumbo of sorcery. They modelled themselves on him and his demands.

He had learned his lesson about whipping them. When he wanted their cooperation, he negotiated through Mammy. The cane was cut at a more leisurely pace than he wanted but he could do nothing about it if he was to harvest the crop.

The sugar he sent to England had been received with indifference. The report said it was inferior in quality to sugar from the West Indies. The soil, which he had thought ideal, was too moist to produce good sugar. As a result, his receipts fell short of the expense of shipping it. He had to make up the shortfall with the sale of some of Prince Gamunu's gems.

Bart pondered what to do about the season's crop as he surveyed the acres of cane rippling in the breeze. There was a local demand for sugar as a sweetener but the price was uneconomic for him. He would have to make more rum instead.

His Singhalese distillers with their experience of producing arrack from the fermented sap of coconut flowers, made a fine rum from the uncrystallized syrup drained from raw sugar. Bloodheart rum was a popular tipple among the garrison of Galle. It would have to be produced on a larger scale to cover his expenses.

Bart sighed, troubled by what to do with his land. He had fought for his dream of having his own plantation and now he could see it becoming a nightmare. Yet until he found an alternative crop that was profitable, he was obliged to continue growing cane to maintain the plantation routine.

Every day he rode through the fields, plagued by growing dissatisfaction. His life, like the plantation itself, had settled into a pointless routine. With Jessica, he enjoyed a warm companionship. With his mother, although there was the distance of their different generations, he had a trusting relationship. He knew he should be content. He wasn't.

He wheeled his horse around and galloped back towards the house, ignoring the startled glances of the slaves. The routine that Mammy hated to see disrupted, needed disruption.

'Jessica!' he bellowed as he jumped off the horse, flung the reins at Jagath and strode onto the verandah. 'Jessica!'

'Yes, Bart?' She rose from her seat where she had been rocking the wooden cradle placed out of the sun to catch the breeze.

Garth was playing with Ranita close to her chair. He tottered towards Bart and he picked the boy up, swinging him above his head. He placed him back on the floor and the child pleaded to be lifted up again. Bart kneeled down and held him off with his hands.

'Get the baby dressed,' he said. 'We're going to Galle.'

'Now?' Jessica looked alarmed. 'It's the sugar season. You said you couldn't go to Galle until the harvest is over.'

'It's over for me. Tissa can handle it. It's routine. I'm not needed here really. Let's go.'

'What about the children?'

'Can you look after the baby yourself?'

She smiled at the silliness of his question. 'Of course I can.'

Her proud manner amused him. Since the boy was born, Jessica had not let him out of her sight. She insisted he slept in their bedroom instead of the nursery. She was jealous of anyone holding or even touching him.

'Malika can stay here with Garth and Ranita. We'll leave them and go to Galle by ourselves.'

'Without slaves?'

'I'll be your slave.'

She glanced at him scornfully, not seeing any humour in his joke. It was as he expected. 'It will take me some time to prepare,' she said. 'It would be better to go tomorrow.'

He looked up at the sun. 'You're right. We'll go before dawn when it's cooler. I'll send Nimal to Galle to order a passenger cart.'

Mammy was furious at his intention and she showed her disapproval of the upset in her orderly running of the house by sulking and burning the dinner. Jagath, waiting at table without Nimal, dropped plates in his nervousness. Daisy pouted, casting long glances of reproach at Bart when Jessica was looking the other way.

His mother alone was calm. She sat with him on the verandah as the stars shone brightly in a cloudless, deep blue sky and the breeze blew gently on them both.

'Do you mind staying here to run the plantation?' he asked her, considering her feelings for the first time since he made his decision.

'I'm flattered you have confidence in me in the middle of the sugar season.'

'Mother!' He laughed sardonically. 'You knew long before I did that this plantation does not need me. My presence makes no difference. The slaves follow the routine and produce sugar and rum without my help.'

'That's untrue, Bart. Why denigrate yourself? Without you here, there would be no plantation. Oh, a few days off in Galle is all right but the Caffres, the *salagamas*, Tissa, Mammy, the children and myself, we all need you. The plantation exists only because of you.'

He gazed at her in amazement. 'I feel better hearing you tell me that.'

'The natives call you Bloodheart because they admire you, Bart. Only you know your shortcomings. They don't.'

'Do you?' His mother had always been a good listener and he found it reassuring to talk to her.

'Have you any?'

They both laughed. He relaxed, leaning back in his chair and crossing his legs, gazing up at the stars. Jessica was in their chamber with the baby.

'I suppose . . .' his mother said slowly, preparing him for the question he might not like. 'That you will see Prince Gamunu?'

146

'It's the purpose of going to Galle,' he said. 'I want him to name the baby.'

His mother sighed, relieved that he had raised the subject of the baby himself. She had been shocked when Mammy showed her the child and pointed out that Bart was not the father.

The household had been on tenterhooks about his reaction. When he saw the baby that first time, he knew instinctively that he was not his. The evidence of his tiny black scrotum, contrasting with the whiteness of the rest of him, confirmed it.

He had gathered the baby up in his arms while Mammy watched him nervously. He held the baby to his lips and kissed him. He kissed his whiteness and his blackness, making it clear to Mammy, to Malika and to Jessica that he knew, but he did not care.

He had said nothing, and expected them to say nothing. Prince Gamunu's gems had bought his silence.

Jessica expressed her gratitude by being a loving and dutiful wife. She no longer queried his absences from her at night, although she must have known that these coincided with Daisy's own absences from the kitchen quarters.

Occasionally, he wondered if he would have been complaisant about Jessica's infidelity without the bribe of a casket of gems. He liked to think he would. He regarded the child with awe, as someone special. He did not think of himself as having been cuckolded, and relished his position as adopted father to a boy who might one day be a king.

He was well rewarded. The gems, of which only a few remained, had paid the plantation expenses for the year and the cost of the new wings that transformed the pavilion to a villa.

Instead of condemning Jessica's conduct, he saw it as a licence for his own dalliance with Daisy and – if he was lucky on his trip to Galle – with Raven.

His mother broke into his thoughts with a cautious observation. 'Mr Radley has informed me in confidence that Prince Gamunu is finally to be sent off to exile.'

'Tissa told me that.' Bart sighed. 'That's why I want him to see the baby before he goes.'

'You've taken it very well. You've changed, Bart.'

147

He was touched by her comment and tried to explain. 'Mammy expected me to throw a fit. She nearly had one herself when I kissed the baby's balls. You probably thought I'd go mad. You all overlooked that I knew from the beginning. I trust Jessica. What happened had to happen. I'm proud of the child.'

His mother seemed relieved. 'He'll be a companion, a play-mate for Garth. There will be no scandal as he looks like your son to outsiders. No one will guess he has native blood.'

'His bride might,' he said mischievously, wanting to shock his mother. 'When she sees him naked on her wedding night.'

'If his bride is a virgin,' Charlotte replied with a twinkle in her eyes, 'how will she know he is different from other men?'

Havis was the first to call on Bart and Jessica when they were installed in the Henricuses' house in Galle. He was shown into the sitting room by Mrs Henricus within half an hour of their arrival.

Bart welcomed him warmly. 'You've put on weight!' he said, punching him in his chest like an old comrade. He was a man now, with the swagger that suited his status.

'That's because I got married.' Havis grinned as he shook his hand. 'Marriage agrees with me as much as motherhood does with your wife.' He bowed to Jessica as she held the baby across her lap.

She acknowledged his compliment with a smile then returned her attention to the child.

Bart drew Havis away to the other side of the parlour to talk to him without Jessica hearing. 'I didn't know you were married. What happened to the Burgher whore I introduced you to?' His loins prickled as he thought he might be able to see Stella again.

'I married her.'

'By the devil, you are a rogue!' He clapped Havis vigorously on his shoulders to disguise his faux pas. 'Why did you do that?'

'To make an honest man of me. Mr Radley's obliged to treat me with respect and he doesn't call Stella a whore any more. His nose was properly out of joint when Mr D'Oyly himself came to our wedding.'

'You have become important.'

'My grandfather has influence. I'm to go to Kandy as writer to Mr D'Oyly as soon as Prince Gamunu leaves here.'

'Congratulations. Is Stella going too?' He tried to make the question sound casual so Havis would not suspect his motive for asking it.

'Yes,' said Havis, causing Bart to bite his lip to hide his disappointment.

'She speaks Singhalese and I've been having lessons in it from Prince Gamunu. It's because of my friendship with the prince that Mr D'Oyly wants me in Kandy. He believes I can understand the etiquette of the aristocracy.'

Bart was curious. 'Why does he want to exile Gamunu? Surely he knows Mr Radley's reports about him fermenting unrest are falsehoods.'

'Are they, Bart? The prince is enormously popular. There is a movement to put him on the throne. Some of the Kandyan provinces refuse to accept British rule.'

'You've become an expert. Where are those provinces?'

'In the mountains by Kataragama. That's along the coast, east of here.'

'Is the prince really involved?'

'We don't know. To be on the safe side, Mr D'Oyly wants no member of the Kandyan royal family remaining in Ceylon.'

Bart glanced across the room to where Jessica was changing the baby's nappy. He saw the flash of black skin, his royal birthmark, and turned hastily back to Havis to distract his attention.

'Will it be possible for us to see Prince Gamunu?'

'You're just in time. He's to be boarded on a vessel for Mauritius tomorrow. I'll escort you to see him myself.'

'Is that necessary? Jessica and I can call on him after the baby's rested. We have no maid with us so we'll take the child too.' Bart smiled broadly, hoping to lull Havis's objections. If he asked outright to see Gamunu alone, Havis might suspect something.

'Well, I am rather busy. I'll tell his guards you are coming.'

'He has guards? The poor chap. Are they inside his chamber or outside?'

Havis hesitated before speaking. 'That's the sort of question

149

Mr D'Oyly told me not to answer. We think there might be an attempt to free him.'

Bart laughed, despite the trickle of sweat that ran down his spine. He spread his hands wide to emphasize his innocence. 'I'm not interested in adding a prince to my menagerie of Caffres and *salagamas*!'

'It's rumoured the prince has friends among the Burghers. Some of them would like to see the Kandyan kingdom revived and the British thrown out.'

'I'm not a Burgher,' said Bart, leading Havis back into the centre of the room. 'Although our wives are.' He smiled at Jessica and the baby who was now clothed and waving his hands happily as he wriggled in her arms.

'Havis says we can visit Prince Gamunu this afternoon. He's being exiled to Mauritius tomorrow.'

He searched Jessica's face keenly for a sign of regret. There was none.

'Keep that information to yourself,' Havis said anxiously, glancing around to see if Mrs Henricus had heard. 'We don't want him to try and escape before he's sent away.'

Prince Gamunu was sitting on his makeshift throne when they were shown into his chamber by a bored British soldier. He waited for the soldier to withdraw and the door to be closed before he descended from the dais. He came towards them with his arms outstretched. Jessica thrust the baby into his hands.

Gamunu halted, found he was holding the baby and raised his eyes, glancing first at Jessica and then at Bart. He could not utter the words of welcome that had been on his lips.

'We would like you to name our son,' said Bart quickly. Jessica's fingers reached for his and he squeezed her hand. An overwhelming feeling of love rushed through him. He felt proud.

Gamunu nodded. 'I never knew . . .' His voice dropped, he swallowed and began to speak again. 'You are indeed Blood-heart, a man courageous and forgiving.'

'They are sending you to Mauritius tomorrow,' Bart said

curtly to hide his embarrassment at the prince's praise. 'Is there anything we can do?'

'You have done it. If I had known, I would never have planned . . .' He stopped speaking and stared at the child. He raised him level with his face and held him for a long minute before whispering in his ear.

'Your name is Kirti! I name you after Kirti Sri Raja Singha who was King of Kandy for over thirty years. May you grow strong like a Royal Lion.' He kissed the baby's lips then handed him back to Jessica. He turned away, wiping his eyes.

There was a drumming on the door, two sharp knocks, a pause, and another knock. Bart remembered the code and looked around, expecting to see Havis.

The door opened. Outside it was dusk and the person who stood in the doorway was in silhouette. Bart saw the outline of a woman wrapped in a cloak, her face hidden by the veil of her bonnet. She closed the door behind her and raised her head.

'Raven!' he exclaimed as Gamunu placed his palms together in front of his bare chest and bowed to her. She ignored Bart and returned the prince's greeting in the Singhalese manner.

Bart felt Jessica tense. He smiled to calm her but she turned to Raven.

'I thought we were to have a *private* audience with Prince Gamunu,' she said scathingly.

'Ladies!' Gamunu raised his hands. 'Raven gave the official knock which means that Havis or Mr Radley himself attends me. What is their message, Raven?'

Bart realized he was treating her like a young girl. To him, though, Raven was almost a woman with her eager, heaving bosom and her wide, excited eyes.

'I'm sorry to interrupt, Jessica,' she said with mock sweetness. 'I have to speak with the prince urgently.' She turned back to face him.

'I heard daddy say that the soldiers are coming for you tonight. They want to forestall any attempt to rescue you.'

There was silence in the gloom of the room. Gamunu looked majestic, towering over Raven. He was hatless with his long hair drawn into the bun at the back of his head, revealing the firm line of his jaw, his straight nose and his high, royal cheekbones. A vein pulsed in his temple in time to the quickening rise and fall of his chest. By the flickering light of the candles, his eyes were opaque.

He moved abruptly, swinging around and stalking to the back of the room, the stiffened calico that covered his body snapping as it flapped at his ankles. He bent for a moment over an elaborately carved wooden chest, raising its lid and plunging his hand inside.

He drew out a gun which he placed on the chair that served as his throne. It was an old Singhalese flint-lock gun, with a long barrel and a wooden handle decorated with ornate overlay in the Kandyan style.

Bart eyed it warily. When he realized it was no threat to them he glanced back to see what the prince was doing.

He was crouched on his haunches before the chest rummaging among its contents. He found what he wanted, an embroidered pouch like a bag used for carrying betel, the leaf and parings of areca nut favoured by the Singhalese for chewing instead of tobacco. He stuffed the pouch into his waistband.

'What are you doing?' asked Bart, intrigued why a betel bag was so important. The prince ignored him, picked up the gun and primed it.

'By the devil! That gun might go off.'

'It is from the King's armoury. The British, with their inestimable good manners, did not search my possessions.' His face was serious.

'Bart, Jessica, you must go now. With Kirti. He is our hope for the future.' He laid the gun back on the seat of the chair and turned to Raven.

'You must leave too. I'm grateful for your warning.'

Bart was puzzled. 'Are you going to resist the soldiers? You'll be killed. Better to go into exile peacefully. Mauritius is similar to here. I stocked my plantation with canes from that island.'

'Ah, your plantation, Bloodheart! How I would like to see it. Jessica has told me so much about it. On the coast road to Kataragama, is it not?'

'Kataragama?' Bart pulled his ear, trying to remember what Havis had said about that place. It seemed to be a code word. Gamunu was watching him intently, expecting a reply.

'The plantation lies on a plateau above a lagoon beyond the bay,' said Jessica softly. 'There is a pass to Kandy through the mountains. It is a haven away from Galle.'

'Go,' said the prince, his eyes glinting. 'I shall think of you there when I need friends.' He stepped onto the dais and turned to face them. Placing his palms together, he bowed to each of them in turn, saying, '*Aybouwan*, may you live long.'

Bart ushered Jessica towards the door, casting a glance at Raven to see if she was coming too. Prince Gamunu was sitting on his throne, his hands bunched into fists on his knees, his face hard and eyes menacing. He had dismissed them from his mind as well as from his presence.

As Bart opened the door, they heard the soft chant and shuffling feet of palanquin bearers halting outside. He peeped around the door cautiously. The guard had gone and the verandah was deserted.

There were two palanquins at the steps. One had its curtain raised ready to receive a passenger. A man was being helped from the other by two tall Caffres. Bart closed the door softly and drew back into the room.

'Who is it?' Raven demanded.

He scowled and walked over to the prince, shouting to draw him out of his trance. 'Marcus Van Dort is outside. What is he doing here? Are you in league with him?'

Jessica cried out in fright. She clutched the baby to her bosom, her eyes widening with her fear. 'Bart –'

The door burst open, pushed in by a Caffre who positioned himself like a guard by the side of the doorway. He was followed by Marcus Van Dort, waddling into the room and panting with the effort of dragging his fat body up the steps.

His tiny eyes flared with anger when he saw Bart. He wrung his hands in distress instead of greeting the prince in the customary manner.

Prince Gamunu stared at him impassively.

Van Dort struggled to get his breath. 'You must come at

vunce, prince,' he said in a strangled falsetto voice. He took a deep breath and regained his self-control. 'The soldiers are comink for you tonight!'

He beckoned a second Caffre to his side. The slave was holding a cloak and a lady's bonnet. The first Caffre closed the door, plunging the room into gloom again.

'Put on these clothes. I haf a palanquin for you. You vill come vit me as my vench. I haf a pass for two palanquins to leave the fort.'

'Good!' exclaimed Raven, rushing over to the prince and gazing up at him. 'Havis said you'd find a way to outwit daddy.'

Bart stepped stealthily back into the shadows behind the throne. Van Dort clearly thought that he and Jessica were party to Gamunu's plan to escape. He peered into the darkness by the bed, searching for a way out of the chamber. There was no side door and all the shutters were bolted.

Gamunu rose to his feet, towering over them all on the dais. 'No!' His soft, deep voice was thick with menace.

'Come on, prince,' said Van Dort, flapping his hands in agitation. 'We haf no time to argue.'

From the corner of his eye, Bart saw Jessica edging to the door. If she could slip behind Van Dort and the Caffre, she could get free.

'I am not going.' Prince Gamunu's defiance halted Jessica. Bart looked at him uneasily, sensing the tension in him.

'You must!' said Raven. 'It's your only chance.'

'It's vat ve haf arranged!' Van Dort's voice rose to a shriek.

'I have changed my mind.'

'Vat!' Van Dort swelled up, his face turning purple. 'You cannot change your mind. I haf risked my reputation to help you. I haf expenses. You vill come.'

'No.' Gamunu shook his head slowly, his eyes glinting with evil. 'You help me because you want the *gaja mutu* as your price. Not because you believe that I will be King.'

'I do, prince, I do.' Van Dort bobbed his head obsequiously, his eyes darting around the room. They widened when he sighted the wooden chest with its lid open.

'Ve haf our agreement. If you stay here or if you come, you

pay me, yes? You haf taken the pearl from the chest?' He took a step towards the prince, wobbling on his short, fat legs.

Jessica sidled closer along the wall to the door.

'I will pay you,' said Gamunu angrily. 'With this!' He reached down to his seat and picked up the gun. He pointed it at Van Dort.

Bart signalled with his hand for Jessica to make a dash behind Van Dort while he was covered by the gun.

Van Dort was gulping with fear, his cheeks puffing in and out like a cobra's cowl. 'You vouldn't shoot your partner, prince!' he whined. He glanced around as Jessica tried to slip past him. He grabbed her with a snort of triumph. She had the baby in her hands so she could not struggle.

'Heh, heh!' he chortled, snuffling with relief. 'You von't shoot a lady. Not ven she haf your baby.' He gripped Jessica firmly, hiding what he could of his bulk behind her.

Bart lunged forward. His sudden movement startled Gamunu who tightened his grip on the gun. It exploded.

Van Dort squealed like a wounded pig. Bart hit the floor. When he raised his eyes as the smoke cleared he saw Van Dort still on his feet.

Jessica was slipping slowly from his grasp. She fell to her knees, holding out her hands to Bart for him to take the child.

Before he could reach her, she toppled forwards and Kirti dropped out of her hands to the floor.

There was a gaping hole at her side, spouting blood where the ball from the gun had torn into her womb.

Raven picked up Kirti and cuddled him to her bosom, murmuring softly in his ears to still his frantic crying.

Prince Gamunu snatched the bundle of clothes from the startled Caffre, pulled the cloak around his shoulders and dashed from the room. Van Dort struggled out after him.

Bart crawled over to Jessica. He knelt beside her and nursed her in his arms. He lowered his lips over hers and kissed her tenderly.

She did not move. She was dead.

CHAPTER SIXTEEN

Even the normally garrulous Mammy was silenced by the sad procession that wound its way up the long trail from the mill road. During the absence of Mistress Charlotte and Tissa in Galle where they had joined Bart for the funeral, she had been in charge of the plantation.

The *salagamas* had stopped cutting cane and worked instead in their *chenas* in the jungle. The Caffres passed the time sleeping contentedly under the shade of the suriya trees, only waking to move back into shadow when the sun changed.

Mammy stood at the edge of the verandah with her arms folded over he wide bosom. Daisy was at her side, trying to prevent Garth and Ranita running into the path of the bullock carts. Little stood beside her, squinting at the sun. Nimal and Jagath waited to run forward and help Mistress Charlotte and Malika descend from the carriages when they halted. The Caffres watched idly from a shaded corner of the garden.

Bare-breasted women stood in silence opposite the villa, the bright patterns of their *comboys* adding to the multi-hued colours of the bougainvillaea bushes. Their men, spindle-shanked and slightly built with sinewy arms, waited behind them.

Two *bhikkus*, Buddhist monks, moody and abstracted, stood apart from the others. They drew their yellow robes about them as the carriages approached, and cast down their eyes. Their ears appeared unnaturally large because of their heads being closely shaven. They clasped ornamented fans of talipot leaf across their chests.

Bart gazed at them from the cart he was sharing with his mother. The solemnity of this homecoming without Jessica caused the details of the scene to be fixed in his mind.

When he first came to this land, Jessica was at his side. It was jungle and plateau then where leopard prowled and deer grazed. Now there was a fine villa with slave cabins, a lawn, a flower garden, breadfruit and mango trees. The cane fields were green where the ratoons of the new crop were growing between the stubble of the old.

The carts lurched to a stop, the bullocks shook their heads and snorted with relief. The sounds blended with the whistling and warbling of birds swooping through the trees surrounding the villa. The sun was setting, throwing its slanting beams on the verandah where its light caught Mammy's plump face as she puckered up her eyes watching anxiously for Bart and his mother.

'Wait,' said Bart softly, indicating with a nod of his head the scene as the sun struck the verandah. 'It won't be the same in this house without Jessica. The slaves sense it too. She was with me from the beginning. She was part of me, and of them.'

'You must show them you're not downhearted.'

'It's odd to think of her in Galle by herself while I am here.'

'The Dutch church is very beautiful. The cemetery is in the best part of town, next to the mansion where Prince Gamunu lived. She'd like that.'

Bart sighed at his mother's mention of the prince's name. Gamunu had escaped through the fort gate in the palanquin and disappeared into the native quarter. Van Dort claimed to Mr Radley that he had tried to prevent him getting away and denied involvement in his escape.

Since neither Raven nor Bart contradicted him, the fat Burgher wriggled out of being punished. He did not attend Jessica's funeral.

Raven did, pale and swathed in black. She accompanied her father and said nothing to Bart in words but her eyes, when she lifted her veil to gaze at him, were deep with a meaning that set his heart thumping. She was gone from the church before he could speak to her.

'They are waiting,' he heard his mother say.

He looked out of the rear of the carriage. Nimal's eager face was sombre as he held open the trap door. 'Let me go first,' he said, pushing past his mother. He jumped out and strode over to the second cart where Jagath was waiting to help Malika descend. He reached inside.

'Give him to me,' he said.

'Yes, sir.' Malika obeyed immediately. 'Go to your papa, Kirti.'

'Thank you.' He smiled at her for what she said.

Taking the child firmly in both hands, he balanced him in the palm of one and steadied him with the other. He raised him above his head. The sun fell on him, emphasising his pallor, Jessica's colour. The baby gurgled.

'Here is Jessica's child,' Bart shouted, strolling around the lawn so the *salagamas* could see him. 'He is named Kirti, after one of the Kandyan kings, and also Charles, after Charlotte, my mother.'

'Praise de lor'!' Mammy raised her hands and cried out with glee. Her shriek of delight broke the tension.

Garth and Ranita began crying, not understanding the reason for the excitement. The Caffres and *salagamas* murmured among themselves. The two monks who had come to pay their respects, listened gravely to Tissa while he recounted what had happened to Jessica.

'A drink, Mammy, to welcome us home,' cried Bart, escorting his mother onto the verandah.

'This is hardly the cause for a celebration, Bart.' She took off her bonnet and handed it to Nimal. 'But a light rum punch is a good restorative after a long journey.'

'Jessica never approved of rum drinking.' Bart shook his head and chuckled to dismiss his sadness. 'Punch, Mammy!' he cried again, slapping her bottom.

'Yessah!' Mammy shimmied at his touch, shrieking with delight.

'Bart!' His mother was surprised at his behaviour. 'Jessica would not approve of you flirting with the slaves.'

He shrugged and turned away from her so he could wink at Daisy without her seeing. 'Tonight,' he mouthed at the slave. 'In my chamber.'

*   *   *

158

The routine of the plantation was soon re-established. Bart was troubled at how little he missed Jessica. When he saw the children were unconcerned and neither his mother nor the slaves grieved, he was less ashamed of his lack of sorrow.

The atmosphere in the house changed for the better. Mammy was delighted. Her beaming face set the others grinning. Smiles came naturally to the Singhalese. Nimal and Jagath no longer glided through the house with measured tread and serious faces. They moved swiftly to Bart's commands, smiling brightly as they served him and his mother.

Malika, without Jessica to criticise her, lost her nervousness with the children and laughed and played with them like an elder sister. Kirti settled down happily with her. Garth and Ranita soon forgot to ask for Jessica.

Since he no longer had to be careful of what his wife would say, Bart was less circumspect in his affair with Daisy. She graduated from being his bedwench to the housekeeper. He sent Delta to live at the mill as the night watchman and installed Daisy in a cabin of her own adjoining the villa.

Mammy's joy was unrestrained. She could now exert her influence over him through Daisy. He knew it, and was content for it to be so.

The relaxed atmosphere at the villa affected the whole plantation. Bart's temper mellowed. He discussed problems sensibly with Tissa instead of reacting with impatience at hitches in the sugar and rum production. He spent evenings planning the future with his mother, something he had never done when Jessica was alive.

'It would be wrong of me to say I'm pleased she's no longer with us, Bart,' Charlotte said one evening, three weeks after Jessica's death. 'However, I approve of the changes since she's gone.'

'You never liked her much.'

'She and I had nothing in common. She made me feel I was intruding. I was lonely.'

'Do you still feel lonely? You could visit your friends in Colombo.'

'I have no wish to join the Government House set. My place is with you. I was a planter's wife in Barbados. This is the life I understand.'

Bart snapped his fingers for Nimal to bring another rum. He watched his mother carefully. She had worn well in the tropics. Despite her love of rum punch, her figure was slim for her age and her face was unlined. She had taken to wearing her hair long, which softened the determined cast to her chin.

The sparkle had returned to her eyes since Jessica's death. Bart suspected that she was drinking a lot now she could do it openly without risk of Jessica's disapproval.

She sipped the punch Nimal brought her and resumed speaking. 'I am pleased by the way you have adapted, Bart. The planter's way.' She held up her glass, forestalling his protest.

'I know about you and Daisy. A single man needs a female companion.' She sipped at her drink. 'We are so isolated here. Be careful lest you fall too much under her influence. Slaves take kindness for weakness. Be always on your guard.'

'You've found a philosopher's tongue, mother,' he said, noticing the glazed look in her eye. 'Bloodheart rum is strong, is it not?'

'It is.' She gleamed at him. 'It's good for my backache.'

When she had gone to bed, helped by Nimal and trying to disguise her unsteadiness, Bart walked to the edge of the verandah and stared out into the night. His own mind was befuddled with the rum he had consumed, yet he was lucid enough to be concerned about his mother.

She was too young, he thought, to degenerate into a rum-swilling plantation widow, the type who flourished in Barbados, lashing the slaves by day and taking them to bed at night.

He loved his mother. She was seventeen when he was born. The age difference was small and a bond of friendship existed between them until his marriage. He saw the solution to his mother's loneliness lay in reviving that bond.

He belched, giggled to himself at his own drunken theorizing, and lurched off the verandah. The cool night

160

embraced him as the breeze rustled the leaves of the bougainvillaea bushes and sighed in the boughs of the suriya trees.

He swayed in front of the bougainvillaea and fumbled with his breeches. He sighed with contentment as the stream of urine hit the soil at his feet, splashing his boots.

An arm snaked around his waist, clasping him tightly. At the same moment, a hand clamped across his chest, lodging thumb and forefinger at the base of his throat. His arms were trapped at his side, his breeches open and his loins exposed.

'*Aybouwan*,' a deep voice whispered in his ear.

An intoxicating aroma of sweet spices tingled his nostrils, adding to his muzziness. The scent of the man trapping him in a bear hug, that threatened to squeeze the life out of him, was familiar. He was not alarmed because he reasoned that someone who was going to kill him would not wish him 'long life'.

'Gamunu!' he said confidently. 'Release me. I must fasten my britches.'

'No trickery?'

'I am an English gentleman.'

He was released as suddenly as he had been grappled. He refused to show the prince that the attack had shaken him. He calmly completed urinating, shook himself dry, pulled up the flap of his breeches and fastened his belt. Only then did he turn around.

His calm behaviour flummoxed Gamunu who had crouched down low, expecting Bart to take a swing at him. Bart put his hands on his hips and glared at him instead.

'Is this what you killed my wife for? To assault me in the garden of my home?'

'It was an accident. A part of me died with Jessica.'

'I told you the gun would go off.'

'You startled me. I meant to frighten Van Dort, hold him at bay while I escaped.' Gamunu rose to his feet.

The rum Bart had drunk added to his perception. He guessed why the prince had come to the plantation. He needed his help but was too proud to ask for it.

He had the appearance of a man on the run. His ill-fitting shirt was torn. His sarong was gathered up around his crotch and tucked in at his waist, leaving his thighs and shins exposed for fast movement in the jungle. His hair was uncombed, the bun loosened, with strands hanging down to his shoulders.

'Why have you come here?'

'Jessica told me of this plantation, of the pass through the hills to my kingdom.'

'You could take that pass without coming to me. I am not the guardian of the road. I should kill you!'

'You won't.' Despite hs bedraggled appearance, the prince conveyed a haughtiness, an air of being totally different from Bart and other mortals. He was peering down his nose at him, his hard features softening with a supercilious smile.

'How can you be so sure?' Bart was amazed to find himself on the defensive because of his colossal arrogance.

Gamunu waved his hand airily, dismissing the question as too petty.

'Why did you come here?' Bart demanded again. 'Take the pass and leave me. Go and claim your wretched kingdom.'

'You must show me the road.'

'Me?' Bart sobered up as he realized Gamunu intended more than just to taunt him. 'You don't know where it is? Jessica didn't know so she couldn't tell you!'

'It is known only to a few. You are one of the privileged.'

'Why should I help you?'

For answer the prince reached into the waistband of his loincloth. It was dark in the glade with only the vague light of the lanterns on the verandah for illumination.

Bart could not see what he pulled out and held up in front of him. If he invited him to the verandah where the light was brighter, there was a danger that Nimal or Jagath would wake up and see him.

'What is that?' he asked suspiciously.

Prince Gamunu waved the object briefly to tantalize him and then concealed it in his huge fist. 'This is the *gaja mutu*, Bloodheart. It will be your reward for helping me.'

The gems the prince had given him had dwindled to six. He could use something else valuable to boost his finances.

'Show me,' he said eagerly, unable to conceal his excitement. 'I can't see.'

'Let us go to your verandah. Welcome me as a guest.'

'I can't!' He was horrified. 'The slaves will see you. The *salagamas*. Some of them might be prowling in the garden even now. Mother might wake up. There's Tissa –'

'You sound like Collector Radley. So many objections.'

'Do you want him to find out you are here?'

'The *salagamas* know it. They showed me this villa. They are honoured by my presence, as will be your slaves. Tissa worships me. Your Caffres are of no consequence.'

Bart was angered by Gamunu's audacity. He strode out of the shadows of the bougainvillaea and jumped onto the verandah. He did not look behind to see if the prince was following. Nimal was on the floor, dozing in front of the main door. Bart kicked him awake.

'Two rum punches,' he said when he sat up.

Nimal scrambled to his feet and scuttled off into the parlour, ashamed at being discovered asleep.

Bart turned around and was amazed to see the prince relaxing in his favourite chair, sitting back at ease and enjoying the verandah with obvious satisfaction. It made Bart cross to see him there, especially because it was greed that prevented him booting Gamunu in his backside and chasing him off the plantation.

'Show me this gadger thing!' he snapped, taking a chair close to the prince and sitting by his side.

The prince's eyes flickered with disapproval at his lack of respect for the gem. 'The *gaja mutu* is what you call in English an Elephant Pearl.'

'Is that what Van Dort wanted from you?'

'He is a shrewd man.'

'You offered him this pearl so he would help you escape?'

'He forced his services on me. I declined.'

Bart pursed his lips, recalling that moment in the prince's chamber. 'Why did Raven come to you? Was she in the plot too?'

163

Prince Gamunu shook his head and placed his hand gently on his shoulder. 'Raven is an impressionable young girl, fired with idealism. She wanted to help me because her father would not. She was a source of information, nothing more.'

Bart felt he had been betrayed. 'You used us all!'

'Not without reward.'

'What did you give Raven? A black cat's eye?'

'A wise man's guidance. Inspiration. She is not interested in material gain.'

'I am.' He scowled. 'You bought my connivance but you caused the death of my wife. Show me this elephant pearl. It must be valuable if Van Dort wants it.'

Van Dort's desire for the pearl inspired his interest. If he possessed something that Van Dort coveted, it could help him get his revenge. He blamed Van Dort for Jessica's death, not Prince Gamunu.

Nimal returned to the verandah with a tray of drinks. He fell to one knee in front of the prince, bowing his head as he offered the tray. The prince raised his eyebrow at Bart, smirking to show he was right. Nimal backed out of his presence, keeping his head lowered.

'Elephant pearls,' said the prince when Nimal was out of earshot, 'are large, brilliant and variously shaped. They are beyond reckoning in worth. They confer on the possessor victory, children and good health.'

'What are they?'

'What is a pearl from a small oyster in the sea? Is it not valuable? Consider how much more valuable is a pearl from a creature as large as an elephant.'

'Do you have to open an elephant to get one?'

'Yes. Not only one elephant, possibly tens of thousands. Only a few elephants have this gem. That is what makes it so precious, so rare.' His voice dropped and his eyes sparkled with reverence.

Bart felt himself being drawn into the magic of the story.

'According to Kandyan legend, only special elephants, those animals gifted with extraordinary powers of memory, loyalty and strength – noble, royal elephants – are likely to have this pearl. It is concealed within their tusks, so only when they are dead can it be found.

'Thousands of elephants have been killed by avaricious kings for the sake of this pearl. It is never found that way. The pearl only comes to those for whom it is destined.'

Bart sipped at his punch and watched Gamunu do the same. He was not so drunk that he was going to be fooled easily. 'If this pearl is as you say, why would you give it to me? Showing you the pass to the Kandyan kingdom is a small matter.'

Prince Gamunu lowered his glass from his lips and stared at Bart with manic eyes that burned right into him. 'For Kirti,' he said. 'It is destined for him.'

Bart was silent. When he got the pearl he would sell it. The money would pay his debts. Kirti would benefit, so in a way the prince was right.

'Give me your hand.' The prince roused him from his thoughts.

He held out his hand while Gamunu wiped his palm with a piece of cloth. In his fist was the embroidered pouch he had taken from the chest before Jessica was killed. The prince opened the pouch, plucked the gem from within, and placed it with grand ceremony in Bart's hand.

'May you be blest!'

He stared at the pearl. It was larger than any of the gems Gamunu had given him, but not as pretty. It was spherical in shape and yellow with age. It was smooth although it lacked polish or shine. He had never seen or felt anything like it. He was scared to close his fingers because of the energy emanating from it.

'The *gaja mutu* is both a gem and a charm with us. It is a talisman according to our traditions.'

'I want it!'

Bart and the prince looked up in astonishment. Standing in the doorway, clothed in a long white muslin nightgown with a gay red ribbon knotted under her bosom, was his mother. Her eyes gleamed as she stared at the pearl in Bart's hand.

'I want it!'

She lunged towards them both, drawing out a sword she had hidden behind her back. With both hands clasping its hilt, she raised it above her head and sliced down at Prince Gamunu.

He leapt out of the chair with a startled cry. The sword whistled past his ear, smashed into the chair and split it in two.

Bart ran to his mother and seized her. She struggled in his arms and then went limp as the pearl, still in his hand, touched her breasts.

'I want it . . .' she gasped woozily before falling in a swoon at his feet.

CHAPTER SEVENTEEN

The blinding light hurt her eyes. She rolled over to bury her head in the pillow. It made no difference; the light was in her skull. She moved fretfully on the bed, hating to be awake, struggling to sleep but conscious of a nauseating agony. The light and the pain gradually resolved into shock at her behaviour the night before.

She drew down the pillow and clasped it to her bosom. She tried to staunch the remorse washing through her, to avoid the awful truth of what alcohol and her passion had made her do. She moaned.

'Miz Charlotte?'

The slave's whisper of concern sounded to her like a squawk of accusation.

'I bring yuh coffee.'

Slowly she opened her eyes, blinking away the stickiness of sleep. The shutters were open and she saw bright daylight outside. The shrill chattering of a flock of Ceylon babbler birds hopping through the branches close to her window added to her discomfort. She waved her hand at Daisy to dismiss her, wincing at the pain the effort caused.

'Mas Bart say let yo' sleep,' said Daisy, anxious to explain why she was bringing the coffee later than usual. 'Nimal done serve him breakfas' a'ready.' She sniffed to show her scorn. 'De boy does be frighten' de coolie –'

'That's enough, Daisy!' Charlotte's head reverberated with her strident reprimand. 'He is not a coolie, he's a prince.'

'He have coolie hair.'

Charlotte pursed her lips, lacking the energy to upbraid Daisy for her rudeness. She eased herself to a sitting position and reached out blindly for the coffee. Daisy placed the bowl in her hands. She sipped the lukewarm, bitter liquid slowly, waiting for it to clear her head and rid her of the unpleasant queasiness that came from having drunk too much sweet rum punch the night before.

It was a feeling she was becoming accustomed to. She enjoyed rum since being introduced to it by her fun-loving husband on his plantation in Barbados. Bart's manufacturing of rum, and Mammy's recipe for punch, was an opportunity for her to drink it in quantities without incurring his disapproval.

It was so easy in the loneliness of sitting on the hot verandah, day after day, to sip more rum than she intended. With Bart's bright company since Jessica's death, it was even easier to over indulge since he enjoyed drinking too.

She opened her eyes, aware that Daisy was still in the room, watching her quizzically. 'Mas Bart say yo' took sick las' night.'

'Really?' She handed back the half-empty bowl, unhappy that the coffee did nothing to ease her distress. 'What else did he say?'

'Yo' suffer heatstroke so he put yo' to bed.'

'Heatstroke?' She remembered guiltily. The shame brought a flood of colour to her cheeks.

Daisy clucked with pleasure at the improvement in her appearance. She fussed around the room, tying back the muslin curtains of the bed and putting out fresh linen for her to wear.

The normality of the slave's actons made her own behaviour the previous evening seem even more bizarre. She had taken the sword to the verandah when she heard raised voices and assumed Bart was in trouble. The sight of the elephant pearl in his hand stirred her to a madness. Why she tried to attack Prince Gamunu was still a muddle in her mind.

'Daisy,' she said in a firm voice to forestall the slave's objections. 'Give me my bottle.'

Daisy silently placed the bottle of rum beside the water pitcher within her reach by the bed.

She leaned over and filled a quarter of the glass with the

amber liquid and topped it up with water. She drank thirstily, ignoring its strength, longing for it to work its magic so she could face the day, her son, and the unexpected visitor.

Daisy stalked out of the room, leaving her to dress herself.

She remained in the chamber until after dinner. It was her custom to spend part of each day in her boudoir, a habit acquired during Jessica's regime when she liked to keep out of her way.

She did her office work there. She sent and received many letters and every other day a bullock cart or runner would go to Galle on her behalf. As well as keeping the plantation books, she was active in her own affairs.

The first consignment of gems and trinkets she sent to her agent in London earned not only profit but orders for more. She conducted her business through Tissa and the dealers he recommended. She sent several more selections to London. Her keen eye and formidable talent for bargaining aided her. She had learned the value of gems. At the sight of the elephant pearl, she had known instantly what it was – and that it was priceless.

She stared at the papers and letters in her escritoire but the pounding of her head made concentration difficult. Eventually, as the hours passed, she knew she would have to face up to Bart and Prince Gamunu and laugh off her behaviour of the night before.

After a strong measure of neat rum to fortify her, she left the room to join Bart and the prince on the verandah.

'Please don't stand up,' she said, smiling sheepishly. She had deliberately chosen a pale blue dress that revealed her figure to her advantage. Powder lightened the dark shadows under her eyes.

'Charlotte!' said Prince Gamunu warmly, leaping from his chair and dashing to her side. He offered his arm to escort her to sit with them in the shaded end of the verandah where a flagon of rum and glasses were on a table.

'How are you today?'

'Quite well,' she said with a simper, uncertain how he would treat her. She refrained from apologising for her conduct as this would place her at a disadvantage. It was better to pretend nothing unusual had happened.

'I have been attending to paper work so could not join you for dinner.'

'A glass of rum, mother?'

'Oh no, Bart.' She laughed politely. 'It's far too early.'

He eyed her suspiciously. 'We were waiting for you to witness Prince Gamunu give Kirti the elephant pearl.'

She opened her fan and fluttered it. Bart and the prince were clearly wondering how much she remembered. She merely smiled graciously.

'The *gaja mutu*,' said Prince Gamunu, apparently sensing her predicament, 'affects people in strange ways when they see it for the first time. Even the most genteel person can be overcome with a powerful compulsion to possess it. A lady of perception and passion could be expected to act quite irrationally.'

'Can a single pearl,' she said, lowering her fan and her voice as she returned the prince's probing look, 'really have such power?'

'Indeed it has. The *gaja mutu* is not coveted for its beauty, Charlotte, but for its potency.'

The way the prince uttered her name, drawing it out in his deep drawl into a word of three syllables, set her flesh tingling. She wondered if it was him or the pearl in the pouch dangling at his waist that had the potency.

She raised her eyes from the pouch and was dismayed to see him watching her intently. He seemed to understand more about her than a man should. She felt herself blushing under his stare and lifted the fan to hide her face. His eyes were fierce and demanding, his smile wickedly beguiling.

She shifted in her chair. Bart, who had seen the prince's hypnotic glare, looked angry.

'Shall we go to the nursery?' he snapped, breaking the spell.

She took the prince's arm and followed Bart. He said nothing as they walked across the courtyard together. Instead, the pressure of his fingers on hers and the spicy fragrance of his body dispelled the throb of pain in her head and replaced it with an ache of desire. She was bemused that a man should have this effect on her. Was it him or the pearl?

'Prince Gamunu must leave tonight,' Bart said at the door to the nursery. 'I will show him the trail to the pass.'

She glanced up at Gamunu without speaking, reluctant to release his arm. He was wearing one of Bart's frilled shirts, his hair flowing to his collar. With his coppery, craggy features and hard eyes, he resembled a pirate not a prince.

She quivered when he drew his arm away from her. She sensed his ruthlessness and was intrigued by it. She followed him into the nursery, ignoring Bart's glance of outrage.

As the prince bent over Kirti, her eyes fell on the outline of his limbs under his sarong. He was agile like Bart, despite his age which was closer to hers than to her son's. She felt at first a pang of regret that she would probably never see him after Bart took him to the pass.

Then an inexplicable fear gripped her. He was withdrawing the pearl from its pouch. He held it between his finger and thumb before rolling it in the palm of his hand.

Suddenly she understood the reason for her wild behaviour the night before. She saw in Prince Gamunu a dreadful evil that threatened her son.

Intuitively, she knew that Bart's survival depended on her. He was too weak to withstand the prince's baleful influence alone.

'Touch this pearl,' Gamunu intoned as he pressed it into Kirti's tiny fist, 'that you may be blessed.'

He added a rapid incantation in Singhala and removed the pearl from the baby's grasp. He slipped it back into the bag and turned to Bart.

'Take it,' he said, holding out the pouch. 'You are the pearl's guardian.'

Charlotte was worried. She was an emotional woman, sensitive to full heartedness in others. The prince's manner was bereft of warmth, too coldly calculating to be genuine.

Bart failed to notice the black glint in Gamunu's eye, but Charlotte did. She drew him aside to warn him.

171

'Come to my chamber,' she said, pretending her interest was in the pearl. 'Let me see Kirti's talisman in private.'

She smiled coyly to distract the prince and saw the hard gleam change to a suggestive twinkle that sent a shiver down her spine.

'What is it?' Bart asked irritably as soon as he closed the door and stood alone with her in her chamber. 'I don't want to leave the prince.'

'Ah,' she said with relief that he shared her doubts. 'You don't trust him either?'

'Of course I trust him. It's bad manners to leave a guest.'

'Be careful, Bart. He worries me. I'm sure he's planning something evil.'

'You're imagining it. Why are you alarmed? The pearl's just a chunk of ivory. The rest is superstition. Van Dort believes in it, though. He'll be sick with jealousy when he knows I've got it.'

'People in London will pay more than Van Dort for an elephant pearl. I know someone –'

'Is that why you went berserk last night?'

'I wasn't myself.'

'Well, I am! After I've taken Gamunu to the waterfall, I'll have nothing more to do with him. Does that satisfy you?'

She was unconvinced. 'I'll stay in my chamber,' she said to get rid of him so she could think. 'A rest . . .'

As soon as he was gone, she poured herself a large measure of rum and added water. She would have liked the fruit syrup Mammy added to make it a refreshing drink of punch, but to ask Nimal to bring the syrup would alert Bart to her private drinking.

It was clear to her that Bart was in danger and that Prince Gamunu had no intention of letting him keep the pearl. It was a trick to get him to show him the pass. She sought in her mind for a solution.

Her chamber adjoined the parlour. With her door ajar she could hear the murmur of conversation on the verandah. When she overheard Prince Gamunu telling Bart he wanted to be alone to meditate, she held her breath and strained her ears to catch Bart's reply.

'I have to go to the mill,' he said. 'I'll be back at sunset. We'll leave then.'

She smiled with determination as she studied herself in the looking glass at her dressing table. Slowly she brushed at her hair, fluffing it out to lend more femininity to her strong features. She wanted to conceal her nervousness so she could resist the prince's influence and twist his needs to her advantage.

She pushed the door open further so he would see into her chamber when he went to the guestroom in the courtyard. She lay, fully clothed, as though resting, on top of her bed.

She fought back her impatience to look for him. The only way she could exert any power over him would be if he sought her. The rum she had drunk gave her the boldness for her plan; it also made her anxious. If he declined the invitation of her open door and Bart's absence, then she had misunderstood the message of his glinting eyes.

The room darkened as someone closed the shutters; the only light came from the rays of sun filtering through cracks at the shutters' edges. She peered into the gloom in alarm. Even the door was closed.

'Who's there?' she asked, swallowing to ease the dryness of her throat.

'Who do you expect?' a deep voice answered close to her ear.

'I didn't hear you come in!' She felt the pressure on the mattress as he sat on the bed. Too late she realized she should at least have expressed surprise at his presence.

Her eyes adjusted to the gloom and she saw by his outline that he was looming over her. She tried to keep calm. 'What do you want?'

'What do *you* want, Charlotte?'

Again the drawling resonance with which he uttered her name enchanted her. He seized her hand and raised it to his mouth and kissed it, his lips lingering at her fingers.

She remained still, thrilling to the sensation the touch of his lips stirred. Slowly, he turned her hand over and kissed his way up the inside of her arm to her elbow. She squirmed.

173

'Your attempt to cleave me in two last night, Charlotte, impressed me. You are a resolute woman.'

She gasped, dismayed that he understood her distrust of him. 'If you were a gentleman,' she said sternly, 'you would not mention it.'

'If I were a gentleman!' He laughed, a low mocking sound that frightened her. 'Then I would not be in your boudoir while your gullible son has obligingly left us alone.'

'Why did you come to our house?'

'To bring the *gaja mutu* for Kirti.'

'That's the excuse, not the reason.'

He paused and looked at her, amused by her remark. 'You are a challenge to my survival, Charlotte. This makes our encounter more piquant.'

'Spare Bart,' she said with the dread of comprehension. 'I'll do anything in return.'

'It does not become you to play the strumpet.'

'If you kill him,' she said in despair, guessing that was his intention, 'I will throw Kirti into the lagoon. He'll be eaten alive by the crocodiles.'

The prince drew back with a start. Her hand was still in his and he squeezed it viciously, causing her to whimper with pain. 'You should not have said that!' He growled with rage.

'I'll scream,' she gasped. 'The boys will come in.'

'They would not disturb their prince.' He eased his hold on her, thinking aloud. 'You leave me no alternative. If Bart dies and you live, Kirti is at risk. So if I am to save Kirti, you must die too.'

He reached for her throat. She felt as fragile as a humming bird caught in his huge hand. It would not take him many seconds to choke the life out of her. Her death would be useless unless it saved Bart.

'Who will care for Kirti without Bart or me?' she said quickly as his thumb and forefinger closed over her windpipe. 'He has Bart's name . . . Not even Mr D'Oyly suspects a royal heir remains in Ceylon to claim the kingdom.'

'You will raise him to be king?' His fingers relaxed their hold.

'If you spare Bart.'

He flung himself on the bed beside her. She sensed his bewilderment at her proposal. Gently she drew away from him, hoping to escape from the room. Instead his hand grasped her wrist.

'Where are you going?'

'What is it to you? You don't want me!'

He jerked her down so she fell across his chest. 'Damn you, woman!' He encircled his arm around her and pulled her face towards him with his hand at the back of her neck.

She resisted yet her heart longed for the embrace.

Their lips touched. She was riven with the blade of his tongue cutting into her mouth. She bled inside as he stirred in her passions that had lain dormant since her husband died. She surrendered to his fury.

When he raised her skirt and his sarong in the same swift movement, she trembled. Their thighs clashed, naked flesh against naked flesh. She arched her waist and wrapped her legs around his, binding herself to him.

She waited eagerly, fearfully, for his thrust. It was dry and agonizing. She withered, screaming, desperate to withdraw.

He held her prisoner in his arms, pinning her to the mattress with the weight of his body. He smote his lips against hers to still her screams. The pressure grew.

She struggled until he abandoned his brutal assault and melted in her limbs. She knew then her life was saved, and loved him for it.

They lay in each other's arms, pausing together before rising to the rush at the end. She flowed with him as his strong, brave body pumped into her.

The door burst open and Mammy stood there with a cutlass in her hands. Daisy was behind her holding the long wooden pestle used for pounding chillies in the kitchen mortar.

'Oh my lor'!' said Mammy. 'It does be rape.'

'No . . .' gasped Charlotte, unable to move. Gamunu lay on top of her with his sarong rucked up to his waist, his buttocks twitching.

Daisy, inspired by Mammy's yell, pushed her way into the room and struck the prince with the pestle on his backside, forcing him into Charlotte. She shuddered at this final thrust then winced as he scrambled off her, shaking down his sarong and confronting them.

'Get out!' he commanded, his eyes flashing anger.

Daisy cowered backwards but Mammy anchored her bulk in the doorway and refused to budge. 'You a'right, mistis?' she asked defiantly.

It took Charlotte a few moments to realize what was happening. Should she agree with Mammy and accuse the prince of rape? To do so would oblige him to escape. He could turn vicious and kill them all.

She decided on bluff, to lure him into thinking she was his ally. Somehow she would alert Romulus to run to Galle with a message for Mr Radley.

'Mammy!' she said boldly, feigning her anger. 'How dare you disturb me in my own boudoir!' She propped herself up in bed, smoothing down her skirt. She throbbed with the feel of him inside her.

'Mix two rum punches at once. Prince Gamunu and I will take them on the verandah. It's almost sunset.'

She smiled at the prince and he stared back at her curiously. He was drained of energy and his eyes were no longer menacing.

CHAPTER EIGHTEEN

'Life in Kandy is based on the monarchy. The King is not merely the political head, he is the sacred symbol that holds society together.'

Prince Gamunu's words, declaimed in his deep, passionate voice, reverberated over the verandah to where Bart was concealed behind a screen of bougainvillaea. He had walked up to the house through the cane fields instead of using the main path where he would have been observed approaching the villa.

Sunset was less than an hour away. Bart was keen to see what the prince and his mother were doing before he revealed himself. The way his mother had watched Gamunu in the nursery had made him wary.

'The British will find that by abolishing the monarchy they have actually reinforced the Kandyans' deep commitment to it. Every Kandyan wants a king. Without a king there is no order or harmony, only confusion and dissension that will prove fatal to the conquerors.'

'Oh dear,' said Charlotte breathlessly. 'Will there be a rebellion?'

'There is already. I am to lead my people from the south. There the loyalty to the old regime is the strongest.'

'Mr D'Oyly will be upset. He has great plans to open up the kingdom.'

'His grandiose ideas are doomed to failure. The British have no sensitivity to our traditions or religion. The monks and nobles are disenchanted, and the people are too. There will be bloodshed, Charlotte. It may be a long battle but one day a king will rule in Kandy again.'

'Oh, I do hope so!'

His mother's gushing support for the prince alarmed Bart. It was all right to murmur words of encouragement when he was incarcerated and harmless. To do so now he was free showed Bart that she was either under pressure to appease him or had succumbed to his demonic charm.

He broke through the bougainvillaea and stormed onto the verandah. In his haste, he failed to notice the glow of affection in Gamunu's eye and his mother's glance of adoration. They were startled by his arrival and their expressions quickly changed. The prince looked tough and his mother anxious when he scanned their faces.

'I heard what you said!' He wagged his finger at Gamunu. Now he had the elephant pearl, he was no longer in awe of him. 'The only way you or your line will be king is if the British want it. Not by rebellion.'

'If the people are ungovernable without a king, they will be obliged to restore the monarchy.'

Bart scowled, puzzled by his own position. The British soldiers were seeking the prince and yet he was harbouring him. 'I should turn you over to the authorities,' he said, reaching for the rum flagon on the table and pouring himself a drink. 'I believed you were being sent into exile unjustly. From what I've just heard, I see I was wrong.' He threw himself into a chair.

'Bart . . .' His mother pleaded, her face tense and a warning gleam in her eye. 'You have an agreement for which you have been paid with the pearl. It is your duty as a gentleman to honour it.'

'I'll show him the pass.' He twisted in his chair. From the corner of his eye he saw Mammy beckoning him to the parlour. Charlotte saw her too and angrily waved her away.

'Do not disturb us!'

His mother's tone worried him. She was on edge. There was an air about her that something was changed. Her face was flushed – that could have been due to the rum – and her hair dishevelled. The customary care she showed in maintaining her neat appearance was lacking. It was strange when she had a visitor to impress. She looked distraught.

'I'll show you the pass,' Bart repeated to bolster his own confidence and to calm his mother. 'After that I will help you no more, Prince Gamunu.'

The prince stared at him impassively. 'It is as I expect.'

'Sah!' Mammy wrung her hands with agitation. She was standing in the doorway with Daisy behind her. 'I does want to see you, sah.'

'Take no notice, Bart. I shall deal with her.' His mother pointed to the setting sun. 'You must leave at once for the trail.'

'Yes.' Bart downed his rum and leapt to his feet. 'The sooner the better.'

'It is time.' The prince rose, glancing at Mammy ferociously. She refused to be deterred. She waddled towards Bart and put her hand on his arm.

The crack of a whip startled them both. Mammy erupted with a shriek of outrage, staring at her hand where the whip had stung her. Bart turned to see his mother coiling the whip dextrously, her mouth set in a thin line of determination.

'Slaves,' she said in a voice that dropped an octave with her anger, 'must not interrupt their betters.'

'Mother, why did you do that?'

'You're too easy on the slaves, Bart. They need more discipline.'

He looked from his mother to the prince and back again, wondering what dreadful thing had happened to make her change so radically. He shrugged his shoulders, preferring to deal with one problem at a time.

'Mammy,' he whispered encouragingly in her ear. 'Do what the mistress says. Go to your kitchen. I'll come later.'

'Later too late,' she said defiantly. 'De coolie –'

'Bloodheart, have you got the *gaja mutu*?' Gamunu took him by his arm and hastily drew him away from Mammy.

'Yes.' He turned back to hear what Mammy was saying.

'I don't believe you!' The prince tugged his arm viciously. 'You want to trick me! You hid it when you went to the mill.'

'That's nonsense!' He forgot Mammy and shook his arm free from the prince's grasp. He was angered by the accusation.

Tissa had told him to substitute a piece of ivory in the pouch in case the prince tried to get it back. Bart had refused.

'I am honourable in my dealings. The pearl is here.' He patted his pocket.

'Let me see it!'

'Why are you so concerned?' He drew out the pouch and handed it to him. He watched carefully as Gamunu shook out the gem in case he tried to substitute something in its place.

Behind him he heard Mammy arguing with his mother until the crack of a whip made her bawl. He dared not take his eyes off the pearl to look.

Prince Gamunu caressed the gem lovingly, enclosing it in the palm of his hand. Bart stared at it, ignoring the commotion behind him. Mammy's cries grew less as Daisy led her off the verandah. She was apparently mollified by whatever his mother told her. It was very odd.

The prince held up the pearl between his thumb and forefinger, offering it to the setting sun. The opaque surface seemed to glow. Bart watched fascinated, all thought of Mammy's outburst forgotten.

'This *gaja mutu* has been mine all my life. Yet each time I look at it, I see it anew. It is constantly changing. To you it is dull and disappointing. If you knew the pearl like I do, you would see beauty that is invisible to the eye.'

'I am honoured that you entrust it to me. For Kirti.'

Prince Gamunu's eyes rested on him, studying him to see if he was being flippant. 'You must keep the *gaja mutu* with you when you need protection. Especially when you go on a mission like tonight.'

'I was going to leave it here with mother.'

'No!'

'She needs protection. I'll not be back until daybreak.'

'You must take it with you! Shall I hold it?'

'No.' Bart grinned as he recalled Tissa's warning and put out his hand. 'I'll hold the pearl. I'll take it with me tonight if you insist.'

'I do.' Gamunu's eyes bored into his as though he was trying to put him in a trance. 'Charlotte has no need of protection. She is capable of more than you know.'

'Glad to hear it.' Bart wanted to be on his way. He walked over to his mother. She was toying with the whip in her hands.

'What was Mammy so excited about?'

'She'll tell you tomorrow. Take this.' She passed him a knife, small and sharp with an ivory handle.

'What the devil is it!'

'For protection.'

'I've got the pearl.'

'Watch Gamunu carefully, Bart. He's wily.'

He dismissed her concern, slipping the knife into the side of his boot to humour her. He kissed her briefly on her cheek. The distinctive aroma of spice, the prince's body odour, came to him as his nose brushed against her hair. He was puzzled but forgot it as the prince himself stepped up to them.

'May you live long,' he said, placing his palms together and bowing as he faced her.

'*Aybouwan*,' his mother replied with a hint of irony in her voice.

The trail to the pass was a difficult one. It began with the path to the river through the fields of young cane shoots. Bart had waited until night to climb for the sake of secrecy. Despite the prince's belief that the low-country Singhalese were his supporters, Bart wanted as few people as possible to know where he was going.

'We must take two Caffres to cut our path,' said Bart, when they reached the river after walking in silence through the cane fields. He halted, raised the flambeau above his head and whistled softly. 'They'll meet us here.'

Prince Gamunu looked worried as two Negroes emerged from the darkness. Romulus carried Bart's gun, while John wielded a cutlass which he banged against a sapling to show his prowess. The tree toppled out of his way.

'I thought we were marching alone.'

'If we do that,' said Bart, 'who will clear the trail? Will you shoot if a leopard attacks us?'

'We are quite safe together.'

'Perhaps. However, I would have to return alone.'

'I had not considered that.'

The prince's remark made Bart realize that he had no regard for anyone other than himself. His mother was right, as usual. He would have to watch Prince Gamunu very carefully.

John led the way from the field path to the trail beside the river. He swung his cutlass easily, hacking at overhanging branches and thrusting them aside. The Caffre's years of experience cutting cane gave him the ability to cut a path through the thickets of bushes and trees with ease.

They marched at a fast pace. Romulus walked behind John holding the flambeau. Bart carried the gun, alert for animals. Gamunu brought up the rear, making it plain by his sulky manner that he regarded slaves and a gun as unnecessary.

They climbed hard for nearly two hours. Gradually the trail disintegrated from an overgrown path to an ill defined scree that had them scrambling with hands and feet to surmount it. Gamunu complained vociferously which irked Bart as he was tired of the journey himself.

'Do you doubt that this is the way to your kingdom?' he challenged the prince after hoisting him with his hand up the sheer face of a boulder the size of an elephant.

'How can you be sure this is the way? There is no path.' Gamunu glowered as he hunkered down to catch his breath. The Caffres leaped ahead with the agility of natural bushmen. Bart did not bother to restrain them.

'We are close to the waterfall. Kingdom Falls, I call it. Can you hear that rushing noise? We're climbing around it now.'

The prince listened. 'You speak the truth. I was told a waterfall marks the pass. I didn't believe there was one because it can't be seen from the plateau.'

'It's hidden, even in daylight.' He was uncomfortably aware of the eager glint that had returned to Gamunu's eye. 'It is enclosed in an outcrop of rock. Like a funnel. It's visible only from a certain point out at sea.'

'You have the *gaja mutu* safe?'

Bart gripped the shaft of his shotgun for reassurance. 'I have,' he grunted, moving away sharply.

The prince was in a crouching position on top of the boulder. The magnetism of his glance was emphasised as a cloud drifted away from the moon and its vague light shone on him. Bart was reminded of a stalking cat preparing to pounce.

A scream echoed out of the jungle. He gulped with fear and tore his eyes away from the prince's stare. The flambeau was lying on the ground ahead. The jungle resounded with the noise of something rushing through the undergrowth towards them.

Bart tensed, lifting the shotgun to his shoulder, ready to fire.

'Massa!' Romulus burst out of the jungle. 'Leopard take John!'

'Stay here,' he ordered Gamunu, running immediately into the jungle where Romulus had come from. He preferred the challenge of a leopard ahead of him to the menace of the prince behind.

The flames from the dropped flambeau magnified the trees creating a flickering cavern of light in the undergrowth. The leopard was moving out of the cavern, holding John's arm in its mouth as it dragged him into the darkness. John must have surprised it as it lay in wait for prey, or perhaps the leopard mistook him for a monkey as he jumped from stone to stone. Leopards were usually afraid of humans.

Bart eased down on one knee and raised the gun. John was lucky the leopard had his arm in its teeth and not his throat which was the usual hold. He aimed carefully and fired.

The shot was true. It took the leopard between its eyes. It yelped, sprang back and landed with a squelch on John's writhing body. Bart sank back on his haunches with a sigh of relief.

Prince Gamunu emerged from the undergrowth. Romulus cowered behind him. Bart was conscious of the prince watching him warily, waiting for him to make the first move. He sprang to his feet and walked over to John.

He pulled him from under the leopard, shouted at Romulus to bring the flambeau. The Caffre's forearm was mangled to a pulp of torn flesh and bone where the leopard had chewed. There was a deep claw gash on his right shoulder.

'Can you stand?' he said, pulling John to his feet. He turned to Gamunu. 'I'll have to take him back.'

'You can't leave me here!'

'Follow the river through the jungle. When you find the waterfall, you'll see the pass half way up it.'

'You must show me!' The prince sounded desperate.

'Very well.' He decided to take him to the waterfall and then hurry back to help John. 'Romulus, tie your shirt around John's arm to stop the bleeding. Wait for me here. I'll be back soon.'

'Give the boy your gun,' said the prince, making it sound like a command instead of a suggestion.

Bart thought it an odd thing to say but did it anyway to give Romulus confidence.

He was annoyed at having to leave the two Caffres in such a hurry. They were both scared witless and he wanted to make sure they understood they would be safe. However, Gamunu's impatience and his own desire to see the last of him were compelling reasons. He clapped young Romulus on his shoulder to encourage him and headed off into the darkness.

The prince followed closely, so close that at times his hand touched his shoulders, then his buttocks and even as they scrambled up a stone-strewn slope, his ankle. He felt Gamunu was measuring him, sizing him up for combat.

At last, with the roar of falling water deafening him, he found the way around a jagged outcrop of rock and stood on a wide ledge overlooking the waterfall. The prince scrambled to his side, grasping his arm and clinging to it in the face of the sheets of spray that showered over them.

They were standing on a ledge about halfway up the falls. The ledge continued until it disappeared under the overhang of the water itself. The moon was bright and gave the falls a ghostly sheen where water plunged past them to the river a hundred feet below.

'There's your pass,' said Bart, pointing into the falls. 'The ledge leads to a cave. It opens onto a trail to the mountains.'

He tried to shake off the prince's grip on his arm.

'Show me the *gaja mutu*!'

Bart faltered, drawing away.

'For the last time.'

'I must get back to John.' He took out the pouch and opened it into his palm, holding the pearl carefully.

Gamunu jerked his arm and he felt himself sliding on the slippery surface of the ledge. He clutched at him to keep his balance.

The prince grasped his hand and Bart thought he was going to help him. Instead, he snatched the pearl, palming it into his own hand. He flung Bart aside and took a step along the ledge towards the falls.

Bart was on his knees but when he saw Gamunu was making a dash for it, he hurled himself at him and grabbed his ankle. His fingers slipped but Gamunu tripped and fell heavily. Bart scrambled onto his shoulders. Spray from the falls soaked them both.

Blinded by the water stinging his eyes, and by the madness that seized him at being tricked, Bart pounded the prince's head against the rocky wall at the side of the ledge.

Gamunu moved almost lazily, shrugging his broad shoulders and striking out with his fist. He had something sharp and hard in his hand that connected with Bart's skull. It was the *gaja mutu*.

It tore a gash in Bart's brow. He screamed with agony. His legs buckled under him and he collapsed. A paralysis spread through his limbs.

Gamunu kissed the *gaja mutu* and chuckled. He stood up, slipping the gem into the folds of his loincloth. He was drenched from the waterfall, his long black hair dripping wet around his shoulders. His eyes blazed, his lips curling over his teeth in a demonic grin.

'It is death to attack me,' he boomed, his voice sounding hollow to Bart in his concussed state. 'I was going to spare you for Charlotte's sake.'

Bart bit his lips, summoning his strength. His limbs were heavy, slow to respond. If he kept Gamunu talking, he hoped to gain time to shake off the effects of the blow.

'What about Kirti?' he gasped.

'Your mother said she will feed Kirti to the crocodiles if I kill you.'

'She will!'

'No, Bloodheart.' Gamunu laughed confidently. 'She won't. She loves me too much for that.'

'Loves you?' Bart felt sick. He was lying close to the outside edge of the ledge. It would be easy for the prince to tip him over it into the blackness of the spuming river far below. He tried to roll away. His limbs would not respond.

'Charlotte has my seed inside her. That's my spell. She is my slave. She will raise Kirti to be a King. He will be her son to replace you!' He advanced towards Bart, chuckling maniacally.

The memory of Mammy's frantic appeal to warn him flashed into his mind. His mother had bartered herself to save him.

'She was good in bed, Bloodheart. Better than your wife!' Gamunu put his foot under Bart's waist and prepared to roll him over the edge.

Slowly Bart managed to raise his hand. He reached up, touching Gamunu's hairless leg, wet with spray. The prince beamed at him, resting his foot under his buttocks.

He needed only to kick and he would plunge to his death on the rocks below.

Bart's hand crept up Gamunu's thigh. The prince stood motionless, gloating at Bart, enjoying the moment of his death.

With a desperate effort, concentrating all his energy on his hand, he stretched upwards.

Too late, Gamunu realized what he was searching for. He brought back his foot to propel him over the edge as Bart's fingers touched the *gaja mutu* in his loincloth.

The strength returned instantly to Bart's body. He flipped out of the way as the prince kicked. Rising to his feet, he caught Gamunu off balance and, with the weight of his thrust, flung him to the ground. The prince fell badly, cracking his head on a sharp outcrop of rock. He was stunned. Bart pushed him under the outcrop so he was trapped by it.

Frantically, he scrabbled in his sarong for the *gaja mutu*. The prince moaned and struggled to free himself. Bart could feel the pearl in the tangle of cloth at his waist. He tried to unfasten it.

He remembered the knife. He pulled it out and sliced at the loincloth. His fingers were numbed by the spray and his eyes blinded with the blood that poured from the gash in his head.

He found the pearl resting in the hair of the prince's crotch. He plucked it away and placed it in the pocket of his breeches.

He felt his strength rushing back. He took deep gulps of air while he gazed at Gamunu lying naked at his feet. He was overwhelmed with loathing for the man because of what he had done to his mother. Death was too good for him.

He bent down and cupped Gamunu's testicles in his hand. The prince stirred in panic and tried to push him away.

'Bloodheart, no! Please, no!' he screamed, trapped by the rocks and unable to shake him off.

Bart held the black scrotum in his left hand, pulling it downwards. With deliberation, he cut through the stretched skin with his mother's knife. Each stroke was her revenge.

He tossed the bloody sac into the waterfall and crawled backwards off the ledge out of the spray.

Gamunu's screams were louder than the roar of the thousands of gallons of water plunging past the ledge where he lay. Bart heard them all the time he was scrambling down the screes of the trail in search of John and Romulus.

Later, he returned to the waterfall with Tissa. He was too late. Prince Gamunu was gone.

CHAPTER NINETEEN

The flowers of the frangipani tree, called temple tree in Ceylon because one can be found near every Buddhist temple, have five white petals. They open in perfect symmetry from buds which are, by contrast, crimson. The flowers have the sweet, pervasive perfume of jasmine, filling a garden with an almond-like aroma that lulls the senses into contentment.

They were Raven's favourite flower. There were dozens of temple trees in the garden of the Collector's residence. The blooms dropped to the ground where they lay to be crushed underfoot by the careless tread of her father, or gathered by Raven and placed in clay bowls of water in rooms where they imparted the fragrance of romance to the staid atmosphere of the bungalow.

Raven was stirred to romantic longing by the perfume because when she plucked at each petal one by one, she whispered 'He loves me, he loves me not,' and always ended with 'He loves me.'

Her familiarity with the flowers grew from many lonely afternoons strolling in the garden while her father and his new writer, a dreary gentleman who had damp hands and a large nose, pursued their duties.

It was not the new writer she considered when she pulled a flower apart or held one to her nose inhaling its erotic aroma. Sometimes she brushed the petals against her lips, the softest touch, pretending it was a kiss.

Her yearning was for a man as yet undefined. During those sultry afternoons of wishful thinking, she formed an image in her mind of the one who would bring glamour and excitement to her life. He would have the manners of Havis but not his fussiness, and the authority of her father without his pomposity. He would have the haughtiness of Prince Gamunu, and the swagger of a dashing young man like Bart Taylor.

He would be physically strong, robust and passionate; he would be taller than her and dress with panache. People would turn their heads to look at him as he passed but he would ignore them nonchalantly. He would be a man of property and be able to provide her with more than an armful of fragrant white frangipani flowers.

He would be attractive to look at, with an open face, a fine head of hair and an engaging smile. He would look, she came to realize over the weeks, somewhat like Bart Taylor.

'He loves me, he loves me not.' Bacause of the flower's five petals, he undoubtedly loved her. All that remained of the flower when she pulled the petals apart was a hint of the perfume, not even a stem.

Although Bart seemed to be the epitome of what she craved and it was his face that hovered in her dreams night after night lending her a sense of wellbeing when she woke, she was loath to admit it. The mystery of who would be the one the flower foretold loved her, was more intriguing than actually knowing.

So she exhibited towards Bart an ambiguous attitude that kept them both guessing. She feared she might have spoilt the game by her apparent lack of interest in him. Hence her reliance on the flowers for self-assurance.

He had come several times to the bungalow to speak with her father about Prince Gamunu's death. Each time he barely acknowledged her presence.

She was furious with him when he did nothing more than nod his head curtly at her and proceed to talk with her father. She supposed it was his revenge because of her rash behaviour with the prince. She wondered if he was jealous.

Or perhaps he was cross with her because of her coldness at his wife's funeral. She wanted to offer him comfort but secretly she was excited by Jessica's death.

The network of slaves and servants who boasted about the doings of their masters and mistresses to each other, ensured there was an interesting supply of gossip about Bart.

He was reported to be missing his wife dreadfully, to have a slave bedwench, to have a whore at Madam Gudde's, to be close to bankruptcy, to be making a fortune with his Bloodheart rum.

She listened avidly to everything she heard about him while being careful to feign scorn in public. People believed him to be a foolhardy ne'er-do-well and that thrilled her.

It was a year since her visit to the plantation when Jessica monopolized her to keep her away from Bart. She had allowed her to do so because she thought it added to her allure. It did not.

She had matured since then, with the body, and certainly the desires, of a woman. She had begun to attract the bloodhounds, as her father called them: hearty, middle aged military men who called to sniff out her intentions. She told her father to refuse them all. She had no intention of marrying until she was ready.

She smiled to herself as she sat under the temple trees. She was ready, oh yes . . . but for the right man.

There was no plan in her mind. She trusted providence to arrange matters for her. She knew Bart made occasional visits to Galle to deliver barrels of rum to the military garrison. The officers' mansion in Church Street, where Prince Gamunu had lived, was a favourite haunt of his.

Sometimes Bart was to be seen on the verandah drinking with the officers in broad daylight, joining in their coarse laughter and childish jokes and revelling in their foul-mouthed company.

She disapproved of him acting rambunctiously in public because he was superior in every way to the army braggarts. Yet his devil-may-care attitude and his contempt for what people thought of him were some of the reasons why she found him attractive.

If only he would notice her, she sighed, crushing the flowers to her bosom.

He saw her walking up Church Street in her sensible afternoon gown that revealed no flesh except her hands. Her bonnet was of recent fashion with side flaps like a horse's blinkers to keep the sun off her face. The light tan of her complexion showed she was not shy of the sun and only wore the bonnet for propriety's sake.

She walked without a chaperon, glancing around her casually as though partaking of an agreeable afternoon stroll to view the sights of the town. With exaggerated indifference she passed close to the colonnaded verandah where Bart was drinking with a group of officers. He eyed her with equal indifference.

She affected a weariness and climbed up the steps of the embankment to rest on the rampart bench opposite the mansion.

Her aloofness infuriated him. She had said scarcely a word during their encounters at her father's house. She would turn her wide, dark eyes on him scornfully, making him feel he was unfit to be seen by her. If she was left alone in a room with him for a moment, she would bolt into the garden to escape. Yet her startling beauty and her proud personality fascinated him more each time he saw her.

'After I hacked off the prince's ballocks,' Bart said loudly so his words carried above the clatter of the street to where she was eavesdropping from her seat, 'I tossed them over the falls.'

The officers laughed heartily and swigged at their rum. He had told the story several times, even to Collector Radley. It no longer seemed to be about him.

'By Jove!' said a stout captain, his face puce with joy at Bart's savagery. 'The bounder deserved it for shooting your wife.'

Bart said nothing. None of them knew the agony his mother still suffered because of what Gamunu had done to her. Jessica was dead and forgotten.

'Why didn't you chuck him over too?' another officer asked.

'I didn't have to.' Bart's eyes twinkled. 'In his state he was relieved to do it himself.'

Across the street he saw Raven's shoulders twitch and her nose tilt up with disdain. Whether she was shocked by what he had done, or merely expressing disapproval for their loud conversation, he did not know. He wanted to shout out to her that she should move if she found their conversation distasteful.

'Excuse me, gentlemen,' he said, nodding across the road and winking. He lowered his voice so she could not hear. 'Some sport!'

The loud guffaws of the soldiers caused her shoulders to stiffen. She was too well-bred to turn and stare openly at them. Since she was ignoring them, Bart ignored her too.

He sauntered across the road and up the steps, walking over to the battlements where he faced the sea and opened his breeches. He whistled jauntily and urinated over the wall.

'By old horny!' he said, shaking himself as he turned and pretended to notice her for the first time. 'Raven?' He fastened himself with an air of insouciance. 'Taking a breather?'

She turned her head without speaking, avoiding his eyes. She was blushing furiously.

'Ah, well,' he said, determined to treat her in the same cavalier fashion, despite the embarrassment he was causing her. 'I'll be about my business and leave you to yours.'

He belched, releasing a gust of rum-soured breath in her direction as he swaggered past her.

'I overheard,' she said softly, 'a reference to Prince Gamunu.'

He struck his brow with the palm of his hand in an exaggerated gesture and looked down at her mockingly. 'You sit here to snoop, miss? That is your habit, is it not?'

Her lips trembled at the insult.

He derived no pleasure from causing her distress. He regretted his words. He was treating her like a whore instead of an impressionable and spoilt young lady.

'Forgive me,' he said, ashamed of himself. 'The company of soldiers ill-prepared me for this encounter.'

She raised her eyes and he grinned sheepishly. She ignored his apology. 'Prince Gamunu may be gone but he used to say his line would live on,' she said.

Her seriousness alerted him to her mood. This was not to be the robust flirting he expected. He sat on the bench beside her, deaf to the barracking from the rum-sozzled officers leaning over the verandah rail behind them.

'He said many things . . .' He watched her eyes carefully.

She was frowning with disgust at the guffaws from the mansion. Suddenly, she rose to her feet and began to walk off.

He jumped up too, annoyed at the soldiers for frightening her just as he was about to make some progress. He shook his fist at them and chased after her.

'What have I done?' he demanded peevishly. 'I sit beside you and you take off in a huff. Do you let the jeers of those jackanapes in uniform upset you?'

'Of course not!' Her eyelashes flickered and she cast an astonished glance at him. 'I am surprised to hear you speak of your comrades in such a disparaging manner.'

'Comrades? They are customers for my rum. Is that why you took offence? You don't approve of my companions? I would much rather spend time with you, Raven.'

'You jest.'

He noticed the quiver of her lips and the softening of her haughty manner. 'It would be folly to joke with a highly strung lady who has a grand opinion of herself.'

'You speak of someone unknown to me. Perhaps you confuse me with her?'

'By the devil!' He pulled his ear lobe. 'Perhaps I do.' He was delighted that she could relax the pompous behaviour she must have copied from her father. 'May I walk with you to the bungalow?' he asked.

'You appear to be doing so.'

'I trust it is with your consent?'

She nodded, peering at him around the blinkers of her bonnet. He wished he had drunk less rum so he could be more appreciative of this moment. After waiting months to talk to her, he was tongue-tied under the impact of her dark-eyed gaze.

'The prince,' she said pointedly, 'gave your wife's son a royal name.'

'Kirti? He's just like him –' He broke off, coughed to disguise what he had said, and added in a rush, 'Just like he said he would be.'

Raven stopped and stared up into his eyes. 'Thank you for telling me.'

'Telling you what? It was a slip of the tongue . . .'

'You've confirmed what I suspected. Your wife was unfaithful to you, with the prince.'

'That's no concern of yours.' He shifted uncomfortably under her gaze.

'Oh, it is!' She sounded pleased. 'How ashamed you must have been.'

'I don't want to discuss it.'

'The baby, who looks after him?'

'His maid.' He shrugged off the question although he was perturbed that she had discovered his secret. 'Why do you ask so much? For your father's information?'

'No, no!' Her manner changed subtly. 'I will never tell anyone else.'

He was suddenly angered by her condescending attitude. 'Don't!' he said. 'I bid you farewell, Miss Radley.'

She was flustered. 'I thought you were walking me home?'

'Another time!' He turned on his heels and strode off in the opposite direction.

He longed to continue talking with her but he wanted his revenge, to give her a taste of her own medicine. Her questions rattled him and made it easier for him to leave her in the lurch. He hoped she felt as humiliated as he did when she treated him off handedly.

Dusk was fast approaching the town and he decided to take a turn around the ramparts to cool down his temper. Raven had annoyed him in several ways: by her intimate knowledge of his private affairs, by her assumption that he would fall at her feet in adoration, and because she was right. It drove him to churlish behaviour, and he was baffled to know why.

His attention was caught by the sight of a man emerging from the porch of his house the way a water monitor scrambles out of a ditch, his head swinging from side to side, his pink tongue darting out between his ugly lips, and his legs straddling the street uncertainly. It was Marcus Van Dort.

His slave, Malie, Tissa's younger brother, stood at his side.

Bart dodged behind a parapet so he would not be seen.

'Vich vay did she go, boy?' Van Dort demanded.

'On the ramparts . . .'

'Heh, heh!' Van Dort clouted Malie around his head with his cane. 'Fetch a light and follow me, I haf vork to do.'

Bart heard him puffing as he climbed the embankment path to reach the top of the ramparts. He kept in the shadows of the swiftly darkening twilight.

Van Dort waddled onto the ramparts and set off in the direction Raven had taken. He moved surprisingly fast for a man of his size but Bart had no difficulty following him. He never looked around but forged ahead with indecent haste.

The ramparts at dusk were popular with the townsfolk for promenading. Muhammadan women, secure in the privacy of their all-embracing robes in the gathering darkness, walked in groups with mothers and grandmothers chaperoning daughters. Singhalese families of children and parents chatted and played together on the lawn of the ramparts.

A European settler and his wife took the air with elaborate informality, accompanied by their slaves and dogs. Bart declined to return their greetings. He was keeping his eye on Van Dort.

In his wake, he smelled Van Dort's perfumed flesh. The expensive lotions were insufficient to disguise the body odour and sweat generated by the wobbling of excess weight on his short, fat frame.

Van Dort had the blood of the lowlands people in his veins. However, the lithe grace and beauty of his *salagama* ancestors were lost in him. His shape more closely resembled a round red Dutch cheese than a human being.

People hurried out of his way as he bowled along, showing no intention of changing his course for anyone. Although he had been deprived of his official position as Registrar, he continued to inspire fear in the town's population.

His wealth and influence were formidable. He boasted he could buy, control or outwit everyone; native, Burgher or British. He would stoop to any evil to get what – or who – he wanted.

Raven was sitting on a bench, staring mournfully out at the sea, a frangipani flower in her hand. She was idly pulling off its petals, her thoughts clearly lost in dreams.

Bart cursed himself for abandoning her in his fit of pique instead of escorting her all the way home. Van Dort's pace quickened.

'Raven!' he cried, wheezing to a halt and, without a word of apology, plumping himself down on the bench beside her.

Bart sidled into the darkness of the battlements so he could hear without being seen. He was intrigued how Raven would handle this obnoxious man.

She seemed startled. The loose petals of the flower fluttered from her hand.

Van Dort was gulping for breath after his dash along the ramparts. He tapped his cane on the ground, impatient to begin speaking.

'Raven!' he cried again. 'I haf vaited long time for an opportunity . . . to speak vit you . . .' He sucked in air and looked at her, his tiny eyes gleaming.

Raven gazed at him as though he had crawled from under a stone. Van Dort was not intimidated.

'You haf been in my thoughts for months, Raven!' He reached out to grasp her hand. She moved along the bench.

Bart wondered why she did not get up and walk off. She was favouring him with more attention than she had ever given him.

'The moon,' said Van Dort in a vain attempt at small talk. 'It is beautiful, heh?' He craned his neck up at the sky, expecting her to do the same. She stared frostily ahead. 'Almost as beautiful as you.'

'You are very kind,' Raven said, finally acknowledging his presence.

'I can be, yes. I haf much property, a fine house. The only man as important as me in Galle is your father. Ve vould make an ideal marriage, Raven.'

'What are you suggesting, Mr Van Dort?' She put her hand to her mouth, stifling a giggle.

'My darlink!' Van Dort pounced and seized her hand in his.

He held it firmly, raising it to his lips. 'I shall ask your father. He vill give his consent, yes?' He puckered his mouth, preparing to kiss her fingers.

'No!' Bart leapt out of the darkness and pushed Van Dort aside.

The fat man squeaked with surprise. He released Raven's hand. She stood up and glared at Bart.

'Why do you interfere?' she asked crossly.

'He was slobbering all over your hand!' Bart glared back at her.

At that moment, Malie arrived with a flambeau. It lit up the scene to the delight of the promenaders who stopped to watch.

'It's *my* hand,' shouted Raven, waving it at him. 'Not yours.'

Van Dort recovered his wits. 'Is this lout troublink you?' he said cunningly. 'I shall call out the guard.'

She smiled at him, ignoring Bart. 'Marcus, perhaps you should speak to my father? If he gives his consent . . .' She let the words trail off suggestively.

It was too much for Bart. 'Raven, you're not serious!' Angry despair gripped him because she seemed determined to humiliate him publicly. 'Would you really give yourself to this Burgher pig?'

'Yes! Anything to keep you and every man in Galle from pestering me when I go out for a walk.'

'He's not worthy of you. Raven. He's a lecher –'

'Who is worthy is for me to decide, not you!'

Van Dort gloated. He placed his pudgy finger on Bart's chest and prodded him. 'Go back to the jungle vit your slave venches.'

Bart clenched his fists. It would be easy for him to smash Van Dort's fat face to a pulp. Each prod of his finger in his chest was goading him closer to losing his temper. He glanced at Raven and saw that her dark eyes were bright with excitement as though she was eager to see him fight over her.

'By the devil!' he roared angrily, thrusting Van Dort's finger away and lunging at her. He scooped her up in his arms

197

with one hand under her knees and the other cradling her shoulders. She screamed.

With a swift movement, he sat down on the bench and flipped her over so she was lying across his lap.

She struggled in vain, flailing her arms wildly and kicking at him with her feet. Calmly, he raised his hand and delivered a sharp smack to her bottom.

'Heh, heh!' Van Dort honked and rubbed his crotch obscenely.

His laughter brought Bart to his senses. He raised Raven to her feet, put his arm around her and marched her off to her father's bungalow before she could protest.

Van Dort stared after them, his eyes bulging.

'If your father won't reprimand you,' said Bart, 'then take notice of me! You cannot walk in public alone. You're cheapening yourself.'

She stared at him, incapable of speech.

'You dropped this,' he said when they reached the gate of the bungalow.

He placed the five petals of a crushed frangipani flower in her hand and dashed off.

CHAPTER TWENTY

Marco Polo, on returning to Europe in the thirteenth century, told of the sapphires, topazes, amethysts, garnets and other costly stones of Ceylon, and a ruby which belonged to the king of the island that was 'a span in length, without flaw, and brilliant beyond description'.

During the dynasty of the Kandyan sovereigns, the right of digging for gems was jealously guarded by the kings themselves. The inhabitants of certain villages were employed in their search for gems under the superintendance of hereditary officers known as *Mudianse*.

This royal monopoly was abolished by the British as a source of income. A licence to mine gems, Charlotte learned, was no longer required.

Charlotte's purchases from the Muhammadan traders in the bazaars and back streets of Galle had sharpened her curiosity about the beautiful stones she was collecting. She realized that the price was regulated by the rank and wealth of the purchaser and there was no standard market value. Tissa, Nimal and even the rugged Jagath were enrolled by her to secure gems at the lowest prices.

She was eager to bypass the traders and purchase direct from the source. A lot of gems came from the district of Saffragam where the capital had been given the name Ratnapura which means 'the city of rubies'. The Moors of Galle journeyed to Ratnapura carrying cloth and salt to exchange for gems at the annual Buddhist festival when a gem fair was held.

The sapphire, because of its exquisite colour and its size, was the most valuable gem of Ceylon. Charlotte heard of gems which the Muhammadans valued at upwards of four thousand pounds, like Marco Polo's ruby.

'Those are the stones I want,' she told Tissa.

'The Moors won't sell,' he said with a bow of apology. 'They retain them as investments. Besides, the rajahs and native princes of India have a passion for jewels and will pay extravagantly for them.'

'I wish I had the wherewithal to lavish in such a manner.' She lapsed into silence.

Bart was in Galle delivering casks of rum to its devotees among the military. Since the failure of his sugar exporting to England, he was concentrating on marketing his rum locally instead.

Charlotte filled the time during his absences with pursuit of her hobby. Bart knew of it and gave her the stones remaining from the gems given to him by Prince Gamunu.

She was dismayed to learn he had sold the others to the Muhammadans. She herself could have sold them through her agents in London. The fault had been hers for not divulging to him the extent that her hobby was a business, one she hoped would significantly boost her finances.

She chose to keep Bart ignorant about her trading in gem stones because it was her own idea. It gave her pleasure, especially in the loneliness of the villa where she had only the children, the slaves and the rum for company.

Tissa was her collaborator in the enterprise. She was sitting with him in the parlour with a new selection of gems spread out on the table between them. She turned to him in despair.

'What are we to do? If the Muhammadans would sell their most valuable gems, which they won't, their prices would be too high. In London and Paris there are enough gems from all over the world to establish a proper market value. I can only compete if the gems I buy cost me less, a lot less, than what they fetch in London.'

Tissa smiled brightly but said nothing. She wondered if he understood.

'Tell me,' she said, putting her hand in a pile of quartz-like chips that he had acquired for a few pennies, 'Where did these come from? They are cheap enough.'

Some of the stones were uncoloured while others had

yellow and pink tints. They glistened as they showered through her fingers back to the table. They were zircons, much favoured by the native jewellers, but of low value.

'From Matara.' Tissa referred to the town on the coast, a few miles east of the plantation.

'The pink ones are like rubies,' she said thoughtfully, pushing them around the table top with her forefinger. 'The others glitter like diamonds.'

'Matara diamonds,' murmured Tissa.

She repeated the name to herself. 'Matara diamonds. Yes!' she exclaimed. 'Buy more! There are ladies of the lower classes in England who might find these splendid. Diamonds indeed. We will send a shipment.'

'Better than sugar.' Tissa's eyes glinted. 'Less work.'

She ran her fingers through the other stones on the table. Tissa had a good eye and, by pretending he wanted a gem for his sister or girlfriend, was able to buy at a low price.

'What's this?' Charlotte picked up a stone that was polished so it shone with the colour of gold. It was oblong in shape, an inch in size. Its warm glow was compellingly attractive.

'I call it a cinnamon stone. It was given to me without charge.'

'It's probably a variety of garnet. Buy more if they're cheap.'

'They're free!' Tissa laughed. 'I took a small piece of rock to the lapidary myself. This is what he produced from it.'

Her fingers closed over the stone and a *frisson* of excitement tingled through her. She swallowed, wanting a rum to steady her nerves. 'Where did you find the rock?' she asked, barely able to wait for his answer.

'By the river,' he said casually.

'Our river?'

'Yes.'

She wondered if he was feigning his indifference just to tease her. 'Tissa!' she cried, giving way to her excitement. 'Are there more rocks?'

'There is one.'

'Is it large?'

'About the size of a temple.' He shrugged his shoulders. 'I

saw the glitter at the side of the rock when the sun struck it. I chipped off a piece. The whole rock has lines in it this same yellow-brown colour.'

'Tissa!'She leaned over and embraced him, kissing his cheek. He squirmed with embarrassment but she was too thrilled to consider her own reaction to the salty taste of his cheek on her lips.

'We shall mine the rock ourselves! I shall ask Bart for Mark and Romulus to chip out the stones. You must hire two gem cutters. We'll polish the stones and send them to England. Since they are ours, the profit will be substantial.'

The discovery filled her with joy and she sat rolling the stone in the palm of her hand, considering the fortune to be made.

'Why didn't you tell me?' she asked at length. 'What I've been searching for is right here.'

'I did not think it was important.'

'Instead of sugar, we have gems. Tomorrow I must see this rock. Now it is time for punch.' She scooped the stones off the table into a casket.

Tissa excused himself to return to the mill. She was left contemplating her good luck while she waited for Nimal to serve her. He brought her a glass and she sipped at it eagerly.

She lowered it from her lips in disgust. 'Did you mix this?'

'Yes, ma'm.'

'It needs more rum.'

'Mammy says you are taking a light rum.'

She gazed up at Nimal, frowning at his announcement. His dark hair flowed over his ears, framing the lean, soft beauty of his face. He was a slim-waisted youth, dressed only in long white cloth. He was a slave without chains, bonded to the house by his own wish. He performed his duties with a silence and efficiency that made him almost invisible.

'More rum!' she said, irritated at being dictated to by Mammy.

Nimal's smile faded. He padded out of the parlour and returned in seconds with a measure of rum in a small glass.

She held her punch out for him and he deftly tipped the

extra rum into it. She was conscious of him watching her warily.

'Does Mammy expect me to get drunk and disgrace myself?' she snapped. 'There is no opportunity for that in this lonely house.'

She waved him away, saddened by his lack of English that prevented him appreciating her distress. She sipped at the punch, waiting for its sweet, spicy taste to lift her depression.

Mammy had been acting as the self-appointed guardian of her virtue since Prince Gamunŭ's visit. The old cook had been shocked at her succumbing to the prince without even pretending it was rape.

Charlotte was pleased Mammy had been upset. Her proprietorial air had inhibited her for too long. Despite the shame she was supposed to feel at being violated, she had enjoyed Gamunu's brutal loving. She drank deeply from the punch, knowing in her heart that life for her could not be normal any more. Gamunu had roused a thirst that rum punch alone could not quench.

Even as she pored over her collection of gem stones in the privacy of her boudoir, the solace she used to find in their beauty was gone. The serenity she used to capture sitting on the verandah with Bart while she worked at a sampler of embroidery and he talked of his plans for the future, escaped her too.

She drained the glass and rose from her chair, pacing restlessly around the parlour. She missed Bart. This would be the third night he had been absent from the villa. To her dismay, as she thought of him, she felt her thirst returning. It began in the depths of her vitals, tugging at her heart, searing her lungs and tormenting her brain.

'I am a woman,' she muttered to herself, bursting through the doorway onto the verandah. That was the damage Prince Gamunu had done. Her reputation was intact with the secret known only to Mammy, Daisy and Bart. It was her self-control that was broken by his arousal of her passion after years of chastity.

'I am a woman,' she cried aloud, leaning against one of the

white-washed columns and staring defiantly across the lawn to the stubbled cane fields. In the far distance beyond where the plateau dipped to the coconut groves, the sea and the sky merged.

She was thousands of miles from London, from the society of her peers. In Ceylon, who cared what she did?

A Caffre strolled with a jaunty gait across the lawn. Swung over his shoulder was a broom made out of the stems of dried palm leaves. He wore a loincloth. The sun shone on him, highlighting his broad chest, thick waist and bulging thighs.

'Mark!' she called, her voice sounding unexpectedly loud in the gentle stillness of the hot afternoon.

The slave stopped in the centre of the lawn, lowered the broom to lean to it, and regarded her quizzically. 'Yessa?' he said in his imperfect English, making no attempt to move closer to the house to see what she wanted.

She eyed him greedily, studying his muscular body without shame. He was originally from Madagascar and had a lighter skin and longer nose than the Caffres from Mozambique. He had a roguish eye and a liking for amusement.

As she watched, he moistened his mouth. The bright pink of his tongue against the black-purple hue of his lips seemed to threaten her.

She sighed and pulled away from the pillar. 'Where are you going?' she asked for the sake of something to say.

'De kitchen,' he said, cocking his head on one side and flashing his teeth in a broad, knowing grin.

'Be on your way!' she shouted, disturbed that he seemed to understand her need.

She laughed at herself when he had gone. Why did it matter what a slave thought?

'Nimal!' she called hastily, pacing up and down the verandah to calm her agitation.

She longed for the company of a man – it was her right as a woman. Why should she be denied one? Bart was away, she could do what she wanted. Yet his absence was the cause of her loneliness. She flung herself into his chair. It had a deep pitch and long arms where he would sit and dangle his legs rakishly. She scanned the horizon the way he did. She loved him, more than Jessica ever did, and more than any whore at Madam Gudde's was capable of.

Nimal coughed at her side. She scowled at him. 'A punch!'

'Yes, ma'm.'

'Make it strong enough for me to taste. The way you mix it for Bart.'

He nodded politely and seemed to float towards the door to the parlour. She watched him idly, seeing the outline of his spindly shanks under his sarong, his thin arms and slender shoulders and his mane of straight black hair. He lacked Mark's brute strength and that Caffre's sardonic grin yet his lightweight body and careful manners did not attract her either.

Never sleep with your slaves, had been one of her husband's maxims. Her brother, the present Earl of Lindsay, ignored its wisdom. He had left his wife for one of his serving maids who swindled him until he was an impoverished roué haunting the salons of St James's. She hoped her own reckless yearnings were not leading her along the same downward path.

'Drink, ma'm?' The voice was huskier than Nimal's and she raised her eyes with interest. Jagath stood before her, proffering the tray and smiling eagerly. She took the glass and laid her hand on his arm to detain him when he tried to move away.

'Jagath, how old are you?'

He shook his head but his smile did not waver. She interpreted it to mean he did not know. He was shorter and tougher than Nimal with a darker skin and a mass of unruly black curls. There was a shadow of down on his upper lip and soft black hair on his arms. He was a sturdy young man with an obliging manner that made up for his lack of English.

He tightened his sarong nervously under her gaze. The realization that he was naked under the thin garment both intrigued and appalled her.

'Are you wanting something, ma'm?'

'No, no!' she turned away and sipped at the punch to

absorb her attention until he left the verandah.

She wondered if there were any real men on the plantation. In Barbados it was not unknown for lonely widows to take a personable young field hand as a lover. She had only two Singhalese boys and Bart's Caffres to choose from. And Tissa.

She sat up in the chair with interest. Tissa was a year younger than Bart. He was handsome and intelligent and clean. He was slightly built and wore his hair in the womanish Klowland style with combs to secure it. He was respected by the natives and trusted by Bart. She liked him, but placed beside Prince Gamunu or Bart he was inadequate.

She finished her punch and looked up as the heavy plod of Mammy stomping across the verandah interrupted her thoughts.

'Mammy!' she said, her voice slurring slightly. 'I was jus' go'n send for 'nother drink.'

'You was?' Mammy dragged a chair out of the sun and plumped herself down on it beside her. She wheezed with the effort. 'I de one does need a drink.'

'Really?' She stared at the old cook through bleary eyes. She wished she was more respectful.

'In Barbados,' said Mammy, hitching at her bosom to emphasize her displeasure, 'de massa don't drink till de sun go down. I ain't go'n drink till den.'

Charlotte blinked. Instead of beaming as usual, Mammy's face was wrinkled with concern. She was dabbing at her brow with her apron, about to launch a tirade of reproval.

'Mammy,' said Charlotte hastily to put her off. 'I know you find me difficult these days. I upset your routine, don't I? Well, I need a drink because I'm *thirsty*.' She clutched her bosom.

'I feel the heat here, and here.' She rubbed her lips. 'There's this desire, Mammy, to . . . to drink!' she straightened up in her chair, banging her knees together under her skirt, feeling the ache in her loins. 'Do you understand?'

'Oh my Lor'!' Mammy shook with laughter. 'So dat de reason!' She leaned over and pinched her cheek. 'You got de fever.'

'I'm not sick, it's –'

'Mammy ain't never let you down, Charlotte-girl! Dere be fever an' fever.' She clapped her hands loudly and within seconds Nimal, who must have been listening in the parlour, was at her side.

'De sun goin' down,' she said happily. 'You bring two rum punches, boy, an' make dem strong!'

'Like Bart's,' Charlotte added, bemused by Mammy's reaction to her confession. She felt better now she had spoken out.

Nimal gave her an odd look and hurried off the verandah.

'I know de cure for you, Charlotte, my dear!' Mammy chuckled. 'You go'n be fine.'

Charlotte leaned on Daisy as the slave helped her across the parlour to her boudoir. Mammy rolled along in front of them, holding a candle. Charlotte swayed. She felt she was walking down a long tunnel with the candle flickering at the end of it.

She clung to Daisy to stop falling over. Someone was singing and she was amazed to discover when the singing stopped that it was her.

'I'm so happy,' she trilled, falling against Daisy. She straightened when the slave's hands grasped her firmly around her waist. 'Mammy's my friend.'

'Dat right,' said the old cook, holding open the door. 'Help de mistis undress,' she said, winking at Daisy. 'I goin' now, Charlotte. Daisy take care of you. She lonely too, widout Bart.'

'Bart ...' Charlotte uttered her son's name dreamily. 'He's a man, a Blood . . . Bloodheart!' She staggered, giggling to herself as Daisy eased her through the doorway into the room.

Mammy closed the door on them and Charlotte saw she had reached the end of the tunnel. She fell drunkenly onto the bed, dragging Daisy down with her.

'Oh dear,' she said with a belch. 'Oh dear, dear.' She made no attempt to move and kept her arms around Daisy. Her fingers crept to the slave's hair and she stroked the soft, tight curls affectionately.

'I know what you do with Bart,' she gushed, closing her eyes.

Daisy wriggled out of her grasp.

She felt Daisy's fingers unfastening her dress. She was relaxed on the bed, letting Daisy remove her clothes as Mammy had instructed. Mammy knew the cure. She was going to be fine.

The night air from the open shutters was cool on her naked body. She stretched her arms behind her and rolled her hips, glad that Daisy was with her.

The soft touch at her breasts thrilled her. She opened her eyes and saw Daisy's lissom body lying beside her. The slave's mouth closed over her nipple, gently teasing it with her tongue.

She closed her eyes again as Daisy's hands crept between her thighs. She reached out and pulled Daisy on top of her, smothering her face with desperate kisses.

'Bart,' she whispered, drawing up her legs as Daisy's fingers entered her. 'My boy, Bart . . .'

CHAPTER TWENTY-ONE

'The rebellion's begun!' Bart took his mother in his arms and kissed her dutifully. She tried to cling to him but he slipped out of her embrace.

'Good heavens, mother, I'm all right. Let me into the house!'

In his eagerness to tell her the news, he was inattentive and missed her frown of disappointment at his perfunctory greeting. He flung himself into his chair, noted that it was not in its usual position, and shifted it. He liked to see the path to the mill instead of the view across the lawn.

'What's this?' He was amazed to find Nimal at his elbow with a glass of punch. 'You serve without being asked?'

'I thought you'd be thirsty after your ride, Bart. I instructed him to bring you a glass the moment you arrived.'

He glanced at his mother with disbelief, wondering if this was an excuse to have one herself. 'Are you drinking too?'

'Mammy reminded me that your father would wait until sunset before he imbibed.' She arranged herself daintily on the edge of her chair, impressing Bart with the care she had taken over her appearance. 'I shall wait for the sun to go down.'

'Very sensible.' He was eager to tell her his news. 'The rebellion started in July. The Buddhists had a festival at Kataragama. Some native fellow said he had been chosen by the god of Kataragama to be King of Ceylon. Instead of being laughed at, the people believed him.'

'That's hardly a rebellion.'

'It was the beginning. The people miss their king. Mr D'Oyly is no substitute and the Prince Regent is a myth for them. They want a real king with a grand robe, gold necklaces and a jewelled crown.'

'Prince Gamunu was right.'

'This native would not have got very far, even with the rebels on his side, without the support of the chiefs. The British sent the Governor of Uva province, he's a Kandyan called Keppetipola, to arrest the upstart. Instead of that, Keppetipola joined him. The whole of Uva is up in arms.'

'Our soldiers will deal with them.'

'They've been caught napping. Mr D'Oyly and his spies failed to see how unpopular the British are. Keppetipola is related to most of the Kandyan chiefs. The rebellion could spread. Uva's lost for the time being.' He sipped his drink and watched her, waiting for the moment to spring his surprise.

'Uva is a long way off from us, Bart.'

'It's not so far if you travel through the mountain pass.'

She smiled. 'I have no intention of doing that.'

'Someone did . . .' He paused to see if she would guess what he had to say.

'Gamunu?' She clutched her bosom. 'He's dead.'

'That's exactly what Mr Radley said. I told him I didn't know for certain. He was alive when I left him at the falls. He was gone when I went back to look for him.'

'Is he *still* alive?'

'Yes! Some of his men must have found him. Don't worry, mother. He'll never come back here. He's leading a section of the rebels. He's rivalling Keppetipola and the upstart to become king.'

'Perhaps he will . . .'

'Mr Radley's in a flap. Gave me a wigging. His daughter's cross with me too.'

'Why are you concerned about her?' She glared at him.

He chuckled ruefully. 'I'm not. She ain't likely to speak to me for a long time, that's for sure.'

'I missed you, Bart. Won't you take me with you next time you go to Galle? I long for intelligent company, people to talk to.'

He smiled to show he understood. There was a passionate gleam in her eye that made him feel uneasy. When she put her hand on his arm and squeezed, he moved so he was beyond her reach.

'Did anything happen while I was away?' he asked to break the tension.

'Tissa found a rock with some pretty stones in it. By the river. Would you let me send Mark and Romulus to break it up? I will hire a couple of gem cutters to polish the stones.'

'Of course!' He was relieved she had found something to do. 'Is it for your collection?'

'Yes.' She smiled enigmatically. 'Bart, where is the elephant pearl? You won't sell it, will you?'

'And spoil my fun with Van Dort? No mother. I've heard Van Dort is in contact with Gamunu. The prince told him I have the pearl. He's livid.'

'Where is it?'

His mother's keenness to know the hiding place surprised him. 'It's safe. I've decided to keep it for Kirti.'

'I'm glad. If you do want to sell it, tell me.'

'What do you want that pearl for?'

When she did not answer but turned her head and gazed out across the lawn, he guessed she was thinking of Prince Gamunu. He expected the news of the prince's survival to cause her anguish yet she seemed more concerned about him having spoken to Raven Radley.

Raven was constantly on his mind. Since he smacked her and took her home, he had not seen her. Mr Radley gave him a dressing down and the townsfolk delighted in the scandal.

He had been furious with her for encouraging Van Dort and for expecting him to fight over her. He smacked her to protect her, so she would see the folly of her behaviour.

He had tried to apologise when his temper cooled so he could explain how his hatred of Van Dort had made him act so caddishly. Raven remained sequestered in the bungalow garden. He sent her a note which was returned unopened.

He was conscious of his mother's eyes on him, studying him intimately. It annoyed him and he stood up. 'I'll go for a ride to the mill,' he said. 'I want to see how Tissa is getting on.'

'You've only just arrived. You must be tired. Stay here with me.'

'I have work to do, mother.'

'Let it wait until tomorrow. I want to hear all about your visit to Galle.'

He spread his hands helplessly. 'Galle is the same.'

'Where did you stay?'

'With a . . . a friend.'

'At Madam Gudde's?'

'Mother!' The question shocked him. 'You don't usually pry into my private affairs.'

'I wish you wouldn't associate with such people.'

'I'm not a child! I'm a widower and a father.'

'You're my son, Bart, and I *love* you.'

He was puzzled by the emphasis in her voice. 'I love you too, mother,' he said to calm her down. 'I'll be back for supper.' He hurried off the verandah and went in search of his horse.

The following weeks brought news of the spread of the rebellion. The British efforts to confine it to Uva were unsuccessful as other provincial governors joined the uprising. The provinces were erupting at a time when British forces were depleted and there was a shortage of native auxiliaries.

It was the rainy season in Uva and communications were hampered by swollen rivers. The interception of the mail service by the rebels made coordinated action by the British forces even more difficult.

A proclamation from the rebels was shown to Bart. It read:

'We have received a King for this Country by the favour of the Gods from four parts of the world and from the God Kandasami of Kataragama . . . It is known to all that the eighteen British forts shall be taken by him . . . The English will never have any success.'

The soldiers who were sent to the hills to quell the rebellion were unused to the conditions and style of fighting. It was a guerrilla war in which regular troops, traversing damp forests by jungle and mountain passes, were easy prey to the natives.

Exposure, privations and disease were the rebels' allies.

The period was one of prosperity for Galle. Reinforcements were landed from India and their presence brought business for the traders and merchants. Bart was obliged to make frequent visits to the town to supply rum to the dealers. At his mother's insistence, he did not stay overnight.

The rebellion was her excuse for making him return to the villa at night. Bart knew the real reason and dreaded the outcome of it. She had become possessive and was using her loneliness to blackmail him into staying with her.

Although he was appalled by this development, he was obliged to submit to her pleas lest she break down like the plantation widows of Barbados and run amok among the slaves.

He was grateful for Daisy's support. She visited his chamber if he wanted her and was a boon in the way she handled his mother.

He had seen her escort Charlotte to her room at night when she was confused through too much rum. She would undress her and put her to bed. She even stayed with her until she was asleep. He found Daisy's devotion to her was touching.

Bart encouraged his mother's interest in her gem project although he regarded the cutting and polishing of the stones that Mark and Romulus chipped off the golden rock by the river as a waste of time. Since it occupied her, and freed him from her demands during the day, he accepted it.

As a result of his mother's desperate need for company, his visits to Galle were too brief for him to pursue his hope of friendship with Raven. The town was hectic with the army's preparations to fight the rebels. He seldom saw Raven in the streets and never had a chance to talk with her.

He was gratified to see she no longer walked alone in the town and was accompanied by an awesome woman, the childless wife of an army officer. He prayed she would keep out of trouble.

From Malie, he learned that Marcus Van Dort had abandoned his attempt to marry Raven. He was too preoccupied with schemes to turn the rebellion – and the ensuing influx of British soldiers into the town – to his advantage.

Bart himself tried to avoid contact with the newcomers. Whenever he completed his business in Galle he would spend an hour at Madam Gudde's before taking the trail back to the plantation to arrive there at sunset.

One afternoon, as he was leaving Madam Gudde's, he felt a light tap on his shoulder. He turned sharply to see a white man in his thirties with a straggly ginger moustache. The man's light blue eyes looked honest and he began his introduction with an apology.

'Forgive me for disturbing you. Mrs Gudde said you might be able to help me.'

Bart had learned to be suspicious of strangers. This one gave the impression of being down on his luck. His clothes were patched and a size too large. He was Bart's height but with a stoop that made him look smaller. He was a weak-looking, unprepossessing character whom Bart would have ignored but for his mention of Gretchen Gudde's name.

'I am in need of accommodation for three or four nights. Every spare bed in Galle is taken. Even here,' he smiled wryly. 'Mrs Gudde suggested I ask you if you can recommend somewhere. I cannot pay much.'

'Are you English?'

'Albert Lindsay, sir. I was a private tutor in Colombo. I'm returning home on the next sailing.'

'Lindsay is my mother's maiden name!'

'How interesting. Perhaps we are related?'

'She would be pleased to welcome you to stay at our villa.'

'I wouldn't dream of imposing on you. I am a stranger.'

'Not at all! Maybe you are related, as you say.'

Bart was pleased. The sad looking man was just the person he needed. A few days of his company would be a fine diversion for his mother. Her possessiveness would vanish if she had someone else to be interested in.

Since Lindsay appeared cultured, even if he was down and out, Bart hoped that his presence in the villa would give him the chance to spend at least a night in Galle. He wanted to try again to apologise to Raven.

* * *

Charlotte viewed the unexpected guest cautiously at first. 'Albert Lindsay? One of the Sussex Lindsays perhaps. Who was your father?'

'A cobbler of no consequence.'

She sniffed at this poor start. 'Where were you born?'

'In London.'

'I doubt that we are related.' Charlotte pursed her lips as she contemplated Mr Lindsay. She did not want to make it obvious that, despite his shortcomings, she was delighted to have him as a guest.

In the clothes Bart lent him, and after a bath to wash away the grime of his journey from Colombo, Mr Lindsay looked presentable. His moustache was combed, and his fair hair brushed back neatly. Even his stoop was less pronounced.

'Where have you been employed in Colombo, Mr Lindsay?' she asked, continuing her interrogation.

Bart rose from his chair with relief. 'I shall leave you and Lindsay to talk.'

'Must you, Bart? I am just getting to know our guest.'

'You will enjoy his company more without me in the way. Have a drink, Lindsay?'

'You are very kind.'

'Tell Nimal to bring two, Bart.' The prospect of an evening discovering all about this stranger pleased her. He seemed agreeable and she warmed to him as the evening progressed.

He was far more interesting than she had thought at first. Nimal was kept busy refilling their glasses as he entertained her with stories of Colombo society. He was quick witted, with an enchanting smile and an infectious laugh.

She noticed, however, that he became subdued whenever Bart strolled on to the verandah.

'Mr Lindsay is quite the raconteur,' she said when her loud laughter at one of his stories brought Bart out to see what was going on.

'I'm pleased you are enjoying his company.' Bart nodded in a satisfied way that made her suspect he was planning something of which she might not approve.

Since Mr Lindsay had put her in a good humour, she did

not mind. She was, in fact, delighted by his company and soon began to think of him as Albert.

When he asked her to show him over the plantation, she did so without hesitation, even though that was Bart's prerogative. She was curious that Albert seemed in awe of Bart for he clammed up and was quite a different person when he was present.

On the third morning of Albert's visit, Bart explained he would have to go to Galle on business.

Charlotte was pleased instead of disappointed as usual. 'I shall be fine, dear,' she assured him. 'Albert will keep me company, won't you?'

'With pleasure.' He half rose from his place at the breakfast table and bowed in her direction.

Bart caught the lobe of his ear in his fingers and tugged at it, frowning doubtfully. 'I may have to stop overnight in Galle if my business takes a long time.'

'That's all right, dear.' She smiled her consent. 'We shall just have to amuse ourselves without you.'

Later, she stood on the verandah to watch him ride off. She ought to have been cross that he was going to Galle so soon after his last visit. However, the prospect of spending her time in Albert's company dulled her discontent.

She suspected Bart would disapprove if he knew she was growing fond of Albert. He was a plausible stranger. She did not quite trust him. There was something odd in the way he was constantly trying to charm her. But he was exciting.

It crossed her mind that he might try to assault her with Bart out of the house. Mammy and Daisy would be too zealous to let that happen. Unless she wanted it . . .

As Bart rode off, she was uncertain what she wanted. Daisy's dexterity and care had calmed her wildest yearnings over the weeks. Now the presence of Albert had roused her again. He was, after all, a man.

Physically, he did not match up to Bart or Gamunu. However, he used his wit and charm to flatter and flirt with her in a way she had not experienced since she was a debutante. She suspected that he was a philanderer, and she rather enjoyed it.

'Come, Albert,' she said, turning away from watching Bart jog on his horse down the path to the mill. 'This morning I shall show you something special.'

'Charlotte,' he murmured, taking her hand in his and raising it to his lips. 'There is nothing as special as being with you.'

She giggled at his absurd attempts to impress her. She knew it was insincere but she loved it. It continued that way the whole morning. She showed him her collection of gem stones in the privacy of her boudoir instead of the parlour. He was unimpressed.

'The only jewels that delight me,' he whispered while sitting beside her on the couch, 'are the opals of your eyes, the rubies of your lips . . .'

'Stop it!' She wriggled as his breath in her ear sent a thrill through her. 'You are teasing me. These stones are very valuable.'

'Not as valuable as you!'

She eased to the end of the couch, out of his way. She returned the collection of gems to the chest in which she kept it. She was reassured by his lack of interest in the stones. A fortune hunter would have betrayed himself by excessive enthusiasm, handling the largest stones covetously, eager to know their worth. Instead, Albert seemed genuinely interested in her alone.

She sighed at the pleasure that was in store for her if Bart stayed away from the plantation for the night.

CHAPTER TWENTY-TWO

They took dinner late that afternoon. During the meal, as Albert was eating, Charlotte tried to study him. To her consternation, when she looked in his direction, he ogled her.

His pale blue eyes were intense with a desire that radiated across the table, making her forget her food. She was drawn to his penetrating gaze and stared back at him, heedless of her surroundings. Nimal cleared the table without her noticing.

'Rum?' she uttered huskily when she realized the meal was over. 'Bart has an after dinner rum in which aniseed and cinnamon have been macerated. It's very strong.'

'It sounds romantic.'

She blushed, amazed at the effect he was having on her. He took her hand to help her from her chair and squeezed her fingers so she was helpless in his grasp. She was standing facing him and could feel the pulse of his body by his closeness.

'Shall we go . . .' She swallowed. 'To the courtyard?'

He shook his head, narrowing his eyes suggestively. 'Not private enough. Let's go back to your boudoir.'

She gasped. 'The slaves! What will they think?'

'Do you let them rule your life?'

'No!' She was annoyed with herself for giving him that impression. She drew her fingers out of his and clapped her hands smartly, hoping to break the spell he was having on her.

'Nimal! Bring the bottle of *rhum d'arrangé* and two glasses. To my chamber.'

Nimal nodded with only the slightest twitch of his eyebrow and padded softly out of the dining room. She sighed with relief that he did not disgrace her by querying her instructions in front of Albert.

'Come,' he said, catching her arm and leading her out of the dining room.

She was overwhelmed by the change in him from the diffident man Bart had brought to the villa three days before. There was a ruthlessness in him now, a vibrant determination to get what he wanted. The beat of her heart quickened as he led her to her chamber.

They sat decorously side by side on the couch while Nimal brought the bottle of aged rum with flowers, twigs and bark floating in it. He poured two small glasses and stepped back hesitantly. Albert ordered him to go.

'Shut the door behind you, boy,' he added quietly as Nimal withdrew.

Charlotte hoped she was dreaming. She raised her glass to her lips, needing the courage the rum would give her. Albert leaned forward and linked his arm around hers so that they sipped the rum together, their eyes and lips close.

The warmth of the rum – or was it the proximity of his face? – made her shiver all over. She giggled happily.

'Do I amuse you?' he asked, looking crestfallen.

'Yes. I'm not laughing at you, because of you.' She put out her hand and toyed with the collar of his coat. It was one of Bart's. Even his breeches, she saw as her eyes gazed down at his thighs, were Bart's. She sighed.

'You make me feel very happy.'

'That is what I want!' He moved closer to her.

She reclined against the head board of the couch so that her face was beyond his reach. She sipped at her drink again, tingling as the taste of the fiery rum seeped through her, mellowing her.

Albert rose from the couch and shifted to sit at her side, trapping her against its back rest. He leaned close. His moustache tickled her and she could feel his breath on her cheek.

'I *want* to make you happy,' he whispered.

She was fascinated by the brush of his moustache and faced him so she could see it. His eyes were opposite hers, his nose touched hers and then, as she parted her lips, he kissed her.

She tensed for a second at those strange lips on hers.

219

Instead of the velvet caresses of Daisy's mouth there was the bristle and hardness of his demanding touch. The kiss kindled her passion and instantly her body was aflame with wanting.

He withdrew. 'You feel it too!' he said. 'I thought you would spurn me.'

'Why should I do that?' She wound her hand around his waist.

'I am a poor man, you are a woman of sophistication, of beauty, of –'

'That has nothing to do with it.' She pulled him towards her, parting her lips so he would stop talking and kiss her again.

He embraced her tenderly, kissing her and fondling her breasts with a sure touch that stirred the same excitement she knew with Daisy. Only this time she had a real man to hold and love her.

She felt the throb of his hard body as her fingers stroked him. His own hands were at her thighs, drawing up her skirt. She moaned and stretched herself full length on the couch as he touched her. 'Kiss me again,' she begged, pulling his face to hers.

He hesitated. 'Do you really want me?'

'Of course!' She thrust herself against him.

'Why? I'm such a poor man. I'm nobody.'

'Albert!' She moaned, twisting her body as his fingers teased her.

'No,' he said, withdrawing his hand. 'I can't.'

She gasped, aching, longing for his touch. 'It's all right, Albert.'

'Will you . . .?' He paused, tracing his fingers around her thighs. 'No. I don't like to ask you.'

'Ask what?' She put her hand down and it brushed the hardness of his breeches. 'Albert, ask anything. Don't feel ashamed.' She wanted him to take her, quickly, while she craved him.

'You'll be cross with me.' His hand massaged the inside of her thigh, sending her shimmering with desire.

She shook her head, unable to speak.

'A small token,' he said. 'Something worthless. It would mean so much to me . . . to remember you by.' His hand moved higher.

'Yes . . .' she sighed, thinking he meant one of her gems. It would be worth it.

His fingers opened her. 'I've always wanted one of those old ivory things. You've got one, haven't you?'

The exquisite anguish as he rubbed and teased her was driving her to distraction. She heard him vaguely as she breathed, 'I want you, I want you!' and wriggled against his fist.

He laughed. 'They call it an elephant pearl. It's nothing important.' He pulled out his hand. 'Give it to me.'

She reached out to seize his shoulders, desperate for him. He smirked and brought his face close to hers.

'Where is it?' he demanded.

The haze cleared from her mind when she saw him leering at her. His eager eyes were bright with triumph.

She stroked the hair at the back of his neck, drawing him down. Her free hand groped on the floor by the couch. She smiled at him.

'Here it is.'

She jerked up her hand, plunging the rum glass into his face. It shattered, slicing its jagged edge into the flesh under his eye.

She screamed, thrusting at him with all her might and pushing him off the side of the couch. He fell with a bone-shaking thump to the stone floor. Blood streamed from the gash in his face.

He bellowed loudly and scrambled up, raising his arm to strike her. There was a knife in his hand.

The door burst open. A cyclone of waving arms, broom sticks and rolling pins gusted through the doorway. Mammy and Daisy charged him, shrieking in unison. He was knocked back to the tiles by the force of their blows.

The knife flew from his hand as Mammy's broomstick struck it. Charlotte leaned over from the couch and plucked it quickly from the floor.

Mammy stood over him, beating him with the broomstick.

He put up his hand to grab it from her. Daisy dashed the rolling pin against his arm, smashing it. His cries of anguish were drowned by the wild shrieks of the two slaves.

'Mammy!' Charlotte laughed hysterically, her shame receding at the sight of her fat old cook belabouring Albert. She brushed down her skirt and stood up, gingerly, her legs weak behind the knees. 'Don't kill him!'

'De man rape! I ain't sparin' him.'

'Mammy, we need to know who he is.'

'Who he is!' Mammy stopped pounding Albert and stared at her in outrage. 'You ain't been introduced?'

Albert whimpered at her feet, stunned almost unconscious. Daisy stood guard over him, ready to clout him with the rolling pin at the slightest movement. Charlotte was giggling with relief and weeping with shame at the same time.

Mammy shook her head with exasperation. 'You ain't learn nothin' Daisy an' I done tell you, Charlotte! Men ain't to trifle wid. Dey snakes in britches.'

She turned towards the door where Nimal and Jagath were watching in amazement. Garth clung to Nimal's legs and peered into the room from behind the shelter of his sarong.

'Jagat'!' Mammy's booming voice made the houseboy flinch. 'Fetch me dat rope from de store where we does hang meat.'

Charlotte murmured to excuse herself. 'He was so polite and charming . . .' She felt foolish in front of Daisy.

'Yo' done do right!' Daisy patted her on her shoulder which made her feel better. 'He hurt yo'?'

She shook her head. How could she describe the hurt when she realized what he really wanted? What sort of woman had she become to lie with a stranger so willingly?

Jagath returned with the rope. While Daisy sat on Albert's legs, Jagath slipped the noose over his feet, tightening it so his ankles were bound together. With Daisy's help, he and Nimal dragged Albert by his legs from the room. Charlotte followed, anxiously asking Mammy what she was going to do.

'String him up by his ballocks!'

'Cut out his vitals an' give 'em to de dogs,' said Daisy, cackling gleefully.

Albert moaned as he was bounced over the tiles and across the courtyard to the store room. His lips were swollen from the blows and blood gushed from his cheek onto his moustache. His left arm hung uselessly at his side.

'Can he speak?' asked Charlotte, hurrying along behind him.

'You want know 'bout him?' Mammy jammed the broomstick in his crotch.

'I wish there was a way we could make him tell us why he came here. I'd like to know before Bart returns. He'll be too angry to question him sensibly.'

'I do it, ma'm.' Jagath smiled brightly as he hauled Albert on the rope over the store room threshold.

'You?' She stared at him in disbelief. Jagath was strong but he was too slight to be able to persuade Albert Lindsay to speak if he did not want to. She suspected that he was only showing off in front of Nimal.

'What will you do?'

'I am showing you.'

She followed them into the store room. Jagath spoke to Nimal in Singhala. The elder boy looked surprised then grinned. He dashed out.

Jagath climbed up some crates to the roof where a hook was fixed into the rafters. This was where Mammy hung the carcasses of deer while they seasoned. He looped the rope around the hook and climbed down.

'Help me?' he asked Daisy shyly.

Together they pulled the rope through the hook so it tightened where it was fastened around Albert's ankles. Mammy jerked up Albert's body and he was hauled feet first into the air.

He yelled, striking out with his good arm and slapping Mammy around her cheek. She grunted and punched him in his waist as he hung upside down.

'He like a fruit bat hangin' from a tree.' Daisy giggled. 'Let we take off his britches.'

Jagath shook his head, to Charlotte's relief. She had no wish to see Albert naked. Even as she gazed on him swinging from the rafters, she shrivelled inside with shame at how close she came to giving herself to him.

Nimal entered the room with a lighted taper. He handed it to Jagath.

'You ask him, ma'm,' Jagath said confidently. 'He is answering.'

Albert was poised three feet from the floor, high enough to stop him supporting himself on his good arm. Despite the pain and the indignity of being upside down, his lips curled over his teeth in a defiant snarl.

'Put me down,' he cried. 'I ain't done nothink.'

Charlotte noticed how this cultured accent had disappeared. 'Who are you?' she asked.

'You know who I am. Get these damn savages off me.'

Charlotte nodded at Jagath, intrigued by what he could do with the taper to force him to talk.

Jagath opened a sack and took out a handful of chilies. They were dried bright crimson, the hottest kind of chilies used in curries for the Singhalese. He threw some of them on the floor under Albert's head. He held the taper to them, keeping his nose away.

Smoke drifted upwards. Albert swung around on the rope to avoid the fumes but the pungent odour soon reached his nostrils. When he tried to thrust himself away, Daisy pushed him back over the smouldering pile. He was forced to inhale the smoke.

The chilies of Ceylon are the hottest in the world. One bite brings tears to the eyes, burns the tongue and, if swallowed, sets the stomach on fire.

Although Albert fought against inhaling the smoke, the harder he struggled, the deeper his gasps of it. The acrid fumes seared his lungs and burnt his brain. He wept, shrieking for the fire to be doused, begging for water.

Charlotte enjoyed his agony. It was justice after he had preyed on her weakness.

'Who are you?' she asked again, signalling to Jagath to continue burning the chilies under him.

'Albert Van Dort,' he cried, choking. 'Cut me loose!'

'You're not even English!' She was appalled.

'Who de one sen' you here?' Mammy demanded, prodding him with the broomstick to make him breathe in more fumes.

'My uncle Marcus.'

'Why?' Charlotte dreaded the answer.

'For the *gaja mutu*. He said you'd give it to me if I rogered you. Prince Gamunu told him you'd do anything for a good poke.'

Her cheeks reddened and tears came to her eyes. She backed out of the store room in a daze. The humiliation, not the sting of the smouldering chilies, caused her to burn with remorse.

She turned and ran across the courtyard, through the house and down the steps of the verandah and out into the garden. She pushed past the bougainvillaea bushes and made for the cane fields.

As she ran, the sneer of Albert when he loomed over her on the couch returned to her mind. Her ears rang with what he had said, branding her for ever with her disgrace.

She fled blindly towards the jungle, heedless of Daisy chasing after her, calling her name and begging her to come back.

She wanted to die.

CHAPTER TWENTY-THREE

To celebrate his release from his mother's constant demand for company, Bart went straight to Mr Radley's bungalow when he reached Galle. He had confidence that Albert would be an engaging companion for her during his absence from the plantation. He prided himself on being a shrewd judge of character and thought Albert to be an inoffensive scholar whose occasional boorishness could be blamed on his lower class origins.

He was in a relaxed mood as he waited on the Collector's verandah. He intended using his concern at the rebellion as his excuse for visiting Mr Radley at his house; his real reason was to talk to Raven. He had timed his visit to coincide with dinner and was gratified when the servant, having announced his arrival, invited him inside.

Mr Radley was seated at the head of a long dining table. A place was set at his side with a plate containing a half eaten meal. The curtains covering the doorway to the garden billowed open where someone had rushed through as he stepped into the room. Raven had flown.

'Come and join me, Bart.' Mr Radley indicated a chair at the other side of the table. He snapped his fingers for the servant to set a place. 'Not English victuals, of course, although Raven does try to train the boys how to cook properly.'

'Is she sick?' he asked, nodding at the vacant seat.

Mr Radley look distracted. 'Can't understand her sometimes. Moody, restless. Spends most of her time in the garden.' He popped a piece of beef into his mouth and chewed energetically while Bart helped himself from the dishes presented to him by the servant.

'I came to you at home instead of your office,' said Bart, using the lie he had rehearsed, 'at my mother's insistence.'

'She well?' Meat splattered on the table from Mr Radley's mouth as he spoke.

Bart nodded, waiting until he finished eating before he said, 'She hopes you will visit us again soon.'

'Wish I could. Far too damn busy. Can't rely on anyone here for me to take a few days' leave. This confounded trouble with the Kandyans.' He continued to stuff food in his mouth while he was speaking.

Bart ate sparingly, occasionally glancing into the garden. He was disappointed that Raven still hated him so much she fled at the sight of him.

'Mother is worried about the Kandyans,' he said. 'Their mountains encircle the plantation. She's become absolutely terrified of being left in the villa alone. She's apprehensive about what might happen.'

Mr Radley finished his meal with gusto and pushed his plate away. He leaned back in his chair, picking his teeth with an ivory toothpick.

'Bart,' he said, 'I will tell you the truth, although what you tell Charlotte is up to your discretion. The uprising is out of control. It's become national. In the Kandyan provinces only the Muhammadans remain loyal to us.'

Bart frowned. 'I had no idea Prince Gamunu was so popular.'

'He isn't! Thank God you let him escape.'

'I don't understand.'

'Mr D'Oyly and his minions, that pup Havis among them, have mishandled the Kandyans. They should have ruled them firmly from the beginning instead of toadying to their customs and letting them keep their religion. They've had an inch, now they want their whole kingdom back.'

'The army –'

'Useless! If they had a proper battle to fight, they might win it. The Kandyans use guerrilla tactics. Some of those yellow-robed monks have run off with the tooth of Buddha from its temple in Kandy. That's the true symbol of Kandyan independence, not those pretenders to the throne.

'Until we get back that tooth, the revolt will continue. Imagine, a kingdom lost for a tooth!'

He jabbed his toothpick in the air. 'I'm glad you're here, Bart. I can't talk to my writer or to the garrison commander. They're too stupid to understand.'

'So Prince Gamunu is not important?'

'Yes, he is! Although no one agrees with me. Gamunu wants to be king, so does Keppetipola and this chap from Kataragama. There's another of them, Ehelapola, used to be the King's chief minister. The more the merrier!

'They all have their supporters. As long as each of the rebel leaders wants to be king, they'll be too busy fighting among themselves to fight us.'

Bart stroked his chin. He was relieved to find that inadvertently he was back in the Collector's favour for having spared Gamunu. 'What do *you* see as the solution?' he asked to ingratiate himself even more.

Mr Radley beamed at the question. 'We need a lot more soldiers from our forces in India. We need that tooth. If one of the claimants looks like beating his rivals, we should support his rivals by concentrating our attacks on him.'

'You have strong views. You should be in charge of the Kandyan provinces instead of Mr D'Oyly.'

'Have a cognac, Bart! I seized a consignment last week in lieu of duty. It's one of the perquisites of being confined to Galle.'

When he returned with the bottle from his locked cabinet, he poured some into a snifter and passed it across the table to him. He sipped at his own glass. 'Excellent, isn't it?'

Bart agreed, although privately he preferred his Bloodheart rum.

'You say Charlotte is apprehensive.' Mr Radley looked serious. 'So am I. Our forces cannot contain the guerrillas. The only way is to harass the Kandyans, destroy their villages and cattle, create famine and fever and fear. Then the Kandyans will despair and submit.' He paused. 'Do you know what we are going to do instead?'

Bart shook his head, growing more appreciative of the cognac's qualities.

'Mr D'Oyly is talking of withdrawing our forces to the Maritime Provinces. That's defeat!'

Bart gasped. 'Won't the Kandyans go on the offensive then? Even Galle could be under threat.'

'Exactly.' Mr Radley leaned back. 'You're worried about your mother. I'm concerned about Raven. You showed me what she was becoming, wandering about the fort making a fool of herself. She's chaperoned everywhere now. I'd like to marry her off.' He sighed.

'There's a shortage of eligible bachelors here. She's a strong-willed girl. I think she declines the most suitable men just to spite me.'

'She has many suitors?' Bart tried to keep the anxiety out of his voice.

Mr Radley nodded, contemplated his empty snifter and poured more cognac into it. He glanced at Bart, hesitated, then passed the bottle over to him. 'How are you faring on the plantation since you stopped shipping sugar?'

'Well enough. I'm concentrating on my Bloodheart rum. It's a steady earner.'

'Your expenses must be high.'

'The slaves keep themselves.' He resented Mr Radley's probing. 'We manage.'

'Of course. I understand your mother has wealth of her own?'

'Good gracious, no!' He laughed heartily, wondering why Mr Radley was so interested. 'Whatever my father left her went in setting up the plantation.'

'Isn't there any family money?'

'My uncles and aunts finished that. Spendthrifts all of them.'

Mr Radley frowned and pulled back the bottle of cognac. 'Your mother is still a young woman. She's bound to feel insecure when she's alone on the plantation. You should bring her to live in the fort.'

Bart was perplexed by the twinkle in Mr Radley's eye. He

had thought the Collector was enquiring about his own prospects, not his mother's. 'I could suggest it to her,' he said with a slow smile as Mr Radley stood up, inviting him to leave.

'May I pay my respects to Raven before I go? Mother would be disappointed if I don't.'

Mr Radley shrugged, taking the bottle and returning it to his cabinet. He pocketed the key. 'She's in the garden . . . if she'll see you. I shall be on the verandah,' he added sternly.

Bart hurried out of the dining room. Raven was seated in the shade of a temple tree with a book open in her lap. She looked up as Bart strode over the grass towards her. Her lips were taut and her eyes blazed with fury.

'I've waited months for this chance to apologise!' Bart said hastily before she could tell him to go away.

'I'm not going to marry you!'

'By the devil!' He halted and stared at her. 'That's a relief!'

'I told daddy I will choose when I am read –' She gaped at him as she realized what he had said. 'You don't want to marry me?'

'Good heavens! Why do you think that?'

'You saw daddy. I thought you were talking about me.'

He laughed at her downcast expression. 'You *were* mentioned in the course of the conversation. I came to see your father because of the uprising, not about you.'

Raven blinked and turned away sulkily.

'He seems to be sweet on my mother.'

As he expected, she reacted immediately, throwing off her sullen expression and glancing at him in amazement. 'Daddy does? You're making it up.'

'He was asking about her prospects, not mine.'

'That's his way. He's a snob.'

'I'm afraid I gave him some discouraging answers.'

She laughed for the first time and some of the tension in his guts subsided at the sound.

'What do you want with me?' she said. 'I never expected to see you again.'

'I was so angry that night. You didn't know about Van Dort. I wanted to teach you a lesson.'

230

'You made me the laughing stock of the town. People say I'm your *mistress*.' She shuddered as she uttered the word. 'Mr Van Dort told people that's why you spanked me.'

'At least you've discovered what kind of man he is.'

'What kind of man are you? Bloodheart!' she sniffed scornfully.

He swallowed, unhappy at the way the conversation was going. 'I meant it for the best.'

'It's not as if you and I even had an *understanding*.'

'You are right to be offended. I apologise again. And again.'

She eyed him archly. 'Did daddy tell you to make it up with me?'

'Why should he do that? It's my own wish.'

'Then perhaps I'll forgive you.' She pouted. 'Only perhaps.'

He grinned, wanting to ruffle her ringlets for her cheekiness. 'You make me very happy.'

'I should disgrace you in public instead. For revenge.'

'Are you vengeful?'

'Very. It's the dark side of my nature. I sit here all day planning the evil things I will do to people.'

He squatted down on his haunches facing her, toying with a blade of grass. He was enchanted by her childish chatter. Despite being in Galle, in the midst of local society, she seemed to be lonely like his mother.

'What people?' he asked.

'As well as you? There's that mean Mrs Dixon.'

'Your friend?'

'My duenna! Am I to be chaperoned for ever? I should have married Mr Van Dort when I had the chance.'

This time he saw the glimmer of mischief in her eye and did not lose his temper. 'Very soon a beau will arrive on your verandah and be smitten your beauty. You'll fall in love with him instantly, be married within the week and sail away to fortune and happiness. Your chaperon and myself will be desolate without you.'

'Bart!' She sounded breathless. 'Are you flirting?'

He frowned, uncertain what to reply.

'Well, you are on your knees, almost, and making pointed references to my happiness. How do you know what will happen? I believe I will never escape Mrs Dixon's clutches. I cannot even go to church without her.'

'Church?' Bart hoped to make her laugh. 'Church is the most dangerous place. Young men look harmless in their Sunday best.'

'I am not interested in young men.'

He exchanged banter with her for several minutes until his thighs began to ache from squatting in the grass. He rose stiffly to his feet, shaking his legs. He was exhilarated by being with her. Her talk was inconsequential yet beneath her blithe manner there was an iron will that was waiting to be tested.

He left her playing with a flower from the temple trees, murmuring softly to herself as she pulled it apart. Mr Radley was waiting for him on the verandah.

'I'm sending Raven to England with Mrs Dixon on the next sailing,' he announced. 'She's to live with her aunt in Bristol.'

Bart's good mood was shattered. 'She didn't mention it,' he said, feeling bitter but trying to appear unaffected by the news.

Mr Radley chuckled as he escorted him down the steps. 'She doesn't know. I'll have to drug her to get her on the ship without protest. Sending her home to England is the only way to keep her out of mischief.'

Bart was plunged into despair. He moped about the villa, too dejected to talk. He declined the glass of rum Mammy tried to press on him to revive his spirits. He spent an hour languishing on the verandah and then retired early to his chamber.

He lay on top of the mattress, rolling from side to side with anguish, too confused to know what to do. When he heard the creak of his door opening, he scowled into the darkness and lay still, pretending to be asleep.

There was a pressure on the mattress as someone sat beside

him. He tensed, waiting for the hand to descend on his shoulder. When it did, he reared up angrily, pushing her away and flinging himself to the other side of the bed.

'I'm sorry, Bart.' Daisy's voice was remorseful. 'Mammy an' me both. Why yo' vex wid us?' Her hand reached out for him again and he wriggled to escape it.

'Miz Charlotte go'n be a'right by mornin', yo' see.'

He shook his head to clear it. There was so much to worry about. 'It isn't that,' he answered sadly.

He sensed her relief that he had spoken at last. His depression had developed during the ride from Galle. He was in no mood to speak to anyone by the time he reached the villa. The commotion that greeted him when he arrived pushed him deeper into despair. Daisy was the one who suffered most from his moodiness.

'I ain't never seen yo' like dis before.' She lay down on the bed beside him.

'Keep away from me, Daisy.'

'Why, Bart? 'Cause I hit yuh mam?'

'You misunderstand me,' he said, praying for her to leave him alone.

'Den tell me what wrong, Bart. Mammy say a man need to empty his head as well as his loins. She send a rum for yo'.'

'I don't want rum.'

'Yo' go'n tell me why yo' blue vex?'

'It's not because of you, Daisy.' He lapsed into silence.

When he had arrived at the villa, his mother was in her room, watched over by Mammy. Daisy had explained how Charlotte had gone berserk, running wildly towards the river, shrieking and pulling off her clothes.

Daisy had hit her with her fist, stunning her sufficiently for Jagath and Nimal to carry her back to the villa. Mammy had given her a draught of laudanum to make her sleep so her hysteria would burn itself out.

In the circumstances, Bart was pleased with the way Daisy and Mammy had acted. They had realized that Albert's presence, even strung up in the store room, was the cause of his mother's panic. They had released him. After the blows he had received and the chili roasting, he fled from the plantation as fast as he could.

'You did right, Daisy.' His sigh reverberated in the stillness of the darkened chamber. 'I don't want you tonight. I have to think.'

'Mammy be pleased 'bout dat. She say yo' love sick.'

'Get out!' He pushed her off the mattress and she tumbled to the floor. 'Leave me in peace.'

'I hope yo' over yuh 'lancholy by mornin', Bart. Yuh mam go'n need yo' den.'

In her innocent way, Daisy had chanced upon the crux of Bart's despair. He waited for her to leave the room before he concentrated on his problem again. With his mother's desperate need for companionship, he could not leave her by herself in the villa for fear of what might happen.

Yet at the same time as his mother needed him, he needed his freedom. He needed to see Raven again. He wanted more than to see her. He wanted to take her by storm, challenging the wild and wilful spirit lurking behind her affected manner. He wanted the fight and the spoils. If Raven left Ceylon, he saw himself becoming old and crotchety, desperate like his mother for excitement, and with no one to consume his passion.

He pounded his fist into the pillow. He could not leave his mother's side to gallivant after Raven. If she was going to England on the next sailing, there was too little time to begin his campaign to woo her. He was outmanoeuvred on all sides. He cursed himself to sleep.

Concern for his mother kept him too preoccupied to mope the next day. She had more cause to be depressed than he, and he respected her mood. Daisy reported she was awake, was dressing and then, later in the morning, that she was sorting through her collection of gems.

Bart, who had been waiting for her on the verandah, decided to face her in her boudoir instead.

'Mother,' he called as he knocked on her door. There was a sound of panic inside.

'Yes?' she answered hastily. 'What do you want?'

'To talk to you.' He waited, hearing her slam down the lid on her chest of gems.

He was amused that she wanted to keep the contents of the chest hidden from him. The stones she was collecting were worthless. The gems Mark and Romulus were mining by the river could be bought for pennies in the Street of Moorish Traders.

'What do you want, Bart?' His mother's tone was brittle when she opened the door and peered around it. 'I've vowed never to have a man in my chamber again.'

'Very sensible.' He strode in, seizing her in his arms and kissing her warmly on both cheeks. 'Will you ever forgive me, mother, for bringing that scoundrel here? I was completely fooled.'

Tears welled in her eyes. 'So was I, Bart.'

'We've survived,' he said.

'I'm so ashamed.'

'Of course you are. I feel the same way. Fancy me being hoodwinked.'

'It's not the deception that shames me.' Her lips trembled. 'It's what I did.'

'I should never have left you alone with him. You can't blame yourself. He was sent here by Van Dort deliberately to deceive you.'

'That's no excuse for my *wanting* to give in to him.'

He was startled by her confession. They were standing in the centre of the room, close to each other. She avoided his eyes, twisting her fingers nervously.

'That's because you're still young and attractive,' he said, instinctively choosing the words she needed to hear. She raised her face to his and smiled gratefully.

'Yes,' he said, understanding. 'It's true. Mr Radley's quite taken with you, himself. He suggests you go to live in Galle. Would you like that? They'd be plenty to do and there would be no likelihood of trouble with the Kandyans.'

'You mean Prince Gamunu. Do you think he'll come back?'

'What for?'

'For the elephant pearl . . . and for Kirti.'

'He can come but he won't have them.'

'No,' said his mother emphatically. 'He won't!'

'Then you will go to Galle? We'll rent a house there. I could go this very afternoon to enquire.' He smiled at the chance of another visit to Raven.

'No, Bart.' She clung to him, wrapping her arms around his waist. 'Not Galle. Stay here with me.'

'If you wish,' he replied wearily as his hopes of seeing Raven before she left vanished. He embraced his mother dutifully.

She reacted with a fierceness that astounded him. 'Kiss me!' she said, raising her lips to his and pressing herself against him.

He shied away. Then it occurred to him that she was acting oddly because she needed reassurance. He kissed her affectionately on her lips before prising himself from her arms.

She gazed at him wistfully. 'You look so like your father.' She sighed. 'It's not strangers I'm afraid of, Bart. It's myself.'

CHAPTER TWENTY-FOUR

Bart's anger festered inside him. He was cautiously polite to his mother during the days that followed. He wanted her to regain her confidence without noticing his own bitterness and frustration. At times he was close to shouting at her when she whined for his company. Somehow he managed to control his rage, bottling it up instead.

When his mother was out of the way in her boudoir, he vented his anger on Nimal and Jagath, bellowing at them while they stood glumly until his rage passed. They shrugged off his abuse and continued with their work.

He could not intimidate Mammy and Daisy so he swallowed his anger with them. However, he did bar Daisy from his bed. He preferred to yearn for Raven at night to squandering himself on his bedwench.

The children were scant consolation for his thwarted desire. Garth and Ranita were nearly four years old, at the inquisitive age. Malika was fully occupied looking after Kirti so the children often pestered him for attention. He directed Jagath to take care of them so he could wallow in self-pity without being disturbed.

His anger drove him out of the house. In the mill, Tissa's competence in producing the rum with his Singhalese helpers made his own presence unnecessary. He sensed the timid *salagamas* were unsettled by him and, remembering the law of slaveholders not to upset the rhythm of work, he left Tissa to manage the mill by himself.

He was thoroughly disgruntled as he stalked along the river trail from the mill slashing at the cane shoots with his whip and cursing his bad luck. It was a week since he had seen Raven. By now she would have sailed.

The chip-chip of metal striking against rock rang down the trail. He headed towards the noise, spite welling up from his guts at the sound. It symbolised his mother's hold over him. He burst through the trees surrounding the glade and glared at the sight, moistening his lips with rage while he decided what to do.

Mark and Romulus were stripped down to their loincloths, poised half way up the face of an enormous rock, hacking at it with makeshift tools. They did not hear him and continued to work, Romulus holding the chisel while Mark swung the hammer.

Squatting under the shade of a *cadjun* thatch awning were two natives, old men with scraggly beards and skeletal bodies. They wore flat hats and sarongs and muttered carelessly together, unaware of his presence.

They were sitting on a mat of dried reeds, sharing it with a curious contraption placed between them. It was a wooden engine secured to a wooden base, with a metal plate at one end, driven by a bow.

One of the men sat at its side, pushing the wooden shaft of the bow forward and pulling it back at great speed. This activated a wooden spindle which revolved and turned the metal plate like a wheel. The other man squatted in front of the plate, holding a piece of rock at its edge. As the spindle turned, the wheel shrieked, cutting into the rock. The man's fingers seemed in danger of being lopped off. Instead, shards and powder ground from the rock fell to the box beneath the wheel. As the man's fingers twirled, the piece of rock was shaped into sparkling facets.

The tools of the gem cutters' trade lay on the mat before the two men; wooden mallets, hammers with metal heads, files and chisels as well as wheels of granite used as grinding stones. Behind them was a heap of chippings, the result of the attack on the rock face by Mark and Romulus.

This was his mother's industry. Bart was incensed with a savage and pointless bitterness as he gazed on it. He wanted to smash it all out of pique.

'Mark!' he shouted. The Caffre did not hear above the

shrieking of the cutting wheel and the thud of his sledge hammer on the chisel.

He stormed into the centre of the clearing, flaying the whip wildly. The shrieking of the wheel died as the two Singhalese abandoned the machine and scurried to the back of the shelter for safety.

Mark raised his eyes at the same time as he swung down the sledgehammer. It missed the chisel and sparked against the rock. Mark was thrown off balance by his badly timed swing and toppled onto Romulus.

'Monkeys!' shouted Bart, seeing at last a way to vent his rage. 'Come here!' He cracked the whip above their heads as they scrambled over the rock face.

Romulus was the nimblest. He trotted over to Bart with the assurance of unspoiled youth. He was the youngest of the Caffres, a boy when Bart had bought him off a slave trading vessel in the mouth of the river eight years before. He had developed since then into a faithful and hard working slave, proud of the strength in his slight, compact body.

He was smiling as he stood in front of Bart. He was from Mozambique, dark skinned and wiry haired. He was afraid of nothing and regarded Bart as his family, having left Africa too young to remember his people.

'Yes, massa?' he asked cheerfully.

'Why did you let go of the chisel?' Bart demanded, looking for a way to punish the boy and hating himself for the madness erupting within him.

Romulus's confidence wavered but he was too bold to shrink away like the Singhalese in the face of danger. He had no dread of shame, nor of bodily punishment. He ignored the whip in Bart's hand and grinned.

'If I hold it, Mark go'n burst my hand.'

Mark ambled over and stood behind Romulus. Bart felt his heavy gaze and refused to look at him. The Caffre was taller than he was with a high sense of honour. To try to lash him would result in Bart himself being humiliated as the Caffre would probably grab the whip from his hand and run off with it until his temper cooled.

Romulus was different. He was younger and fresher. His loincloth hung loosely around his waist, exposing his muscular buttocks. Bart's fingers itched.

'I go'n burst yuh ass,' he said imitating the youth's slave speech.

Romulus grinned again, enjoying what he thought was a joke.

The flash of his brilliant white teeth and his snigger of scorn was all that was needed to set off the volcano of wrath in Bart's mind.

'Damn you!' he said, stepping back and raising his hand. The whip was weighted in its handle so the thong of finely plaited leather could tear through the air with a flick of his wrist. He cracked the leather above Romulus's head. The slave looked impressed.

Mark moved out of range and strolled across the glade to squat in the shade with the gem cutters. His casualness added to Bart's fury.

'I'm going to thrash you, Romulus,' he warned again, half hoping the slave would run away and save him from his own madness. Romulus shrugged his shoulders, standing stoutly in his place.

He tried again to intimidate him, cracking the leather thong so it whistled close to his ear. Mark's deep throated chuckle mocked him. Romulus blinked, the smile frozen on his face.

Bart danced back two steps, turned sideways and scythed the whip at waist height. It smacked against Romulus's rump, catching his loincloth and tearing it off. He flicked the whip upwards so the cloth flew into the air and landed at the side of the glade.

Mark chortled with glee, encouraging Bart's rage.

The sun shone on Romulus's naked body, lighting up the sheen of perspiration so it gleamed, its blackness transformed to gold. His penis hung down in a sheath with a rosette of skin at its head. He stood with his arms akimbo, making no effort to protect himself.

Bart roared with anguish and sliced the whip against his

thighs. The force spun Romulus around. He stumbled but regained his balance and stared back defiantly at Bart. Blood trickled from a cut on his right buttock.

'Sah?' Romulus said pathetically. 'What I done do?'

'This is for your boldness!' He cut another stripe across his thigh. 'This is for your rudeness!' He drove at him again, wanting to slice off his swinging penis for its mockery of his own frustration.

'Sah!' Romulus crouched down, pointing along the trail behind Bart. He tried to speak but the whip cut him off.

Bart raised his hand to lash again. Suddenly Romulus leapt at him in a flurry of waving arms. Bart stepped back, holding the stock in front of his face to protect himself. He was too late.

Romulus held his throat, smashing his naked body into his chest and knocking him to the ground. He plucked the whip from his hand.

Bart tried to grab his body but it was slippery with sweat and blood and slid from his grasp.

Romulus jumped away and stood panting just out of reach. Raising his hand, he pointed urgently down the trail. 'Look, massa,' he cried. 'Someone comin'.'

Blood from the boy was smeared on Bart's face. He wiped his eyes, refusing to turn and look. He was disgusted with himself. 'No there ain't,' he shouted furiously. 'Give me my whip.'

To his surprise, Romulus handed it back without fuss, handle first.

'Bart!' a frantic voice called. 'Bart!'

He grasped the stock firmly in his hand, his senses tingling at the sound. Slowly he turned, blinking with disbelief at the sight of the woman stumbling towards him. Her hair was dishevelled, her white dress muddy and torn.

He flung the whip aside and ran to catch her before she fell.

'Bart . . .' she gasped, swooning in his arms.

He stared at her in amazement. 'Raven . . .'

Romulus strolled over, wiping the blood off his crotch with

his loincloth. 'I help you, massa,' he said affably. 'Carry her to de river. She need water.'

Raven trembled as Bart lifted her. All the energy and will power flowed from her body. Her head fell back, her bonnet tumbling off and hanging by its ribbon from her neck. She heard the Caffre tell him to carry her to the river and she felt herself being borne in his strong arms through the jungle.

She listened to his anxious breathing, the snap of twigs under his boots, and the gurgle of the river. She sighed, pretending to have fainted as he laid her out on the grass of the river bank. She kept her eyes closed to see what would happen.

'What the devil's she doing here?' Bart asked abstractedly of the Caffre.

'Come for yo',' the youth replied, showing he was quicker witted than Bart. 'Splash water on her face.'

She felt sorry for the confusion Bart was in. Her unexpected appearance when he was alone with his Caffres must have given him a shock. She had been startled to see him grappling with the Caffre youth, his clothes smeared with the boy's blood.

She gasped at the impact of cold water on her face. She forgot her feigned swoon and opened her eyes. Her first sight was of the naked Caffre trickling water from his cupped hands onto her. She shut her eyes tightly and moaned.

'Are you all right?' Bart sounded gruff and she wondered if she had done the right thing in coming after him.

She moaned again, peeping under her eyelashes to assess the situation. Bart was kneeling at her side, wiping his brow with the back of his forearm. He seemed agitated. The Caffre was squatting by the river, gathering more water into the palms of his hands.

She spluttered when he drenched her again. She opened her eyes fully and struggled to sit up. She tried to ignore the youth's nakedness since it troubled neither himself nor Bart.

'Enough water,' she gasped, waving her hand at the Caffre to restrain him. The water seeped under her bodice to her breasts. She shivered, even in the heat.

'You gave me a fright!' Bart sounded cross with her for upsetting his routine. 'Can you talk?'

She nodded her head, at the same time loosening the ribbons of her bonnet which were nearly choking her. She shook out her hair, its black ringlets tangled and damp. She tried to primp them into tidiness, worried at how she looked.

Bart himself was no better. His shirt and face were bloody, his hair wild and his eyes glazed. The Caffre was in the river, splashing himself and inspecting the cuts on his thighs.

'Why were you whipping that boy?' she asked impulsively, instead of playing on his sympathy.

'What?' He jerked back, glancing at the youth as though seeing him for the first time. He gulped. 'Romulus?' He lapsed into thought.

She was disappointed by this side of Bart's character. She expected him to be dynamic instead of dumbfounded. 'I'm sorry to disturb you,' she said tartly.

He grinned and stood up without replying. He strode to the river's edge, hunkered down and sluiced his face, letting the water pour over his hair and down his chest and back. His shirt was soaked. He shook himself dry like a dog, sending spray in all directions.

'Did you come alone?' he asked, surprising her by the question.

She nodded. She was piqued by his casual reaction to her arrival.

He turned away from her and spoke to the Caffre. The youth emerged from the river, wiping the water from his body with his hands. He picked up a cloth from the river bank, wrapped it around his waist and ran off through the trees.

'Romulus is going to the mill so Tissa will prepare the bullock trap to take you to the villa. Do you think you can walk?'

'Yes, I'm not hurt.' She scrambled to her feet to prove it. Her feet were sore and every step caused her pain. She clenched her teeth and took a step towards him. He saw her wince.

243

'Did you walk all the way here?' he said, his voice showing a trace of sympathy at last.

'I ran.'

'Without an escort?'

'I had to get away.'

'From whom – Van Dort?' He moved closer and held out his arm.

She grasped it eagerly, supporting herself against him. His arm slipped around her waist and she felt less guilty about what she had done.

'From daddy.' She bit her lip to stop the tears. If he saw her crying, he would think her a useless female who swooned and wept at every crisis. She took a deep breath and a step forward, letting him lead her gently to the path.

'He was going to send me back to England,' she said bitterly.

He seemed unconcerned by her news. 'Why?'

'Is that all you have to say?'

He shrugged his shoulders, continuing to urge her along the trail.

At her side she saw the field of sugar cane. A dense grove of trees grew on the other side separating the path from the river and giving shade to the trail. She was exhausted and puzzled by his attitude. She sighed.

'Daddy was tired of me, I suppose. It was all right for me to be his housekeeper but when I wanted some fun, that awful Mrs Dixon was enlisted to see I didn't have any.'

'Fun?' He mused on the word, his dark blue eyes twinkling roguishly. Her heart beat faster at his sardonic smile.

'Won't he be distraught at what you've done? Coming here alone –?'

'I could do nothing else,' she said crossly, interrupting him. 'If I stayed in Galle I would be . . .' She paused, trying to remember a word she had heard the soldiers use. 'Shang-haied!'

His chuckling annoyed her. 'It's true,' she protested. 'I was to go with Mrs Dixon to live with my aunt in Bristol. I overheard daddy discussing with her how to get me on board.'

'I know,' he said, deflating her indignation. 'Your father told me of his plan.'

'You knew, and you didn't tell me!'

He was startled until gradually an inkling of comprehension entered his eyes. He tightened his grip around her waist. 'How did you get away?'

'I slipped out of the house before dawn. The sentry at the fort gate let me through. I said I was going to the Buddhist temple. I managed to pass the native quarters without anyone stopping me. The worst part was the road along the coast. I had to hide in the jungle every time a carriage came in case daddy was in it looking for me.'

'He might be at the villa now.' Bart scratched the lobe of his ear.

'I don't mind if he finds me *now*,' she said. 'The ship would have sailed by now. With Mrs Dixon on it.' She felt less agitated at the thought; she was safe.

'Why didn't you hide in a coconut grove near the town until you saw the ship sail? There was no need to come all the way here.'

She pulled away from him, dismayed by his heartlessness. 'I . . . I . . .' She was overwhelmed, furious with him for asking the question, and cross with herself for not knowing the answer.

'I'm pleased you came, Raven,' he said, reaching out to hold her again. 'But I don't know what mother will say.'

CHAPTER TWENTY-FIVE

Charlotte viewed Raven's arrival at the villa with acute misgiving. She sat quietly, her serene smile belying how she felt, while Bart and the girl talked softly together on the verandah.

The moon was full, its glow casting a luminous calm over the garden and the cane fields. It affected all of them in the house. Nimal moved soundlessly, replenishing her empty glass. Even the chatter of Mammy and the Caffres in the kitchen was muted by the atmosphere.

Charlotte considered Raven while pretending to contemplate the moonlit vista. She had grown into a young woman of ravishing beauty; her cheeks were radiant and her dark hair lustrous now she had recovered from her flight from Galle.

The keen sparkle in her eyes when she watched Bart gave her an air of zest and of adoration. It added to Charlotte's apprehension.

'What do you think of her, mother?'

Charlotte was surprised to see Bart standing beside her chair, leaning over her. She glanced beyond him to where Raven had been sitting. 'Where is she?'

'I took her to the guest room. She's exhausted, poor girl. You had dozed off so we didn't disturb you.'

Her empty rum glass was on the table beside her. She blinked to give her time to gather her wits. 'She seems, er . . . charming.'

'What do you really think?'

'She's using you, Bart. To fight her father. What a pity she didn't go to England with Mrs Dixon.'

'You don't like her. You didn't like Jessica at first.'

'A flighty young miss who disobeys her father and traipses

246

through the jungle without a chaperon is hardly worthy of my commendation.' She raised her hand to touch Bart on his arm.

He moved beyond her reach and paced the length of the verandah, his shoulders hunched showing his displeasure. He swung around and returned to her side.

'She's brave,' he said. 'I admire her for that.'

Charlotte was saddened. In a way, she had seen it coming. Bart craved the company of people his own age. She could not compete.

'Pluck is admirable if applied in a worthy cause,' she said stiffly. 'I trust you will show more sense than she does in decision making.'

'Mother! How pompous you sound. She's a game young miss, headstrong as hell. Don't worry about her staying here for long. Her father will come for her tomorrow.'

She frowned. 'I don't think I want to see Thomas Radley.'

'No one knows about you and Albert, mother, nor about what Prince Gamunu did. You can hold your head high.'

She pursed her lips. 'How do you know Mr Radley will come here?'

'I sent Tissa to Galle with a message for him. Raven doesn't know.'

A wave of affection for him gushed through her. 'How thoughtful of you, Bart. You are quite right. She must leave here as soon as possible. It is so much better when we are alone together, just you and I.' She succeeded this time in grasping his arm before he could slip away.

He bent down and bussed her on both cheeks, gently easing himself away when she tried to prolong the embrace. 'I'll send Daisy to your chamber,' he said. 'I'm going to bed.'

She was filled with an inexplicable dread. 'Bart!' Her cry halted him at the door to the parlour.

'Raven is under our protection . . .' She shuddered, unable to voice her thoughts.

Bart was angry. 'Do you think I would take advantage of a lady in distress? You have a very poor opinion of me!' He stormed off through the doorway without saying goodnight.

His fury confirmed to Charlotte what she feared.

Bart was a gentleman and ought to be able to resist the temptation of Raven spending the night at the villa. Yet he was foolhardy too. If Raven wanted to trap him into marriage, here was the perfect opportunity. She need only suggest he come to her chamber and then she would complain to her father that she had been compromised. The banns would be read before Bart realized what had happened.

'Daisy!' Charlotte cried excitedly as the slave emerged from the darkness to take her to her room. 'I want your help.'

'Why, Charlotte, can't yo' stand?'

'Of course I can.' She rose to her feet indignantly. 'This is a matter of importance. We have to save Bart from that girl. She wants to lure him into marriage.'

'She's a sweet young virgin, Charlotte. Mammy say she make a good wife for Bloodheart.'

'You ought to be upset.'

'Bloodheart young an' lustful. He need a wife as well as a bedwench.'

'I won't have it! She's a scheming busybody. I can see that in her calculating eyes.'

'I doubt yo' go'n stop it. When dey get together de sparks sure go'n fly.' Daisy chuckled gleefully.

'Then they must be prevented from, er, getting together.'

'She sleepin' in de chamber next to Bart own.' Daisy nodded her head with satisfaction. 'Jagath sleep on his mat outside. De boy ain't hear if Bloodheart creep in dere in de dead of night.'

'That's exactly what Raven expects to happen! We must stop it.'

'How?' Daisy snorted with scorn which only increased Charlotte's determination.

'You'll see in the morning,' she said as an idea suddenly occurred to her. 'Now close the shutters and go to bed.'

'I go'n come to yuh bed tonight, Charlotte. Bart don't want me.'

'No, you mustn't do that. Not tonight.'

She hurried into the house and across the parlour to her boudoir before Daisy could follow. Once inside, she prepared

248

herself for bed, donning her primrose yellow nightdress and applying perfume liberally to her breasts, under her arms and between her legs.

She listened to the sounds of Daisy closing the windows overlooking the verandah and onto the courtyard. When she heard the courtyard door being closed she opened her own door.

She had to hurry because Bart would be listening for the same sounds of the house being closed up for the night. She walked across the parlour to the liquor cabinet where the rum was kept. Deliberately, she made a lot of noise as she opened the cabinet, took out a bottle and poured a drink.

She pulled a chair across the floor scraping its legs on the tiles with a screech. However, she did not sit down.

The chink of light under Bart's door showed he was awake and listening to the noise. If he thought she was drinking in the parlour, he could not leave his bed room. She banged the glass down on the table, clinking it against the bottle.

She was pleased with her ruse. In her bare feet, she padded across the tiled floor to the courtyard door. She held her breath and eased it open slowly, frightened lest its creak give Bart a clue that she had left the parlour. She slipped into the court-yard and closed the door gently behind her.

The night air was refreshingly cool. The moon was shining on the leaves of the temple trees, giving them a waxlike sheen. The fragrance made her light-headed as she breathed in deeply. She clutched the door handle to steady herself and glanced anxiously around the garden.

Jagath was curled up on his mat outside the guest room door. The room next to it, the nursery, was where the children were sleeping. Malika slept with Kirti while Garth and Ranita shared a bed of their own.

At the other side of the courtyard, the dining room was shuttered. There was a faint glow of light from the kitchen at the end of the dining room. She paid no heed to that as Daisy and Mammy would be too preoccupied with gossiping to notice her.

She dodged across the moonlit lawn and stood underneath

the boughs of a temple tree, letting its shadows absorb her. She watched Jagath intently in case he was awake and had seen her move. When he did not stir, she raised the skirt of her night-gown in one hand so she could move more easily, and glided over the lawn to Raven's door.

Jagath was snoring peacefully. She reached for the door. Holding her skirt high, she stepped over Jagath into the room. She closed the door behind her, scarcely daring to breathe.

There was a noise in the darkness as Raven turned lazily in bed. Charlotte was convinced she was expecting Bart. That was why the girl did not cry out in alarm when she entered the room. It confirmed that her suspicion about Raven was right. Fortunately, by getting to the guest room before Bart, she had foiled Raven's scheme.

She moved hesitantly towards the bed, still clutching the skirt of her nightdress in her fingers. She was not sure what she was going to do. It was enough that she was there before Bart's foolish ardour led him to fall into Raven's trap.

She stood over the girl, listening to her breathing. It was a soft, regular sound with no murmur to indicate that she was awake and lying in wait for Bart. Charlotte's heart quickened, thumping loudly in the stillness. Fury almost choked her as she thought how Raven was trying to snare her son into marriage.

She felt faint. The hem of her nightdress slipped from her fingers and she stumbled. She put out her hand to steady her-self and fell against the bed. There was a large mattress on it, filled with down. She sank gratefully into the space at Raven's side.

She was appalled when she realized this was where Raven was hoping Bart would lie. She could not stand up. Instead, she eased herself into a sitting position, struggling to catch her breath and cast off the rage that gripped her.

She waited for Raven to speak but the only sound in the silence was the girl's sigh as she stirred in her sleep. A power-ful longing to seize her suddenly swept through Charlotte. She was torn between an urge to punish Raven and an over-whelming desire to crush the girl in her arms and share her love for her son.

She peered into the darkness to see where Raven was lying. Slowly, she stretched out her hand, inching it across the mattress. She was driven on by hurt and anger that could no longer be controlled. Her heart was hammering, her breath ragged. She raised her hands and lunged for Raven's naked body.

'Charlotte!' someone shouted as the door banged open. Mammy and Daisy rushed into the room.

Charlotte shuddered, overcome by shame and despair. She swooned and fell forward into Raven's arms.

'She does need 'scape de devil dat here,' Mammy pronounced.

'There is only one devil here,' said Malika, surprising them by speaking since she was normally reticent. She had left the children in the nursery to join in the discussion about Charlotte.

'What dat?' Mammy demanded fiercely at this challenge to her authority.

Malika smiled to soften her criticism. 'Bloodheart rum.'

Mammy sucked in air, hissing as she prepared to rebuke her for her naivety. The lantern flickered in the draught from the open courtyard door. All the slaves were gathered in the parlour with Bart, except for Daisy who was with Charlotte in her boudoir trying to soothe her. They could hear her sobs of anguish. It added urgency to their search for a solution to her unhappiness.

Malika perched on the edge of a chair, wary of relaxing comfortably in the presence of her betters. Her straight black hair was braided in a single plait that hung down her back to her waist. She wore a loose fitting cotton robe over her *comboy* cloth. She had spoken out because she considered it important.

'I am seeing the same madness with Mr Van Dort,' she said, her face serious and her wide eyes shadowed with a frown. She had been Van Dort's servant until Bart bought her as wet nurse when Ranita was born.

'He was doing cruel, evil things when he was under the influence of strong liquor.'

'Mistis Charlotte an Van Dort ain't de same!' Mammy snorted.

251

The old cook had the settee to herself, her bulk almost filling it. Bart was pacing backwards and forwards across the room, his hands clasped behind his back. Jagath was standing by the door keeping watch on the guest room, while Nimal and Little were sitting together on a chair.

'Charlotte was be drinkin' rum long before she come here.' Mammy's eyes narrowed until they were almost hidden in the fleshy folds of her face. 'Dere does be an evil here dat menacin' her, leadin' her to foolishness.'

'I am seeing it happen to Mr Van Dort,' Malika insisted, knowing she was right.

Bart put his hand on her shoulder which made her flinch. She was not scared of him, she loved him, although in a different way to her secret affair with Jagath. Bart was the kindest white man she had ever known. She doted on his son and on Ranita and the baby Kirti. She would do anything for him. It hurt her to speak against his Bloodheart rum.

'You are right, Malika,' Bart said, his sombre voice assuring her that he was not offended. 'So are you, Mammy.'

He spun around as the door to his mother's chamber opened and Daisy came out.

'She finish cryin',' Daisy said. 'She sleepin' now. De laudanum do dat.'

Bart sighed. 'In the morning, she'll think it was a bad dream. So will Raven. She was so tired, she went back to sleep in Mammy's arms.'

Mammy clucked her tongue. 'Mistis Charlotte goin' from bad to worse. De rum help her. She need to leave here.'

'Yo' only sayin' dat 'cause yo' want to go back to Barbados!'

Daisy's angry voice startled Malika. She glanced at Jagath for support but he ignored her. She found the Caffres were so aggressive when they spoke. It contrasted with the gentleness of the Singhalese. She was in awe of Mammy and Daisy and Little because of the harsh way they addressed each other.

'I don't want to stay here, dat for sure. No more do Mistis Charlotte.' Mammy pulled herself off the settee and stood defiantly in the centre of the room, wagging her finger at Malika.

'Even a coolie girl can see dat.'

Malika stared back meekly, unable to see why Mammy was excited. She had a suspicion, which she preferred to bury out of the way at the back of her mind, that Mammy was jealous of her because she was in charge of the children. Many times Mammy had muttered about Garth growing up more coolie than English. Coolie was her word of contempt for the Singhalese.

'Enough talking for tonight,' said Bart, clapping his hands to dismiss them.

Malika walked back across the courtyard with Jagath. They were silent in the moonlight as they paused outside the guest room door. Malika wanted Jagath to come to her in the nursery. 'The children are sleeping,' she told him.

He shook his head. 'I am guarding Miss Raven.'

'You didn't stop Charlotte going in.'

'Why should I?' he asked. 'I was to keep out intruders. Charlotte was not my concern.'

'Am I your concern?' she asked simply, affected by the moonglow on his handsome features and tousled hair.

'You are going to be my wife,' he said just as simply.

Malika's day with the children was always a hectic one. Garth was impulsive and impatient like his father and egged on Ranita to copy him. Jagath helped her with them when he could so she could concentrate on Kirti. She adored the baby. The experience she gained bringing up Garth and Ranita enabled her to care for him better. She felt she understood him.

He was a beautiful baby with his mother's placid temper but a fierce determination to have what he wanted. There was an aura about him. Malika knew he was going to be special.

He was naked on her lap and she was changing him when a shadow fell across the open door of the nursery. She looked up in surprise to see Raven staring at her.

'Good morning,' she said politely.

Raven smiled. She was fully dressed with her hair combed, the ringlets framing the delicate beauty of her face. She looked nervous despite the assured glint in her dark eyes. Malika liked her instinctively.

'I hope I didn't wake the children last night,' said Raven, stepping into the room. 'May I hold him?'

Malika offered Kirti to her without hesitation. He gurgled happily in her arms.

'I like babies,' she said.

'He senses that.'

Raven bounced him in the air then frowned suddenly. 'Why is he . . .?' She hesitated with embarrassment. 'He's black, just there . . .' She nodded at his genitals.

'That's because he's special. I call him Bloodheart royal.'

'I see,' said Raven as though she knew the truth. 'I'm going now, Kirti. I don't know when I'll see you again.'

'You are leaving, miss?' She was sorry.

'My father has come for me. I'm going back to Galle. Perhaps you can bring Kirti to see me there. I doubt I'll be allowed to return here.'

'Is your father angry?'

'No.' She smiled as she handed Kirti back. 'I've calmed him down and Bart's rum helped. As long as he doesn't hear about last night. Poor Charlotte.'

'Oh no, miss, he won't.'

'I haven't seen Charlotte. She's in her room. I hope she'll be all right.'

'You are forgiving.'

Raven's smile took on a hard edge and her eyes glistered with determination. 'I am not forgiving, Malika, but for now I must be. I'll tell you a secret. One day, I am going to marry Bloodheart, whatever his mother does to stop me.' She leaned forward and kissed Kirti on his cheek. 'Look after him . . . for me.'

'Oh yes!' She stood in the doorway holding Kirti as Raven strode across the courtyard lawn. She watched her pick a frangipani flower and hold it to her nose, smelling it deeply before she entered the parlour.

She was exhilarated by Raven's visit, and by her interest in Kirti. She did not tell anyone, not even Jagath, what Raven had said about marrying Bloodheart. Her concern was the children and she looked after them conscientiously.

The tension in the villa eased after Raven's visit. Charlotte remained secluded in her chamber for two days, then she sent for Tissa and gave him instructions about buying more gems for her collection. Malika was always pleased to see Tissa and he spent time with her and the children.

From Tissa Malika learned the latest news about the rebellion in the Kandyan provinces. 'Prince Gamunu is doing well,' he said as they romped with the children in the shade of the temple trees. 'The British are on the run.'

'Will he come back here?' she said fearfully.

'Charlotte asked me the same question.'

'Of course, she's worried. What did you tell her?'

'The Kandyans have to win back their own kingdom before they will try to take the Maritime Provinces.'

'Yes, yes.' Malika nodded, growing more apprehensive. 'What about Kirti? Prince Gamunu might come for him.'

'That's what worries Charlotte.'

They both looked towards the baby who was crawling over the grass, trying to follow Garth. 'We must protect him,' Tissa said gravely. 'It is our duty.'

The weeks passed bringing conflicting news about the rebellion. Prince Gamunu's forces were said to be harassing the British troops sent to flush them out of their mountain lairs. Then Keppetipola's forces were rumoured to be gaining control in all the provinces.

Prince Gamunu seemed to be losing popularity. This was confirmed when Keppetipola supported the coronation as king of a former monk with no connection to the royal family.

Malika listened to all the stories eagerly. At night, when she was alone in the nursery with the children, she swore Garth and Ranita to secrecy before relating the latest rumours to them. She did it for Kirti's sake, bouncing him on her knee as she recounted the deeds of Prince Gamunu.

'One day,' she whispered into his ear as she laid him in his cradle to sleep, 'you could be a king, my little Bloodheart royal.'

Charlotte came every day to see Kirti. Malika was pleased by the interest she showed in him. She encouraged her to play with him. She believed that by involving Charlotte with the children, she could help her shake off the depression that bedevilled her. Maybe she would drink less rum too.

'Isn't he growing strong!' Charlotte lifted Kirti from her arms. They were on the verandah. It was mid-morning, when the heat of the day was at its height. Bart was in the mill with Tissa. Garth and Ranita were playing together under a suriya tree.

'You are looking after him like your own child,' said Charlotte.

Malika felt proud. She saw it as a sign that Charlotte was getting over her shame at what she had done by this interest in Kirti and the children.

'He is growing strong like his father,' she said contentedly.

A gleam of panic entered Charlotte's eyes. She cuddled Kirti close to her. 'Oh, Malika,' she said, sounding agitated. 'I am so thirsty. Run to the kitchen and ask Mammy to mix me . . . a fruit juice! I'll hold Kirti while you're gone.'

Malika was pleased by her request for a fruit juice instead of rum. She ignored the wildness in Charlotte's eyes, lulled into complacency by her obvious delight at having Kirti in her arms. She hurried off the verandah without a qualm, through the living room and down the long dining room to the kitchen.

'Lor'!' Mammy greeted her. 'You look pleased wid yourself.'

'Miss Charlotte is wanting a fruit juice, not a rum.'

'Dat what she say to sweeten you, child. She have plenty rum in her boudoir.' Mammy poured the contents of a clay pitcher into a glass.

'Passion juice,' she said, handing it to her. 'Dat go'n sweeten de mistis. You watch. She go'n pour a shoot of rum in dat when she t'ink you ain't lookin'.' She chuckled.

'I am not thinking so,' Malika said confidently. 'She is enjoying herself too much with Kirti.'

She carried the juice at a leisurely pace to the verandah. It was a peaceful day, with only the chirping and whistling of birds in the courtyard to disturb the villa's tranquillity. When she walked through the parlour onto the verandah she saw Charlotte's chair was empty.

She looked around, expecting Charlotte to be playing with Kirti on the lawn. She was not there either. Garth and Ranita were under the tree alone.

She placed the juice on a table and ran across to them. They looked up at her in surprise. 'Where is Kirti?' she asked, a chill hand of fear clutching her heart.

Garth looked puzzled. Ranita, sensing her fear, burst into tears.

'Where is your grandmother?' Malika begged, kneeling down in front of Garth. 'She and Kirti – where did they go?'

The boy was thoughtful. He bit his thumb, then shook his head.

'You must have seen her!'

'No,' said Garth shyly. 'I no see my grandmother.'

'Then she must be in her boudoir!' She was foolish to worry, she told herself as she left the children and hurried back into the house.

Charlotte's door was closed. She hesitated before she opened it and peered inside. The room was gloomy. She was about to withdraw when a shadow of movement caught her eye.

There were two candles burning on top of a great chest, like the altar of the church in Galle. Charlotte was standing before them.

Kirti lay between the two candles. He was naked and still, his mouth, arms and legs were bound with strips of gold-coloured cloth. Charlotte's hands were raised in the air above him. The blade of a knife glinted in the candle light.

'Gamunu shall never have you!' Charlotte cried with a mad shriek. 'When you are dead, he won't come here!' She poised, ready to plunge the dagger into the baby's heart.

Malika leapt at her with the strength of a pouncing leopard. She caught Charlotte's arm and deflected the knife so the blade flashed within an inch of Kirti's tiny body.

She pulled her to the floor, screaming for help while Charlotte stabbed her repeatedly, tears of madness streaming down her face.

CHAPTER TWENTY-SIX

The clank of the anchor chain being winched on board the *Swift* (captain John MacKeiver) could be heard clearly above the din of creaking masts, shouting sailors and the sound of the sea slapping against the wooden hull of the vessel as it bobbed in the bay.

Bart was grim faced watching the sails being unfurled and the wind billowing in them. He blinked to keep his eyes dry lest he disgrace himself with tears in front of Raven, Mr Radley and the children.

He glanced at Garth and Ranita to see if they understood. Tissa was holding Ranita, helping her to wave, and Jagath struggled to support Garth in his arms while the boy waved furiously. Malika, her arm bandaged, nursed Kirti who was staring at the sea with intense delight.

From their vantage point on the battlements adjoining the Collector's bungalow, they had a clear view across the harbour as the *Swift* sprung from its anchorage in the stiff breeze.

Bart scanned the decks for a sign of his mother. She had cried when he kissed her farewell in the privacy of her cabin. She had looked long into his eyes without speaking. It was a look of incomprehension, of shame, at their separation when she needed him most. He had hugged and kissed her again to assuage his guilt at sending her away.

'You will be fine, mother,' he had said to console her. 'Too long in Ceylon. A few months in England, seeing your friends, completing your business, and you'll be fit again.'

'I worry about leaving you, Bart.'

'Don't.'

'The rebellion, Prince Gamunu . . .'

He had kissed her on her mouth. 'I shall be very cross,' he

said to distract her, 'if you don't sell my rum for a good price.'

'And the gems,' she said, her eyes clearing. 'I've only agreed to go so I can interest my friends in the cinnamon stones. I shall have a gorgeous necklace made up, and bracelets and pendants, and wear them to the balls and soirées. Simply everybody will want them. The stones will sell for large sums. You'll see.'

'I know,' he had said, keeping the doubt from his voice so she was encouraged by her fantasy. 'I know.'

He had left her standing in the centre of her cabin surrounded by the wooden coffers containing her collection of gems and the cinnamon stones cut by Mark and Romulus from the rock by the river.

He regarded her obsession with what she called gems as part of her madness. No one would pay more than a few pennies for those pretty stones. They were not real gems like the prince had given him. However, because he realized how important her belief in them was for her, he said nothing. She had suffered so much already.

None of them really understood her madness. Dr Barry, more accustomed to treating soldiers' maladies and wounds than prescribing a cure for a woman who was physically strong and healthy, recommended a change of climate for her 'blackouts'. Bart could only hint at what his mother had done to avoid the disgrace of her attacks, first on Raven and then on Kirti, becoming public knowledge.

Bart loved her and shared her bewilderment at her odd behaviour. He was relieved when she agreed to go home to England. He would miss her, but the strain of guarding her and constantly wondering what she would do next was inhibiting. She was taking Mammy with her as her companion.

'There's Mammy!' Garth's shout brought Bart's mind back to the view across the harbour of the *Swift*.

'The lad has a sharp eye,' said Mr Radley.

'He'll miss Mammy more than he'll miss my mother.' Bart waved at the sight of Mammy's bandanna fluttering in the breeze as she stood by the ship's rail. 'I wonder if she'll come back?' He knew how terrified Mammy was of the sea, and of her dislike of the Singhalese.

'She will,' said Raven, warning Bart by her glance that he ought to be careful what he said in front of the children. 'Mammy wouldn't let your mother go anywhere without her.'

'Goodbye!' Garth shouted and they all joined in. Even Kirti cried out in the excitement.

When the ship rounded the point of the harbour and disappeared from view, they all followed Mr Radley from the ramparts to the bungalow gardens.

Raven held her hands out for Kirti. 'May I hold him?' she asked Malika. The girl's eyes widened and she looked anxiously at Bart.

He smiled to reassure her. 'Let Raven have him, Malika. You must be tired holding him so long.'

'I am not,' she said softly.

The obstinacy in her voice impressed Bart. Her eyes were still haggard from remorse. She had blamed herself for entrusting Kirti to Charlotte. She bore no grudge against his mother, believing her to have been possessed by a demon.

'How is your arm?' asked Bart, walking with her to show he appreciated her concern for Kirti. 'Have the stab wounds healed?'

'It was nothing.' Malika pouted. Raven was embracing Kirti and the boy chuckled contentedly in her arms.

'Kirti likes Raven,' said Bart, aware of Malika's continuing disquiet at letting anyone else hold him. 'Raven likes him. You need have no fear for him now.'

He hoped what he said was true. His mother's fear had been that Prince Gamunu would return because of Kirti. It was still possible. The boy had more claim to the throne than any other rebel pretender. The prince might seek to crown Kirti to boost his flagging popularity.

Bart left Malika with Raven and the children and joined Mr Radley on the verandah. His relationship with the Collector had not deteriorated when Raven fled to the plantation to avoid being sent to England. Mr Radley's relief at finding his daughter safe and unviolated was greater than his wrath over her behaviour.

'Raven could have gone with Charlotte,' Mr Radley sounded grave as he handed Bart a snifter of cognac. 'They would have been company for each other on the voyage.'

'Yes.' Bart frowned, keeping his disagreement to himself.

Mr Radley sighed. 'She refuses to leave Galle.' He paused. 'She's very fond of you. Every day she mentions your name.'

'She likes the children. That's why I brought Kirti today. She's very good with him.'

'She could do with a child of her own.'

He ignored Mr Radley's hint and turned the conversation to his own concern. 'We hear only rumours on the plantation. What is the latest news about the rebellion?'

The Collector looked smug. 'It's as I prophesied. Now we have reinforcements from India, the rebels are reeling. We have the fire power and the men to starve them into submission.'

'It will soon be over?'

'Thank God! The tooth relic has been recovered. The Kandyans see it as a sign of our destiny to rule them. Their morale is low. Keppetipola's pretender has been exposed as an impostor. They will need something sensational to rally them now.'

Bart sipped at the cognac thoughtfully. 'If they had a real claimant, a new king for the future, would that help them?'

'Damn sure it would! The factions would unite if he was descended from the royal line.'

It was as he feared. 'Anything new of Prince Gamunu?' he asked casually.

Mr Radley pursed his lips and stared at Bart. 'He hasn't been seen for some weeks. The rumour is that he is preparing to unite the rivals somehow. He's a slippery character, as you know.'

Raven walked onto the verandah interrupting Bart's thoughts. He watched her sitting close to her father, with Kirti snuggling in her arms. Malika hovered anxiously behind her. Tissa and Jagath strolled across the lawn with Garth and Ranita. They sat in the shade by the carts where the bullocks were grazing.

261

'When will you bring Kirti to see me again?' asked Raven. Her dark eyes flashed with amusement that implied it was him she hoped to see instead of the baby.

'When I can.' He shrugged, wanting to avoid the trap he suspected was being laid for him. 'There is so much work on the plantation. Without my mother, I will be the bookkeeper too. I have to see that Daisy and Little can do Mammy's work.' He saw the glance Mr Radley gave Raven.

'You need a wife, Bart!' the Collector said with a noticeable lack of tact.

'When I'm established.' He was intrigued by the flush on Raven's cheek as she hurriedly became absorbed in Kirti.

'Maybe when my mother returns. She is bound to have plans to find me a bride in England.'

'Good God!' Mr Radley spluttered over his cognac. He coughed to clear his throat. 'Can't you find a bride for yourself? Nearer home.'

'Daddy!' Raven sounded embarrassed. 'Why must you be so personal?'

'I like to see things organized, that's why.' Radley studied Bart suspiciously. 'Why do you say when you're established? You have your plantation. It's in your name, isn't it?'

'I have a number of commitments . . .'

'Don't say another word, Bart.' Raven looked cross. 'He's prying.'

Mr Radley stood up and Bart jumped to his feet. The Collector sniffed disparagingly. 'Not established, eh?' He nodded to himself, glanced at Raven and sighed. 'Give him back the baby, Raven. He has a long journey.'

Malika took Kirti and fussed over him. Raven's lips formed a moue of displeasure and Bart felt her eyes searching for his.

'When shall we see you again, Bart? Even if you are busy, could you not spare an afternoon to dine with us?'

'Leave him alone, Raven! He'll come when he can. Didn't you hear him?'

'Yes, daddy.' Her lips tightened and she glowered at her father behind his back.

Bart was struck once again by her dark-eyed beauty, lent a

depth by her pique at being rebuked. He grinned sardonically to disguise his yearning. She gave him a withering look in retaliation so he took his leave quickly.

He intended to put Malika and Kirti in the carriage with Jagath and ride with Tissa and the children himself. He changed his mind however and got into the first trap instead with Malika and Kirti, leaving the others to take the second one.

The traps jolted over the ridges and ruts in the muddy streets. He was sitting opposite Malika and Kirti. A leather canopy protected them from the sun. He clung to the side of the cart to prevent him being jostled onto Malika. Kirti began to cry.

He was thinking of Raven as he glanced along the street over the head of the bullock pulling the trap. There was a palanquin being carried jauntily down Church Street towards them.

'Van Dort!' he said aloud, his thoughts of Raven crumbling. He waved Malika to take Kirti to the far corner of the trap where she would not be seen. He had recognized Van Dort's palanquin by its bearers, the four hulking Caffres who were his bodyguards.

The driver pushed against the bullock's head to keep it on a straight course. There was space for the palanquin to pass if the bullock took the side of the street instead of the centre. Bart groaned.

'Move over!' he shouted to the palanquin bearers.

They continued to jog towards the cart, making it plain they demanded the right of way. The bullock was alarmed by the relentless advance of the bearers and their chanting. It veered to the right and blocked the palanquin's path.

The Caffres lurched to a halt, supporting themselves on their sticks while their shoulders took the strain of the litter. There was a squawk of protest from inside and the curtains were pulled apart. A face, blotched and perspiring with the heat, appeared.

'Vat is this?' Van Dort shrieked at the bullock driver in his high-pitched voice. 'I'll haf you thrashed for blockink the

263

highvay.' He shook his fist at the hapless man who was trying to get the bullock to move. He raised his eyes to see who else he could threaten.

'Bart Taylor!' he exclaimed, his cheeks turning puce. He jerked on the litter so it swayed. 'Put me down!' he shouted to his bearers.

They lowered the palanquin sharply to the ground, adding to his discomfort. He leaned out as Malie, his slave, ran up and opened the curtain for him to descend.

'Heh, heh, Bart! Your mother haf fled?' He wheezed with grim laughter. 'You are stayink, no? I shan't let you escape.'

Bart jumped down from the cart to help the driver guide the frightened bullock aside. Because the palanquin was parked in the centre of the street, the cart could not pass.

'Move your master out of my way!' Bart shouted angrily.

The Caffres, trained to obey loud orders, immediately strained and raised the litter. Van Dort was thrown back onto the cushions. He grasped the curtain and leaned out so his eyes were level with Bart's.

'I haf your mother's notes. She has gone so you vill pay!'

Bart was disgusted. 'I owe you nothing.'

'If you don't pay, I seize the plantation!' Van Dort laughed triumphantly as the Caffres bore him away through the narrow gap between the trap and the side of the street.

Bart shrugged off his dismay. 'What does he mean?' he asked Tissa who jumped from the second cart to join him in the street. 'What is he scheming?'

Tissa frowned, nervously touching the tortoise shell comb that held his hair in place.

'By the devil, Tissa! You know something about this.'

'Miss Charlotte promised she would discuss it with you.'

'Discuss what? Did she sign some promissory notes?'

'Yes, Bloodheart.' Tissa backed away as though fearing his wrath. 'Several.'

'To Van Dort?'

'To gem merchants. That was how she bought the gem stones in her collection. She intends to pay when she's sold them in England.'

The fear that gripped Bart made him choke. He put his hand on Tissa's shoulder, staring after Van Dort's palanquin. He imagined he could hear Van Dort's chuckle of laughter on the breeze gusting down the street.

'They are demand notes,' said Tissa hesitantly as the enormity of what he was saying occurred to him. 'Van Dort must have bought them from the Moors . . .'

'How much?' He scarcely recognized his own voice.

'Thousands of dollars,' said Tissa glumly. 'Nimal and Jagath bought gems for her too. The traders were so willing to accept her notes without question. They know you are wealthy, no?'

'No! I've got no money!' He beat his hand against his brow in anguish. 'How can I possibly pay them off? Van Dort's right. He could seize the plantation.'

The lantern in Charlotte's cabin swayed with the rolling of the *Swift*. The sea was calm close to the coast but Mammy looked unhappy as she clung to the door handle to keep her balance. Charlotte smiled at her.

'Go to your quarters, Mammy. You'll be fine when you get your sea legs.'

'I ain't leavin' you.'

'Fiddlesticks.' She looked at her sternly. 'I shall go to sleep.' She gestured at her bunk. 'So much excitement. I need the rest. You do too.'

Mammy regarded her suspiciously. The ship rolled and she rolled with it, only her hold on the door saved her from being pitched into the coffers of gems stacked at the side of the cabin. Charlotte laughed.

'Mammy, I declare you're green.'

'Ooh!' Mammy blenched. She clutched at her bosom, her tiny eyes signalling her distress.

'Go,' said Charlotte soothingly. 'I'll be all right.' She waited until Mammy succeeded in opening the cabin door and was steadying herself for the next rise and fall of the ship.

'Thank you, Mammy,' she said as the motion carried the old cook away from the door and sent her bouncing along the passage.

Charlotte sighed, rose up from her chair and hurriedly closed the door. She was content, drawing succour from being alone after the weeks of panic. At last, in that cabin with its lantern swaying to the accompaniment of shipboard creaks and clatters, she felt at peace.

She opened the lacquered ebony writing box that Bart had thoughtfully placed on top of a chest to serve as a table for it. She regretted the cabin was so small. She felt restricted after the openness of the villa but supposed that she would get used to it. From where she sat in the cabin's only chair, she could lean across and touch the bunk bed or the door.

She searched in the box for a quill and the inkpot and some paper. Once the *Swift* left the shelter of the coast, the sea would get rough and it would be impossible to write. She spread out the paper on the sloping surface of the box. She sucked the end of the quill for a few moments, marshalling her thoughts before she leaned forward and began her letter.

It was late when she finished. She knew by the increased movement of the ship that they were leaving Ceylon far behind. She closed the box and stood up, stretching herself. The ceiling was low enough for her hands to touch it. She felt cramped.

She opened the door. Her cabin was on the main deck with one adjoining cabin and two opposite. She had not met the other passengers when she boarded due to the sadness of bidding goodbye to Bart and the children. She stepped out, firmly holding the rail running at hand height along the side of the passage.

She was queasy after writing so much in the constant motion of the vessel. She was sorry for Mammy. She reached the end of the passage and looked across the deck. Mammy would be aft with the other servants. She heard their moans.

It was dark on deck, the only light coming from the lanterns swinging wildly in the wind. She felt herself being drawn one way by the motion of the ship and rolled back another. She clung to the rope that replaced the wooden railing as a handhold, and used it to guide her to the ship's rail.

She was in the shadows at the side of the ship. It seemed too far to walk and search for Mammy in the dark so she decided to take a few mouthfuls of the fresh sea air before going back to her cabin to sleep.

At the taffrail a seaman was emptying a bucket of fish entrails into the sea. She ignored him. It was a dark night with a quarter moon suspended like a baby's cradle in the sky. She assumed Galle lay behind in the distance, under the moon.

A man was walking towards her from the shadows. She took no notice of him, letting her thoughts dwell on Bart, wondering if he was gazing out at the moon from the villa's verandah, thinking of her. It would be at least a year before she would see him again.

She was aware that the man had stopped by the rail close to her and was gazing up at the moon as well. She glanced at him. In the dark, it was difficult to see him clearly. She gasped.

For a moment, she thought he was Prince Gamunu in European clothes. There was something familiar about the way the man was standing. She shook her head and gripped the rail to compose herself. She was determined not to let her imagination upset her. She was free of the prince's influence now.

'Hello, Charlotte,' a cruel voice said.

Before she could call for help, a hand closed over her mouth and jerked her head back. She saw the pale blue eyes, the ginger moustache and the hard leer of Albert Lindsay Van Dort.

She released the rail and beat him with her fists, wriggling frantically to break free of his grasp. The ship rolled and she found herself suddenly launched in the air. She screamed.

She was falling through the night, spinning wildly. It was wet. The lanterns of the *Swift* were above her, in the stars. Suddenly she was in the sea.

She screamed again, shocked by the cold that swamped her. She was outraged.

Somebody was lying in the water beside her, nudging her. She turned gratefully. A double row of pearl white teeth grimaced, then the wide jaws of the shark snapped off her scream in a single bite.

Her last glimpse was of Albert Van Dort calmly turning away from the rail and walking across the deck to her cabin.

CHAPTER TWENTY-SEVEN

The weeks after the departure of his mother and Mammy from the plantation were strange ones for Bart, days loaded with foreboding. He was able to divert his mind to the cane harvest, riding through the fields at a fast pace so the breeze would cool him, and urging the cane cutters to work harder.

He carried his whip furled under his arm. It was a symbol only. If he used it on the *salagamas* they would dwindle away since none of them were compelled to work. His three remaining Caffres – Delta, Mark and Romulus – toiled at crop time with a will inspired by their keenness to show the Singhalese they were better than them. Bart left them alone.

With his mother's departure he had stopped the gem cutting which he regarded as a futile venture. Mark and Romulus were better employed in the cane fields. It was only through cane, he believed, that he could survive.

Tissa agreed with him. 'The canes are juicy this year,' he said when Bart visited him in the mill. He pointed at the copper cauldrons bubbling with boiling liquid squeezed from the canes by the huge grinding stones. 'We'll have rum and sugar in plenty.'

Half-naked natives swarmed around the mill with an industry that amazed Bart. 'Your boys work well,' he said, not to praise Tissa but out of admiration. 'I wish I could pay them.'

'You give them food and shelter. They are proud to toil for Bloodheart. You can pay them when the sugar is sold.'

Bart pursed his lips to hide his misgivings from Tissa. 'Come to the villa this evening!' he said. 'Drink some rum with me on the verandah. Like the old days.'

He wiped his brow. It was hot in the mill and the cloying smell of boiling sugar added to his discomfort. Yet he was reluctant to leave the activity and return to the torpor of his home.

Tissa eyed him shrewdly. 'Daisy is not enough for you?'

He bridled, offended by his familiarity. 'You would not dare to speak to me like that in the old days.'

'You were never so melancholy then, Bloodheart. What troubles you?'

Tissa led the way out of the millhouse to the yard where bullock carts creaked with their loads of cane from the fields. Natives rushed to unload them and feed the canes to the grinding stones. It was more frenetic than inside the mill, but cooler.

He followed Tissa to the river bank where the water wheel turned rhythmically and the noise of the natives was less intrusive. 'Daisy is wonderful,' he said helplessly.

'I am thinking she is unable to replace your mother and Mammy together, and still be your bedwench.'

He clapped Tissa on his shoulder, delighted by the comment. 'You see how I need someone like you to talk to? You understand me better than I do myself.'

'Your loneliness will pass. You have the children. Malika looks after them better than a mother. It is only for a few months, a year at the most, and Charlotte will return.'

'You won't come tonight and drink with me?'

'Another time. I have the boiling to attend to.'

Bart sighed, watching the swirling of the river. 'Yes, that is more important. We need the income.'

'Are the debts very great?'

'Until I hear from Van Dort, I cannot say. He is probably buying up all the notes he can find to create a large sum that I'll be obliged to pay the moment he demands it.'

He shook his head, too perturbed to explain to Tissa that it was not money alone he was worried about. There was Kirti and the constant threat that one day Prince Gamunu would return and demand the boy, and the elephant pearl too.

That Van Dort had tried to trick his mother into parting with it showed Bart how valuable the *gaja mutu* was. She had pleaded with him to let her take it to England to sell. He had refused. Only he knew where it was hidden. He was keeping it for Kirti.

'What of Miss Raven?'

Tissa's question, asked casually but heavy with meaning, startled him. He picked up a pebble from the ground, studied it pensively, then flicked it into the river, trying to skim it over the surface. It bounced once before hitting a ripple and sinking.

'Raven?' He knew the significance of Tissa's question but tried to ignore it. 'I know nothing of her.'

Tissa looked at him scornfully. 'Perhaps you should learn. She intends to be your wife now your mother's in England.'

He flung another stone into the river and turned on Tissa crossly. 'You pry too much in my affairs! That was Mammy's weakness. By the devil, I'm glad to be ride of her. Are you taking her place in gossip and conjecture?'

Tissa grinned, pleased to have aroused his anger. 'By your retort, I am seeing you do know of Raven. That is good. She will cure your loneliness.'

'Hold your tongue!' It was his despair that made him angry. 'I cannot marry her. Without wealth and with my mother's debts hanging over me, what kind of life can I offer her?'

'You have the villa, the mill, the plantation . . .'

'Do you forget Van Dort? He has sworn to break me.'

Tissa looked at him impatiently. 'What has become of Bloodheart, the courageous man? Is he dead? Is there only a spineless English settler who whimpers for his mother like a suckling pup?' He turned away sadly, his sarong swirling as he strode back to the mill yard.

Bart heaved, shaking his head at the river. Yes, he wanted Raven. Yes, he wanted to outwit Van Dort. But somehow he could not summon up the defiance Tissa's words were supposed to inspire in him.

He turned away and pushed through the jungle to the path winding by the river bank. He wandered aimlessly. Behind him he could hear the steady chopping of cane by the faithful *salagamas*. The sound depressed him because he knew it added to his obligation to them.

He would be lucky to find a market for the sugar so he could pay them what they expected. He wondered why the optimism with which he started the plantation should have deserted him when he needed it most.

A man moved ahead of him on the path. Since he opened up the plateau, many strangers wandered its trails. The natives of Ceylon were great travellers, journeying from one end of the island to another on the flimsiest pretext. They enjoyed religious pilgrimages or trips to view some phenomenon of which they had heard and wished to see for themselves.

Bart assumed the man ahead of him was an inquisitive traveller until he was struck by the odd way he was behaving.

The man was walking slowly, his head on one side as though listening. Then he trotted a few paces, stopped, listened again, and peered into the bush at the side of the trail. He began to walk again, his tread so light not even the birds were disturbed by his progress through the jungle.

Because the path led eventually to the waterfall that gave access to the Kandyan mountains, Bart suspected this man could be a spy bound for the pass. He might even be carrying a message for Prince Gamunu.

The prospect filled him with dread. He slipped behind a tree when the man halted, hoping the broad trunk would hide him if he glanced back.

From his appearance, the man was a Tamil. He was dark skinned with a waistcloth that was dyed and ornamented in the manner favoured by the Tamils of the north of the island. His hair was black, long and straight, tumbling over his brow. He carried a basket made of plaited reeds.

The Tamils were industrious people, prone to leave their home districts to seek opportunities elsewhere, often carrying curry stuffs, betel leaves and other produce to sell in villages as they travelled. They were skilled in agriculture, intelligent and eager to learn.

For several minutes, as Bart watched him, the Tamil remained crouched motionless on his haunches at the side of the trail. His basket was on the ground beside him. If Bart had not seen him take up that position, he would have walked straight past him. He had become so effectively part of the jungle.

Suddenly the man pounced. His agility was astonishing and he disappeared beyond view in a twinkling. Bart scratched his head, wondering if he had imagined the man's presence. But his basket was still on the ground. He waited.

There was a rustle in the undergrowth and the Tamil emerged, holding in both hands by its head and tail, an enormous *cobra de capello*.

The man shouted and a boy ran down the trail to join him. He was naked except for a thread tied around his waist. He had glossy black hair and the slender graceful limbs of his race. In his hand was a small piece of white wood resembling a root. He passed this gently to and fro over the snake's head, ignoring its darting tongue.

The cobra gradually inclined its head as though in a trance. The boy raised the lid of the basket and the man coiled the snake into it.

Bart stepped out from his hiding place. The two Tamils clasped palms together and bowed. Neither seemed concerned by his sudden appearance. He guessed if they could hear a snake slithering through the undergrowth, they would have known of his presence long before he became aware of theirs.

He spoke with them but nothing he said was understood. Their humble manner convinced him that the sole purpose of their presence on his land was the trapping of snakes. They could not be spies for the prince.

His obsession with Prince Gamunu was different from that of his mother. She had been scared to face him again. Bart was afraid of losing Kirti. Every day as the boy grew, he revealed some remarkable new feature of his personality that endeared him to Bart.

His concern for the baby's safety kept him at home. He used that as his excuse for not going to Galle. While part of him, the sensual side, longed to see Raven again, the thoughtful side prevailed.

His scrutiny of the ledgers left by his mother showed how parlous were the plantation's finances. Since he could not afford to marry Raven, he resolved to avoid her.

The household settled into a new routine. Daisy managed the house while Little attended to the cooking. Jagath helped Malika with the children and Nimal waited on him. Romulus and Mark tended the gardens when they were not working in the cane fields.

Bart was fond of Daisy for her rough, practical ways. Her energy in bed drained the passion from him at night although it could not dull the yearning for Raven that haunted his waking hours.

In his mind he treasured a picture of Raven sitting under a temple tree, her ringlets ruffled by the breeze, her wild eyes momentarily pensive and a flower in her hand. That memory helped him survive each day's loneliness.

He was relieved one evening when he heard the sounds of people approaching the house. He craved company and was pleased to see Tissa emerging from the dark. He was sitting on the verandah playing with Kirti, waiting for the boy to be tired enough to put to bed.

Tissa seemed hesitant about disturbing him.

'Dammit, man! Come in.' He clapped his hands for Nimal. 'Come to join me for a punch?'

Tissa waved his hand in refusal. He stepped onto the verandah with an air of reluctance. Bart was puzzled by his lack of ease.

'What is it?' he demanded, gathering up Kirti from the floor and holding him close to his chest. He saw a movement beyond Tissa.

A boy stepped out of the shadows carrying a basket. Bart frowned with recognition.

'Why, isn't he the snake-catcher's boy?'

'Yes.' Tissa shuddered as though he was scared to speak.

'What is he doing here?'

For answer, Tissa signalled the boy to place his basket on the floor. 'He has a message for you.'

Tissa's fidgety manner and quick glance into the darkness at the side of the house, alarmed Bart. He hugged Kirti closer, filled with foreboding.

He had known Tissa since the day he arrived in Galle nearly ten years before. He had watched him like a brother, growing from a timid slave to a man who commanded respect as the plantation overseer.

He trusted Tissa, yet that flicker of his eyes into the darkness made him sick with dread that his trust was about to be betrayed.

'What message?' He stood up, squaring his shoulders, pretending greater confidence than he actually felt.

'See for yourself!' Tissa angrily kicked the basket.

Bart clasped Kirti tightly as he waited for the lid to spring open and a snake to slither out.

The Tamil boy bent down and pulled off the lid, tipping the basket on its side.

A round, bloodied object rolled across the verandah floor towards Bart's feet. He jerked back, ready to leap on a chair if the thing moved to attack him. He stared at it in horror.

Malika screamed. Kirti started to cry, beating his tiny fists against his chest.

He looked from the object to Tissa, and saw his eyes were glistening with tears. He handed Kirti to Malika who hurriedly bore him away to the parlour entrance.

He crouched down and gingerly prodded the object with his finger. It rolled over and he saw he was staring at Prince Gamunu's severed head.

Gamunu's scalp had been shaved. It was a mass of pulpy flesh smeared with congealed blood. Only the eyes were recognizable. They stared up at Bart and seemed to be appealing to him.

Instinctively, he shied away, kicking out at the head to escape its evil. It bounced over the floor and lodged under a chair. The snake boy dived to retrieve it.

'The rebellion is over,' said Tissa in an anguished voice. 'The British executed Prince Gamunu last night.'

'How did you get the head?'

Tissa was silent.

Bart was bewildered. He sat down to think. With Gamunu dead at least part of his worries were over. Kirti was safe and his mother need not fear returning to Ceylon.

He watched the boy stuff the head into his basket with an air of indifference. He wondered if there was a snake in there to keep it company.

'Why the devil did you bring that here?'

'For you to know I speak the truth!'

The high-pitched voice that screeched from the side of the verandah caused his heart to leap. He shuddered as the fat, vile figure of Marcus Van Dort waddled out of the shadows, clambered onto the verandah and sat down, panting, in a chair.

Malika fled to the parlour, covering Kirti's face to shield him from Van Dort's evil eye.

Tissa and the snake boy edged away from Van Dort. Bart tried to understand what was happening. He guessed Van Dort's Caffres were lurking in the dark, waiting for their master's order to attack. He had no weapons to hand; he was at Van Dort's mercy.

Daisy bustled onto the verandah. Bart glanced at her, hoping she was going to repel Van Dort with her broomstick but she carried a tray of drinks. She offered one to Van Dort and one to Bart. Tissa declined.

'Mammy al'us say white folks does like a drink even when dey quarrellin'.'

'Quarrellink?' Van Dort chuckled, pleased by Daisy's reference to him as a white man. His *salagama* background was his constant shame.

'I come as a friend, Bart, not to quarrel.' He raised his glass in a toast and sipped at it. His pudgy face beamed with pleasure. 'Your slave haf better manners than you.'

'Better than yours too. What the devil are you doing here?'

'Tut tut. Alvays the hasty boy. You haf not changed.'

'You have. You're fatter and uglier.'

'Bart, that is not vorthy of you. I haf come as your friend. To do you a favour.'

'The only favour you can do me is to remove yourself from my verandah and fall on your fat backside in a cobra's nest.'

'Spiteful, Bart? Vy? Haf I not come to help you?'

'The more you say that, the less I believe it's true.' He took a swig of the rum. 'What happened to Prince Gamunu?'

'Tissa spoke the truth. Gamunu was my friend. I bribed the executioner because I thought you vould like his head for a

275

souvenir.' He chuckled, the rolls of fat on his belly wobbling obscenely.

'Tell me why you're here and get out.'

Van Dort finished his drink and glanced around the verandah. He held out his glass for Daisy to take from his hand. He nodded approvingly. 'Vat a pleasant home you haf built here. I like the air.'

'I don't. Not with you polluting it.'

Van Dort's cheeks shook with mirth, not at Bart's remark but at what he was going to say. 'Bart, I know you haf the *gaja mutu* that Gamunu left vit you inadvertently. That is mine. I vant it.'

Bart leaned back in his chair, pleased that the threat was in the open at last. He knew how to fight it.

'Damn, Van Dort,' he said with a grin of mock disappointment. 'You're too late. My mother took it to England. She should be there by now. Probably sold it already for a few shillings to a costumier.'

'You lie!' Van Dort's eyes narrowed. 'I happen to know your mother haf not the pearl.'

'It's not here!' He spread his hands wide to demonstrate his innocence.

Van Dort pushed himself up from his chair. He staggered and looked around, expecting someone to come to his aid. No one moved. He reached inside his coat. Bart jumped out of his seat.

Van Dort pulled out a sheaf of papers and offered them to Bart. Bart refused to give him the satisfaction of accepting them so he tossed them to the ground at his feet.

'These are copies of the promissory notes dear Charlotte signed. I haf registered them all in my name. I vill cancel them in exchange for the elephant pearl.'

'You're crazy!'

'I am more than fair.'

'I don't have the pearl, I tell you!'

'Then, Bart, I must demand payment in full.' He paused and spread his chubby hands to embrace the darkness beyond the verandah.

'If you don't give me the pearl, or pay the value of the notes, this plantation vill be mine.'

CHAPTER TWENTY-EIGHT

'Garnets, rubies, sapphires, Matara diamonds ... By the devil, what are they?' Bart groaned with disbelief. He shook the promissory notes at Tissa. 'There are thousands of dollars' worth of bills here!'

Tissa regarded him blankly.

His lack of concern riled Bart as much as the notes did. 'That's money, Tissa! Real money.' He released the papers so they fluttered onto his desk.

For the whole morning he had been checking the bills and the total against Van Dort's summary. Since Van Dort left the villa the night before, he had barely slept. At first light he summoned Tissa from the mill to help him examine the notes and to explain the purchases.

When Tissa said nothing, Bart rose to his feet and stretched. Tissa flinched, which softened Bart's anger. The Singhalese were sensitive people, alarmed by unexpected movements. He tried to explain.

'These pieces of paper represent half the value of this plantation. That's half the house, half the mill, half the land and even half of you because you're still a slave.' He saw Tissa's bland expression harden.

'Van Dort can own me again? Half of me?'

'All of you, Tissa. To cancel the debts he wants everything, even though I value the plantation at double.'

'I won't go. I'm yours.'

He was touched by Tissa's loyalty. He strode around the room, pulling the lobe of his ear. 'I don't understand why Van Dort will accept the elephant pearl in payment. Why is it worth so much to him?'

'It is priceless.'

Bart thought aloud. 'He probably bought those notes at a percentage of their face value. If the dealers owed him favours or he blackmailed and bullied them, he could have acquired them for a lot less. His total outlay is much lower than mother will have to pay.'

'Bart . . .' Tissa sounded hesitant at interrupting him. 'When your mother sells the gems in England, she'll have the money.'

'I wish I had your faith.' He sighed with exasperation. 'Even if she makes back the full amount, Tissa, it will be too late. Van Dort's given me a week.'

'Then borrow the money yourself.' To Tissa it seemed simple. 'Sign your own promissory notes.'

'Who will lend to me? You can be sure Van Dort has spread the word around Galle to prevent that happening.'

Bart left the stuffiness of the parlour and strolled out on to the verandah. It was deserted. He had forbidden Malika to bring the children outside. The unexpected arrival of Van Dort had made him realize how vunerable he was, even there. Anytime Van Dort's Caffres could ransack the villa.

He stood at the verandah's edge, scanning the plantation. With the fields shorn of cane he had a clear view across the stubbled earth to the brink of the vast plateau. Beyond the distant boundary of trees, the land sloped through jungle to the coconut groves along the coast. He thought of the years he had toiled, with Tissa at his side, to create the plantation.

'What do you think, Tissa? What should I do?'

Tissa smiled politely. 'What do *you* think?'

'Dammit!' He knew Tissa would never commit himself before him in case he would be accused of disloyalty. 'This is my plantation. Why should Van Dort have it? I'll give him the pearl instead.'

Tissa's eyes widened. 'Do you have it?'

'I know where it is.'

'You told him your mother has it.'

'Yes, and he seemed to know I was lying. He's shrewd.'

Tissa looked troubled. 'It would be unlucky to part with the *gaja mutu*.'

'Do you want me to give him the plantation – and you?'

'If you give him the *gaja mutu*, Van Dort will still find a way to drive you out.'

'No, he won't.' Bart was growing weary of the struggle. 'That's only his threat.'

'Don't trust him! He's evil. The *gaja mutu* will give him a potency no one can resist.'

'Superstitious nonsense!' He smacked his fist into the palm of his hand. 'By the devil. I *will* give him the pearl. It'll be a relief to get him off my back and to know the plantation is secure.'

He turned to Tissa eagerly, expecting to see him smile with approval. Instead, Tissa stared back with eyes that were moist with disappointment, as though Bart was betraying him.

'Cheer up, man!' He jabbed him in his chest which made Tissa even more upset. 'It's only a piece of old elephant's tusk.'

Tissa turned and slunk off the verandah, showing his dismay at his decision by the slope of his shoulders and his listless gait.

Bart made his preparations. He instructed Daisy and Nimal to keep the outer shutters and doors closed. No strangers were to be allowed into the villa, not even the Singhalese who worked at the mill.

'I will be away for a few hours,' he explained. 'No one will know where to find me.'

'Is it dangerous?' asked Daisy.

He was gratified by her concern. 'The danger will be here unless you do as I say. I don't expect Van Dort to try anything yet. Just in case, we must be careful.'

Daisy nodded dutifully.

'I shall be back by nightfall.'

As well as his pistol and cutlass, he took a packet of food that Little prepared for the journey, wrapped in a leaf of wild plantain. He wore his boots, breeches and shirt, no coat or hat.

He was about to leave when Daisy rushed out to the verandah and gave him a bandanna. He lowered his head and let her tie it around his neck. She seemed to expect a kiss of farewell. He drew away irritably, waved at her and stepped off the verandah, taking the path to the mill.

He was aware of Daisy and Nimal watching him as he walked. He shrugged off their curiosity. His only fear was that something might happen to the children. Until Van Dort was satisfied, everyone was at risk, especially himself. The thought made him pause.

Perhaps Van Dort had planted spies? He remembered Junie, the Caffre at Madam Gudde's who was in his pay. Was someone in the villa reporting what he did to Van Dort? If they guessed he was going for the pearl, someone could follow him and, when he retrieved it from the hiding place, attack him and rob him of it. Without the pearl to pay off Van Dort, he would lose the plantation too.

His loss of nerve perturbed him. Tissa was right. Bloodheart had died. His courage had evaporated so he viewed even this solo trip into the jungle with alarm.

He glanced up and down the path. In the distance, gathered around the mill, were the Singhalese busy with the cane harvest. Behind him was the villa where Daisy was still watching him. He resumed his walk, whistling to himself to raise his spirits.

At the fork where the path led to the mill yard, he turned left onto the trail through the jungle. The trees provided shelter and after walking a few paces, he darted into them to hide. Looking back, he could see where the villa path entered the mill yard. He did not have to wait long.

Jagath, clutching his sarong up to his waist so he could move faster, ran down the path. He rushed over to Tissa. Bart saw him talking to him, pointing in the direction he had taken.

Bart waited half an hour to see who would walk along the trail to follow him. He was surprised when no one did. Tissa was in view most of the time, directing his men in their chores. The bullocks brought the cane, the men unloaded it and fed it into the grinding stones. The rhythm of work at the mill was undisturbed.

Eventually, he was convinced that he was not going to be followed. He cut his way energetically through the undergrowth. Branches and creepers snagged his hair and tore his shirt. The trail became worse as it rose from the canefields. He listened carefully for strange sounds above the noise of the jungle. He was certain he was alone.

He climbed for two hours. The path was overgrown, which reassured him. He heard the roar of the waterfall drawing him closer.

When he reached the outcrop of rock that shielded the falls, he rested. He opened the packet of rice and curry Little had given him. He was too agitated to eat much and threw the plantain leaf packet on the ground.

It was cool in the jungle, damp and gloomy under the dense foliage that kept out the sun. He shivered, conscious of being alone in an alien atmosphere. He scrambled to his feet and hurriedly completed the climb up the scree leading to the lookout over the waterfall.

He hacked at the creepers blocking the final approach and then, as he entered the glade that opened into the vast chasm, he stopped and stared.

He was five feet from the side of the waterfall. It tumbled down the cliff face with a roar that deafened him, spray drenching his hair and clothes like being in a rain storm. He was stunned by its magnificence.

The sun filtered through the gap where the funnel of rock was open to the sky, blazing against the white wall of water. The arc of a rainbow hovered in the middle of the chasm. He was drawn to the edge.

He held on to a vine hanging from a tree and leaned out to gaze at the water plunging down into the whirlpool below. Beyond the wild cascade of water was the ledge of rock giving access to the pass. He ignored it, pulled back from the edge with a sigh of sorrow and looked around the glade.

He saw the boulder he remembered from his last visit. It was covered in slimy green moss nurtured by the dampness of the place. He scraped off the moss with his cutlass and found the arrow that he had carved there as a marker.

281

He paced three steps in the opposite direction to that indicated by the arrow's head. The soil was covered in vines and clinging plants that gave off a foul vegetal odour when he hacked at them.

He dug quickly, using the blade of his cutlass to turn up the earth. He uncovered the five stones he had buried in a circle to guard the elephant pearl and there, nestling in the centre in its decayed leather pouch, was the pearl itself.

It looked like a ball of clay. He glanced around nervously before bending down to pick it up.

As he touched the pearl, a change came over him. .

He plucked it out of the soil and rubbed it against his shirt, over his heart. The mud sticking to it fell off but it still looked dull and uninspiring. He slipped it into his pocket.

He was astonished at the confidence and optimism that soared through him. The damp, eerie glade and the dripping jungle held no more terror. He chuckled at that fear that had made him nervous. His strength and courage were restored.

After a final, brief glance at the waterfall, he retraced his path to the scree of stones. He lowered himself down the slope, slithering on his backside to the rocks at the bottom where he had rested during his climb up.

He was eager to get back to the villa. The thought of Marcus Van Dort's demands now seemed preposterous. He was fired with a new energy, a resolve to deal with the fat Burgher so he could be left to run his plantation in peace. He was a man courageous again. Tissa would be pleased.

As he paused at the resting place, he sensed something was wrong. He looked carefully on the ground and then into the tangled undergrowth beside the rock where he had sat. His lunch packet had disappeared.

He touched the hard nut of the pearl in his pocket, pressing it against his thigh. A monkey must have taken the food, he reasoned, or any number of scavenging jungle creatures. He tightened his grip on his cutlass and stepped down onto the path. The ground slid from under his feet.

He gasped, clutching at the air in vain to regain his balance. The cutlass flew from his fingers and he fell backwards. He had trodden on something that moved. There was movement in the undergrowth as he put his hands down to push himself to his feet. He touched something slippery.

He saw the snake the instant before it struck. It was an enormous cobra, its yellow eyes livid with evil. It seized him by his forefinger, retaining its hold for a few seconds as if unable to retract its fangs. He shrieked with horror and tried to shake it off.

He felt the blood flowing. The pain was intense. The snake released him and slid off into the undergrowth, its tail crossing the path a long while after its head.

Time was suspended for Bart. Dimly, he saw the jungle closing in on him; a paralysis crept into his hand. He raised himself to his feet, took a few steps forward and then fell down, face first in the mud.

In a few minutes he would be dead.

The shadow looming over him became a boy. He moaned, struggling to rise, pleading through half-closed eyes for help.

The boy grunted, pulled off his waistcloth and crouched down naked at his side. He took from the cloth two stones each the size of a small almond. They were black and highly polished though of an extremely light substance. He jerked Bart into a sitting position and made a soft, hissing sound when he saw the bite.

He applied the stones to the wounds inflicted by the teeth of the snake so that each stone covered a fang mark. The stones seemed to adhere to Bart's finger of their own accord. Blood oozed out. The boy indicated with gestures that Bart himself should hold the stones in place.

His initial shock had passed and he was comforted at having someone to aid him. The boy's lack of panic and air of calm self-assurance, despite his nakedness and youth, made him believe his magic would work.

He touched the stones lightly as the boy directed. Blood flowed from the bite and was rapidly absorbed by the porous texture of the black stones.

The boy clucked his approval and rubbed Bart's arm downwards from his shoulder towards the fingers. He maintained the massage steadily for three or four minutes. Bart's vision cleared and the paralysis flowed out with the blood. Suddenly the stones dropped off.

The boy gripped Bart's fingers, twisted and pulled them until the joints cracked.

'*Pamboo-kaloo*,' he said, picking up the stones and wrapping them in his loincloth. He grinned and held out his hand for Bart to stand.

'Snake stones?' guessed Bart, his voice hushed at the miracle. The snake boy's stones were actually bone that was sufficiently porous and absorbent to extract the venom from the bite before it had time to be carried into his system.

He gripped the boy's hand, restraining him when he wanted to bound off down the trail.

'No, boy,' he said. 'Stay with me.' He unwound Daisy's bandanna from his neck and tied it gingerly around his sore finger.

He tapped his pocket, believing it was the elephant pearl that had protected him. He froze. The pocket was empty.

The boy was grinning at him like a Galle street urchin. He held up his fist, opened it and showed Bart the *gaja mutu* in his palm.

'Give that here!' He lunged for the boy. He was still weak. The boy darted easily from his grasp.

'Come here!' He reached for his pistol and then realized that had gone too.

The boy grinned again, opened his waistcloth and showed Bart the weapon hidden in the garment.

'How the dev –'

The boy danced to his side, took his bandaged hand and placed the *gaja mutu* firmly in it. He returned Bart's pistol to the other hand.

He danced away, leaping from rock to rock like a black fawn. He paused atop a large boulder and placed his palms together at chest height, bowed briefly and was gone, swallowed up by the shadows of the jungle.

* * *

Bart expected the bullock trap lumbering up the path to the villa to be carrying Marcus Van Dort. He had the elephant pearl ready for him, in an ebony box. The promissory notes were laid out on the escritoire with pen and ink at hand for Van Dort to sign a receipt. When he cancelled the notes, Bart would give him the pearl.

He drummed his fingers with impatience on the rail of the verandah as he waited for the slow moving carriage to reach the villa. The sooner he dealt with Van Dort, the better. Tissa was with him, strangely subdued.

'See how bold he is,' Bart said sarcastically. 'He comes without his Caffres. He thinks he owns the plantation already.'

Tissa squinted down the path, shading his eyes from the sun. 'It's not Van Dort!' he yelled with delight. 'It's Miss Raven.'

'Raven?' He clutched the rail. 'What the devil does she want?'

He had to wait for his answer until Raven was seated in a chair in the cool and shaded atmosphere of the parlour. She was dressed in black and declined Daisy's invitation to remove her bonnet. A Singhalese girl who had travelled with her waited outside on the verandah.

Bart was puzzled by how sombre she looked, and by her reluctance to talk.

'What's wrong, Raven?' he asked repeatedly while she composed herself.

'I have bad news, Bart.' She hesitated, making an obvious effort not to cry.

'Daddy is coming to tell you officially. I hurried to be the one to bring you the news. Now I'm here I don't know how to tell you.' She sniffed, holding her handkerchief to her nose.

He jumped up from his seat and strode to her side impatiently. He put his arm around her. 'Don't cry, Raven, for God's sake. I can't stand it.'

'I'm crying for your mother, Bart. She's dead.'

A silence descended on the room. Bart nodded his head and sighed heavily. They were alone. Tissa was on the verandah and Daisy was in the kitchen preparing refreshments.

He felt Raven's hand searching for his. He held it and was surprised when Raven rose from the chair and came to him so that she was in his arms, her cheek resting against his chest. He patted her shoulders affectionately.

'She was drowned the night she sailed from here. It's taken until now for the news to reach us from London.

'Drowned?' He guessed what had happened. 'Suicide?'

'She was murdered. They found a man in her cabin searching for something. A report was made at the Cape.'

'Whatever did he want?'

'An elephant pearl, the man said. He was put in irons but someone poisoned him.'

Bart nodded grimly. 'That must have been Mammy's doing.' He clung to Raven as she sobbed against his chest. He was too angry for tears.

'I wondered how Van Dort knew Charlotte didn't have the pearl.' He bit his lip.

'My God!' he exclaimed, releasing Raven and dashing to the escritoire. 'I was going to give this to Van Dort. My mother died because of it, because of me. I was going to give it away!'

'It's all right, Bart. Keep calm.' Raven hurried over to him. Her bonnet was askew and she untied it quickly and cast it onto a chair as she reached him.

'Don't do anything silly.' She put her hand on his arm.

He clasped the ebony box containing the pearl to his chest as she leaned against him. Her face was close to his. He saw the tears still moist on her cheeks and the blaze of determination in her eyes.

'Let me help you!' she whispered.

'Help me?' He pulled away from her, waving the box in her face. 'What can you do? If I don't give this to Van Dort he'll take the plantation.'

'Fight him!'

He paused and stared, wondering if he had heard her properly. He was fascinated by the wild glint in her eye and by her shimmering ringlets as she tossed her head with fury.

He placed the box on the escritoire and turned back to her. He put his arms on her shoulders and shook her.

'Fight him? By the devil, I will.'

Her hands snaked around his waist and she pressed close to him. He stopped shaking her and opened his mouth to speak. She raised her lips to his.

'No,' he said, breaking away. 'No!'

'I want to help you, Bart.'

'Then leave me alone. This is my fight!' He stood ill at ease in the centre of the room, ashamed at the hurt he was causing her.

Daisy bustled in from the kitchen, carrying a tray of refreshments.

He pushed past her and strode out of the parlour into the courtyard. He grabbed a flower from the branch of a temple tree that hung in his away. Angrily, he tore the flower apart, crushing the petals in his fist.

Raven sank down into a chair where she could watch him pacing the lawn. She murmured softly to herself under her breath as Daisy set out the tea things.

'He loves me, he loves me not, he loves me, he loves me not, *he loves me!*'

CHAPTER TWENTY-NINE

'The legal way,' said Mr Radley brandishing the sheaf of papers Bart had given him to study, 'is to oblige Mr Van Dort to prove his case in the courts. These are copies of promissory notes, not the real ones. How do you know your mother signed the originals?'

'I don't.' Bart stared across the desk at Mr Radley. He had come to see the Collector at Raven's insistence. She sat beside him in her father's office.

'Bart's a gentleman, daddy. He accepts Mr Van Dort's word as an honourable man.'

It made Bart sound stupid. He gawped at her. 'Have I been foolish?'

'It is always prudent to seek advice on these matters.' Mr Radley steepled his fingers. 'If you wish to settle this without protest, you can give Van Dort the pearl he covets so much.'

'He's not giving Van Dort anything!' Raven's eyes blazed.

Bart shook his head to contradict her. 'I have to pay mother's debts.'

'When they are proven.'

'I will still have to pay.'

'Bart!' Raven glowered at hm in desperation. 'Court procedures take a long time. Daddy can make sure of that. You'll have the opportunity to find the money without selling the plantation.'

'How?' He raised his eyebrows, disturbed by her innocent trust that everything would be all right. 'I have nothing.'

'You'll find a way,' she said. 'I know you will.'

The look she gave him stirred a longing in his heart. He turned away from her sharply. 'I'll do what you suggest, Mr Radley.'

'An advocate must represent you. When Van Dort comes to see you, refer him to your advocate. Do nothing else.'

Bart listened without enthusiasm as Mr Radley, obviously relishing the legal niceties of his predicament, outlined his defence. For Bart it was a futile procedure. His concern was raising the money, especially now his mother was dead.

In the past he had grown accustomed to borrowing from her, even though he knew one day he would have to repay. That he should have to pay Marcus Van Dort instead offended his sense of decency.

He knew Van Dort had arranged his mother's murder although it was impossible to prove. Albert had expected to find the pearl in her cabin and would have returned to Ceylon with it from the Cape. When the official report arrived from England, he would know the full circumstances.

After the interview with her father, Bart joined Raven for a walk in the garden. He enjoyed her company. She was young yet she had the mettle of an older, maturer person despite her naivety that all his problems would resolve themselves.

'Daddy likes you,' she said brightly. 'That's why he's helping. I told you we could fight Van Dort.'

'We?' He grimaced. 'You seemed to approve of him a year ago.'

'You saved me from myself. I must have been horrid.'

'Young and foolish, yes. Now I'm the foolish one for allowing you to involve yourself in my affairs.'

'I want to be involved.'

'Why?' His challenge made her falter in her stride.

She gazed at him speculatively, as though assessing what she could say to him without being rebuffed. 'It's not because of you. I feel a special bond for Kirti.'

'That's a relief!' He laughed harshly to disguise his real feelings.

Strolling at her side, in the tranquillity of the garden with the only sounds being the lapping of the sea on the rocks below the battlements and the gentle song of the Ceylon magpie-robins, he longed to tell her how he felt. Yet he dare not.

His desire to possess her, to add her to his list of conquests, had changed to a genuine affection. It was a fondness that made him wary of speaking the truth. He knew she yearned for marriage but that was impossible for him to contemplate.

'Why is it a relief?' she asked unexpectedly, causing him embarrassment with the abruptness of her question.

He pulled the lobe of his ear. 'You're young, Raven. Why get involved with me?' He shrugged, trying to extricate himself. 'I'm only thinking of you.'

'I'm quite capable of thinking for myself!'

He was startled by her tart retort. He was about to retaliate when the loveliness of her face, turned towards the sunlight, distracted him.

'By the devil, Raven!' he blurted out, not caring if his oath upset her. 'Why don't you leave me alone?'

'If I did,' she smiled sweetly, 'you would have handed over your plantation to Van Dort.' She raised her hand to still his protest.

'If I am interfering, tell me. I'm concerned about Kirti, not you. He can't fend for himself when you do something stupid that affects him.'

'Why should you care about my son?'

'Your son, Bart? Remember I know the truth. Yes, he is yours, but he's royal too. I was a little bit in love with Prince Gamunu myself.'

'You didn't . . .' he stopped, ashamed at the indelicacy of his question.

'No, I did not, Bart.' She darted a glance of scorn at him. 'Jessica did. I admired you for accepting Kirti as your own.'

He longed to explain to her that he accepted Kirti because he was bribed by the prince, not because he was the kind, forgiving man she thought him.

'I am not worthy of your admiration or even your help,' he said bitterly.

'I know your faults, Bart. You're proud and obstinate. You act rashly without thinking. You're cruel to those who serve and love you.'

'Dammit, Raven!' He stepped away from her, astounded by her criticism.

'You're foul mouthed and blasphemous too, and you hardly treat me like a lady. Yet you're a gentleman, Bart, with your own standards of what is right and wrong. You're a pioneer, an outsider, a courageous –'

'Stop it, Raven!' He grasped her wrist tightly, bewildered by her catalogue of his shortcomings. 'Who put those words into your head, your father?'

He felt her swaying towards him so he released his grip. Her eyes looked longingly into his, causing a tremor in his loins.

'I told you I am capable of thinking for myself. I want you to realize that you're not deceiving me by your airs. I'm not a little girl any more. I am a young woman with passions that stir here.' She patted her bosom.

'Listen, Raven!' He held up his finger – the one the snake had bitten – and wagged it in her face. 'I'm an impoverished settler of no consequence. I'm a widower responsible for three children. I'm not courageous and I certainly don't know what is right and wrong any more.'

He hesitated at the gentle way she was looking at him. 'I care for you, Raven, yes, I do. I'm grateful for your help, your friendship. I had a sister once, I wish she'd been like you. That's all it can be between us. Like brother and sister.'

'Yes, Bart,' she said, smiling serenely and not believing a word of what he said.

'Give me a whore,' he said gruffly to Madam Gudde. 'I'm in a hurry.'

Gretchen Gudde scrutinized him over the rim of her gin glass. He could feel her disapproval as he sat in a chair opposite her. He cracked his finger joints impatiently.

'I see you so seldom, Bart, but I hear of you often. Won't you join me in a gin?'

'No.' He was deliberately curt. He had walked straight to the brothel from the Collector's bungalow. Raven's words still burned in his ears. He wanted to distance himself from her, to still the influence she was trying to gain over him. He also wanted to purge his body of the desire that throbbed within him.

'Have you had an argument with Raven?' Gretchen asked nosily.

He rose from his seat in anger and then fell back, cradling his head in his hands with despair. 'Am I so transparent?'

'You are a man.' Gretchen grinned knowingly at her gin.

'Does everybody in this town know my business?' He shrank with shame.

'What can you expect when you make it public by racing from Raven's house to mine? When are you going to stop teasing the girl and marry her?'

'Never!' He raised his head and flung his hands up in the air to push aside all his problems. 'Are you going to give me a whore?'

'Be patient, Bart. You cannot jump my girls like they're bedwenches. You need someone to soothe the ache that's bedevilling you. What is it, Bart? Won't she lie with you unless you marry her?'

'Gretchen!' He spluttered, his anger cooled by her mistaken assumption. 'You don't know everything! I've never even kissed Raven Radley. She's like a sister to me, that's all.'

Gretchen drained her gin glass and stood up. She was wearing a flimsy robe and, judging by the flash of white flesh from her thigh when she moved, was naked under it. She walked over to the bed and sat on its edge.

'Very well, Bart,' she said, primping her hair coquettishly. 'Since you're in such a hurry, and obviously determined to prove how you don't care for Raven . . .' She opened her robe. 'You can have me.'

He gawped at her nakedness. Her body was the white of lard, her breasts pendulous to the folds of flesh bulging above her shrivelled thighs. She reclined on her pillow and beckoned him with one hand while the other stroked herself. Her lips parted in a horrendous leer.

'No!' He jumped to his feet in dismay, clawing at the air like a nervous youth.

'It's all right, Bart. If you're in a hurry, I can spare a few minutes.'

'I've changed my mind,' he cried, not caring about hurting her feelings. 'I don't want *you*!'

To his relief, she covered herself with the robe. She swung off the bed and stalked across the room towards him. 'There is something your mother neglected to do to you, Bart.'

'What's tha –'

She smacked him hard across his cheek with the open palm of her hand. The blow stunned him, knocking him onto the chair.

'That's for insulting me,' she said. 'And this,' she added, slapping his other cheek, 'is for cheapening Raven. Now get out! Go to her! Tell her you're sorry and beg her to marry you!'

The courtship, like the court case, lasted seven months. As soon as he stopped fighting his feelings for Raven and concentrated instead on resisting Marcus Van Dort, the pressure on him lifted. He was on the offensive and enjoyed it. He was Bloodheart again.

'Half of those notes were spurious,' he told Tissa after the final hearing. 'Van Dort backed down. I only have to pay half of what he claimed at first.'

Tissa was alarmed. 'It was not my fault, Bart. I could not remember every purchase exactly.'

They were walking up the path to the villa together. Bart led his horse by its reins. He had just returned from Galle.

'I trust you, Tissa,' he said breezily. He had no option. The success of the plantation depended on him. 'Van Dort forged the notes thinking I'd give him the pearl, not the plantation.'

'How will you pay him off?'

Bart slapped the stock of his whip against his thigh. 'I'm waiting for news from the agents in London. Mammy delivered the gems to them. Charlotte left letters of instruction. She had a premonition that something might happen.'

'You are keeping the *gaja mutu*?'

His suspicions were aroused by Tissa's interest in the

pearl. 'Yes, Tissa, I am keeping it. I've taken some precautions. Van Dort will never have it, by fair means or foul.' He glanced at him sharply. 'Why are you so concerned?'

Tissa's sparkling eyes clouded over with shame. 'Do you doubt me after all this time, Bloodheart?'

'Dammit, Tissa, I never said that. Van Dort's cunning. He tried to trick me, maybe he'll try with you too.'

'We have a way to deal with our enemies.' Tissa's smile was precise but it did not fool Bart. He glimpsed the toughness in Tissa and it made him regret his distrust.

He clapped him heartily on his shoulder. 'Raven says I don't appreciate those who are loyal to me.'

Tissa's smile broadened. 'Raven is wise. I hope you bring her to live on the plantation soon.'

'We shall marry when my debts are cleared.' He withdrew his hand from Tissa's shoulder and glanced up at the villa.

In the rays of the setting sun he saw it as others viewed it when they visited for the first time. It lacked the grandness of a mansion but with flowers and shade trees growing around it, disguising the haphazard way it had been built, it was a pleasant and reassuring sight.

Malika was on the verandah with Kirti waiting to welcome him. Garth ran down the path towards him ignoring Daisy calling him to come back. Bart stooped to pick him up and placed him on the horse's saddle, holding him there carefully.

'Were you a good boy today, son?'

Garth's eyes widened with excitement at being on the horse. He pouted at the question. 'Daisy not good,' he said. 'She don't know enough for me.'

Tissa chuckled. 'Garth's another one who needs Raven here. She'd answer his questions properly.'

'Raven's not soft like Jessica or my mother, Tissa. When she's here we'll all have to behave ourselves.'

'Including you?'

Bart gazed at Daisy standing on the verandah with her arms akimbo. She was tall and proud with the glow of the dying sun emphasizing her statuesque figure. His loins stirred at the sight.

'Yes,' he said sadly, 'including me.'

They chuckled together with the understanding of mango friends – good comrades – as Daisy bustled towards them and lifted Garth from the horse. Ranita ran out to greet Tissa and Malika brought Kirti for Bart to hug and toss in his arms.

Bart's reluctance to ask Raven to marry him had been dispelled by Gretchen Gudde's timely slap. He reacted immediately. He had stormed into Mr Radley's office and demanded to be allowed to marry Raven when his affairs were settled.

Despite his rakish instincts, the courtship was restrained and conventional. His clash with Van Dort had brought him close to Raven, giving him a greater understanding of her than could be learned from whispering sweet nothings under temple trees.

He grew accustomed to Raven. Although he ached when he kissed her, shielded by the trees in her father's garden, he controlled his desires like a gentleman. He marvelled at the passion they shared without actually doing anything. The way she held her fan when they were in company said secretly, 'I love you'. Her glance while he and Van Dort confronted each other in court was as satisfying to him as a kiss.

The garrison officers took bets about when he would marry. In Madam Gudde's his affair was the talk of all the whores. They envied the way Raven retained his interest when she was so obviously a virgin. They had difficulty understanding that love could thrive without the succour of regular pleasuring.

Bart was indifferent to the speculation of gossips and to Raven's own entreaties about when they would marry.

'When I've settled my debts,' he told her yet again as they sat in the garden one evening idly watching a vessel dropping its anchor in the harbour.

'Let us marry now,' she said, her fingers pressing against his. 'Daddy agrees. You sold the sugar crop profitably and the demand for rum means you can set your own price. Paying off your mother's debts to Van Dort will be easy.'

He hugged her close to him, bolstered by her confidence. 'Van Dort isn't finished yet.'

'Is he going to keep us apart for ever?' She kissed him on his cheek. 'Forget him, Bart.'

He smiled at her lovingly. 'We can't afford to be married yet.'

'Fiddlesticks!'

'When your eyes spark like that I know I have no choice.'

'I will give you one month, Bart Taylor!'

'Oh dear,' he said, moderating his usual oath. 'It's unseemly to be so impatient.'

'Is it?' She fluttered her eyelashes. 'At times I feel possessed. I wake up in the middle of the night crying your name.' She bit her lip, avoiding his eyes. 'Is impatience a sin as well as unseemly?'

He grasped her chin between his thumb and forefinger, forcing her to look at him. He kissed her gently on her lips, feeling the energy soaring in her breasts as she thrust against him.

'I love you, Raven,' he whispered. 'Be patient just a little longer.'

'A month, that's all . . .' she said firmly.

The ship they saw dropping anchor carried a complaining passenger who made her way in great haste to the Collector's bungalow. Her shouts to the driver to make his bullock go faster on the short journey from the harbour could be heard through the darkening streets of the fort.

Boys who watched this determined woman landing at the wharf, ran after the cart in amazement. No one in Galle had ever seen such a sight as this grandly dressed lady of huge girth with her scathing tongue and skin as black as a crow's.

In the garden, Bart heard the woman's strident tones as she stood on the verandah and demanded to see the Collector personally.

'By the devil!' he exclaimed, forgetting Raven's sensitivity. He pushed her from him and spun around to listen. There was no mistaking that strident voice.

He seized Raven's hand and dashed with her into the parlour. Mr Radley was retreating as the woman advanced on him brandishing her parasol.

Bart halted in the doorway, gazing at her with disbelief. 'Mammy!' he exclaimed.

'Thank de Lor' I find you, Bart!' She accepted his embrace, proudly preening herself in front of Mr Radley.

'Lor', how I suffer! Every night I cry myself to sleep on 'ccount of Mistis Charlotte. I been to London, I done her business, an' I come all de way back.'

She was dressed in a gown of red velvet trimmed with white tassels hanging across her vast bosom. This extraordinary ensemble was topped with an outlandish bonnet as wide as she was with an overflow of feathers. Bart gaped at her, not knowing whether to laugh or cry.

'Mammy, that dress! That hat!'

'Dis be how ladies does dress in London,' she said scornfully. 'Made 'special for me. De nice macaroni say it 'hances my charms.' She giggled and waggled her backside at him. 'Cost plenty, but no matter now I'm rich.'

Bart glanced at Raven at the same moment as she looked at him. He reached for her hand. Mammy continued speaking in a rush.

'Charlotte left me 'nuff an' I grateful to her even dough I have to work for it. I take de gems to de agent an' I see dat white *makak*, de monkey, don't swindle her jes' 'cause she dead. He pay a fair price.' She sniffed. 'De lawyers give me one packet of mail for you, Bart. An' a draft 'cause Charlotte leave you rich too.' She fumbled in the depths of her enormous travelling bag, wheezing and grumbling with the effort. She found the papers she sought and thrust them at Bart.

'Ain't no one go'n offer a lady a drink?' she shouted scornfully at Mr Radley. 'In London, dey treat me like a black queen.'

'So you are, Mammy!' Bart kissed her great wobbling cheeks and hugged her until she wheezed with delight.

'I does be too old for you, Bart,' she said, pushing him away and straightening her bonnet. 'Ain't you marry dat wench yet?' She nodded her feathers at Raven.

'I was waiting for you.' Bart waved the papers at Mr Radley. 'There's a draft here for twice the value of the plantation. My mother's left me rich!'

'Dat what I say,' said Mammy, advancing on the drinks

cabinet where she had spied the bottle of cognac. 'Dat what I say.'

'How does it feel to be a planter's wife. A rich planter's wife?'

They were riding in the bullock cart through the coconut groves on the road from Galle to the plantation. They were alone. They had been married by the Registrar that morning with Mr Radley and Mammy and Gretchen Gudde as witnesses.

'I'll tell you tonight,' she said. 'When I'm really your wife.'

His loins leaped and this time he did not try to pull away from her or cross his legs with embarrassment. He held her tightly around her waist and she nestled her head on his shoulder. When the bouncing of the carriage made that uncomfortable, she sat at his side and giggled happily.

'I shall never forget daddy's face when he saw Madam Gudde,' she said. 'Why did you invite her? I thought you wanted to keep the wedding secret?'

'She was a friend of mother's.' His eyes twinkled and he kissed her on her mouth to stop her asking any more awkward questions.

The carriage lurched to a halt, throwing them against each other. Bart looked beyond the bullock as the driver jumped down.

'Damn, there's a coconut tree in the way. It's fallen across the trail.' He scrambled out of the cart. 'We'll have to wait until enough people come to move it.' He helped her to descend.

She looked up and down the trail with disappointment. 'There's no one in sight. Couldn't we walk the rest of the way?'

'Am I to take my bride home on foot?'

'It's a lovely afternoon. It's very romantic, just the two of us.'

He sighed, knowing he could not defy that glint in her eyes. 'I'm not carrying you,' he said, clasping her hand in his. 'We'll walk to the lagoon. I can send a boy from there to tell Tissa to bring the horses for us to ride home in style.'

They walked in silence, accompanied by the piping of mynah birds swooping through the trees. Bart's happiness made him careless. He did not see the gang of men emerging from the jungle behind them. It was Raven's gasp of fright that made him turn.

He was too late to resist. A sack was thrown over his head and he was pitched onto the ground in the sudden blackness. He heard Raven scream as her hand was torn from his.

He lashed out blindly. A sharp blow at the back of his neck knocked him senseless.

When he recovered, the bullock driver was leaning over him splashing sea water in his face. It was dusk.

'Raven?' he said fearfully.

The driver shook his head.

He looked around. She was gone.

CHAPTER THIRTY

Bart read the note Tissa handed him when he arrived at the villa. His head still throbbed from the blow. As soon as he had realized Raven was not on the trail, he had rushed home. Kirti and the children were safe and there was nothing amiss in the villa. Tissa had been waiting for him.

'Where did you get this?' he demanded, disturbed by Tissa's possible involvement in the kidnap.

'A boy brought it to the mill.'

'Did you hold him?'

'Why should I? I didn't know what it said.'

Bart read the note again. He could hear Van Dort's swinish voice in its sinister message. 'The pearl for Raven. Mill in one hour. Alone or she dies.'

He gazed at Tissa, sick with doubt that he had something to do with the plot. 'Why the mill?' he thought aloud.

'He is making his escape quicker from there.'

It was an ingenious plan. There was no time for Bart to summon help from Galle. The mill was surrounded by trees and was dark. It was by the river, isolated from the rest of the plantation. The nearest dwellings were the *cadjun* shacks of the *salagama* peasants.

'What will you do?' Tissa asked anxiously.

'I have no choice.'

'You are giving it to him?'

'To save Raven's life. It is all he wants. He will go away afterwards. He can't stay in Galle because I'll see he's arrested.'

'If you are still alive.' Tissa pulled at his hair in anguish. 'Don't trust him. When you give him the *gaja mutu*, he'll kill you. And Raven too.'

'What about you? You don't seem to be afraid.'

'This is not the time for fear, Bloodheart.'

'You're right. We must think of a plan.'

He darted inside the house, took the ebony gem box from its hiding place in a secret drawer of the escritoire, and hurried out again. He gave Nimal and Daisy instructions to close the shutters and doors and let no one enter the villa. Although he still harboured doubts about Tissa, there was no one else to help him. He told him what to do.

'You are brave,' said Tissa with a grin. 'The *gaja mutu* is giving you courage.' He looked pointedly at the box in Bart's hand.

'The pearl will give me Raven!' He opened the box and displayed it to Tissa. The pearl lay swathed in blue silk. It was lacklustre in the lantern's glow. He heard Tissa's swift intake of breath as he reached for it.

He pulled the box away from him and snapped the lid shut. 'Go now, Tissa. I'm depending on you.'

He watched him disappear into the darkness of the trail. At least, he decided, if Tissa was in league with Van Dort, he would tell him he had the pearl. That might help Raven.

So many possibilities entered his mind as he stepped off the verandah. Van Dort's men could attack him before he reached the mill, kill him and disappear with the pearl. He was being too hasty, yet there was no time to spare.

He turned back and hurried over to the parlour door. Nimal opened it immediately. Everyone was in the parlour, including Malika and Kirti. He stared at Daisy in surprise.

'What are you doing?'

'We see dis note.' She held up the scrap of paper. 'Tissa read it for us.'

'We are wanting to help,' said Malika. 'Kirti does too.'

Despite his despair, Bart was amused. Kirti was straining at Malika's hold on him, stabbing the air with his tiny fists.

'You help by staying here, Malika.' He counted the slaves. There were Daisy and Little with Malika and the children and Jagath and Nimal, eight of them in all. Mammy was still in Galle.

'Jagath,' he said sternly, 'if anything happens to me, you are to take Malika and the children to the *salagamas* huts. Hide there. You must save Kirti and Garth and Ranita whatever happens. Nimal, you are to go to Galle and seek Mr Radley's help. Explain everything to Mammy.'

'What 'bout me?' Daisy demanded. 'Me an' Little comin' wid yo'.'

He touched her cheek tenderly. 'Stay here, defend the villa.' He gave her his pistol.

'Yo' ain't takin' no weapon?'

'What use will it be? Van Dort has Raven. I can't do anything.'

'Take your whip.' Daisy thrust it in his hand and grabbed him suddenly around his waist, pulling him close to her. She hugged him, chewing the lobe of his ear.

'You're a grand wench,' he told her gruffly, patting her backside with the whip handle.

There was a lump in his throat as he left the villa wondering if he would ever see them again. He carried the box under his shirt close to his heart.

There was a young moon; its glow in the early evening was enough to show him the path through the cane fields to the mill. The year's crop was almost ripe for cutting. The canes were as tall as he was, their leaves fluttering in the breeze like ribbons.

He moved cautiously, listening for unusual sounds, his whip ready to repel any attackers. He guessed that Van Dort, or his henchmen, were holding Raven in the jungle close to the mill.

It was only two hours since he and Raven were walking together along the coastal path. He rubbed his head ruefully, cursing himself for his lack of precaution. Raven's faith that everything would be all right had dulled his instincts.

His anger mounted at the thought of Raven in the hands of Van Dort's Caffres. She pretended to be strong but she was like a temple flower that could be crushed with rough handling. She had no experience of hardship.

She would be terrified in the jungle in the dark. What would the Caffres do to her? He snapped his whip in the air in his rage. The sound cracked through the stillness of the evening.

The months he had courted Raven seemed wasted. He had

respected her, hardly daring to touch her in case she felt defiled by his wanting. Now, on the verge of taking her to his bed as his bride, she had been snatched from him because of Van Dort's greed.

He reached the mill compound and glanced around. He was relieved to see Tissa had carried out his instructions. There were lanterns ranged around the yard, hanging from the branches of trees and throwing an eerie light on the millhouse and grinding shed. The rush of the river drowned the noise of the jungle. He stood at the edge of the rim of light thrown by the lanterns, keeping in the shadow of a tree trunk. If he stepped into the light he would be an easy target for anyone who wanted to attack him.

He strained his ears at the sound of people moving in the bushes at the other side of the yard. There was a flurry in the trees. He almost stepped out of his hiding place when he heard Raven shouting vigorously.

'You black ape! Take your hands off me.'

He saw her being dragged through the undergrowth to the edge of the jungle that surrounded the mill yard. She was panting, her bonnet had gone and her beautiful white gown was torn. Her ringlets were tangled and her face smeared with mud.

He had never desired her more than at that moment as she stood, angry and dishevelled, defying the two Caffres who held her.

He wanted to dash from his hiding place, wielding the whip above his head, and tear her from the hands of the Caffres. But he waited. Raven's bravery inspired him.

He sensed the presence of other figures lurking in the trees behind her. The Caffres were waiting. They were holding Raven's arms tightly, their heads alert as though they were listening for orders.

Bart felt someone close to him. He tensed with fear, his palms damp as he clutched the whip and turned to defend himself. There was no one there. He stared into the darkness of the trees and heard a sound like the hiss of a snake. He jumped back in terror and looked down.

Squatting close to his feet was the Tamil snake boy, his basket in front of him. He held up a warning finger to his lips.

Bart swallowed. The noise of his pounding heart seemed to reverberate through the glade. He drew back his shoulders, emboldened by the boy's friendly presence.

Raven was struggling. One of the Caffres raised his hand to hit her. Using the arms of her captors for support, she swung off the ground and drove her knee into his crotch. He winced and bent double. Bart recognized him as Junie, the Caffre who used to be the guard at Madam Gudde's.

He shook off the hand of the snake boy who was trying to restrain him and burst out of the hiding place. 'Raven!' he shouted to her across the yard.

'Don't give it to them, Bart!' Her cry echoed around the walls of the millhouse before it was swallowed up by the roar of the river.

Standing in the circle of light, he was uncertain what to do. The grinding shed was in the centre of the yard, between him and Raven. She was still struggling and another Caffre came out of the darkness to hold her arm. Junie removed his loincloth and massaged himself where she had kicked him.

'Van Dort!' Bart called. 'I'm here. I've got the pearl. Show yourself.'

There was no answer, only Raven's frantic cry: 'No, Bart, no!'

'Look at me, Van Dort!' He drew the box from his shirt and held it up. 'Let Raven go. I'll put the box on the grinding stone. I'm alone. You can come for it.'

He was puzzled at the lack of response from the darkness. Raven had stopped shouting. She was staring in horror at Junie who had massaged himself until he was hard.

'How interestink . . .!' a high voice said.

Bart swung around to see Van Dort emerge from the mill house. Delta, the watchman, was with him, a pistol in his hand pointed at Bart's chest.

'Take the pearl and let Raven go!' Bart shouted with relief at being face to face with him at last.

'You disappoint me, *Bloodheart*.' Van Dort sneered. 'I expected some resistance from you, not from the girl. I haf arranged a divertissement to persuade you to cooperate.' He waved a flabby hand at the Caffres.

They moved swiftly. One of them placed his hand on the corsage of Raven's dress and pulled. The sound of ripping fabric set Bart's teeth on edge. He gaped as the dress fell away from Raven's shoulders and she stood naked in the lantern light.

Her pale body contrasted with the gleaming black skin of Junie who stalked towards her, holding himself as though bearing a heavy sword in his hand.

Another Caffre held a knife to Raven's throat. She opened her mouth but refused to scream. Her eyes watched the naked Junie with disgust.

'Don't move, Bart!' Van Dort's voice cut into the silence like the crack of a whip. 'If you do, she dies.'

Delta cocked the pistol. Bart froze, believing Van Dort's threat.

'Drop your vip, Bart.'

Helplessly, he let the whip fall to the ground at his feet. 'I'll give you the pearl if you let her go,' he said. 'She's done nothing.'

'Vat! Spoil my chance of a little entertainment to revard my Caffres? You should thank me the boy vill break in the vench for you.'

Junie put his hand between Raven's thighs, drooling as he rubbed himself against her.

There was a creaking sound from the shadows by the river. Van Dort looked disconcerted and the Caffres, startled by the curious noise, hesitated.

Raven tried to wriggle free. Junie pushed her to the ground. He clambered on top of her as the grinding stones began slowly to revolve.

Bart gritted his teeth, ready to act. Tissa had done his part by engaging the waterwheel so that it turned the piston-rod driving the grinding stones. The distraction was enough.

He leapt across the yard waving the gem box in the air. Before Delta could take aim, he flung himself down behind the plinth in the grinding shed.

'I have the pearl,' he shouted, extracting it from the box and

305

holding it up for Van Dort to see. 'Release Raven or I put it in the grinder.' He held it against the lip of the rollers. One slip and his hand would be drawn in with it and mashed to a pulp.

Van Dort snuffled like a truffling pig on heat. 'Bart . . .' he said, his voice quavering.

Bart pressed the pearl closer to the churning stones. From the corner of his eye he saw Junie on his knees beside Raven. 'Call off the Caffre,' he shouted.

'I'll exchange her for the pearl! You can trust me.' The whine in Van Dort's voice sickened Bart.

Suddenly the Caffres guarding Raven shouted and leapt away from her. Junie struggled to stand. A monstrous cobra slithered through the grass towards him. He fell backwards with a bloodcurdling shriek of agony as the snake sank its fangs into his groin.

Raven jumped to her feet and ran across the yard to Bart's side. She was unharmed.

The Caffres fled into the jungle, leaving Junie writhing in his death throes on the ground. The Tamil boy danced out from his hiding place and gathered up the cobra, coiling it back into his basket.

'Keep down!' Bart pulled Raven to his side behind the plinth. 'He has a gun.'

He tore off his shirt and covered her shoulders with it. Slowly he raised his head. Van Dort was waddling towards them.

'Bart!' he squeaked between gasps for breath at the unexpected activity. 'You haf your vife . . . now give me the pearl. You are a gentleman of honour, no?'

Bart looked at Raven helplessly. She shook her head.

He leaned out, holding the pearl against the mouth of the grinding stones. Delta was facing him with the pistol gripped tightly in both hands.

'Don't move, massa!' Delta's teeth flashed. 'I go'n shoot off yuh ballocks. Yo' stole Daisy so I go'n kill yo'.' His fingers tightened on the trigger.

Bart let the pearl slip from his hand between the stones. He lunged at Delta as he fired.

Van Dort howled and flung himself at the grinder. He thrust

his hand in, reaching for the pearl. His fingers clawed over it. He squealed with pain as the millstones chewed on his hand.

Bart peered at him from where he lay on the ground. Delta's shot had passed above his head. A whip whistled close to his ear.

He ducked and looked again. Raven stood over him with his whip in her hand. She was lashing Van Dort's backside as he squawked in agony and tried to break away from the grindstone's grip.

Tissa and Romulus rushed out of the jungle and pounced on Delta, throwing him to the ground and beating him with his own pistol.

'Help me pull Van Dort free!' shouted Bart as he rose to his feet.

'No!' Raven flicked the whip and its lash passed near Bart's face. 'Keep away from him.'

Her dark eyes glistened with fury and a kind of rapture as she sliced the whip into Van Dort's flesh. His breeches were in shreds and blood oozed from the cuts on his buttocks. He was shrieking.

Frantically Bart looked around for an axe to cut off his arm to save him from being drawn into the grinder. 'Help me,' he begged Tissa. 'We could cut him free.'

Tissa raised his head from where he and Romulus had succeeded in subduing Delta. He brushed the hair from his brow. 'I'm not hearing you good,' he said cheerfully.

Bart watched in horror as the stones heaved and drew Van Dort deeper between them. His shoulder followed his arm and then his head was dragged in until the screaming ceased and his whole body was digested by the giant cane crusher.

Raven threw down the whip in the sudden hush that filled the yard.

Bart grabbed her, pulling her close to him to cover her nakedness. She was shaking hysterically, her lips quivering as she tried to speak.

'Bart, Bart . . .' she cried.

He drew her away from the lanterns' glow into the darkness beside the river. She stumbled as she walked with him. He bent to pick her up, scooping her into his arms and carrying her to the water's edge. She began to sob.

Gently, he walked with her into the river, lowering her naked body into its cooling water. Behind him the waterwheel creaked as it continued to drive the millstones. The remains of Van Dort's body, crushed to a bloody pulp, were spewed out into the sugar troughs.

Tissa ran down to the river bank and offered Bart some gunny bags to cover Raven as they emerged from the river.

Bart's breeches were soaked and his boots full of water. He nodded, directing Tissa to spread the jute sacks on the ground. Tissa crept away silently as he laid Raven down on them.

'It's over now,' he said, holding her in his arms.

The faint light from the quarter moon shone on the white ripples of water. Raven's ringlets hung damply over her bare shoulders. Water trickled from her breasts down to her thighs.

'It's just beginning,' she said.

'No, Raven.' He protested in vain as she loosened his belt and slid his wet breeches down his thighs.

'Yes,' she said, closing her lips over his.

Later, when they lay side by side on the gunny bags and the moon had dropped from the sky, she mused softly into his ear. 'What a shame the pearl got crushed.'

He reached for his breeches and fumbled in the pocket. He held up something between his finger and thumb.

'What's that?' she muttered dreamily.

'The elephant pearl. It was an old piece of ivory that got crushed.'

He leaned over her. With a chuckle of triumph, he brushed his hand against her breasts. Lowering his fingers, he forced the *gaja mutu* into her navel.

'I love you, Bloodheart,' she cried, opening her arms to embrace him. She pressed her body tightly against his, feeling the firmness of the pearl penetrating her flesh.

'I love you!'

308

A selection of bestsellers from Sphere

FICTION

THE PANIC OF '89	Paul Erdman	£2.99 ☐
WHITE SUN, RED STAR	Robert Elegant	£3.50 ☐
A TASTE FOR DEATH	P. D. James	£3.50 ☐
THE PRINCESS OF POOR STREET	Emma Blair	£2.99 ☐
WANDERLUST	Danielle Steel	£3.50 ☐

FILM AND TV TIE-IN

BLACK FOREST CLINIC	Peter Heim	£2.99 ☐
INTIMATE CONTACT	Jacqueline Osborne	£2.50 ☐
BEST OF BRITISH	Maurice Sellar	£8.95 ☐
SEX WITH PAULA YATES	Paula Yates	£2.95 ☐
RAW DEAL	Walter Wager	£2.50 ☐

NON-FICTION

INVISIBLE ARMIES	Stephen Segaller	£4.99 ☐
ALEX THROUGH THE LOOKING GLASS	Alex Higgins with Tony Francis	£2.99 ☐
NEXT TO A LETTER FROM HOME: THE GLENN MILLER STORY	Geoffrey Butcher	£4.99 ☐
AS TIME GOES BY: THE LIFE OF INGRID BERGMAN	Laurence Leamer	£3.95 ☐
BOTHAM	Don Mosey	£3.50 ☐

All Sphere books are available at your local bookshop or newsagent, or can be ordered direct from the publisher. Just tick the titles you want and fill in the form below.

Name _____

Address _____

_____

Write to Sphere Books, Cash Sales Department, P.O. Box 11, Falmouth, Cornwall TR10 9EN

Please enclose a cheque or postal order to the value of the cover price plus:

UK: 60p for the first book, 25p for the second book and 15p for each additional book ordered to a maximum charge of £1.90.

OVERSEAS & EIRE: £1.25 for the first book, 75p for the second book and 28p for each subsequent title ordered.

BFPO: 60p for the first book, 25p for the second book plus 15p per copy for the next 7 books, thereafter 9p per book.

Sphere Books reserve the right to show new retail prices on covers which may differ from those previously advertised in the text elsewhere, and to increase postal rates in accordance with the P.O.

A REVOLUTIONARY APPROACH TO FOOD AND FITNESS

TASTE of LIFE

JULIE STAFFORD

THE DIET THAT SAVED A LIFE

Julie and Bruce Stafford thought they had the perfect life and family until, out-of-the-blue, 30 year-old Bruce, who had never missed a day's work through illness in his life, was struck down by cancer.

As Bruce's health steadily deteriorated, Julie decided to investigate the link between diet and disease. She came up with an eating plan based on the principle of low-fat, salt-free and sugar-free foods but applied it to inventive, delicious and mouth-watering recipes. The result? A miraculous recovery. Within two weeks Bruce's health improved and now he is completely cured.

Julie Stafford shows you how to eat like a gourmet and be healthy too. TASTE OF LIFE is truly a revolutionary, life-sustaining breakthrough.

0 7221 8105 1   HEALTH/COOKERY   £3.50

Danielle Steel

A captivating bestseller . . .

WANDERLUST

At 21 Annabelle Driscoll was the acknowledged beauty, but it was her sister Audrey – four years older – who had the spine and spirit. She had talent as a photographer; she had the restless urge of a born wanderer.

Inevitably it was Annabelle who was the first to marry, leaving Audrey to wonder if life were passing her by. The men she met in California were dull, worldly. Even in New York, they failed to spark her. Only when she boarded the *Orient Express* did she realise she was beginning a journey that would take her farther than she had ever dreamed possible . . .

0 7221 8307 0   GENERAL FICTION   £3.50